P9-EKY-722

THE
PUZZLE BOX

Opening it will change your life. Forever...

BY THE APOCALYPTIC
FOUR

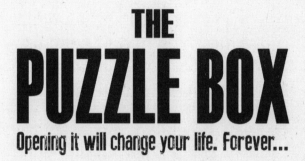

EDGE SCIENCE FICTION AND FANTASY PUBLISHING

AN IMPRINT OF HADES PUBLICATIONS, INC.

CALGARY

Edge Science Fiction and Fantasy Publishing
An Imprint of Hades Publications Inc.
P.O. Box 1714, Calgary, Alberta, T2P 2L7, Canada

by Randy McCharles, Billie Milholland,
Eileen Bell and Ryan McFadden
Interior design by Janice Blaine
Cover art & Design by Neil Jackson

ISBN: 978-1-77053-040-9

EDGE Science Fiction and Fantasy Publishing and Hades Publications, Inc.
acknowledges the ongoing support of the Alberta Foundation for the Arts and
the Canada Council for the Arts for our publishing programme.

Library and Archives Canada Cataloguing in Publication

The puzzle box / Apocalyptic Four, Eileen Bell ... [et al.].

ISBN: 978-1-77053-040-9
(e-Book ISBN: 978-1-77053-041-6)

1. Science fiction, Canadian (English). 2. Fantasy fiction,
Canadian (English). I. Bell, Eileen

PS8323.S3P89 2013   C813'.08760806   C2013-900449-1

FIRST EDITION
(H-20130523)
Printed in Canada
www.edgewebsite.com

TABLE OF CONTENTS

ACKNOWLEDGEMENTS

Four stories; four dedications. Randy wishes to dedicate *The Awakening of Master March* to the musically talented Val King. *Autumn Unbound* is dedicate by Billie to women everywhere who get blamed for stuff they didn't do. Eileen dedicates *Angela and Her Three Wishes* to her father while Ryan dedicates *Ghost in the Machine* to his mother.

The Apocalyptic Four also wish to acknowledge the fictional French toymaker, Philip Lemarchand, for making the puzzle box the scariest artifact on and off Earth, as well as Erno Rubik for taking that fear and turning it into frustration.

❖   ❖   ❖

The First Piece of the Puzzle

❖   ❖   ❖

No-one will miss it...

Professor Albert Mallory felt no guilt about taking the puzzle box. He'd worked nearly a month in that dirt-water town, trying to pull history from the flotsam and jetsam of a place that didn't have any history worth saving. As far as he was concerned, it was a town best forgotten. He shouldn't have accepted the contract, sight unseen, but desperation makes men do foolish things. One month. Each day spent digging through the garbage of other people's lives, and each night playing poker with the four ghouls in the back room of the Nevermore pub. By the time he'd been paid, he barely broke even.

Albert stared at the small metal box sitting on his desk and tried not to think of the backroom of the Nevermore and the four smiling men at the poker table, taking him for every hard earned penny with never a thought for the life they were ruining. Every night. Plenty of history in that room— even if it was his own.

That's why he'd taken the box. He had expenses.

He stretched, reached for the half-empty bottle of Jim Beam and poured himself a drink. He swallowed and grimaced at the familiar burn, then poured another. Fortification for the phone calls he had to make. One bad, and one with the potential for good. A lot of good, if he played his cards right.

"So which one?" Albert whispered, putting the bottle aside. "Good or bad?"

He fumbled in his pocket for a coin and flipped it in the air. "Heads," he said, then shook his head when it landed tails.

"Just my luck."

Albert finished the bottle and then called Morley Van Rosen, the local loan shark to whom he owed money. A lot of money. He'd have to do some fast talking, buy himself a little time, then make that second phone call and set up the sale of the box.

Once he sold the box, everything would be all right.

"Albert, you scamp," Morley hissed. "You are late. Do you have my money?" And then he mentioned a sum that almost forced Albert's heart to stillness.

"I— I," he stuttered.

"That won't do it, Albert. I need to hear the words: 'I have your money, Mr. Van Rosen.'"

"Tomorrow," Albert whispered. "You'll have it tomorrow night."

Silence. Then, "Rosemont and Claireborne will be at your door at 7:30 p.m."

The line went dead and Albert dropped the receiver on the desk as though it were diseased. Not Rosemont.

After several futile minutes tearing apart his tiny kitchen in search of another bottle, Albert sat back down. He had one more phone call to make. The good one.

Albert had almost pulled himself together by the time Julian Gabareaux, his best and only customer, answered.

"Julian!" he said, but the cheer in his voice sounded cracked and ridiculous as he pushed back his hair, greasing it with the sweat from his forehead. "I'm back! And I have an amazing find for you."

"I was beginning to think you'd decided to return to academia full time, Albert. So, what do you have for me? Something Egyptian, I hope. I'm beginning to collect some divine—"

"Yes, Egyptian. Absolutely!" Albert cried, looking at the small box on the corner of his desk and hoping that the tiny marks etched into the sides were close enough. "It's a beautiful gold-alloy metal box. Nothing as ordinary as a jewelry box. This is a secret lock box, with religious and magical significance. Used in rituals. Very rare. A fantastic find. And in perfect condition."

"Not too perfect now," Julian laughed. "You know I want—"

"The patina of age. Yes." Albert pulled the phone away, afraid he would scream into the receiver and frighten off his best customer. He sucked in a quick breath and put the receiver back to his ear. "It's perfect."

"Wonderful," Julian said. "Bring it over as soon as you are able. I'll be leaving the country at the end of the week, and I do want to have my people look it over. Verification, you know."

"Julian, you can trust me," Albert said. "You know that."

"Albert. This is just business."

"Business."

"Of course. Now get some rest. You sound tired."

What Albert felt was exhausted. "I'll see you tomorrow, early," he said.

"And you will show me how it opens," Julian said. "We can't have another embarrassment, now can we?"

"No." Julian had been unable to make one of Albert's last finds work, a mechanical caged bird, quite possibly a Jaquet-Droz original from the 1850's. The silly prat had embarrassed himself in front of his highbrow friends when he couldn't figure out how to start it. He'd acted as though his failure had been Albert's fault. "It will work perfectly. Trust me."

Albert put down the phone and stared at the box. He had no idea how to open it. Lord knows he'd tried to open the thing, but had only succeeded in getting one small piece to move. It stuck out woefully from one side of the box, like a crippled wing. He hadn't even been able to put it back in place.

I'm a dead man.

He picked up the box and carefully waggled the one piece. His hands shook with frustration. He considered trying to pry it open so he could examine the inner workings then reassemble it. But if he did that and it broke, he'd have nothing left.

"Bloody hell." A doctorate from Boston College and he couldn't open a simple child's toy. It was infuriating.

Albert mentally went through the meager list of people who owed him favors, hoping one of them would have the expertise to open the box. But even as he did so, his hands kept working the wing. He wanted to solve this particular riddle on his own. Wasn't that what had sent him into archaeology in the first place? The desire to solve puzzles and riddles from the past?

Even as he lost himself in the puzzle, he knew he didn't have time for this. In a few short hours he would need to deliver it to Julian, the secret to opening the box in hand. If he failed, Rosemont would hammer on the door, and Albert's legs — or life — could be irreparably damaged.

The pounding on the door startled him so fiercely that he fumbled the puzzle, nearly dropping it. Rosemont! It's too soon.

Van Rosen, while ruthless, was a businessman first. He would want to collect his money over breaking Albert's legs.

He tucked the box on a hat shelf with shaking fingers then stared at his hands, willing them to calm before opening the door.

The man standing in the rain looked as if he'd stepped off a Victorian steamer. The rain ran off his yellow hat and slicker in torrents. His circular glasses were fogged and he carried a wooden suitcase covered with labels from around the world.

"Ah, just the person I wanted to see," the man said.

Albert gripped the door frame to keep his hand from shaking. Perhaps Rosemont had a new sidekick. This one did not look dangerous, but psychopaths come in all stripes. "Do I know you?" Albert asked.

"No, I expect you don't," said the man with a hint of sadness. "Will you invite me in so I can warm myself by your fire? Perhaps offer me some tea? I am soaked to the bone."

"What?" Albert asked, taken aback. "No. I don't think so."

"I'm sorry, but we do not have time for niceties," the man said, pushing himself past Albert, his footsteps leaving puddles on the worn wooden floor. "We have much work to do tonight, Albert." He placed his drenched case on a chair and began unfastening his jacket buttons.

Albert watched his unwanted visitor fuss with his jacket, carefully straightening it before placing it on the chair next to the dripping suitcase, and decided the little man did not look dangerous. Just irritating. "How do you know my name?"

"How about that tea?" the visitor asked.

"Listen—"

"And where is the puzzle box?"

"Box?" A new fear this time. Of being discovered. Albert's mind cycled through possibilities. Spies? Hidden cameras in the warehouse? Had the senile old security guard seen him? Did the police know? His brain whirled. He needed time to think. More than that, he needed his drink.

"Yes. The box. I know you have it, Albert. Now where is it? It has much to show you."

Albert opened his mouth hoping to defend his name but instead made a sound like he had lost his tongue.

"You are going to attempt to sell it, yes?"

"Are you with Julian?" Albert whispered.

"Julian is your buyer?" The old man clucked his tongue and shook his head. "The box does not belong to him. You understand that, don't you? He could no more buy the box than you could buy the borough of Manhattan in New York." He slammed his hand down on the table.

Albert jumped at the sound. "Leave!" Albert demanded, pointing at the door.

The visitor pursed his lips, unimpressed by Albert's false bravado. He removed his glasses and wiped the fog away with a clean white handkerchief he pulled from his trouser pocket. "If you sell the box to Julian, how much will he give you?"

"I'm donating it. Leave. Now."

"This won't work, Albert, unless you're honest with me."

"Who are you?"

"Someone trying to help you. Let me ask you one more question: once you've got your money, how long do you reckon it will be before you end up back here?"

"I'm moving at the end of the month." Albert glanced around the small room that served as his library and his office. Dingy books competed for space with dust-covered artifacts on cheap book cases, the shelves bending from the weight. The fire he'd started to chase away the chill guttered and smoked sullenly. God, he hated this place.

"I don't mean the physical here, Albert. In how many backwater towns do you find yourself? How many times do you end up a victim in the local gambling dens? The scene may change but the tale is always the same."

Albert's knees weakened. He slumped in a chair at the table and eyed the bottle of Jim Beam.

"What do you want from me?" he asked, his voice a weak whisper.

"I'm here to tell you a story— though I'm not much of a story teller, truth be told. I'm more of a chronicler."

"A writer?"

"No, no, no, nothing as banal as that. I collect truths. Would you like to see?"

Albert struggled to fit the pieces of this strange conversation together, but couldn't make them connect in any meaningful way. He shrugged.

"Sometimes, Albert, the story is about what you need, not what you want." Though Albert did not see the old man move, suddenly his left hand held the puzzle box. Albert started and glanced at the hat shelf. Empty. What the hell?

Returning his gaze to the box, he asked, "What are you doing with that?"

The visitor ignored his question, turning the box this way and that, as though admiring it. "How long have you blamed the faceless men for taking your money? Night after night. You in those sinful dens. Losing your money. And your soul, chipped away piece by piece."

"I don't always lose," Albert said.

"You sound like a child." The old man glared, and Albert slumped deeper in his chair. "You do always lose. How long will you wait for the good life to fall into your lap? Face it, you want the rewards without the investment. A dangerous path. But you already know that, don't you?"

The visitor held the box in both hands. "What would you say is the greatest gift I could give you?"

A way out of this jam.

"Untrue," the visitor said and Albert blinked. Had he spoken aloud? Too much Jim Beam. Or not enough.

"This is the greatest gift," the visitor said, holding the box out to Albert. "This."

"I don't know how to open it," Albert said.

"Open it? It's not your task to open it. It's your task to observe."

"It's a box. What's there to—"

Albert's voice stopped as he looked at the box and realized it had changed. It was still a metal box, but he could see new letters and symbols stamped into the bronzed surface. The visitor manipulated the letters by sliding the side pieces of the box around to the back.

"How did you do that?" Albert whispered, and blinked again. A dim blue light began to glow through the cracks in the box, and what at first looked like a trick of Chiaroscuro quickly became a pulsating yellow glow. Then it became as bright as a halogen lamp. White hot light lanced through the loosened seams of the puzzle box.

"Look, Albert." The old man held it out on his outstretched palm. It vibrated with energy.

Albert gasped, but before he could lean forward, the white light exploded into a dazzling rainbow of colors so intense they blinded him. He threw a hand before his face.

"Open your eyes, Albert," commented the stranger. "And observe. Your life shall nevermore be the same."

The next Piece of the Puzzle will be revealed after "The Awakening of Master March."

THE AWAKENING OF MASTER MARCH

❖ By Randy McCharles ❖

The World's Ugliest House

Warlock looked at the house, reread the scribbled address on a torn piece of paper, and then looked back at the house. He immediately knew three things. First, that this was indeed the address he had been given, dead center in the middle of a quiet, older suburb. Second, this was likely the same location he had been brought to the previous evening, gagged and blindfolded and more than a little surprised. And third, that this was the ugliest house in existence, the monstrous concoction of lunatic architects run amok.

The house was large by any standard, two floors of crooked walls and flying buttresses, with gabled windows in places gables had never been intended. The roof zigged where it should have zagged, requiring the later addition of enough eaves to drain a battleship. There was a giant satellite dish that had broken its mooring and slipped downward until now the only signals it could receive would need to emanate from the neighbor's garage.

Warlock frowned at the miniature wooden steps that led from the cement front walk to a brooding oak door surrounded by exterior walls painted blue and pink. Warlock closed his eyes and looked again. Yes, still pink.

It was times like these that Warlock wished he had never discovered the *Discovery Channel*.

Stuffing the address into a pocket of his jeans, Warlock hefted his backpack to fit more comfortably on his shoulders and then approached the fence that guarded the property. The fence was picket. White, thankfully. And all of three feet high. Warlock reached down, carefully unlatched the gate, stepped inside, and relatched it.

The yard, he noted, consisted of grass. Just grass. No trees, bushes, or flowers. In one place the grass held an impression of some mystic framework since removed. There were diagonal lines and rounded corners and a couple of square areas where grass had grown in but failed to completely eradicate the evidence. One patch of grass boasted a rather large quantity of sand.

Shaking his head, Warlock continued up the cement walk and then ascended the very short wooden steps. He couldn't remember the last time he had seen wooden steps, but he clearly remembered stumbling on these ones as his abductors escorted him from their van and into the house. It was the right place, all right. There was even a white van parked on the street.

The oak door had had a five inch square hole cut out near the center at about eye level. He stared at it and knocked.

After a few moments he was unsurprised when a panel that covered the hole from the inside slid back to reveal an eye, a nose, and the edge of a frown.

"Who is it?" demanded a vaguely familiar female voice that apparently owned the partial frown. Its tone was certainly frownish.

He answered. "You can see who it is, so why ask?"

The frown did not like that answer. It continued to exist. The eye, as well, took on a glarish demeanor.

"Speak your name if you desire to enter. That is the rule."

"You should know my name," said Warlock. "I was here last night. You can't have forgotten me already."

"No name, no entry."

Warlock sighed. "Very well. My name is Warlock."

The eye continued to glare, and then the frown had the gall to giggle.

"Something funny?" asked Warlock.

More giggling.

"Look," said Warlock. "Even if you don't remember me, I remember you. Sister August, isn't it?"

The giggling stopped and was immediately replaced by indignation. "Are you mad! Never use our names outside. It is forbidden."

"Right," said Warlock. "And yet here you are asking for my name. If you'd just open the bloody door I wouldn't be outside and we could bounce names off each other all day."

"Idiot," said the now indignant frown. "I can't open the door until you give me the bloody pass phrase. So speak your bloody name!"

Pass phrase? Warlock let the events of last evening roll through his mind. Most of it was gibberish, so he examined the most gibbered parts seeking a pass phrase. Nope. Nothing. There was quite a bit about names, however.

"Oh," he said. "I think I have it." He cleared his throat and then dramatically exclaimed, "I have no name."

Sister August's partial features vanished as the panel slid back to cover the hole. Then came a loud clack as a heavy bolt slid back. Slowly, the door creaked open.

Warlock pushed the heavy door open wide enough to slip inside and saw that all of Sister August had vanished, not just her frown, which was too bad as he remembered her as being rather cute when she wasn't glaring through a five by five hole. He closed and bolted the door. He wasn't sure he was supposed to bolt the door, but it seemed reasonable. Now, if only he could figure out *where* in the world's ugliest house he was supposed to go.

Just A Roadie

Immediately inside the entrance was a large cloak area with a couple dozen light jackets draped on hooks that were a little too low to the floor for Warlock's liking. The architects hadn't even taken advantage of the lower hooks to add additional shelving above them. It was a crime.

Counting the jackets, Warlock smiled at the thought that at least several of his abductors probably lived here, which could almost make up for the ugliness of the architecture. This house was starting to get interesting.

Adjacent to the cloak area the entryway opened into a spacious parlor, the very room where he had been ungagged and unblind-folded last evening only to find himself surrounded by a dozen young woman between the ages of twenty-two and twenty-five. He had felt like Sir Galahad in Monty Python's *Holy Grail*. Only, while he had less scruples than Sir Galahad, these ladies of Castle Anthrax had considerably more scruples than their younger counterparts and had shown no interest whatsoever in his virility. Well, that's what you get for calling on a house full of witches rather than a castle of virgins. But no matter, Warlock's grail consisted of just one of the dozen women. And it was she, alone, who greeted him now in that spacious parlor in the world's ugliest house.

They had found each other two days ago in a candle store. Warlock was browsing for anything that might spruce up his image, but couldn't decide between black candles or red. Valerie held an armload of long white candles she was about to purchase.

Warlock couldn't remember having ever seen a more striking woman, and somehow mustered the nerve to ask her opinion on his candle dilemma. She was blonde, of course. Warlock was mad for blondes. But it was the set of her nose and the shape of her jaw that kept drawing his attention. Valerie kept asking if she had lipstick or a food crumb on her chin. Each time Warlock answered, "No. You're perfect."

Valerie had seemed only vaguely interested in him until he told her his name. That was when she suggested they have lunch and she told him about her interest in magic and witches. After telling each other their life story, Valerie mentioned that her coven needed a twelfth to be complete. Warlock took the hint and told her that he might be interested, which resulted in his kidnapping. He never did buy candles.

"Greetings Initiate," intoned Valerie, the witches' High Priestess.

"Uh, hi, Val," said Warlock. *Damn*. Why did he always get tongue-tied around the woman he was interested in?

Valerie batted her eyes at him, and then shook her head, sending long blonde curls dancing around her brow and shoulders. "If you intend to join our coven you are going to have to follow the rules of the house. You must call me Sister April."

"Right," said Warlock. "But look, you're the High Priestess, right? How come you're just *Sister* April, like the rest?"

Valerie smiled. "We are all just Sisters, even you. *If* you pass the trial."

Sister? Warlock thought, *Even me?* Then his brain caught up to the worst of what Valerie had just said and his heart began hammering. "Trial? Er. Wasn't that last night with the kidnapping and the candles and the chanting and the chickens?"

"Chickens?" asked Valerie, confused.

"That's a joke," said Warlock, mentally kicking himself because women he was interested in never got his jokes, but at least the distraction had slowed his heart. Last night was bad enough. He didn't really *need* a trial. "They only have chickens in the movies," he added. "But wasn't that whole ritual thing my initiation? Aren't I a member now?"

"A joke. I see," said Valerie, allowing a slip of a smile. "Last night was *our* joke, to gauge if you are serious about joining the coven. Your real trial is right now."

Oh crap, thought Warlock. *Now the chickens come out.* "I can only stay an hour," he said, looking for leniency. "I've got a gig tonight."

Valerie widened her eyes. "A gig?"

"You know," said Warlock. "With the Seriously Damp. Loud music."

Valerie ran a hand through her curly blonde hair, the movement sending a thrill down Warlock's back. You couldn't beat blond hair.

"I know what a gig is," she said, half laughing. "I didn't realize you were in the band. I thought you were just a roadie."

Why? thought Warlock, *does everyone insist on putting just a in front of roadie?* Despite his desire to grind his teeth, he tried to sound cool. "Hey. Roadies are important. We set up and tune the instruments and amplifiers so that the band members sound good. They'd sound like crap without good roadies."

"I thought you said the Seriously Damp hated you?"

Damn. Of course I told her. "Sure they hate me. How can they not hate me? They'd sound like crap without me. They're jealous."

"I thought you said that you hated them, too? That it was only a matter of time before you formed your own band."

"Sure, sure," said Warlock. "That's how it's done. You roadie for a while to see how the business works, then you can start your own band without getting screwed by everyone."

Valerie nodded, but seemed troubled. Warlock kicked himself for sounding like an idiot.

"So this is a paying gig, is it?" she asked.

"Sure, sure," said Warlock. "Well, not really. The club is going to feed us after the show. That's payment, of a sort."

Valerie took a step toward him. "Let's see if I've got this straight. You've got an hour to pass your witch's exam before running off to get kicked around by a band that hates you, all so you can get a free meal at two in the morning."

Warlock thought about arguing with her, about trying to win her over to his way of thinking, about getting her to understand the very complex realities of a musician's life, but in a rare moment of clarity in the presence of a woman he was interested in he thought better of it. Instead he said: "Welcome to the music business."

As if to confirm that he had said the right thing, Valerie smiled.

"Well," she sighed. "Since we don't have much time we had better get started."

Trial By Conundrum

Valerie walked over to the fake fireplace. This was not your typical fake fireplace, with fake wood and natural gas and a flue that would never accommodate smoke from a real burning fire. No, this was a fake fireplace befitting the world's ugliest house. It was, in fact, a fireplace painted onto the wall with bright acrylic paint. The stone mantel above it, however, was quite real.

On the mantel stood a small, silver gong. There was an equally small hammer hanging from a silver chain attached to the silver frame that held the silver gong. The hammer was also silver. Valerie grasped the small hammer by its handle and tapped the gong, which created a sound not the least bit reminiscent of *Anna and the King*. It was, Warlock decided, a gong appropriate for mice.

Nevertheless the sound was sufficient to bring ten young women running and soon the room was filled as it had been the evening prior: one witch short of a coven plus one initiate. Warlock craned his neck looking for chickens.

"Behold the initiate," intoned the High Priestess, Valerie.

"Behold the initiate," chanted ten witches.

Valerie walked around behind him. "Having returned to the coven of his own accord after being unafraid by the hazing—"

Hazing? If they call last night's incense and chanting a hazing, not a one of these girls had watched Animal House. *They didn't know the meaning of the word hazing.*

Valerie continued, "—the initiate seeks to pass the trial and earn a coven name."

"The trial," chanted the ten witches.

Valerie must have leaned forward then as her voice was very loud in Warlock's ear. "The nameless one seeks a name."

"A Coven Name," chanted the witches.

Warlock now remembered that bit from last night and from his confrontation at the door. To be a member of a witches' coven the High Priestess had to give you a name. He hoped he'd get a better one than Sister August.

"To be granted admittance to the coven you must solve this riddle," said Valerie. "There are two sisters: one gives birth to the other and she, in turn, gives birth to the first. Who are the sisters?"

There arose a clamor among the witches, sharp intakes of breath, the stomping of small feet, the grinding of teeth. Then Sister August cried, "But that's too easy!"

Another Sister shouted, "Favoritism!"

Valerie walked around in front of Warlock and held her hand in the air for silence. Warlock noticed a slip of paper in her hand. "How dare you speak thus? Am I not the High Priestess? The head Sister of this coven? Duly chosen by all of you to guide us in all things?"

"Yes," said one of the witches. She had red hair and more freckles than Warlock thought any redhead should be burdened with. He seemed to recall her name was Sister January. "But, you have to admit, it's not much of a riddle. The one I got took hours to solve. The answer to this one is obvious."

Valerie stamped her foot and waved her fist in the air. "Well, of course it's obvious. You are a witch. Have been a witch for... how long have you been a witch for?"

"I joined two months ago," said Sister January.

"Right," said Valerie. "Two months. Long enough to grow into your power and solve all the riddles. But our initiate here is not a witch and will not immediately know the answer." She looked at Warlock. "You don't already know the answer to the riddle do you?"

Warlock had been watching all of this with rapt incredulity. A riddle? Wouldn't a witch's trial be to turn someone into a newt or something? Or to bind a black cat as a familiar? This coven was filled with calendar girls and required initiation by riddle. What had he gotten himself into? The things you do for love.

"Let's see," he said. "Two sisters give birth to each other? Can't see how that's possible. So, no I don't know the answer." *But I will after five minutes on the internet.*

"Still," said Sister August, who Warlock suspected had taken a disliking to him after the altercation at the door, "it isn't much of a riddle."

Valerie huffed and glared at Sister August. *Or maybe,* thought Warlock, *Sister August has altercations with everyone.*

The High Priestess lowered her fist and displayed the slip of paper. "Sister November, did I or did I not draw this riddle from the riddle chest as required by our Order?"

"Yes Sister," answered one of the witches who hadn't made a fuss.

"And Sister November, did you verify the riddle and its answer as belonging to the coven riddle chest?"

"Yes Sister, I did." Sister November smiled at Sister August. "Luck of the draw."

"Luck of the draw my a—" muttered Sister August, but she was drowned out by the noise of the witches trooping out of the room, leaving only Valerie and Warlock behind.

"Since you have a gig," said Valerie, again looking troubled, "you don't have much time to solve the riddle. Bang the gong when you are ready to tell us the answer, or leave this House forever."

Then Valerie followed the other witches out.

The Puzzle Box

All things considered, thought Warlock, *that went well.* He hadn't come across looking awkward. Much. He was certain he had made a good impression on Valerie. Hadn't he?

The thought of a trial had had him going, though. Warlock hated tests. And tests hated him. High school had been a disaster. How a guy who knew everything could get no better than a 'C' on a test, every test, only proved that there was something wrong with the system. Right? Warlock had dropped out in tenth grade and spent the next few years watching television. He especially enjoyed old series reruns on RTN, the Retro Television Network. He had learned a lot more on TV then he ever had at school. And there were no tests.

Valerie's threat of a trial felt too much like high school. He'd get a 'C' before he even started. But this riddle thing wasn't much of a test. It should be a breeze.

He glanced about the parlor and immediately knew one thing. No Internet. *Damn.* He considered sneaking around the house in search of a computer, then remembered his cell phone. He could call someone to look the riddle up, just like in *Who Wants To Be A Millionaire. I'll call a friend for help with this one, Regis.*

He pulled out his phone, but before he could hit speed dial, it rang. The call display said: Valerie. He answered it.

"You're probably thinking that you could call someone and ask them to find the answer for you."

"Hadn't crossed my mind," said Warlock.

"I'm glad," said Valerie. "Cheating means automatic expulsion."

"Of course," said Warlock. "I'm just standing here using my witch-like powers of deduction to solve the riddle. I'll have it in no time."

"I know you will," said Valerie. "I have faith in you." Then she hung up.

Warlock grinned. *She has faith in me.* This was going even better than he had thought. He looked at the phone in his hand, then shook his head and put it away. He couldn't call anyone now. If she caught him cheating he'd lose that faith and more. If he failed... well, perhaps she'd lose less faith.

While pondering the silly riddle, admittedly distracted by Valerie's admission of admiration, Warlock's eyes wandered the room. There wasn't much. His backpack by the door. Sofas, chairs and lamp tables against walls painted white with a tinge of pink. An ancient hardwood floor mostly concealed beneath a large black and white carpet that created an image in Warlock's mind of a zebra after an unfortunate encounter with a steam-roller. Only two doors, the one he had used to come in from the front entranceway and the one the witches had used to enter and leave the room. No windows. An acrylic paint fireplace. And the mantel.

There were two objects on the mantel. The silver gong. And an ornate box.

Could the box be the riddle chest the witches had mentioned? If so, perhaps the riddle's answer was inside. Maybe this was not a riddle test at all, but a test of an entirely different nature. How deliciously devious!

Warlock walked over to the mantel and took down the box. It was unexpectedly heavy and looked very old. Unlike the gong it was not silver. Some other metal, but he couldn't tell what. Bronze? He tried to open the lid, but it wouldn't budge. Locked? There didn't appear to be a keyhole. He squinted and couldn't find a seam for the lid. Now *this* was a puzzle.

He turned the box in his hands, applying pressure in different places, trying to find a seam. He never found one, but he did manage to get one end of the box to turn. "Like a Rubik's Cube," he said aloud. *Is that what this is? A fancy Rubik's Cube?*

As a child Warlock had learned to master the Rubik's Cube and impress his friends. Of course, that was before he had taken the stage name *Warlock* and pushed aside childish things. But the box looked much older than any Rubik's Cube and it wasn't really behaving like one. After turning the one end he couldn't find any other bits that turned.

He resumed applying pressure and another part of the box shifted, sliding like a drawer, but unlike a drawer it was a solid piece. There was no open space in which to put anything, such as the answer to his riddle. He realized then that the box was no longer square and that he couldn't just put it back on the mantel and no one would notice. He tried to push the slidy bit back in, but it wouldn't budge.

Warlock looked at his watch. Damn, he had to get to his gig. But he had no answer to the riddle about the two sisters and he couldn't leave the box like this. Valerie would think him an idiot.

Panicking only a little, he continued to poke and prod the box. Ten minutes later it looked nothing like a box. There were bits sticking out and depressions and crevices and still no answer to the witches' riddle. He stared at the painted fireplace and wished it was real so he could throw the box into it.

Warlock immediately recanted. The thought had come from his inner stupid self, that small voice that was a constant wellspring of truly bad ideas. Pay no attention to the fool behind the curtain.

He noticed his hands were shaking. God, he hated tests. He tried again to press the box back into a cube and his trembling fingers fumbled, sending the box bouncing between awkward hands. The harder he tried to hold onto it the more awkward his fingers fumbled the box until at last it slipped from his failed grip.

Warlock watched the box fall as though in slow motion, tumbling through the air, turning through space as though proudly displaying its unboxlike shape, its abundance of angles, numerous fissures and jutting protrusions. Warlock's eyes saw all this and then saw too the carpeted hardwood floor, and his pounding heart slowed with the realization that the box, such as it was, would bounce harmlessly off the carpet. The box was no fragile collection of plastic pieces, a Rubik's Cube, to shatter upon contact with the hardness of the floor. At worst the hardwood beneath the carpet would receive a mild dent.

Even so, Warlock's breath caught as the box hit the floor.

It did not bounce.

It did not shatter.

What it did do is open like a flower. That was when the world's ugliest house came crashing down on him.

The Conundrum Of The Sphinx

Warlock shook himself and discovered that he was somehow not buried in pink siding and excess eaves. There was quite a lot of sand, however. He coughed as it flew into his eyes and mouth. Perhaps more than a lot.

When his eyes ceased watering he knew one thing. He was not in Kansas anymore. The house was gone. As were the neighbors' houses. And the streets. The city. There was nothing but sand for as far as the eye could see, rolling in waves that extended out to the horizon like some stormy ocean, frozen and painted beige. The sun was still there. Perhaps a bit bigger and hotter than Warlock remembered, hanging in a sky so blue that it hurt his eyes. One word repeated in his mind. *Crap. Crap. Crap.*

When, eventually, there was room for more than that one word, he added a second. *Holy Crap. Holy Crap. Holy Crap.*

His whole body was shaking. He rubbed his face with his trembling hands. He closed and opened his eyes. Repeatedly. But the scene never changed. He found room for a third word. *Holy Serious Crap.* Drop a box that doesn't look like a box onto an ugly carpet and what do you get? Warlock couldn't find the words. *Holy Serious Crap.*

Somewhere among those three words it registered in his mind that there was no sign of the box in the sand at his feet. *Crap.*

"Hey Duffas!"

Recognizing something familiar in this alien place, Warlock looked up but saw only sand.

"Behind you, genius."

He had to cover his eyes with a trembling hand as he turned; the sun really was bright. And hot. Warlock found he was starting to sweat. He was pretty sure it wasn't from nerves. When he could see again, what he saw shocked him so badly that he fell backward onto his butt. Fortunately the sand was soft.

"How come I get all the geniuses?"

The creature making this observation stood perhaps forty feet tall, half as wide and twice as long, though it was hard to estimate size given the lack of anything to measure against. Suffice it to say that it sat like a lone, large building in the desert. It had the lower body of a lion, the upper body of an eagle and wore an expression of irritated smugness. It was a sphinx. Even more a sphinx than the Sphinx of Egypt. If anything, the Sphinx of Egypt was a cheap imitation.

Warlock chewed on his tongue, trying to get it to work. "Who? Er. What are you?"

The creature shook its eagle head and ruffled some feathers. "If you have to ask then you really are seven kinds of stupid."

Warlock struggled to his feet and, even though he was trembling inside and out, attempted to look tough. As tough as you could look while glaring up at someone six times taller than you. "Fine, I can see what you are. But how did I get here?"

The sphinx bent down its beak and studied him, like a bird studies a worm before eating it. "I assume you opened the puzzle box."

"Of course," said Warlock, barely stopping himself from laughing hysterically. "I opened the puzzle box."

"And now," said the sphinx, "You must answer the riddle I give you, or die."

Yeah. No surprise there. Between renditions of *Crap, Holy Crap*, and *Holy Serious Crap*, he remembered hearing somewhere that the best defense was a good offense. He felt fairly certain that this was a war reference, and that while the situation he found himself in wasn't a war, he couldn't really say what it was. Besides, it was all he had so he used it. "How about you answer *my* riddle?" asked Warlock.

"What!" The sphinx spread its wings and whipped up a storm of sand.

Warlock gritted his teeth and closed his eyes until it passed, half-hoping that when he opened them again he would be back in the world's ugliest house, the victim of some hallucinogenic drug released when the box opened. The other half wanted none of it. This was the adventure of a lifetime and he didn't want it to end. Right now Warlock was rather unhappy with that other half. He opened his eyes, proving the other half the victor.

"No one," continued the sphinx, "has ever asked *me* to answer a riddle. What a concept! You are either very wise or very foolish."

"Yes," said Warlock. *Got it in two.*

"Very well," mused the sphinx. "Ask your riddle. Since I know everything I shall have no trouble answering it."

Holy Serious Crap, thought Warlock. *Was this going to work?* It was all he could do to keep from falling into the sand laughing. "Then riddle me this," he said. "There are two sisters: one gives birth to the other and she, in turn, gives birth to the first. Who are the sisters?"

The sphinx stared at him. "But... that's my riddle! You can't ask me *my* riddle. That's what I'm supposed to ask *you*!"

"Holy Ser—" said Warlock. "I mean, but I did ask. Now tell me the answer."

The sphinx scowled, as much as a bird can scowl. "Day gives birth to Night and Night to Day." The scowl turned into a sulk. "But you have asked me my own riddle. Now I'll have to come up with a different riddle to ask you."

"Oh, that's OK," said Warlock, his voice beginning to break. He wasn't going to be able to keep this up. "I don't really need another riddle. If you'd just show me how to get back—"

The sphinx took a step toward him, rising on lion legs then settling back into the sand. This act raised a great wall of sand that knocked Warlock down and half buried him. The giant beak loomed toward him. "You cannot go back without answering my riddle. Fail to answer correctly and you die!"

"OK," said Warlock in a small voice. "The answer is *Day and Night*. Now can I go?"

"No!" squawked the sphinx. "You must answer a new riddle. A more difficult riddle now that I have given you the answer to the old one. But what?" Its eye seemed to see something in the sand. "Ah, yes. This one. It has never been asked. Ever. Ha! What has the power to give you endless joy, but if lost, leaves you miserable?"

"Uhm," mumbled Warlock.

"*Uhm* is not an answer," said the sphinx. "Now answer quickly. I grow weary of looking at you."

Warlock ducked his head as he thought about the Day and Night riddle. But his thoughts were crowded out with *Crap, Crap, Crap*. If this was the same kind of riddle there could be any number of answers. *Crap.* But the sphinx would only accept the one it had in mind. *CRAP!* But would it risk the same kind of riddle? *HOLY!* Or was it being devious and doing something else entirely? *SERIOUS!*

"Hurry up," admonished the sphinx. "I grow hungry as well as impatient. Perhaps I shall eat you."

Warlock ducked even more, as if his body could feel the hungry beak approaching. *The sand*, thought Warlock. *The sphinx was looking at something in the sand.*

Warlock fell down to his hands and knees and began searching where the sphinx had looked. He was openly weeping now, his cool façade blown. He was going to be sphinx kibble. *Holy Serious Crap. Sphinx kibble!*

The sphinx gave an annoyed squawk and Warlock risked a glance and saw it lift its wings in preparation to raise another sand storm. But before the sphinx could act Warlock saw a flash of red and dove for it. The sphinx lowered its wings and grumbled in its belly. "Have you an answer for me?"

"Er," said Warlock, wiping his eyes with a sandy fist. "This ring?"

"This ring?" echoed the sphinx. It rolled its eyes. "Sure. Why not. That ring. You humans get stupider with every passing millennium, don't you? No, don't answer. That was an observation, not a question."

Holy Crap, thought Warlock. Only it was a different Holy Crap. It was a Holy Crap that contained a sense of surprise and disbelief and, well, even more disbelief. The way the sphinx had rolled its eyes and said "Why not", Warlock had the feeling that he could have said *garglefarb* and gotten the same response, that any answer he gave would be the right one. He'd had no idea what was going on and now he had less of an idea than that!

From somewhere Warlock's inner stupid self rose to the surface and waved the ring at the sphinx. "Can I keep it?"

"What?" demanded the sphinx, blinking with astonishment. "You want to keep the ring?"

Warlock should have dropped the ring then and there. He should have cried and cowered and said, *please sir, can I have another?* Instead he placed the ring on his right middle finger. His inner stupid self was in its glory.

The ring fit perfectly. It was a very masculine ring; heavy silver etched with what could be runes, holding a large square ruby. If any ring shouted *Warlock*, it was this one.

"You're lucky to still be alive," squawked the sphinx, "never mind asking for trinkets. But go ahead, keep the ring. A lot of good it will do you."

As the sphinx spoke its voice faded, as though it were moving off into the distance. The last words Warlock heard were, "Bloody stupid huma—" And then Warlock found himself once again in the ugliest house in the world. He was on his knees surrounded by a scattering of sand. The ring, which he decided to call the *Warlock Ring* was still on his finger. The puzzle box sat on the carpet in front of him, no worse for wear for having popped open after hitting the floor, but still looking like anything but a box.

A Coven Name For Warlock

As Warlock sat staring at the box he knew two things. First, this coven business wasn't the lark he had thought it was. Not just a hobby that occupied Valerie's time and something he would have to put up with if he wanted to get close to her. There was real magic going on. Sure, verbal abuse by a sphinx wasn't the first thing that came to mind when Warlock thought of magic, but he couldn't think of any other name for it. Well, he could think of *one* other name: psychotropic hallucination. But drug-induced trips didn't leave behind souvenirs like the Warlock Ring. He turned the ring on his finger, just to make sure it was really there.

The second thing he knew was that he was still shaking like an invalid. He needed to take several deep breaths and drive the words holy, serious, and crap from his head, and tell his inner stupid self to get back in its cage. *I could have been sphinx kibble!* No, got to stop thinking like that. His inner stupid self was right for once. The sphinx had been going to let him go all along. Any answer was the right one. *Breathe.* Why was he trying to make sense of this? None of it made any sense. *Breathe. Ring still there? Yup. Breathe. Breathe again.*

Eventually Warlock cleared his nerves and his mind and felt a little more like himself. He looked again at the box and noticed something. It was now stretched out like the folds of an open box laid flat. Only while a normal box would look something like a cardboard crucifix, this box was just a line of twisted metal, like a bunch of chains stretched out and crossing over each other. The jutting parts along the surface seemed to make letters. B-E-L-I-E-V-E. Believe. With a finger he traced each letter. As his finger left the final E the box folded up into its original box shape. Good as new.

More magic? And what was BELIEVE supposed to mean? His inner stupid self shouted: "It's about you, duffas! You need to stop acting cool and instead *be cool*. Believe in yourself for once." But Warlock ignored this bit of faux wisdom. What did his inner stupid self know, anyway?

Instead he considered the box, which was once again a box. Now he could put it back on the mantel with no one the wiser that he had fooled with it. Plus, he now had the answer to the riddle. Or, at least, *an* answer. Suddenly everything was going his way.

After returning the box to what he hoped was its original position, Warlock lifted the silver hammer to hit the little silver gong. But he stopped himself. *The sand.* The carpet was much heavier than it looked and it took several attempts at folding parts of it to shake the sand onto the hardwood floor. Then no effort at all to brush the sand with his palm under the edge of the carpet. Now there was no trace that Warlock had not simply stood and pondered the riddle.

He returned to the mantel above the painted fireplace and tapped the gong with the silver hammer. "Bang Bang," he said.

Valerie and the other witches trooped back into the room. "Have you divined the answer to the riddle?" the High Priestess intoned.

"I'm not sure *divined* is the word I'd use," said Warlock, "but I do have an answer. The sisters are Day and Night."

Valerie smiled while several witches behind her grumbled. Barely audible was Sister August's mumbled, "Too easy."

Undeterred, Valerie raised her hands and proclaimed, "Sisters, our coven is at last complete. Sister January. Sister December. Come forward and convey upon our new Sister his coven name."

"Uhm," said Warlock. "I'd kinda like to keep my own name."

But the witches ignored him as Sisters January and December stepped forward. Sister January carried one of those cardboard tubes that you put floor plans or art prints in.

"And this *Sister* thing—" said Warlock.

"Unlike other covens," Valerie cut in as the two Sisters opened the tube, "where the High Priestess chooses the coven name for each new member, we allow new members to choose their own coven name—"

"Well," said Warlock, "In that case—"

"—From the coven calendar," finished Valerie. Sisters January and December had removed and unrolled the tube's contents. It was a 1972 calendar proclaiming *The Year Of The Witch*. It featured a head shot of Elizabeth Montgomery from the old *Bewitched* TV series.

"Er," said Warlock.

"January and February are already taken," said Sister January.

"As are April through December," added Sister December.

"That leaves—," said Warlock.

"Sister March," said Sister August, with a smirk.

"Er," said Warlock. Every now and then in the music business, no matter how hungry you are, you encounter what is known as a deal breaker. It could cost you your career, but you have to draw the line. Perhaps you are asked to sing Britney Spears songs, or provide a tribute performance of Tiny Tim. Every musician has a breaking point where they turn down the money and go home. Warlock had just hit such a breaking point. *Sister March* indeed.

"Now Sisters," said Valerie. "I know some of you were opposed to including a male witch in our coven." She looked pointedly at Sisters August, January, and a couple of others. "But we agreed to let Warlock try out and he has passed the trial. So now he will be known among us as *Brother* March."

Better, thought Warlock. The purpose of the deal breaker is to encourage the other party to back off, for the terms to be more amenable. He could live with Brother March, but Warlock felt there may still be room for negotiation. "If I could suggest something."

Everyone looked at him.

Warlock offered what he hoped was a winning smile. "I get the whole calendar thing, and that any name other than March won't fly, but this Brother and Sister business sounds a little, I don't know, monkish, don't you think?"

The looks turned into stares.

"Perhaps even a little... cultish?"

"We don't want to be thought of as a cult!" exclaimed Sister December.

"That's why we use the calendar," added another witch. Warlock thought she might be Sister September. "Everyone loves calendar girls."

Warlock was relieved that someone else said it before he accidentally blurted it out.

"But no one knows our coven names," said Sister January. "We only share those among ourselves."

"Oh, right," said Sister December. She let out a breath.

"Even so," said Warlock, still hoping to make his point, "we may begin seeing ourselves as a cult, on a subconscious level."

There were murmurs among the Sisters, all along the lines of, "No, I don't think that would happen."

"Which can all be avoided," Warlock hastily concluded, "if my coven name was *Master* March."

A silence fell upon the room that was so thick that Warlock supposed it might be, well, magical. Then…

"Mistress January," mused Sister January.

Several other Sisters joined in.

"Mistress May."

"Mistress June."

"Mistress October."

Even to Warlock's ears the coven was beginning to sound more like a bordello than a Sunday School.

"Master March should be fine," said Valerie. "But Sisters, let's not be too hasty to follow suit. When I look at Samantha," she nodded at the calendar, "I don't see *Mistress*."

It took Warlock a moment to realize that Samantha meant Elizabeth Montgomery, the perky witch from *Bewitched*.

"Sisters," said Valerie. "Please welcome to our coven our twelfth and final member, Master March." She raised her right hand and put it on Warlock's shoulder. "Your coven name must be kept secret within the coven and used when we meet and work our group magic."

"Group magic," Warlock echoed. He had watched a few *Bewitched* re-runs on the Retro Channel and didn't remember seeing any group magic. Didn't remember covens either. Weren't the witches all related and trying to get as far away from each other as possible? Didn't they all just cause problems for each other? Especially for Samantha's husband? He still couldn't help but see himself as a Darren to Valerie's Samantha.

There is something about time pieces that make you look at them at the oddest moments. Here was Warlock surrounded by a gaggle of young calendar girls who worshipped a 60's TV show about domestic witches, one of whom was the object of his own amorous worship, with every evidence that magic is real and no clue what the next step would be, when his unconscious mind directed him to glance at his watch.

"Holy Serious Crap!" said Warlock. "I'm late."

The Gig Must Go On

"Hey, Duffas! You're late."

For the briefest of moments Warlock thought that the sphinx had caught up with him, but then realized the voice belonged to Gord Boscoe, the Seriously Damp's bass guitarist. What kind of name was Gord for a bassist, anyway? He'd never go anywhere. Loser.

"Sorry, sorry," said Warlock. "Lots of time left." He found the cable bag and started unzipping it. "I'll have you set up in a jiffy." But the bag was mostly empty.

"Already set up," said Ricky Montana, the drummer. "No skin."

Montana's not a bad name for a musician, but Warlock always believed he should drop the Ricky part.

Warlock looked around the stage and saw that Montana was right. Everything was set up. Guitars in their stands. Cables plugged in. Montana sat Indian style on the floor tapping quietly on some bongos, warming up before he hit the big drums. Gord was leafing through some sheet music. Must be some new material tonight. Crazy Eddie, lead vocal and lead guitar, was nowhere in sight.

Crazy was not Crazy Eddie's real name, but it sucked as a musician name unless you were into Blues. The Seriously Damp was not a Blues band. The Damp was alternative rock.

Warlock had tried to explain to Valerie what alternative rock was. When he finished she said: "So it's like unpopular rock." After he clarified she said: "You mean rock that blows?" It was at that point that he gave up trying to explain it to her and just named a bunch of alternative rock bands, like the Cure, R.E.M and Cold Coffee. "Ah," she said. "It's like rock without the roll." That seemed like a good point to change the subject.

"No Crazy Eddie?" asked Warlock.

The two band members shook their heads. They never spoke much before a show. Conserving their voices, they said. Of course, Gord only provided backup and Montana didn't sing at all. He just didn't like talking.

Warlock looked at his watch. "He'd better get here soon. Not much time for a sound check."

"Did the sound check," said Gord, not looking up from his sheet music.

Did the sound check? These guys were going to sound like crap. And it would reflect badly on the roadie. Badly on him.

Warlock went around and checked the cables. At least *they* were OK. Right cables plugged in the right way into the right ports. He checked the settings on the amps and the mixing board, and then looked out into the near-empty bar. Yeah. Right size. The settings should do to start. He would adjust them on the fly as things got going. He checked the lights and the lighting controls. They looked OK too.

He looked up to see Gord and Montana watching him. Gord said, "You think we didn't spend a year as roadies before starting the band?"

A year? Warlock had been roadie for five years. *Damn.* It should be him up there as front man, not Crazy Eddie. Guy couldn't even pick a decent name for himself.

The awkwardness of the moment was saved by Gord's cell phone going off. The Hallelujah Chorus. My God, but this guy had no class.

Gord grunted into the phone then stuffed it back in his pocket. "Hey roadie," he said. "Tear it all down. No gig tonight."

"What's up?" asked Montana.

Gord shook his head. "Crazy crashed his car. Busted arm. Some ribs. They're takin' him to Grace."

"Bummer," said Montana.

Warlock stood there. Busted arm? That's not just no gig tonight. That's no gig for months, unless they found a replacement front man.

"Hey roadie," called Gord. He was putting his sheet music into his guitar case. "Don't just stand there. Break it down."

"I've got a name," Warlock shouted back. "It's Warlock. Got it? Warlock." But in his mind all he could hear was Master March.

"Yeah, well," said Gord. "Who cares? Right now we need the gear stowed, so it's roadie. Bad enough we had to set up ourselves."

Five years, Warlock thought. *I've been roadie for five freakin' years. They only ever did one year. I'm a better roadie than they'll ever be. And I'll be a better band member.*

Gord was getting visibly irate at Warlock's lack of roadieness while Montana looked amused by Gord's growing ill temper. Gord opened his mouth, ready to harangue, but Warlock cut him off.

"Whatever happened to *The Gig Must Go On*?" he demanded.

"Not without a front man, it doesn't," growled Gord. He started unplugging cables himself.

"But you've got a front man," said Warlock.

Gord stopped pulling cables and looked at him. "Who?"

"Warlock," said Warlock.

"Who?"

"Me." *You idiot who can't even pick a decent stage name for yourself.*

Gord roared with laughter while Montana had the decency to just chuckle quietly. It took Gord a moment to recover enough to speak. "You? I've heard you play and sing during sound check. You're crap on guitar and have a voice only a hound dog could love."

Warlock clenched his fists. He had two choices. Beat Gord until he was in worse shape than Crazy. Or pick up Crazy's performance guitar and start playing. He opted for the least satisfying alternative, but the one also least likely to get him in trouble.

Crazy might be a hack but he had decent guitars. His performance guitar was an ebony Gibson Les Paul Melody Maker. Warlock swung the strap over his shoulder, fingered an experimental strum to ensure that Gord hadn't pulled any critical cables, then turned down the volume a smidge so that it would match his unmiked voice. Before Gord or Montana could stop him he jumped right into *Ice Cold Mama*, one of the Damp's most popular songs.

For five years Warlock had been roadie for the Seriously Damp. In addition to setting up and checking the equipment he had sat through every performance, fine-tuning the sound and controlling the lights for dramatic effect. After all those performances he knew all the lyrics and guitar work by rote.

He didn't own a guitar himself, but had tried out bits of various songs while tuning the band's equipment or messing with equipment in music stores until the staff realized he couldn't afford to buy anything and threw him out.

Despite wanting to be a musician, Warlock had never had a music lesson in his life. You needed your own instrument for that. And you needed money to pay for the lessons, which were expensive. So Warlock had learned the guitar the roadie way, by ear and on other people's instruments. Sometimes this worked. Just look at Jimi Hendrix or Mark Tremonti. Usually it did not. Warlock was as usual as they come.

And yet... *Ice Cold Mama* poured from Warlock's fingers and lips as if he had been born to the song. Gord's fingers froze above the power button. Montana rose to his feet, sat down behind the drums, picked up his sticks, and started tapping along. Gord followed suit, picking up his guitar and adding the baseline. The few heads in the Blue Oyster Bar turned.

Warlock played though his own surprise, afraid to stop in case this moment never came again, and eventually reached the end of the song. The final note lingered in the air and applause from the bar filled the void.

Gord stood staring at Warlock, speechless.

Montana said, "The gig must go on."

A Brief Word About Eavesdropping

Some conversations make no sense, even when you know roughly what it's about and you hear both sides of the conversation. Then there are conversations where is it abundantly clear what is going on, even if only one side of the conversation is overheard. Let's put our ear to the wall and give it a try.

Ring.

"Hello."

"Sorry. Who is this?"

"Warlock?"

"Could you slow down. I can't understand a word you're say—"

"You're what?"

"What's *fronting*?"

"Really. Is this some kind of joke?"

"OK. Sure, sure, I believe you."

"Yes, I could be there."

"Wait! Where is there?"

"What's the name of the bar?"

"Never heard of it."

"Down on eleventh?"

"OK. I can be there in twenty."

Click.

"Who was that?"

"Warlock. I mean, Master March."

"So what's up?"

"I think the chickens have come out."

Yes, well, never mind.

Oh! Oh! It's Magic

The Seriously Damp had never played better. After getting properly in costume and being introduced by the Blue Oyster Bar's owner (who may have been a terrific small business manger, but was a less than adequate MC) the band opened with *Don't Let A little Rain Get You Wet*. Having warmed up the small, but attentive audience, they moved into *River of Love* and *Big Rubber Boots*.

The audience grew as people walking past the bar stopped to listen then came inside as they saw plenty of empty seats. Among them was a group of eleven women in their early twenties who would qualify as groupies had they cheered for the band and gazed longingly at the musicians with adorning eyes. However, since instead of doing this they ordered Cokes and ginger ales and clapped politely after each song, the crowd assumed they were just college students or secretaries, with no real taste for alternative music. They would probably go look for a bar with an 80's cover band after they finished their sodas. All but one did.

Warlock had almost fallen off the stage when he saw the entire coven walk into the bar. He had been watching for Valerie and was worried she might not show up after all. That might have been preferable to seeing the entire coven. Sister August glared at him. Probably hadn't stopped glaring since earlier that day.

When the Sisters arrived he was caressing the strings and singing "into everyone's cereal a little rain must fall." The faltering of the guitar and the sudden pain in his voice could have been intentional. He pretended that it was and continued along in the same vein. It amazed him that he could ad lib a song so seamlessly, especially one he had heard a million times but never played before in its entirety. The bland expressions the coven wore made him look closer at that amazement. Could it be magic? But he hadn't done anything. So he kept playing. The gig must go on.

By the time the band took a break Valerie was on her own. Warlock gave thanks to whatever gods witches prayed to.

"Not bad for a roadie," Valerie said as he sat down next her. A server whisked by and slammed a Coke on the table in front of him.

"I can explain," said Warlock. This was supposed to be a celebration, not an apology.

"I'm sure it will be a good one," Valerie said.

Warlock cut to the chase. "Crazy broke his arm."

"And," said Valerie. She waved her hand in a circle.

"The gig had to go on. I was available. The band asked me to front them."

"The band asked you to front them?" Valerie repeated. "The band that hates you. The band that doesn't even know your name and just calls you roadie."

"There wasn't anyone else," Warlock asserted.

"But you can barely play the guitar," said Valerie. "At least, that's what you told me."

"I…" Warlock stopped. He knew he was crap on the guitar. He had never played like he had tonight.

"How are the blisters?" she asked.

"What blisters?" said Warlock.

"Exactly. You don't have proper calluses. Your fingers should be bleeding."

Warlock looked at the fingers of his left hand. He had never played often or long enough to develop the thick calluses a guitarist needs. When he did play, his fingertips always hurt after even twenty minutes of pressing the strings. He had just played two hours straight with no pain at all. "Cool," he said.

Valerie slammed her palm on the table. "Cool? Are you a child? It's not cool. You're abusing your power."

"My power?"

"You're supposed to be using your power with the coven for good. Not to set yourself up as a rock star."

"Hey wait. I didn't know I even had power. And I'm doing this for the band."

"Really?" said Valerie. "For Gord and Montana?"

"Well, not them personally," said Warlock, surprised that she could remember the band members' names. "For the Seriously Damp. The gig must go on."

"Ohhhh," said Valerie. "You're such a disappointment." She jumped up out of her chair and ran out of the bar.

Warlock rose to follow, but was stopped by a twenty-something who did qualify as a groupie.

"Crazy Eddie! Can I have your autograph?" She pushed a sharpie pen into his hand and exposed the top of her left breast.

Warlock weighed the girl's mindless adoration and decided it was poor compensation for the disappointment he had seen in Valerie's eyes. But he signed anyway.

"Crazy Eddie is history," he said. "Say hello to Warlock."

The Good Witch

Warlock woke up at the crack of noon. Yes it's a cliché, but for a musician it's also a fact of life. His head swam with the mother of all hangovers. Another cliché. No excuse this time. He chugged some aspirin and milk and pondered the eternal question of how you can get hung over from a few Cokes and a 2 AM steak sandwich. Not finding an answer he napped until one o'clock and felt a little better.

As a twenty-something who owned neither car nor driver's license, he took the bus from his basement bachelor pad to the ugliest house in the world and wondered if he would get assigned a broomstick. Or could he just nod his head and blink and be wherever he wanted to be? No, that was *I Dream Of Jeannie*. For now he'd settle for the bus.

The real question was: *How do I make things right with Valerie?*

Warlock had never been good at patching things up. The first step, he knew, was to figure out what he did wrong. Often this was impossible. Even point blank asking the offended party "What did I do wrong?" often failed to produce comprehensible results.

He went through the circumstances in his mind. First, Valerie was happy with him, well, *happier* with him, when he was a roadie. Then when the opportunity arose to be in the band she blew up. She claimed he had misused his power. Did she mean magic? He looked down at the Warlock Ring on his right hand. Was it the ring? He thought back on how well he had played. And sung. It was more than just a *good night*. It had to be magic.

Valerie had called him selfish. Did she want to be in the band too? He pictured in his mind Valerie and the Pussycats, only there were ten Pussycats and it made for quite a racket.

The bus reached his stop and Warlock got out and walked the two blocks to the world's ugliest house. He idly wondered if he could use his magic to make it look more respectable. What if the exterior was a nice rust red? He decided he had better not, at least until he had spoken with Valerie to find out what her problem with him was. Top priority.

"What's the password?" said Sister August from behind the door.

Warlock glared at her through the five by five hole and spoke his coven name.

"That was yesterday's password," Sister August told him with a certain smugness.

"I don't have time for this foolishness." Warlock gripped the doorknob with his right hand, the one with the Warlock ring, and willed the door to unlock.

The doorknob fell apart in his hand. The bolt on the other side of the door, however, remained bolted. "Crap."

"What?" cried Sister August. "What did you do?"

Warlock heard the bolt slide and then Sister August stepped out onto the porch. Her scowl dripped acid.

She frowned at the pieces of doorknob lying on the top wooden step. "I hope you're as good at fixing doors as you are breaking them."

"It was an old doorknob," said Warlock. "Love the scowl, by the way. It's quite becoming." He marched past the unhappy witch and found his way to the parlor.

Valerie greeted him with an unreadable expression. "I see you got past Sister August. Figured out today's password, did you?"

"There are ways to circumvent passwords," he answered mysteriously. "Look, about last night—"

"—I probably overreacted," interrupted Valerie.

The train of thought in Warlock's head instantly ran off the tracks. And he had worked so hard to put it together. He resorted to, "Er."

Valerie took a deep sigh. "I have to remember that you are like a child with a new toy."

"A what?"

"You've had no guidance or training, and Goddess knows the Sisters haven't been any help."

"Well that's—"

"—I was planning on showing you your room today so that you could prepare to move in."

"Move in?"

"But I now think that may be premature."

"Premature."

"You should study this first." She brought out a book she had been holding behind her back and presented it to him. "I think it's for the best."

Warlock took the book and stared at it. The cover said: *The Good Witch by Elizabeth Montgomery*. When he looked up, Valerie was gone.

That went well, he told himself. *I think*.

The Devil You Say

Warlock settled himself on a sofa with his head at one end and his feet at the other, after of course taking off his shoes. Despite not getting in a complete sentence he felt that he was somehow back in Valerie's good books and wanted to stay there awhile.

He'd decided last night, after Valerie had stormed out of the Blue Oyster Bar, that it was time to ask her out on a second date. After, of course, sorting out whatever it was that had upset her, which seemed to have happened though he was even less sure of the solution than he had been of the problem.

Had she really asked him to move in with her? The words had been spoken, but somehow he got the feeling that the meaning was off kilter. But no matter, that was a little fast even for him. He'd read a book first.

Warlock had never been one for reading, so fortunately it wasn't a large book. Well, it was a large book but so too was the type. And there was a photograph or drawing on every page. Most of the photos were stills from the *Bewitched* TV series. Most of the text, too, was about the TV series, but the purpose seemed to be to put the various scenes and events into the context of witchcraft.

After twenty pages Warlock determined the theme: that real world witches are a force for good and have nothing to do with evil or Devil worship.

Fair enough. Warlock had sought entry in the coven only after Valerie had mentioned it on their first, and so far only, date. And he had done so solely for the purpose of getting closer to Valerie, not to become a witch. In fact, the concept of wearing a goat's head or decapitating chickens held no real appeal for him.

He skimmed through to the end of the book and concluded that Elizabeth Montgomery, the actress, had never written it. Either the network had hired a ghost writer or the book was completely unsanctioned. He wondered where Valerie had gotten it.

He then wondered just how devoted to Elizabeth Montgomery Valerie was. Did she see herself as the second coming of *Bewitched*? Had he fallen head over heels for a fruitcake?

But what about the magic? That was real enough. Real enough to play the guitar and defile doorknobs.

He glanced up at the mantel above the fake fireplace. The silver gong and the ornate puzzle box were still there. His visit with the sphinx must have been magic too. And the ring.

Warlock put down the book and rose from the sofa. After the incident with the door he was reluctant to use magic again. He had used it to front the band without even knowing what he'd done. And when he'd consciously tried to use it to unlock a door, things had gone pear shaped. Didn't that happen to Darren when he got magic for a brief time?

He shook his head. He had to stop confusing fiction with real life. He was not Darren Stevens, he was Warlock. A warlock. Had his choosing of that particular stage name been a premonition of what he would become? Why not?

Perhaps he should try some magic. Recalling the book, he should also be a good witch. Do something good.

He could fix the door. But Sister August would be out there and he didn't want an audience in case things went sour. Again.

His eyes fell to the fake fireplace. Why would anyone want to paint a fireplace onto a wall? But maybe they hadn't. Maybe it had been a real fireplace and one of the witches had turned it into a painted wall. That made much more sense. All Warlock had to do was change it back. Easy as pie.

But now that he had made the decision to attempt magic, he felt doubt pooling in his stomach. Suddenly pie was no longer easy. His inner stupid self looked up and said: "Believe in yourself." But Warlock pushed that part of him back down. "I already believe in myself," he muttered, not really believing the words.

Conscious of his Warlock's Ring, and setting aside what had happened with the doorknob, Warlock focused his thoughts on the wall, imagining the painted flames as real flames. He closed his eyes. And when he opened them the flames were real.

But there were rather more flames than the fireplace warranted. The house was on fire!

"Quick to jump to conclusions, aren't we?" said a voice.

Warlock spun around and there behind him, on a burning sofa, lounged Ray Wise, the actor who had played the Devil in the TV series *Reaper*, complete with dark blue suit and perfect hair.

"You're right about this book, though." He held up *The Good Witch*, a corner of which was on fire. "Elizabeth never wrote this. True, she became moderately Wiccan after the show stopped filming, but that was more to sell autographs than from any true belief." He flashed Warlock his patented grin.

"And you're not really Ray Wise," said Warlock. "You just took his form to set me at ease." And Warlock did feel at ease. He should be freaked, but he wasn't. None of this felt real.

The Devil tossed away the burning book and rose to his feet. "Bravo. Bravo," he said, clapping his hands. "Give the man a kewpie doll. But I'm not lying about the book. It would be a *sssin* to lie about books." The *S* in sin seemed to have a life of its own.

Warlock noted that while the house kept burning around him, the flames never advanced. The Devil, if that's who this was, wasn't out to kill him, but to talk to him. "So what it is that you want?"

The Devil chuckled. "Your soul, of course." Then he laughed. "Just kidding. Really. I've had all the souls I can stomach. Overrated, souls. Not worth the ethereal nothingness they're made of. But seriously, I'm here to help you."

"Help me."

"Learn how to use your power. And, oh, you've got a lot of it. Given time you could be called Destroyer of Worlds. Wouldn't that be something?"

"I don't know," said Warlock. "Would it?"

The Devil flashed him a silver tooth. "Take it from me kid, there are lots of worlds out there just begging to be destroyed. And it's fun, too. Didn't you ever play video games?"

"Well I—"

"—Oh, that's right. Grew up poor on the wrong side of the tracks. But now's your chance."

"It is?"

The Devil spread wide his hands. "You can have it all, son. How about stardom? Didn't you enjoy being the front man for the Seriously Damp?"

"You know about that?"

"Know about? I arranged it. You don't think accidents just happen do you? No, that Crazy Eddie is a pretty good driver. Even when I stopped the green light from switching to yellow he knew that something was up. Fortunately, driving is an instinct. If the light is green you keep your foot on the gas. And you can take that to the bank."

"You put Crazy in the hospital?"

The Devil grinned. "And you got to be front man for the Damp." Then his look turned serious. "That was your first and only freebie. From now on it's tit for tat."

"Er…"

"You do a job for me and I make an opportunity for you. How about it kid? It's the grand old Warlock tradition."

One thought went through Warlock's mind. *Crap.*

After he recovered from that one thought he coaxed out a few more. They went something like this:

This is a Deal With The Devil.

Crap.

These deals never work out.

Crap.

But that's in fiction, which is full of uplifting morals rather than real life.

Hmmm.

In real life crooked bankers rob you of your life savings, then get bailed out when their greed breaks the system, and then they retire to tropical islands with hugnormous pensions. No wait, that's too big for even my mind to grasp. Real life is where losers like Crazy Eddie front alternative rock bands while cool cats named Warlock adjust the lighting.

Warlock could picture himself up at the mic while Crazy, arm in a sling, adjusted the lights. *What's wrong with this picture? Nothing.*

' '

Look, there was no crap that time. Things are looking up.

But this is the Devil, man.

Crap.

"Well," said the Devil.

"Er," said Warlock.

"*Er* is not an answer," said the Devil.

"How about I think about it?" Warlock suggested.

The Devil blew air out of his cheeks and tsk tsked and shook his head. "Dangerous," he said. "But, if that's the way you want it..." He clapped his hands and was gone. The fire, too, vanished.

Warlock looked about the parlor and saw that the book was back on the sofa where he had left it, unsinged. The fireplace was still just paint. And his headache from earlier in the day was coming back. He rubbed his eyes. This magic thing wasn't doing him much good today.

He considered banging the gong to summon Valerie when she appeared of her own accord.

"Did you finish the book?" she asked.

"Oh yes," Warlock told her. "Interesting read." He decided not to mention the ghost writer. Or the Devil.

Searching For Souls

Valerie ushered him out the front door and onto the porch. "I think at this juncture you could use some soul searching," she said.

Sister August was also on the front porch, attempting to graft the pieces of doorknob back onto the door by means of applying six miles of duct tape. "Read the book, did he?" asked Sister August.

"Yes," said Valerie.

"A lot of good it will do him."

"Hush," said Valerie. To Warlock she said, "Come back at seven. We're going to do a working tonight."

"Whoopee-do," mumbled Sister August.

Valerie ignored her. "It will be our first working with a full coven. I'm expecting extraordinary results."

"Praise the Goddess," whispered Sister August.

Valerie led Warlock down the wooden steps and to the yard gate.

"Tell me," said Warlock. "Does Sister August ever smile?"

The Coven High Priestess considered for a moment. "I don't think so. No."

Warlock gave Valerie an awkward hug and waved a polite goodbye to the sour Sister then walked to the bus stop. He was already on the bus and heading downtown when he realized that his encounter with the Devil had made him forget to ask Valerie out on their second date. *Crap.*

As the bus lurched toward downtown he resolved to ask her out for dinner tomorrow after tonight's working, whatever a working was. Maybe something Italian. Everybody likes Italian.

He got off the bus a half block from Sid's Guitar Shop. Valerie had said he should do some soul searching and the best way to do that was to strum the strings.

Sid was not happy to see him.

"I thought I told you to stay out of here," Sid growled as Warlock entered the store. "If you're not buying you're not trying."

Warlock showed his palms. "You must not have heard, I'm fronting the Seriously Damp now. I'm in the market for a guitar."

Sid's eyes did a passable impression of dinner plates. "You? What happened to Crazy Eddie?"

Visions of Crazy's car getting slammed by a truck while Ray Wise rubbed his hands in delight flashed through Warlock's head. "Broke his arm," Warlock mumbled. "Won't be playing for a while."

"That's a shame," said Sid. "Crazy's a good kid. Still. I can think of a thousand musicians in this town who would make a better replacement than you."

Warlock thought that *a thousand* was going a little far, but he didn't bother to say so. Instead he said, "I've gotten better."

"Right," said Sid, in a tone that struggled to conceal a guffaw. "What kind of guitar are we looking at?"

"I've got $200."

Sid smirked. "New or used?"

Warlock frowned. "New or used bills?"

"Do you want a new or used guitar? $200 isn't going to get you much."

It had taken Warlock five years to save $200 for his guitar fund. The fact that he ate all his meals in bars said all that needed saying about his money management skills. But fact is that time had just flowed one day into the next and the day to actually buy a guitar always seemed a long ways off. It wasn't until last night with the band that he'd realized that that day was really a long ways off in the past. He'd lost five years.

But today all that would change. Or had changed last night. Warlock was no longer a roadie. He was a front man. And a front man needed strings.

"What do you have in the way of used guitars?" he said.

Sid might be a toad on two legs, but he took guitars seriously and showed Warlock the best he could afford, a well used Jackson Hardtail. Warlock knew Jackson to be a solid if not acclaimed brand, and this one looked in good shape. Some of the better used guitars came with pedigrees of who had played them. No one would admit to having played this one.

Warlock lifted the worn strap over his head and settled the Maplewood body against his stomach. It did have a nice feel to it.

He strummed a 'C' chord.

"That squawk is you," said Sid. "The strings are perfectly tuned."

Warlock played through a simple riff. It wasn't bad, but it came nowhere close to what he had done last night.

"Be right back," said Sid. "Got another customer."

Warlock told himself that this was foolish. If he could play last night he could play today. You don't forget how to ride a bike. He tried to picture that analogy in his mind and failed, but he knew it still fit. He prepared to strum again.

"Eh Eh Ehm," said a tiny voice.

Warlock looked up from the guitar to find a small blonde girl standing in front of him. She looked to be about ten years old. Also, her eyes were glowing.

"Aren't you that little girl," he asked, "from that episode of *The Collector* where the Devil appeared by temporarily taking over the body of various people?"

"You watch entirely too much TV," replied the little girl. Then she grinned an evil grin that could only appear on an angelic face. "But you got me. Have you finished thinking about my offer?"

"Er," said Warlock. "Actually, I haven't begun to think about it."

"Yet here you are," said the Devil, "attempting to reap again the rewards from last night's pro bono."

"Look," said Warlock. "What do you need me for? You can cause *accidents* whenever you want."

"True. True," said the little girl. "But look, I'm the Father of Lies. Father, get it. I need children. Evil is much more fun when you're not the only one doing it."

"The thing is," said Warlock, "I've never been big on evil."

"You've never been much of a guitar player, either," suggested the Devil. "Yet here we are."

From the far side of the store came a crash and a twang.

"What was that?" asked Warlock.

The little girl shrugged. "Just a guitar falling off the wall."

Boom. Crash. Bang. The death cries of several additional musical instruments followed, concluding with a lonesome rattle of cymbals.

"Why are you doing that?"

"What makes you think it's me?"

"Well, it isn't me," said Warlock. "And you're the only Devil in the room."

The little girl smiled. "OK. It's me. I'm doing it because I'm annoyed. With you."

Sid shouted as what sounded like a wall collapsing echoed through the store.

Crap, thought Warlock. *Sid doesn't deserve this. And he's probably just the appetizer. I'm the entrée.* "Well stop it," Warlock said with a confidence he didn't feel. "You're not making any points with me here."

Somewhere a fire ignited.

The little girl offered a pretend frown. "I told you that thinking about my offer was dangerous."

This had to stop. "Fine. I'm done thinking. Not interested."

The little girl's eyes flashed, and behind her instruments crashed to the floor as whole wall racks collapsed and shelves toppled. Smoke drifted among the carnage. Warlock wondered if he might have said the wrong thing. Then the little girl started to grow and darken until she became something that resembled an armored assault vehicle with horns. Warlock assumed that if the Devil had a natural form, this was it. When he spoke his voice was thunder.

"Andrew Potemkin," — which was Warlock's real name and the reason why he needed a stage name in the first place — "after a short lifetime of bad decisions you have made yet another bad decision."

That can't be right, thought Warlock. It was his inner stupid self who made those bad decisions. He was pretty certain that this last decision came from his cool self. He looked at his hands. They were trembling. Yup, cool self.

Then suddenly his right middle finger felt like it was on fire and he shook his hand in the air. Amid the flurry of shaking fingers he saw that the Warlock Ring was gone and replaced by a large red welt. The Devil laughed and Warlock saw that the ring was now on the not-quite-goat's taloned finger.

"Now," boomed the revised Devil in a deep, echoing voice. "You will spend the rest of eternity in my domain suffering every torment imaginable."

"Er," said Warlock, stalling while his brain searched for a way out of this mess. His inner stupid self whispered an idea. It was the stupidest idea he had ever heard, but he didn't have anything else so… "Is it true that you sometimes play chess?"

The Devil paused in his revelry and stared at him. "Chess?"

"It's just that I'm not very good on the fiddle."

The armored goat frowned. "You wish to challenge me?"

"Sure," said Warlock, suddenly hoping that this would play out like his encounter with the sphinx, that any move was the right one. "I win, you give me back the ring and never bother me again. You win…" and here is where Warlock ran into trouble. "Uhm. What do you want if you win?"

The Devil laughed. "You have two problems. First, you could never best me at anything. No mortal could. Second, you have nothing I want." He nodded into the distance. "The lake of fire and brimstone is that way. I think we'll start your torment there."

This can't be right. This was the point where the one thing the Devil wants should leap to the fore of Warlock's mind. And then the Devil would accept his challenge and name the one thing that Warlock could best him at. Problem was, nothing was leaping into Warlock's mind. *Crap.*

"Any chance of your offer coming back on the table?" Warlock croaked.

Suddenly his hand stopped hurting. He stopped shaking it and saw that the ring was back on his finger. He looked up and saw that he was back in Sid's Guitar shop and that it hadn't tumbled to the ground. In fact, nothing was amiss. The Jackson guitar still hung from its strap across his shoulder. The small girl stood silently in front of him.

A reprieve? Well, that was better than the alternative. Warlock took a deep breath and exercised the best cure he knew of for unsettled nerves. He strummed the riff he had attempted earlier. The guitar sang.

"That was lovely," said the little girl with flashing eyes.

Sid walked back over. "Yeah. Not bad at all. Never knew the Jackson could sound that good. Maybe I should raise the price."

Warlock dug his hand in his jeans pocket and pulled out his savings, handing the worn bills to Sid. "Too late. I just bought it."

Sid rubbed his chin and stuffed the bills in his shirt. "I guess a deal is a deal."

"I love deals," said the little girl. Then she spun on her heels and skipped away.

"Friend of yours?" Sid asked Warlock.

"Just a fan."

"Cute kid," said Sid, "Weird eyes though."

The Devil's Number

The number 13 is said to be unlucky. The earliest reference to thirteen being unlucky or evil is from the Babylonian Code of Hammurabi (circa 1780 B.C.E.), where the thirteenth law is omitted. At the Last Supper, Judas, the disciple who betrayed Jesus, was the 13th to sit at the table. And the Vikings believed that the prankster Loki in the Norse pantheon was the 13th god.

If you need a more modern reference, how about Friday the 13th, or Apollo 13, the only unsuccessful mission by the USA to land people on the moon. I could go on.

But 13 is only the Devil's Number in western cultures. In China, India and Italy, for example, 13 is considered a lucky number. Yes, I realize that Italy is a western nation, but Italy never was one to follow the crowd.

This all just goes to show that the Devil is where you find him.

A Short Thought About God

Warlock was in a mixed mood. On the one hand he was pleased with himself that he finally held a guitar of his very own. He was doubly pleased that he could play it as well as he had played Crazy's guitar the night before. Those first sour notes in the guitar shop after his earlier fiascos with the doorknob and the fireplace had worried him that his magic power might be, well, a little rough around the edges might be putting it mildly. At some point he would have to try more magic, but for now he was content just to play guitar.

On the other hand he was scared spitless that he was now a flunky for the Devil. Or worse, that the Devil still had endless torments waiting for him. When he had woken just a few hours ago he hadn't even believed in the Devil.

His inner stupid self would like to think that he was clever enough to make some kind of deal with the Devil that would give him a winning hand, but the rational part of him whispered that the Devil was not only all powerful, but that he had invented cheating and wasn't afraid to use it. No matter how Warlock looked at it he saw himself as screwed.

For the first time in his life, Warlock thought about God. It wasn't a deep thought, nor did it last very long. And that thought was this: In theory good always wins over evil; in practice evil gets away with murder. Besides, didn't the Bible say that all the witches and warlocks should be put to death? He just couldn't see himself entering a church and saying: "I'm a Warlock and the Devil wants to throw me into a burning lake. How about some help?" He suspected the congregation would pick him up and throw him bodily into the lake themselves.

Yup. Screwed.

To make matters worse, having bought the guitar he now had no dinner money.

He had three hours to kill before he would see Valerie again so he found an empty coffee can in a dumpster and went to the park to busk. The knowledgeable musician that he was, he knew that he not only needed a permit, but a permit for a specific location. He also knew that McArthur Park was both huge and busy and that he should be able to busk a couple hours without incurring the wrath of the cops.

Luck was on his side, or perhaps the Devil had created another opportunity. Dangerous Joe wasn't at his usual spot. And a great spot it was. High foot traffic. Nearby trees to shield him from the wind and undo notice. And a Tim Horton's coffee shop right across the street where he could spend his earnings on an inexpensive meal.

Taking the portable Danelectro Bacon and Eggs Mini Amp and micro-speaker out of his backpack — Sid had been so impressed by Warlock's playing that he had thrown a used $30 unit in for free — Warlock turned it on, checked the battery (almost full) and plugged the Jackson in. He strummed a few cords and adjusted the volume. For a busker on foot the setup was ideal. For a front man of the Seriously Damp it wasn't even a suitable practice system. He'd have to buy a better amp and speaker later, a Paul Stanley or a Behringer. That and a guitar case. For now Warlock had no way to carry the Jackson apart from wearing it.

After only a few minutes setup, Warlock played.

There were two reasons Warlock had always wanted to be a musician. First, the near zen-like state of producing music. It was a high better than you could get from any drug. And second, the joy on people's faces as they took in that music. It was the ultimate symbiotic relationship. And it was, perhaps, the exact opposite of what the Devil wanted for him. If the songs Warlock chose to play and sing that afternoon were a little dark, that might be the reason.

An Evening Working

At six p.m. Warlock thanked his audience, emptied the coffee tin, and refreshed himself with a Tim Horton's club sandwich and coffee. Then he jumped the bus to Valerie's.

His mood was atmospheric until he encountered the duct-taped doorknob. He considered using magic to fix it, then thought better of it and knocked on the door instead.

Sister August slid back the panel, saw who it was, yelled "Don't break anything!" and unlocked the door.

"And a pleasant evening to you, too," he told her.

In response she scowled at the guitar strapped across his shoulder. Warlock wondered how long it would take him to save enough money to buy a used guitar case.

Valerie did a double take when he entered the parlor. "We, uh, don't really need music for our working."

Warlock removed the guitar and laid it flat on the floor, insurance against the neck warping if he leaned it against the wall. He set his backpack in front of it as protection. "Just bought it today," he said. "Gonna need a guitar if I want to make any real money."

"That's the spirit," said Valerie.

They sat together on a sofa as the rest of the coven ambled in and began placing tall, white candles on every surface that would support them.

"What should we work tonight?" Sister January asked Valerie.

"How about peace on Earth?" said Sister October.

Sister August groaned. "We did peace on Earth last night. And last Thursday."

"You can never have too much peace on Earth," retorted Sister October.

"How about we magic the doorknob whole," said Sister August. "There are a few other things around here that could use some magicking as well."

"We don't do magic for ourselves," admonished Sister January. "That would be selfish."

Sister August shook her head. "Then how about *you* magic the doorknob fixed for *me*? That would be very unselfish of you."

"Maybe we should work to benefit would-be musicians," suggested Sister December, looking pointedly at Warlock. "Give their careers a boost."

Valerie stood up and held her hands out in warning. "Sisters, we are hardly starting things off in the right spirit. Good works do not include sharp tongues."

This was met with subdued mumbling.

Warlock cleared his throat. "I understand that I'm the newbie here—" All eyes turned toward him. "—but I'm wondering if you're aiming your sights too low."

"What do you mean?" asked Valerie, and by the way she said it Warlock knew that he shouldn't have spoken up.

"I guess what I mean is, if we're going to work some magic tonight, why don't we do something that will have a real impact."

"A real impact," echoed Valerie, in a cold tone that reinforced his first observation.

Warlock saw no way to back down without looking the fool, so he kept going. "Sure, you know, something really big. Something like binding the Devil so that he can no longer tempt the souls of Men."

Warlock may as well have been the only person in the room for the response he received. Was that a forlorn wind he heard slipping down the hallway?

Valerie's voice filled the silence. "I, ah, find your exuberance admirable, Master March, but even if the Devil did exist such a working would be well beyond our simple power."

"Damn right," added one of the Sisters; Warlock couldn't tell which one.

"The Devil doesn't exist?" whispered Warlock.

"Of course not," said Valerie. "All the Gods, Goddesses, and their darker counterparts are just personifications for extremes of the human condition."

Personifications?

The question must have been obvious on Warlock's face. "Metaphors?" Valerie suggested. "I thought you read Elizabeth's book?"

"I did," Warlock half-lied. Skimming is reading, after all. He may even have seen the word *metaphor*. It sounded like a word a warlock would use. He knew he had to say something before Valerie asked about more things he hadn't read. "I guess I failed to pick up on that little nugget."

"Duh!" muttered one of the Sisters; Warlock was pretty certain this time that it was Sister August.

"So no Devil, then?" said Warlock.

Valerie shook her head. "Not really, no."

Warlock needed to make sure. "He couldn't just appear in this room, say, and threaten us all with fire and brimstone?"

"That would be somewhat more than a metaphor could muster," Valerie suggested.

"Right," said Warlock. "So, this peace on Earth idea sounds good to me."

This was met with a shy clapping of hands and several groans.

"We'll save that for another night," said Valerie. "I've thought of a working that we haven't performed yet. We're going to heal the sick."

This was met with a chorus of *ahh*s.

As the Sisters went about lighting the candles Warlock sat wondering if Ray Wise had ever actually read *The Good Witch*. For a metaphor he was pretty handy with the flames and glowing eyes. And tomorrow Warlock would have to decide whether to work for or risk the wrath of a powerless metaphor. *Crap.*

The candles were now all lit, including several on the mantel, their flames bouncing off the silver gong and the metal puzzle box like small lighthouses. It brought to mind the lyrics of one of the Seriously Damp's less popular songs: "Lighthouse of my soul, guide me to safe harbors." Warlock felt that he could use a little of that right now.

Turning off the lamps and taking pillows off the sofas and chairs, the Sisters all began kneeling in a circle. Warlock did the same, but when he tried to kneel next to Valerie she told him to move to her other side. Only then did he notice that the circle was in month order, January though December. He wondered if the coven had left empty pillows for months like himself who had not yet joined or were absent.

Tonight no one was absent, and Valerie — Sister April — took his left hand while Sister February took his right. Warlock had never taken part in a séance, but this sure felt like one.

Then Valerie spoke a chant that the Sisters followed.

"Tonight we seek the Goddess," Valerie intoned.

The Sisters, with Warlock joining in, repeated. "Tonight we seek the Goddess."

It went on like this for a while with the coven dedicating themselves to doing good works in the name of the Goddess.

Finally Valerie said: "Tonight we seek to send our strength to those in Grace Hospital who battle illness or injury." The coven echoed the words. "Give them our strength that they may be strong."

As Warlock echoed these words with the coven he felt suddenly exhausted. As the final word was spoken the candles went out leaving the room in darkness. The Sisters on either side, or witches rather — having just experienced, well, something, Warlock was now inclined to see them as more than just a sorority — he sat in the dark, drained as if he had just run a marathon and, figuratively at least, catching his breath.

After a while he felt his hands set free and then someone turned on a lamp.

"Wow," said Sister December. "That was something."

"Yeah," added one of the other Sisters.

Warlock saw that the Sisters were putting the parlor back to normal, pillows on the furniture and removing the candles.

"We have learned a great lesson here tonight," said Valerie, who looked tired but otherwise in very good spirits. "See what a full coven can do?"

Most of the Sisters began talking together in twos and threes as they shuffled out of the room. The working, apparently, was over. Warlock turned to Valerie trying to think of a good way to ask: "What the Hell happened?" but came up empty. So instead he asked, "What was all that business about the Goddess? I thought you said she was a metaphor."

Valerie smiled at him. "The best of all metaphors. The Goddess symbolizes life and growth."

Warlock tried again. "But why invoke her at all if she is not a real person?"

The High Priestess of the coven gave her newest witch a patient look. "Invoking the Goddess allows us to focus our thoughts and energies so that the coven may work as one. Without focus our working would be chaos."

"Ah," said Warlock. "I understand." Though in truth he understood none of it. Band members didn't have focus. Each member — drummer, guitarists, vocals — knew their part and just coordinated with the others, harmony rather than focus. True, often the drummer set the time and the others followed, but that still wasn't focus.

A jam session was the antithesis of focus, with everyone doing any old thing and often riffing off each other. There was a certain elegance in chaos.

"So what did you think of our working?" Valerie asked, distracting him from these deep thoughts. There was a childlike eagerness in her eyes that Warlock found appealing.

"Well," he said. "I know something happened. I'm just not sure what."

"I thought that was obvious," said Valerie. "We sent energy over to Grace Hospital to strengthen those housed there."

"I got that," said Warlock, "but there's no... visible results. We can't see that we made a difference."

Valerie looked confused. "Why is that a problem? We can see from our own exhaustion that we did good. Seeing the specific results won't make it any more true."

Warlock was at a loss. "Maybe it's a guy thing," he said. "I'm kinda results oriented."

"So why don't you drop by the hospital tomorrow," Valerie suggested. "You should check up on how Crazy Eddie is doing anyway."

"Right," said Warlock. "Crazy."

Grace Hospital

Warlock had never been to Grace Hospital. Had never been sick a day in his life. He used to think of himself as blessed, though now that he expected the Devil to turn up at any moment and drag his sorry ass down to Hell, he wasn't so sure.

After last night's working he wasn't certain what he would find at Grace Hospital. The lame walking? The blind seeing? The poor paying their bills? From what he could tell, based on watching such programs as *ER* and *House* (the Devil was right, he did watch too much TV) everything in the hospital appeared business as usual.

He asked for Crazy Eddie's room. That was a no go. When he couldn't remember Crazy's real name he thought he was out of luck. But then the nurse took note of the guitar hanging off his shoulder and asked, "You mean that guitar player who crashed his car two nights ago?"

"Yeah. That's him."

The nurse frowned. "You musicians should really learn how to drive."

"Hey," said Warlock. "I ride the bus."

She didn't appear to have a snappy answer to that so she sniffed and said, "Room 305."

After a few bad starts Warlock finally found Crazy's room. He figured that the same moron architects who had designed the world's ugliest house must also design hospitals. The place was a maze of identical corridors that turned corners or branched off in new directions for no apparent reason unless it was to confuse patients and foil their escape attempts. When he found Crazy, the injured front man was watching daytime soaps.

"That'll rot your brain," Warlock said.

"Already rotted," Crazy quipped as he clicked the TV off using the remote with his left hand. His right hand was tied to his chest, his arm covered with enough bandages to make a do-it-yourself mummy.

"You're in good spirits," Warlock noted, wondering just how long that would last when he told him the Seriously Damp had a new front man.

"Just got some good news," said Crazy. "Up till this morning the doctors were worried the ligaments wouldn't heal right. Said I might never strum the strings again."

"Rancid," said Warlock.

"It's cool. This morning's X-Rays told a better story. Now they think I'll be good as new."

"Oh," said Warlock. "Wicked."

"Glad you dropped by so I could share the news with someone. I haven't seen Gord or Montana. How's the Damp?"

"Er, getting by," said Warlock. This was the time, the right time, to tell Crazy that he was now fronting the band. But somehow he couldn't. Crazy looked so… happy.

"Are those new strings?" Crazy asked, smiling at the neck of the Jackson visible above his shoulder.

Warlock pulled the strap so that the guitar slid under his arm and over his chest. "Just a used Jackson. I'm not getting near enough practice on borrowed strings."

"'Bout time, man," said Crazy. "You been stuck on roadie way too long. Time to spread your wings."

Another perfect moment to break the news. *Since you mention it…* But what Warlock said was. "I plan to start busking. Get lots of hours in."

"Best way," agreed Crazy. "Go to that closet over there. Yup. Inside. Check the pants pocket and bring me my wallet."

What? Was Crazy going to throw him a couple of bills to busk for him? Here and now?

"You'll have to open the wallet," said Crazy, "on account of I only have one working hand right now. Check under the driver's license."

Warlock felt awkward poking though another man's wallet, especially while he was watching, but he did what he was told and found, to his astonishment, a busking permit.

"I don't use it much these days, but it's still got a few months on it." He waggled the fingers of his right hand. "Lord knows I won't be needing it."

"Crazy, I don't know what to say."

"Say you'll get out there and play up a storm. And if you see either of those errant Damp players, tell him to give a guy a visit, will you?"

"Will do," said Warlock. Busking permit in pocket, he left the hospital.

Hell's Hospital

Or almost left the hospital. The first floor wasn't where it should have been.

Warlock tried retracing his steps, but soon found himself lost. He would have asked someone for directions, but all the people appeared to have vanished.

Feeling he knew what was going on he tried to think of what TV show involved the Devil and this never-ending hospital, but he drew a blank. Possibly it was from a show he hadn't watched.

"No."

The voice was tiny and came from somewhere near his knees. Warlock looked down and saw what might be the world's smallest midget. Apart from his height, or lack thereof, he looked in his forties and was wearing an off-white attendant's uniform.

"No what?" asked Warlock.

"No," said the little man, "this is not from a TV show."

"Then what is it?" asked Warlock.

"It's a hospital," said the attendant.

"Yes, but—"

The attendant's face turned into a hideous leer. "A hospital in Hell!"

"Tell me," asked Warlock. "The Devil writes for television, doesn't he?"

The little man kicked him in the shin and yelled, "Ask him yourself." Then he scuttled away and was gone around a corner.

Warlock reached down and rubbed his shin. This was not as easy as it sounds. He still had his guitar strapped behind his shoulder snugged tight against his backpack.

It was at this point that Warlock figured he knew. Well, he didn't know the whys or wherefores, but he knew one thing, that Valerie was right and that the Devil was just a metaphor.

"A what?"

Flames burst from the doors of an operating theater as they banged open revealing the Devil. Not as a suave actor, nor a sweet little girl. It was the Devil in his armored goat persona.

"A metaphor," Warlock said aloud.

The Devil raised a blood red finger and pointed at him. "You! You don't even know what a metaphor is."

Warlock considered that. "Not in the dictionary sense, no. I couldn't quote a definition at you. But neither could you quote a definition to me."

"I can't what?"

It was a good thing this was a hospital as the Devil looked to be having an epileptic fit.

"I can do anything!" he screamed. "Everything!"

"Then go ahead," said Warlock. "Tell me the dictionary definition of metaphor."

Suddenly a very large dictionary appeared in the Devil's hands. The cover flamed and smoked where he touched it. Then just as suddenly it disappeared. "I don't need a dictionary. And I don't need to play these games with you either. Do you accept my offer or don't you? Time has run out."

"I'll answer as soon as you give me a dictionary definition of metaphor."

"You fool!" screamed the Devil. "How can you anger me so and hope not to suffer?"

"Tell you what," said Warlock. "You tell me the dictionary definition of metaphor and I will accept your deal."

"You'll what?"

"Easy as that," said Warlock. He pulled on his guitar strap and slid the Jackson from behind his shoulder. If you don't give me a definition, then I refuse your deal and am going to sit down here and play guitar until you go away."

The Devil stared at him. "That is the stupidest thing I have ever heard anyone say."

Warlock strummed a chord. "Naw. You've heard lots stupider things, most of them from me."

Through gritted teeth the Devil spoke, clearly, slowly, and very angrily. "Metaphor: something that represents something—"

For a moment Warlock feared that he had gotten it wrong. That he had taken a horribly written song, added an oboe and a violin section, and had only made it worse.

"—that stands for something else—"

It might only be the flames from the burning corridor, but Warlock felt sweat forming on his forehead and nose.

"—that isn't what it really is—"

And now the Devil, too, was sweating. Can the Devil sweat?

"—that is, I mean, isn't—"

The flames were getting higher and hotter.

"—a, a, oh fiddlesticks!"

The fames died away until there was just the hospital corridor. The Devil still stood there, but had resumed his Ray Wise persona, complete with grinning white rictus. "You may think you've won, but I'll always be here, whispering in your ear—"

"—tempting me," concluded Warlock. "Yes, yes. And doubtless I'll give in. To a degree. It's who I am. My inner stupid self is really just me. And if there is anything I'm good at it is making mistakes. But I'm not making this one."

The Devil grinned and rubbed his hands, acting as if he hadn't just had Hell pulled out from under him. "Until next time," he said. "I'll find you when your heart is broken, or when you are at one of life's lowly lows. The timing right now was all wrong."

"Yeah, yeah," said Warlock. "You go ahead and believe what you want. That's what I'm going to start doing. Believing. In myself. Things are looking brighter already."

"Are they?" said the Devil's voice. Not the Devil himself, as he was already gone. "Good luck finding your way out of Hell's Hospital." And then even the voice was gone.

Warlock looked at the unmarked corridor and doors and at the absence of people. The Devil was right; he wasn't really in Grace Hospital. At least, metaphorically he wasn't. Wandering the halls would get him nowhere. So instead he sat down, pulled out his mini-amp, and played his guitar.

His playing wasn't very good, but it wasn't very bad either. It was not his magical playing in The Blue Oyster Bar or McArthur Park. But it was better than *he* had ever played before. The new ingredient, he decided, was belief. Belief in himself that he could play and improve over time without magical aid.

Warlock knew his fingers were getting sore, that he should stop soon or pay with blisters. But at the same time he was caught up in the melody. He wasn't playing any song he knew. He was just riffing. A one person jam. A chaos of one. His eyes closed.

"Excuse me."

Warlock stopped playing and opened his eyes. The nurse who had directed him to Crazy's room stood looking down at him.

"That sounds really lovely," she said, "but you can't play here. If you like you can make arrangements to come back and play for some of the patients. I know they would like that."

Warlock stowed the mini-amp in his backpack then climbed to his feet and swung his guitar behind his shoulder. "I'd like that, too," he said. "I'll be in touch."

As he started to walk off the nurse stopped him. "Wait. What's your name?"

The name *Warlock* almost rolled automatically off his lips. But he thought, *That's the old me. I need to make a new start.* He looked the nurse in the eye and said, "They call me Wizard."

Well, not a huge change, but it was a beginning.

Wizard

Valerie stood reading the busking permit. "So this is your new day job, huh?"

Wizard shrugged. "Well, I can't keep doing gigs in the evening. That's when we do our workings."

Valerie nodded. "What about the band?"

"The Seriously Damp is Crazy Eddie's band. It would be wrong to take that away from him."

"I see," said Valerie, handing him back the permit. "Actually I'm pleased. I didn't really like who I saw you becoming."

"Me neither," he agreed. And then decided to tell her everything. Well, not everything; that would be a bit much. He told her about his run-ins with his metaphorical Devil.

They sat on a sofa in the parlor. It wasn't the type of tale you told standing up.

"You took a big risk," Valerie told him when he finished. "If the Devil had been real you'd be… well, I can't even imagine where you'd be."

Wizard grinned. "Naw. You set me straight on that one. We worked real magic with a metamorphic Goddess. It only made sense that the Devil was no different."

"Yes," said Valerie, "but you couldn't *know* that."

"I didn't have to know it. I just had to believe it. Besides, it bothered me that the Devil was exactly what I expected him to be."

"Bothered you in what way?"

"I never spent ten seconds in my entire life thinking about the Devil, then here he comes, large as life, the embodiment of various TV shows I had watched where the Devil was a character. It was just... so unlikely."

"And," said Valerie.

"And," he conceded, "I had just finished reading how the coven was, well, pretty much inspired by a TV show."

Valerie grinned guiltily. "You know there are studies that prove that television is a strong influence on our behavior. And our beliefs."

Wizard shrugged. "If it wasn't TV it would be something else. Books maybe. Or music."

"Okay," said Valerie. "You've explained where your own personal Devil came from and how you defeated him."

"For now," amended Wizard.

"Okay. For now. But why now? Why did your dark side suddenly metamorphose into life?"

"That's easy," said Wizard. "It coincided with my getting magic. I think my magic gave my dark side life."

Valerie looked startled. "But... you've always had magic."

Wizard sighed and told her the other half of the story, about how he cheated his initiation and found a magic ring.

"This box?" asked Valerie, rising from the sofa and taking the odd metal puzzle box down from the mantel.

Wizard nodded.

Valerie did a few quick twists and turns with the box and opened it. Warlock closed his eyes, expecting a sand storm, or a deluge of rain, or who knows what, but nothing happened. Valerie showed him the box. She had opened it out to show the word B-E-L-I-E-V-E. Then she touched each letter and, after touching the final E, the box closed up again.

"You uhm," said Wizard, "didn't visit a desert the first time you opened it?"

Valerie shook her head. "But I did find a ring inside." She showed him her right hand and on the middle finger was a delicate equivalent of the one he wore. He showed his to her. The rubies looked like a matched set.

"Well that's... something," said Valerie. "But I had magic long before I opened the box and found the ring. Sometimes a ring is just a ring."

"Where did you get the box?"

"It was in the house when I bought it. Actually, it was pretty much the only thing in the house."

Wizard nodded. "The other Sisters. They don't…?"

"No. None of them have magic. That's why I was so excited to find you in that candle shop, and feel the magic within you. I thought I'd be the only one in the coven with magic. Surrounded by witches, I'd still be alone."

Wizard spread his hands. "But if I've always had magic, why didn't I know until I opened the box?"

"I didn't know I had magic either," admitted Valerie, "until I read *The Good Witch*. The book told me to believe in myself. And I did. And then I could do things."

"And the box told me to believe," said Warlock. "I'm thinking now that I must have subconsciously seen the word in the box before my trip to the sphinx. Maybe for me believing comes with a touch of the metaphorical."

"I hope you can get over that," said Valerie. "It sounds exhausting."

Wizard shrugged. "Yeah, never a dull moment with me. Speaking of which…" Last night he had put off too long asking Valerie out for that second date and had then lost the opportunity. No. That wasn't it. He hadn't worked up the courage. He'd been afraid she'd say no. Now that he had some faith in himself he found that nothing was holding him back. "We have a couple of hours before tonight's working. Would you allow me to take you out to dinner? It'll have to be Tim Horton's though. And we'll have to bus it. I'm a little short on cash this week."

Valerie looked at him. "Why, Wizard, I'd be delighted."

"Wizard?" asked Wizard. "Not Master March?"

Valerie shook her head. "Master March is your coven name. Tonight I'm going to dinner with a musician named Wizard."

For the first time in his life Wizard felt as cool and collected as he had always tried to make his Warlock façade appear. As he escorted his date to the door he felt not the least bit awkward, inside or out.

"Oh," said Valerie. "Someone repaired the doorknob."

"Guilty," said Wizard. "I also fixed the satellite dish. Despite Sister January's admonitions, I think it is okay to do for yourself now and then."

Valerie chuckled. "I can see it's going to be a three ring circus when you move in."

Even the mention of *moving in* failed to break Wizard's cool. He knew she meant his own room as part of the coven. But that could change. Over time.

"Oh," he said. "About this house."

"What about this house?"

"It used to be a day care, didn't it?"

"Why yes. How did you know?"

Wizard grinned. "I divined it."

Epilogue

After a modest yet delightful dinner the two witches returned to the world's ugliest house only to discover the puzzle box missing from the mantel. Rather than becoming alarmed or growing angry, they simply shrugged and never again gave the box a second thought.

The Second Piece of the Puzzle

❖ ❖ ❖

As he did nearly every morning, Albert woke with a pounding headache and a thick tongue. What was different today was the smell of frying bacon and the early morning sun shining in his eyes. Most nights, he made sure to draw the blinds because he knew he'd sleep until midmorning before even considering starting the day. He briefly thought he was back in Egypt, but the crumbling plaster ceiling indicated he was in his apartment. He'd fallen asleep atop his covers still wearing his clothing. He shifted and knocked off a stack of books occupying the end of his bed.

His mind fought through the last of a fragmenting dream. Something about the desert, and a huge talking statue, and hellfire. The visions felt so real. He glanced at the clock: 6:30 a.m. He could truthfully say that he hadn't risen this early in years. Sure, he'd been up at the crack of dawn, but that was because he'd be stumbling home from the gambling halls. Drunk and penniless. And yet, this morning he didn't feel that crushing defeat that greeted him when his eyes opened. Today, he was... hungry.

He sat on the edge of the bed. His mind felt cluttered. Too much Jim Beam. *And the box.* The box was in the dream too. Bloody hell, he had to get it to Julian today. Except...

Finally, he put it together. The box, the frying bacon, and the sounds of someone preparing breakfast. Without bothering to change into fresh clothing, Albert dragged himself to his feet and staggered out into the hallway, past the bathroom, and into the kitchen.

The Chronicler stood by the stove, scooping eggs onto two plates already laden with bacon and overdone toast. He turned and nodded.

"Ah, there you are, Albert. I trust you slept well?"

Albert sat at the table and pushed aside the empty bottle of Jim Beam. He usually liked to start the day with a little something to quench his thirst. Hair of the dog and all that. But not today. The Chronicler placed a steaming plate in front of him. Albert didn't want to speak, couldn't speak, as images of the desert and a strange, strange house percolated through his mind. Those memories, they didn't belong to him and yet they floated through his thoughts as if they did. And with them, visions of card games, and Moira. *Why am I thinking of her?* He tried to veer his thoughts from her but the images of her were so real and so painful, as if the wounds were fresh and not years old. What had this man done to him to unlock those emotions and memories?

"Delightful woman that Mrs. Gelderland," the Chronicler said.

"Who?"

"Your upstairs neighbor. Your cupboards and icebox were bare so I had to bother her for something. I'm not much of a cook but I can do a wonderful breakfast."

Albert couldn't answer, barraged with flashes of the dream and of Moira.

She pulled the string on her blouse and the top fell open. He leaned in and tasted her lips, experienced their softness. Her tongue teased him. His hands parted her blouse and touched her skin. She inhaled sharply.

His eyes stung and his throat constricted. He didn't want her memories here. Couldn't have her. Not here. Hell, he had crossed a continent to get away from her. *But the distance never matters.*

The Chronicler stared at him, but Albert didn't want him to see tears so he turned his attention to a piece of bacon and folded it into his mouth.

The older man touched Albert's arm. "The first time can be almost painful. I remember it all too well."

Albert pulled his arm back and said nothing. Painful did not begin to encompass how he felt. But at the same time he was hungry. Ravenous.

The Chronicler watched him eat but never touched his own food. Albert ate quickly. When he looked longingly over at the second plate, the Chronicler pushed it to him. Halfway through the second portion he began to slow.

"You don't understand yet, do you?" the Chronicler asked.

Albert said nothing. He pushed the plate away and realized that the puzzle box sat between them. *Had it been there all along?* He knew it hadn't. Then he remembered what he had dreamed last night. But what exactly? A hallucination? A premonition?

"That... dream. Was it a memory? Or something else?"

The old man nodded sagely. "It was very real, Albert. Real for you."

"The Sphinx, and the ring, and the card games. I understand that, I think."

"Yes?"

Visions of Moira. Her eyes, her skin, and the way she smelled. "Not everything fits. What... did it mean?"

Albert noticed how old the man looked. More haggard than yesterday. Lines etched deeper into his skin, his posture more beaten down. Eyes darker.

"I cannot tell you that. I am only a chronicler."

Albert knew that was a lie. This man was trying to show him something and the lesson wasn't over yet. He stared at the box. The letters and light had faded. It looked exactly as it had before this stranger had walked into his life.

"May I?" Albert asked, reaching for it.

"Of course. You must learn its secrets."

Albert turned it in his hands. His mind felt sharper today, more focused. *Like it used to.* He knew he still had to get Van Rosen the money he owed him, which meant he had to sell the box to Julian, his one and only buyer. Albert glanced at the clock: 7:00. He still had time. Then his gaze returned to the box and those thoughts faded into the background as though *they* were the dream.

"The past can be uncomfortable," the Chronicler said. "Painful even. But like a needle that gives life sustaining medicine, the past can be a powerful remedy."

Albert's hands grew sweaty as the box warmed. Letters materialized on the dull surface. He touched the letters, sliding them around the box, manipulating them and rearranging them. He shifted them from side to side.

"You see? You understand?" the Chronicler asked.

"I don't." Light pulsed from inside the box and Albert paused, worried that he had erred.

"There is no right or wrong, Albert."

"I don't want to do this," he said, even as he continued manipulating the letters. They spelled something, but he did not recognize the words. His hands knew, but he did not.

"Do not fear the past."

The next Piece of the Puzzle will be revealed after "Autumn Unbound."

Autumn Unbound

❖ By Billie Milholland ❖

"Oh, quit whining! Smite the cheeky wench and conjure another."
So spoke ox-eyed Hera, Zeus's long suffering, but loyal, third wife.

Prometheus: "I can't make another, most gracious cow-faced lady. Your irrepressible husband ordered she be the most beautiful woman ever created. If I smite her, I have to replace her with the *second* most beautiful woman ever made. I don't settle for seconds."

Hera picked her teeth with a cricket leg. "Of course you don't. You're a Titan's spawn." She reached for a goblet of wine. "And there's a reason why the most beautiful woman shuns you?"

Prometheus contorted his handsome face just enough to express his displeasure, but stopped short of creating an actual wrinkle. "Zeus forced her to promise my fish-brained brother she would stand by him until his love grew cold."

Hera yawned. "Epimetheus, the fool, abandoned her. Isn't that cold enough?"

"But first he took the blame for her when she opened Zeus's stupid chest. Maybe she thinks that means something."

Hera watched Prometheus over the rim of the goblet until she saw him begin to squirm. She narrowed her eyes. "Did you actually see her open the chest?"

He crossed his arms and glared at her. "Nobody saw her do it. That's not the point. We all know she did it. I designed her with so much curiosity, she had to open that forbidden chest."

Hera leaned back on her throne. "Why do I have the feeling you're telling me only part of the story?"

Prometheus looked away. "The story is the story. That's how it's told. My point is: Epi doesn't love her. She doesn't love him. So why can't I have her now that he's gone?"

"Because you told her Epi loved her, you titanic moron."

"That was when Zeus tried to foist her on *me*. I had to lie."

"So. Tell her the truth."

"I did, but now she'd rather believe my lie. Obstinate woman."

Hera snapped her fingers and a curtain lifted, revealing a woman so beautiful it was said *angels wept as she passed*.

Hera smiled. "Pandora, Prometheus seeks your hand. I want to hear your response with my own ears."

The stunning woman raised her eyes to the foot of the throne. "Prometheus lies," she said, her voice honey smooth. "He has no interest in my hand. His quest is for something lower. I decline."

Prometheus stepped forward and shook a fist at Pandora. "You can't decline. You have to obey."

"Why?" Pandora turned her back to him.

Hera rose from her throne and kicked Prometheus in the shin. "Why, indeed." She linked her arm with Pandora's. "Walk with me, girl."

They strolled through Hera's apple orchard, neither speaking until they reached the lair of Ladon, Hera's hundred-headed dragon. Hera tossed a golden apple into the cave.

"Wake up, lazy one. I need your council."

Two or three dozen heads emerged, blinking and frowning. A half-dozen peered at Pandora.

"She seeks mortality," said one.

"Give it to her. You've got nothing to lose," said another.

"She'll come back soon enough," said a third.

Hera folded her arms across her chest. "Epi's down there wandering the mortal realm and he hasn't returned."

The dragon's big claw dragged back all his writhing heads but one. "Epi didn't relinquish his immortality. That lot never does. But she would have to, wouldn't she? She exists at your whim. Toss her in. Make her mortal. She'll only last a decade or so."

Hera patted Pandora's perfect cheek. "What do you say, girl?"

"Mortality can't be worse than what I have here. I'm despised, Lady. They all believe I opened the chest. They think I *let* Epi take the blame."

Hera sighed. "I know. They're addicted to intrigue, silly twits."

"I need to find Epi."

"Why? Epimetheus doesn't love you. Surely you know that."

"I'm not allowed to know that until he tells me directly. Zeus bound me to him until he declares his love cold."

"Zeus has a dim sense of humor." Hera tossed another apple to her dragon. "Go back to sleep my pet." She fixed her large cow-brown eyes on Pandora. "The mortal realm is dirty, noisy and dangerous."

Pandora shrugged. "The immortal realm is noisy and dangerous for one like me. And, if you don't mind me saying so, clean is over-rated."

Hera nodded. "I know, but the others seem to like it." She gazed out at cloud tipped mountain ranges. "I've never sent a minion down into mortal territory before. I'm sure Zeus has some ordinance against it." She smiled. "But, it might be amusing."

"Please, Lady. Nobody will miss me."

"Prometheus seems to think you might favor him if you weren't bound by your promise."

"Prometheus is a donkey's pizzle."

"Agreed. I like you. It will be fun to see how you fare down there."

"Can you get permission?"

"Permission? I never ask permission. I'll give you thirty years. A tedious long time in the tiresome lives of mortals, but a few moments up here. Of course, I don't know where in that veil of tears the silly coward is hiding. Talk to Iapetos. For reasons lost on me he continues to keep track of his worthless son."

She plucked an apple and shined it on her gown. "I think I'll start you out as an infant. That may save some of your sanity in that slimy place."

Prometheus was not pleased, of course, and he pouted while Hera, Aphrodite and Iapetos made the arrangements. In the mortals' dreary afterlife they found three spirits willing to return briefly to mortality to become guardians. Prometheus reluctantly relinquished a portion of his god silver to keep Pandora mortal for the duration.

"Just as long as I get it all back," he said, his generous lower lip trembling.

Aphrodite blew a raspberry. "Send a couple of Fayal to guard it. Send a whole tribe if you're that paranoid."

"Don't worry," Prometheus called to Pandora as she faded from sight. "When your time is up, I'll be there to bring you back home."

A lingering guilt clung to me after I left Peter. I couldn't shake it, but I expected it to lessen when I walked into the welcoming home of my three aunts. They kept my old room and office ready for my inevitable breakups. Permanent, temporary digs. I expected hugs and their standard assurances: "He really wasn't your type, dear. We saw it right from the start, didn't we girls?"

Not this time. The moment I entered the kitchen the aunts were at me like crows on carrion.

Absentminded Aunt May snapped to attention, shoving aside her Suduko puzzle. "You said Peter was the one. Now you're giving him up?"

"I thought he was the one, I..."

Gentle Aunt June talked over me, her voice pitched high with irritation. "You didn't give him a chance, that's what you didn't do." She slapped a pair of oven mitts against the counter.

Aunt April, usually the queen of glass-half-full, had a frown so deep I could hardly see her eyes. "Autumn Bailey, this is unacceptable." She stretched her short frame until the finger she shook grazed my nose. "You go right back there and say you're sorry to that poor, young man."

I waved my arms. "Hey. Whoa. Ladies!"

Aunt April yanked a chair away from the table, shoved it at me and jabbed with her still pointing finger. "Sit."

Too astonished to resist, I sat. Aunt June set a mug of tea in front of me. I wrapped my hands around it and studied my aunts as they settled at the other end of the table. I waited. My break-up with Peter rankled them. Why? They had never taken an interest in the guys I dated. They always accepted my inevitable break-ups with little reaction. I was surprised they knew Peter's name.

Finally Aunt May leaned forward. "We feel it's time you settled down, dear."

"Why?"

Aunt May cleared her throat. "Well." She sighed. "Oh. You tell her, June."

Aunt June stared into her cup for a moment. Then she drained it in several long swallows and dropped it into her saucer. If the crash of china against china had been a gunshot, I couldn't have been more surprised. Aunt June steepled her hands and tapped her mouth with her pointing fingers.

"To put it bluntly, dear, your reputation is at stake."

I raised both hands. "Shut the front door! I don't have a reputation. Good, bad or indifferent." I squinted hard, trying to get them back into focus. "My reputation for what?"

"Fickleness."

"You've got to be kidding."

Aunt April fluttered her fingers. "It's not good for your career to be seen as fickle."

"I'm a journalist. Nobody cares about my personal life. Why would they? You three have never cared about my personal life. Why now?"

Aunt May, in a rush, "You'll be thirty this year."

Aunt April, pressing her palm against her cheek: "Our time is running out."

Aunt June swatted Aunt April with an oven mitt. "Hush, Rilla." She swung around and glared at me. "What Rilla means is: *Your* time is running out— we think you need some permanence."

I stood up. "Permanence? Are you demented?" I tried to stare down their disapproval, but failed. "You know what? I'm going out on the porch. I'm taking a few deep breaths and then I'm coming back in. When I do, I expect to see my real aunts at the table, not spooks in aunts' clothing."

I didn't make it to the mud room before they surrounded me, grabbing me; pulling me back into the kitchen.

"Don't call us spooks!"

"Who said we were spooks? Did you hear something?"

I shrugged them off. "You're upset. I get that. But I doubt it's got anything to do with my reputation. Why don't we go for a walk? See if we can stroll back to reality."

"She thinks we're not real!" Aunt April wailed. "Tell her we're real, June."

Aunt May wrapped Aunt April in her arms and rocked her back and forth. "She didn't mean it, Rilla. She was just teasing. Autumn Bailey, you tell your poor aunt you were teasing."

"I wasn't teasing. That was sarcasm. I think you're drunk. All three of you."

"Shame." Aunt May scowled. "Accusing your aunties of drunkenness. Maybe *you* should go for a walk and find your manners."

"I'd accuse you of being high if I thought that was possible. You're right. Maybe I should go for a walk."

I needed a good think and thinking required running. I ran ten blocks to the public library and sat on the steps to catch my breath. Senility? Unlikely. Group hysteria? I didn't know what to Google to find out what ailed them. The aunts were my only kin and they had always been rock-solid, unshakeable. Odd and eccentric, yes, but sturdy bricks to lean against. It worried me that they were upset by something as mundane as me messing up another relationship.

Sure, I'd been floundering in the boyfriend department. Trying out men like perfume testers. And, yes. It bothered me. A lot. But the aunts had never had an opinion before. Not once.

Drawing a serious blank about what was bugging them, I decided I'd clean up my loose ends with Peter. Generally, when I dumped a guy, I packed my essentials while he was at work, left a note on the fridge, and disappeared on an assignment for a week or three. I couldn't seem to do that to Peter.

My relationship with him was different. We were at ease together. We made each other laugh. He respected my ideas. It should have worked. He sold his place and I sold mine. We bought the condo so we could start fresh, together. New routines and patterns. I brought all my belongings with me, not just enough to camp out for a few weeks, like I used to do. I made a real commitment. At least I thought I did.

After two months of living well together we were on the balcony on a beautiful spring morning. Peter had just handed me a steaming mug of coffee. Fresh ground, fair trade, organic. It smelled great. Tasted better. I smiled at him across our bamboo table. Peter smiled back.

Then he said it. The 'M' word.

"I know you're allergic to the marriage thing, but I was…"

"Stop!" I failed to keep my smile in place. "Please, Peter. Don't."

"Just hear me out."

"No. I can't. Peter, I just can't."

I didn't know how to explain to him. Crap, I couldn't explain to myself why the thought of marriage made me crazy. I couldn't explain it, but I did warn him. I'd warned all of them, but none of them took me seriously. I had nothing against marriage, but I did have something against a sharp pain in my gut, crazy thoughts in my head and the urge to bolt before I betrayed... That was just it. Betrayed who?

There was nobody to betray. I'd never had a relationship with more than one man at a time, and yet every relationship I'd ever had ended with me walking out, feeling like I had to leave, because to commit any more deeply meant I was cheating on somebody. Each time I was overcome by an insane feeling I had a relationship somewhere else. Totally bonkers, I know. It meant I changed men more often than I bought shoes. My girlfriends complained they couldn't get a guy to commit. I didn't attract the no-commitment guy.

I tried to tell myself— I was a seeker. Forever curious. Not the settling-down type. But I didn't really believe it. Aunt April was right; playing relationship musical chairs was unacceptable. I was seriously messed up.

I jogged to a river trail; it was just a short run to the condo. By the time I hit the walking bridge I knew what I had to do. Swear off men. Maybe not forever, but definitely for a year or two. Good solution. Simple. Clean. I stood on the bridge, frowning down at the swirling water. I glanced over my shoulder to see who else was on the trail. Nobody I recognized.

I leaned forward and whispered, "Ancient River, I call upon you to witness that I, Autumn Anesidora Bailey, do on this day pledge to be blatantly single until such time as I figure out how to screw my head on straight!"

I didn't know why I had to formalize the silly decision, but I felt relieved having done so. The image of me grabbing my head and twisting it like a light bulb also cheered me.

I turned to finish my run, and there it was. A stupid veil, right in my face. No big surprise. The damn things were everywhere. They stretched out like wisps of bilious fog. I'd always been able to see through them to what looked like a different world, but I was never able to cross over. Yet, right then, one second I was on the wooden planks of the walking bridge and the next on a stony path in the foothills of a mountain range.

I stumbled and fell. It took a few moments for my brain to catch up to what happened. As I rubbed my scraped knee, I looked back and saw the veil behind me. A long ribbon of murky mist through which I could see the blurred image of the walking bridge. I knew what I'd done, but I didn't believe it. I approached the veil cautiously and waved at out-of-focus walkers and joggers on the other side, but no one waved back. I saw them, but they didn't see me.

I yelled. "Hey, there!"

Nobody heard me. I pressed my hand against my mouth as an unfamiliar panic clawed at my chest. It couldn't be real. The veils were imaginary. Constructs from my overactive imagination. Leftovers from childhood dreams. Weird, I know. But I'd been a weird kid.

Carefully, I stretched out my hand to touch the veil. I felt a slight tickle, the kind you feel from a freshly poured carbonated beverage. I pushed against the veil and my hand disappeared. I stepped forward and was standing on the walking bridge. My heart beat so fast I had to lean over and brace myself against my knees to catch my breath.

A jogger shrieked. "Where'd you come from?"

I looked up and saw fear on her face. "I… ah… I just jumped, from up there." I pointed to the stout flag pole that towered over the center of the bridge.

"What were you trying to do? Kill yourself?"

She raced away while I collapsed on a bench in the middle of the bridge and stared at the veil. Stress? Hallucination? Had to be. Couldn't be. The startled jogger proved it was some kind of real.

I encountered two more veils before I got to the condo and scared myself stupid by crossing through each one. Something powerful pulled at me. I was able to return, but it freaked me that I couldn't resist going in. What if one time, I couldn't get back? What was that place on the other side? Remnants of old dreams prodded me, but they were too fantastical. Alice in Wonderland stuff. It wasn't the first time I suspected I had a serious mental disorder.

When I finally made it to the condo, I walked in on Peter preparing to pack my Greek statuettes, the last of my belongings still there. He'd insisted on doing it. He wanted it done properly. He was hurting, and still he managed to be infuriately reasonable, when I'd been so unreasonable. He'd even helped move my things into storage. That made me feel twice the bitch.

He'd arranged my little statues along the breakfast bar in rows according to some order that made sense to him. I liked his quirky, obsessive traits. I was going to miss him. Not good. It wasn't my habit to miss a guy once I'd moved on. Peter had lined up the boxes like a kiddie train on the kitchen floor and was sorting bubble wrap. His eyes were sad, but he grinned at me and I wanted to slap myself for making him suffer.

He held up the replica of an early nineteenth century Pandora statue. The one of her holding a box. "Sorry. I haven't got them packed yet. You won't believe what happened."

I stared at his goofy smile. I wanted to smile back, but I caught myself in time. I shook my head. Focus. I needed to focus. We had just split up.

I frowned and shifted down to an *I'm-really-annoyed* gear. He wanted to give me a stupid excuse? I hated stupid excuses. I felt something rising in me. Something unpleasant. I put the breakfast bar between us.

"Yes. You're right, I won't believe what happened."

The chill in my voice startled me. I had the vague notion I was over-reacting, but I ignored it. I leaned across the cold marble until I was forehead to forehead with him.

"I won't believe what happened to you in some elevator." I slapped the counter. "Or on the way to get bread." I slapped the counter with my other hand and felt the sting of it move up my arm. "Or when you had to stop to replace a wiper blade that just might have been defective according to something you found on the internet."

I was yelling by then. Peter opened his mouth. I jabbed my finger at him.

"You shut up. Shut the hell up. I'm tired of listening to your bullshit excuses."

He stared at me like I'd gone out of focus. I felt out of focus. I was not a screamer, yet what came out of my mouth hit twenty decibels over anything I'd uttered before. I was ranting and I couldn't stop.

"I won't believe any crazy-ass story you pull out of your scrawny butt."

Peter backed away until the wall ovens stopped him. He glanced at the stairs to the loft and started to slide along the counter towards them. He was going to bolt. He looked ridiculous. I laughed at him. He sprang for the stairs.

"You're the Father of Excuses," I taunted. "No, you're the stupid father of all fathers of excuses!"

Peter sat down part way up the stairs. He looked scared. "What's the matter with you? Are you nuts?"

"Maybe." What *was* the matter with me? I was actually enjoying my childish outburst. "Father. Of. Excuses."

The father of excuses. *Ohmygawd.* An image of another man, cowering on stone steps eclipsed Peter. Somebody taunted him. It wasn't me.

A dolorous and familiar voice droned through my head. "One son, the Father of Foresight, the champion of humans; the other, Father of After-sight, the champion of nothing. The Father of Excuses."

I swung around. "Iapetos?"

Of course Iapetos wasn't there. He was one of my fantasy people. From a series of recurring childhood dreams. My pretend family. Pure nonsense. But it was childhood, night-time nonsense. Not grown-up, middle-of-a-break-up nonsense.

"Autumn. You're freaking me out." Peter's voice shook.

I blinked rapidly. I was freaking myself out, so I had no words to reassure him. I stared at him. He stared at me. Finally he looked away and out of the corner of my eye I saw a shimmering ribbon form along the living room window. A veil? Inside? I resisted the first tug from it. The second yanked me forward like I was tied to a rope. I stumbled toward the veil.

"What are you doing?" Peter yelled at me.

"I'm not sure." I fell through veil and looked back at Peter, watched his mouth open. For crap sake, now I was really scaring him. I lunged against the force that held me and tumbled back into the apartment.

"Peter, I'm so sorry."

My words were empty comfort, but they were all I had. He leaped down from the stairs, ran to the door and yanked it open. The door slammed shut behind him.

I peered through the veil and resisted the strong pull until I saw Iapetos. One step and I was on a coarse sand beach. Far ahead, looking out to sea, stood Iapetos, crazy old Titan. I wanted him to turn and wave at me. I wanted him to be real.

My dreams used to be full of Titans. Crowded with squabbling Greek gods and goddesses. A tiresome lot, but I was fond of

Iapetos. He was the only Titan penitent for his role in Chronos's murder— at least in my dreams. He told me he had bestowed the gift of mortality upon humans. His siblings thought it was a vengeful act. I asked him why he did it. I didn't remember his answer. Now, I had to know. Dream or no dream, I had to know.

I ran toward him. "Iapetos! Papa!"

Papa? I didn't know why I said that, but it seemed right and proper.

He turned and smiled and in a flash he was standing beside me. "So. You've returned."

I frowned.

"Ah. I see. Not prepared to return." His voice sounded sad. "No matter. I suppose you brought a question."

The urgency of my question eclipsed my confusion. "Mortality. You gave humans mortality. Why?"

"Of course. That's the last question you asked before you left us. It's not surprising you don't remember the answer."

"I need to know." My near hysteria was out of place. My voice belonged to somebody else.

Iapetos sat against a sea-worn boulder. "It's a rare gift that immortals can never have." His voice was deep and mournful. "Human's don't appreciate it, of course, but they make the best of it. Because of it, they often rise to a valor we can only imagine."

I responded, "They also sink to indescribable depravity." I hadn't known I thought that until I heard it come out of my mouth.

He laughed. "Of course. Of course. Depravity is easy. We're consumed with depravity on this side of the veil as well. But, we're immortal. What we do doesn't really matter. We cannot die."

"Mortals don't want to die. I don't want to die."

"I don't want you to die, either. There's no need. You're the best daughter-in-law I have. I don't intend to lose you."

"Daughter-in-law?" I staggered back, snapped back into myself, feeling like I'd been punched. "I'm married? To who?"

Iapetos yanked on his ear. "Oh, my. I had misgivings when you wanted to try on mortal life. But it was only thirty years. A blink of an eye. What could go wrong in that short time?"

"Try on mortal life?" I had a terrible feeling he was telling the truth, but I couldn't grasp what he meant.

The old Titan shook his head. "I knew we should have done it my way, but Hera insisted that you forget everything so that you wouldn't go insane. She thought you couldn't really experience mortality if you remembered your life before. Hogwash. Mortals are made of sterner stuff, I say. But I made Aphrodite promise to bring you up to speed when you came of age. Obviously she had other ideas. Conniving female. Always upsetting the order of things." He turned away.

"But, I *am* mortal. Aren't I?" I whispered, more to myself than to him.

He swung around. His face wrinkled with irritation. "I don't know what you've become. But you'll return to yourself the moment you've completed your thirtieth mortal year. Unless…" He grabbed my chin, pinching hard. "No. Not even you would make that choice." He let go and I was back in Peter's living room. No sign of the veil.

My cell phone rang. Peter.

"Autumn. Look. I changed my mind. I don't want the condo. It's yours." He sounded out of breath, like he'd been running.

"Peter, don't be silly."

"Silly? This is not me being silly. This is me being frickin, frackin, freaked. The place is possessed and you with it."

"Wait, Peter."

"If this is some kind of joke. A holographic trick? How did you do it Autumn? Why?"

"I didn't. I couldn't."

"Okay. Maybe it's me. Maybe I slipped a cog. Gone nutters. I'm calling a shrink, but I'm not coming back to that place."

"Peter!"

He hung up. Crap. I paced from room to room. By then, I knew I was the one who'd gone nutters. I suspected I had always been a little off kilter. Iapetos was obviously a stress vision. Except my chin still throbbed. Was it possible to imagine that? Maybe. Psychosomatic pain was well documented.

I nuked a bag of soup. Couldn't eat it. I phoned Peter. He didn't answer. I phoned his brother.

"Clay. I'm trying to reach Peter."

"Too late."

"Excuse me?"

"He's gone. He told me you'd phone. Told me to tell you to do whatever you wanted with his stuff."

"Gone where?"

"Didn't he tell you? Chile. Doing earthquake relief with his buddy Josh. Thought he'd have told you."

"Clay, I don't believe you. I just talked to him."

"Surprised the hell out me, too. Taking the split hard, I guess. He came over here. Dropped off his Jeep. Called a cab and was gone."

I hung up and stood there, stunned stupid. I was the person who disappeared without a word. I was the impulsive person in my life. Solid, dependable people like Peter didn't do things like that. Something was shaking my snow globe and I didn't how to make it stop. I didn't know what to do. I fired up Peter's computer, wasted time on Facebook, Googled a few topics that might be worth writing about, then phoned a couple of friends and listened while they chattered. I watched day turn to night through the windows in the condo that should have been my home.

Why hadn't I outgrown my childhood fantasies? Everyone else did. The silly business of yearning for the 'real' family. Everyone has a similar story. My best friend, Emily, used to imagine she was adopted and at any moment her real parents would drive up in a limo and reclaim her. Foolish, stupid childish fantasy. But Emily grew up. I was obviously some kind of weirdo who couldn't grow up. I had no clue where to go to get help and I didn't have the fortitude to stay in the condo without Peter. I shut the door softly when I left. The click of it closing sounded horribly final.

The aunts were asleep when I got back, so I tossed all over my bed waiting for morning. The quiet house threatened to crush me.

I was up and out for my run at 7:00 a.m. as usual. I took a new route. Far away from any veil zone, but I expected one to show up every time I turned a corner. Nothing happened. The only thing not normal during my morning run was me. I burst in the door at 8:00 a.m. and found the aunts sitting at the table, fully dressed, eating toast and sipping mugs of tea. Not normal. They were never dressed before noon.

"Did you have a good run, dear?" That was Aunt April, not looking at me.

"Good enough."

I grabbed a towel from the drawer and dabbed my sweaty face. The weird of yesterday had not gone away.

Aunt April stirred her tea, rattling her spoon against the mug. "I hope you're not after a chat this morning. We're going out and we don't have time for talking."

The other two nodded.

I sighed. "If this is about me leaving Peter, snubbing me won't change my mind."

Aunt June took off her reading glasses and waved them at me. "Well, maybe we've changed our minds. Did you ever think of that?" She sounded like a petulant four-year old.

"So, you're not upset at me for dumping Peter?"

She shrugged and buried her head in a newspaper. Aunt April examined her toast.

Aunt May tapped her mouth with her napkin. "When you're done abusing your keyboard this morning, would you drive into the country, maybe out east somewhere. Pick yarrow and Labrador tea for our birthday beverage."

"Sure, I can do that. Why don't I just bike over to Wagner Bog?"

"Autumn Bailey!" Aunt May stood up and flung her napkin across the table. "Wagner Bog? That's west. And it's a protected area. Environmentally sensitive. You know that."

Of course I knew that. "You always pick your wild tea in Wagner Bog."

Aunt May pressed a hand against her face. "That was before." She sat down hard. Her usually soft voice had a hard edge. "We've decided it's time to be an example to others."

"But, you have permission."

"Of course we have permission." Her voice raised a notch. "We have permission to *selectively* harvest medicinal herbs for the Circumboreal Plant Project. It does not include random collection for personal use."

That made no sense. The aunts had always collected tea for personal use in Wagner Bog.

Aunt May gave me the 'look'. "Stay away. From Wagner. Bog."

The other two nodded vigorously.

I raised both hands. "Okay. Okay."

When Aunt May used 'the look', I usually humored her. Not this time. I needed to talk to the Fayal. Wagner Bog was their only habitat.

When I got there, they rose like a swarm of locusts out of grass and shrubs. They teemed around my head, all chattering at once, darting frantically back and forth in front of my face until I couldn't see where I was going. I swatted at them. Useless gesture. They're faster than a wink. I dropped the basket and the little wretches dove for it. They hung it on an aspen branch, just out of my reach.

"Hey!"

I didn't usually yell at them. They were annoying and rude, but their feelings were easily hurt and they could pout for days.

I yelled louder. "What's the matter with you?"

Some of them glanced at me, but they continued to buzz around the hanging basket like angry bees, bickering and pushing at each other. Finally, I had to do it. I knew they hated it, but they left me no choice. Two fingers from each hand into my mouth. A good strong whistle. Instant silence. Naida dropped like a leaf. Flea blubbered. Benthi and Dredge headed right at me. The rest dove down to comfort Naida.

Benthi stopped about a foot from my face. Her wings were a blur as she hovered. She crossed her tiny arms and glowered at me.

"That hurt, Big She."

Dredge hung in the air above her, shaking his tiny fist, chittering like a squirrel.

"I'm sorry, Benthi. I *am* sorry. But you were on a rampage. I've never seen you bugs act so strange."

Dredge exploded out of the air, hit my cheek like an arrow and bit me. The little bugger bit me. Drew blood. Before I could react, he zipped over to a patch of fireweed, lit on the highest stalk and screamed, "Not bug!" He spit at me. "No! Not!"

Crap. They hated being called bugs. I knew that, but I'd called them bugs in jest many times before; I thought it was an acceptable tease between us. I rubbed my throbbing cheek. A Bog Fairy bite is not much worse than a hornet's sting. So, the aunts said, but I'd never been bitten before, so I didn't know if there might be side effects.

Benthi had no sympathy. "Shame." She scolded. "Shame!"

My cheek swelled like a birthday balloon around the bite. My head throbbed. I sat down hard on the trail. Benthi giggled and pointed. Dredge whirled around my head like a mini tornado. I couldn't see him when he traveled that fast, but I heard his mocking laughter. He was a vindictive little fart. Of course, the rest of them flitted over to stare at me as I sat there, disoriented and in pain. I endured a barrage of Fayal glee while I pushed down a rising panic. What had got into them?

My world was warping out of shape. First the veil, then the hallucination at the apartment, then the aunts, and now this. What did it mean? I couldn't tell what was real. I was in serious trouble.

Eventually, mob laughter exhausted, the Fayel plopped down around me like big raindrops and for a few moments everything was quiet. My face throbbed, my head pounded and I could hardly see. To hell with the birthday tea. As soon as I recovered my equilibrium, I was going home. I wrapped my arms around my knees and closed my eyes.

"Big She?"

I felt Benthi tug at my eyelids. I ignored her.

"Au-tum A-nes-i-dor-a Bay-lee?"

"Wha?" I muttered, my tongue swollen. "I don't wanna talk ta you."

"You made this happen, Au-tum Bay-lee."

"I seh sorry."

"Good. Now you help us, and we'll be Stephen's even."

"Even Stephen."

"I like the other way."

"Fine."

I couldn't imagine what help those shrewd little creatures needed. They knew ancient, authentic magic; the kind embedded in photosynthesis and undifferentiated cell division. I opened my eyes. Fayal surrounded me. Hundreds of them, maybe thousands. I'd never seen so many. And they were quiet. Dead quiet. All over the moss and the shrubs and trees they clustered. Quiet and still, like prehistoric insects suspended in amber. Eerie.

Benthi stood tall and serious on my bended knee. "Your three mamas. They want to bring bad on you."

She stared at me and it seemed like the rest of them held their breaths, waiting for my response.

"My aunts?"

She nodded, solemnly.

I frowned and chewed on my tongue where I felt the swelling already going down. "You've been into the fungus."

She shook her head, pantomiming dismay. "Never drink that fusty. Never. Not me."

Of course she drank magic mushroom brew. They made it and I was sure they all drank it. Benthi denied it, because she knew I didn't approve. I didn't approve, because it slowed them down, making them easy prey for owls and hawks.

"Why would the Aunts bring bad on me?"

"Soon you have to go to your home, but they want stay here. Forever and forever."

I rubbed my throbbing cheek. "I *am* home. Benthi. This is where I live. This is where I've always lived."

"Not this home. Your forever home. Old mamas say when you go back they can't follow. They want find the silver, so they can stay."

"My forever home?"

The Fayal just stared at me.

"Come on. Talk to me. My forever home? Silver? This is not penetrating past my ears. Explain!"

The Fayal crowded closer, rustling around me like dry leaves. Benthi leaned towards me and whispered, "The silver. It keep you here. Make you stay. When silver go, you go."

Dredge and Benthi exchanged a look. Benthi frowned. "Boss man put it here, Big She. We guard it. If old mamas take silver; we have to die. How did you forget?"

The whole population whined around my head, squeaking like crazed rodents. I put my fingers into my mouth again. I didn't blow, but I got instant silence.

"Boss man? Are you daft? What boss man?"

"You boss man." Dredge jabbed his finger at me.

They all nodded. Some of them shook fists.

I stood. "And this hidden silver keeps me here?" More nodding. "If I'm not kept here, where do I go?"

Dredge hovered in front of my face, his arms folded. "You know where you go. Everybody know."

I folded my arms. "Really? Everybody except me, it seems."

A ripple of sound moved through the crowd of little creatures and as suddenly as they had appeared they winked out. I wasn't easily surprised, but they startled me with that antic. I listened hard, my eyes darting everywhere trying to spot them. Then Benthi was at my ear.

"Hide, Big She! Now!" Her whisper was barely audible, but the alarm in her voice sliced through me. She darted over to a hump of moss-covered dead fall and pointed frantically. "Lift up. Hurry."

I lifted a thick blanket of moss. It came up in one piece, like a hinged door. Under it, a steep clay chute disappeared into blackness.

"Slide!"

I slid. Wet and slimy with mud, I tumbled off the end of the slide into a gigantic pile of conifer cones. I found myself in a dimly lit cavern surrounded by hysterical Fayal.

"Did they see her?"

"They not see."

"You be sure?"

"They want silver. Not looking for Big She."

I stood up. "Who? What are you talking about?"

"Those three. The magpies."

"Magpies?"

"Old birds. Your old birds."

"Mine? Look, you loopy little lug nuts. Whatever is happening with silver or magpies, it's got nothing to do with me."

They hovered over my head, tiny arms crossed, little faces wrinkled and pinched.

I glared at them. "How long have you been hiding this slide from me?"

They all shrugged.

"Silver and magpies have everything to do with you, Anesidora." A silk smooth voice spoke my middle name. .

The Fayal, instantly silent, bowed their heads and moved apart to reveal a creature the size of a finger joint. The Fayal whispered, awe and reverence in their voices. "Captain Taran. Lady Captain Taran."

Without thinking, I lifted my hand and she landed lightly on my finger. A tiny human form, slim and delicate where the Fayal are round and chunky. Translucent veined wings more like those of a mayfly than the sturdy dragon fly wings of the Fayal. She studied me with lively curiosity.

"The Titans miss you, Anesidora. They say time come back home."

She looked familiar. A wave of longing moved through me and I did want to return home. I shook my head. I didn't remember her from Olympus and that was the only other home I'd known. I shook her off my finger. The Fayal gasped.

I clutched at my head. *Olympus?* Where had that come from? Images of cold stone formed in my mind. Columns, wide enough to house elephants, towered up, nearly out of sight, supporting a dome as vast as the sky. A marble floor, polished and polar. I stood on that floor cold and alone.

The tiny captain chattered. She sounded far away. I think I responded. I think she chattered and scolded more. I can't be sure, because all of a sudden I was back on the Wagner Bog walking trail. Alone. The sun setting. A chill in the air. Fayal out of sight. I touched my cheek. The swelling was gone. Was it ever there?

By the time I returned to the aunts' house I couldn't remember the exact conversation I'd had with the Fayal. It lingered just beyond the tip of my mind; close enough that I wanted to believe it happened, but far enough away that I couldn't bring up the details. I know I asked the captain who she thought I was. I couldn't remember her answer. She blinked out like a lit match in the wind and what she left in my memory was a short, obscure and ridiculous to-do list.

Find what you seek— the person and the treasure.
Beware the aunts; they will forsake.

What I sought was my old, predictable life back, but hope for that was waning.

The aunts got home late, grubby and cranky.

I was considerably cranky, myself. "What happened to you?"

"Muskeg." Aunt April dropped her muddy, garden boots into the kitchen sink.

"Why?" I wanted to ask if they were looking for silver, but I didn't. Maybe I didn't want to know the answer.

"Bog cranberry." Aunt June pulled off her headscarf and shook out her hair.

"A little early for berries, isn't it?" I hadn't even tried to mute my sarcasm.

"Leaves." Aunt May dumped a small paper bag of plant material in the middle of the kitchen table. "We need the leaves."

They went right to bed. Too tired to talk, they said.

The next morning, after my run, I lingered in the sun porch with my coffee. I pretended to read while I observed the aunts. I looked through a different filter now, but I couldn't believe they wanted to 'do me bad'. As I watched them, memories surfaced. The old, elaborate story emerged. Night dreams from my childhood, clear and clean. They couldn't be dreams; they had to be stories I'd read, said one side of my brain. No. Memories, said the other.

One fantastical scene dominated, the one where the Greek goddesses Aphrodite and Hera led me from the immortal world of Olympus into the mortal realm of humans. But in my dreamscapes there were no aunts. The whole thing was bloody ridiculous. I shoved the 'down-the-rabbit-hole' illusions to the back of my brain where they belonged and tried to focus on what was left of my regular life. The aunts' birthday. I could count on their birthday staying the same. I had one more birthday duty to perform. Pick up the birthday gift. Easy. I'd been doing that since I was nine.

He didn't like the box, but couldn't say why. Joanie, who ran his till, said the problem was that he hadn't chosen it. Everything else in *Epimetheus Antiquaries* graced the shelves, because his discerning eye had separated gold from dross.

The box had just appeared. On his front counter. Over the long weekend. No sign of break and enter. Nothing disturbed. No note or any other communication. Unbelievable. The unexpected had not paid a visit to his life for many centuries. He had taken vigorous precautions to make it so.

Not that the box was dross. Far from it. It was ancient. He grudgingly admitted its magnificence, but he didn't want to like it. In spite of his best efforts he was drawn to it by an unreasonable and unbearable attraction. A nail to a magnet. It had happened to him only once before. Fifty lifetimes ago. Another time. Another box. Prometheus and his gang of bullies flattering him, taunting him and then snatching away the treasure he wanted before it was really his. They encouraged her to open it. He knew they made her do it. If she was disgraced, he was disgraced. That's what they wanted.

Well. He fooled them. He confessed. He took the blame and then exiled himself. Their bullying couldn't reach him in the mortal realm. What did they think they'd accomplish? Sending a box? A box was nothing.

At first he hid it in the back storeroom in a water-stained steamer trunk. For several months he resisted the sweet voice whispering to him. He thanked the old gods that nobody else could hear it, and for that reason he thought he could continue to ignore it.

One night he startled awake to hear an especially strident cry from the box. Half-way across town the plea reached him. He resisted a vulgar urge to leap out of bed and go to his shop in the middle of the night. Over eons he'd learned how to resist his primitive yearnings, but he was a beginner again under the persistent beguilement emanating from the box.

The next day, when he took the box out of the steamer trunk, its sigh of relief tore at him; the sound was so pathetic, so familiar. He scribbled a shockingly low price on a tent card and set it beside the box in the front window, confident that somebody would snatch it up within days. A month later it was still there, slowly gathering dust.

The night cleaners refused to dust it no matter how much he threatened them. They said it was a witch box. He told them he didn't deal in necromancy, but they didn't believe him.

Finally he moved the box to the front counter. He didn't want it that close to him, but he had to make it prominent. He had to sell it. A few people glanced at it, but nobody picked it up. Once a customer stretched out her hand, but before she touched it, she drew her hand back, pressed it against her chest and giggled. She turned away, snatched up a vintage bowl with a grape and vine pattern, paid the hefty price in cash and didn't wait for her change. She hadn't shut the door behind her before he decided to lower the price on the box again. The heat of the box's disapproval changed his mind.

He went home early that day, and that night, for the first time in his unremarkable life in the mortal realm, he locked his back door. It had been several thousand years since he'd felt an unease that significant. He went to bed, turned out his light, and stoically waited for the one he left behind to enter his dreams. She was his to bid in dreamtime.

Annie's Antique Mall. It should have been a simple pick up. Annie had emailed a photo of a pair of straw-yellow bottles. She knew how to find a quirky gift for the aunts' birthday. This year it was a 19th Century ether bottle and its companion, a small, drip dispensary bottle. Handsome and peculiar.

I swung the door open at Annie's and stepped in. I would have stepped right back out had my momentum not propelled me forward. I stumbled into a wavy barrier; thick and warped. A veil? There? I burst right through onto a sandy wasteland.

The shop on the other side was out of focus, sounds muffled by the soft, sand-shaker whisper you get when you hold a seashell against your ear. Over that distant shush I heard Annie.

"Hi, Autumn. I found the perfect container for this set. Come and see."

Ohmygawd. I'd been duplicated. One of me on this side of the veil and one of me on the other. I heard my twin respond. Her voice muffled, but understandable.

"Great. Aunt June will love these. Aunt May will hate them. Aunt April will make fun of them. It's the perfect birthday gift, as usual."

Annie's pleasant voice: "You doing anything special for the birthday dinner?"

My voice: "Nah. We'll drink the disgusting birthday beverage; eat currant scones with high bush cranberry jelly, and probably have mango chicken."

Annie's voice: "And cake? No. I forgot. They don't do cake. Did you ever tell me why?"

Me, laughing: "I doubt anybody knows why. They've always done it without cake."

I watched the wavy image of Annie choosing a roll of wrapping paper. Suddenly, I wanted to stop her. It was the wrong gift. I stepped through the veil and I was eye to eye with Annie. She squinted at me and frowned.

"You okay?"

I blinked. Everything had snapped back into focus. The sound of the sea was silenced. Was I okay? I didn't know. I hoped I had become one person again. I smiled— at least I tried to smile. I said I was okay. I looked behind me. The veil was gone.

Annie held up the wrapping paper, puzzlement wrinkling her face.

"You said not to wrap them? Did you mean not in this paper, or not at all?"

I pressed my fingers against my temples. I didn't remember saying that. "Sorry, Annie. Don't pay attention to me. I think I just had a brain fart. A little stressed lately, I guess."

Annie wrapped the boxed ether bottles. I paid.

"You need a vacation, girl." I heard worry in her voice.

I nodded. "Maybe."

I sat in my car trying to understand what had happened. The veil. In Annie's shop. Weird. There seemed to be two of me.

Impossible. What had I done? Split my personality? I needed to research some serious psychology.

The wrapped parcel on the passenger seat beside me was not the right gift. Of that much I was certain. Why was I certain? And, if that was the wrong gift, where was the right one?

"Your aunts need something to remind them who they are." A woman's voice. A pleasant voice.

Who said that? My window was down, but nobody was beside my car. I subdued panic. Nobody in the rear-view mirror. Nobody within a hundred meters of my car.

"Silly girl. It's me. Aphrodite. If you think I'm going to actually sully myself by stepping into your mortal morass, even for a few moments, you're delusional."

I leaned my head against the back of the seat. I nodded, agreeing with the disembodied voice. I *was* delusional. I didn't need more convincing.

"Command your noisy contraption. I don't know how you stand that racket. Follow me."

I drove out of Annie's parking lot following a faint shape. It guided me half way across the city to a tiny antique shop tucked into the cup of a 1960's era strip mall.

I stopped in front. A face appeared in the bow window of the little shop. A face out of focus. A familiar face. A small, tight sound escaped my lips. I caught back my breath.

Find what you seek.

I yanked the car door open and stumbled over to the window, leaning on the sill with my face pressed against the glass. There was no one there. It was just a window between me and an over-crowded arrangement of old things. A heavy velour curtain behind many tiers of collectables hid the interior of the shop from view.

I had to go inside, but I felt nervous. What if…? What if what? I didn't know. As I turned away from the window, my peripheral vision caught a glint of light. At one edge of the clutter I saw it, reflecting sunlight. The right gift. A mourning brooch, framing a piece of braided hair. A macabre gift. But so were the ether bottles. What made the brooch a better choice? I half expected an answer.

Hearing nothing, I shrugged. "Fine." I muttered. "I'll buy the damn brooch. Two ridiculous gifts instead of one."

I strode to the door and stopped. A rush of familiarity. I'd been here before. Impossible. I go into one antique store once a year. *Annie's Antique Mall*. No other. I lifted my hand to push the door open. My heart-rate accelerated. I felt dizzy. I shoved my hands into the pockets of my jeans, stepped back and stared at the door. I was wedged between a panicked urge to flee and an eagerness to burst into the store. Eagerness won. I opened the door.

Inside, the shop was dimly lit and dusty. There wasn't enough air. I couldn't breathe. I heard myself groan. "I can't do this." I don't know if I said that out loud.

I dashed back outside and tried to breathe. Deep breaths. I looked up at the heavily carved board hanging out over the street like an English pub sign. *Epimetheus Antiquaries*. Elaborate letters carved deeply into the wood.

Epi? Iapetos' youngest son, Epimetheus. No. Ridiculous.

I remembered. I was nine. I'd ridden the rapid rail with Aunt June to an unfamiliar part of the city. She was nervous and chatty. She kept saying she'd had too much coffee and shushed me when I pointed out she didn't drink coffee.

We had to walk a couple of blocks to the shop and I remember she held my hand tightly like she thought I might run off. She yanked me over to the grubby bow window and pointed to a teapot. A square, Japanese teapot. A white thing, splattered all over with globs of brown glaze. Ugly. The price: two hundred and sixty-three dollars. Aunt June handed me an envelope of bills and shoved me into the shop. She didn't come in with me. I was used to that. Aunt June often suffered bouts of claustrophobia.

Inside the door I was stopped by a flush of warmth, like I'd stepped close to a hearth fire. It was dark and quiet in the shop. An old man shuffled over. He looked like a character from a vintage movie, wearing a tailored Victorian era suit, a high collared shirt, a brocade vest, and bedroom slippers. He was tall and thin with a sad, blood-hound face. I felt a rush of recognition that embarrassed me. He had to lean down to hear my whispered request. He smelled of the sea. I liked that. I smiled and I looked him in the eye.

When I saw who looked out at me, I was instantly angry. I wanted to spit in his face. The urge was so strong I had to press my hand against my mouth to stop myself.

He stared at me and staggered back a bit. I was sure he'd been able to read my mind. I didn't know what to do. I was a kid with an even temper and long fuse. I wasn't used to a sudden rush white-hot anger. I would have turned and ran out, except the force that was Aunt June waited outside, looming like a stone wall behind me. That was twenty years ago.

I looked at the door. *Trellos Anoydos, proprietor*, painted on the bottom of the frosted window in tall, thin calligraphic strokes. Same name. He'd told me everybody called him Old Anos. I called him old Anus— inside voice, of course. He looked older than Zeus and I decided he was a spook. Zippers that sealed off rips in the firmament that were supposed to contain the restless spirits of those who had passed on were never monitored well. The odd spook leaked out from time to time.

Spook sightings didn't make the news. The aunts told me only the rare person could actually see them.

I remembered standing at the counter, gripping the edge of it with both hands, my chin resting on the top. I'd squinted up at him while he counted the money from Aunt June's envelope. I tried to will him back through a rip. For a moment I actually thought I could do it. I imagined he was afraid of me.

Back at home, the aunts were unusually curious about the man who ran the shop. They seemed surprised to learn he was old, and they were markedly distressed and even a little bewildered when they discovered I had taken a dislike to him.

A flashback of their conversation that evening played in my head like a YouTube video on steroids. Me, a skinny little kid, sitting on the upstairs landing just out of sight, straining to hear what they said.

Aunt June. Imperious. "She's too young. I told you she was too young."

Aunt April. Harsh and accusing. "You didn't say anything. You were just as eager as we were to get it over with."

Aunt May. Husky, whiny voice. "I thought it was supposed to just happen. Get them together and they'd take it from there. Our task is done. Now what are we supposed to do?"

As quickly as it started, the video in my head winked out. Epi. It had to be Epi. Was I ready to see him again?

Anos ran his stylus over the codes on the screen. The Salvation Army on the south side of the river still had pick-up service. He'd donate some furniture and include the box. He started to enter numbers to send the message. The small bell above the door tinkled, the door swung open and a young woman entered. She stood in the light of the slowly closing door, looking bewildered. He caught his breath. He knew her. No. He didn't know her. He blinked rapidly. He'd seen her before. She squinted into his shop, then turned abruptly and walked back out.

He clutched his chest. He did know her. He replayed a scene, instantly as fresh in his memory as if it had been yesterday. She'd hurt his feelings, that little girl. Tiny she'd been then, but tough as Cleopatra's toenails and about as unattractive. She'd disliked him on sight. He was embarrassed to remember he'd wanted her to like him. With great effort, a few thousand years ago he'd weaned himself completely from the debilitating desire for affection and approval. And there she was breaking it all down. Why? She was a plain little thing and aggressive. Nothing like the perfect beauty he'd left behind.

He was surprised to see her again. All grown up. Still scrawny. Still irregularly featured. No curves. The young woman needed a good meal. He stared at the closed door and the lovely face of the other one smiled at him. Sweet and shy with a touch of mischief. He cursed the flood of longing that pulsed through him. They were nothing alike, that scrawny girl and the immaculate one he'd left behind. Just the same, he struggled to resist an urge to run out after her. To call her back.

His computer screen hibernated. He lined up items on his counter in descending order according to size. Make order. He needed to make order. The bell above the door tinkled again. He didn't look up right away, but he knew she'd come back in. He could feel her presence. He had an irrational urge to run to the back room, to hide from her. He palmed a tiny soul jar, a replica, of course, one of his favorites.

"Excuse me." Her voice was harsh. Not a pleasant voice. Not the perfect one's voice.

He glanced at her. Her look challenged him to respond. He gripped the small porcelain receptacle so hard, it cracked apart, slicing his fingers. He welcomed the pain.

"There's a hair snake mourning brooch in your window."

She stood, defiantly, in front of his counter. He nodded and said nothing. Finally he turned away to draw a tissue from a dispenser. He dropped the shards and dabbed at the quickly coagulating blood on his hand. When he turned back, she was staring at the box.

"Is that for sale?"

All of a sudden he wanted to say, 'No!'

"Well, is it?" She picked it up. Her eyebrows rose. Her fingers traced the intricate pattern on the top. She turned it over. "How does it open?" She shook it.

He was unprepared for that question. He hadn't tried to open it. He hadn't wanted to try. He knew if he investigated he would play into the hands of those who'd left it.

He muttered, "I don't know."

He busied himself retrieving the mourning brooch. He could hear the box rattle as she shook it, but it didn't cry out. In fact, he was sure he heard a murmur of satisfaction. He wiped sweat from his forehead. He needed to open a window. It was hot and stuffy in his shop. He set the brooch on the counter and rung it up. He didn't look at the woman, but he could feel her frown.

"Is this a trick box?"

"Possibly." He shrugged.

"Where are the instructions?"

"There aren't any."

"What good is it then?"

"Probably no good at all."

"I want to buy it." The surprise in her voice made that statement sound like a question.

"It's pricey."

"No, it's not. Says right here. Twenty bucks."

"Oh. My goodness."

He snatched the box. It squawked. He held his breath and looked at the girl. She stared at the box. Was it possible she'd heard it? His heart rate increased. Foolish as it was, he didn't want her to have it.

"I must have been half asleep when I wrote this price. I'm so very sorry." He sucked in a deep breath and blurted, "The actual price is two hundred dollars."

"Two hundred?"

She reached across the counter and drew two fingers across the top of the box. It purred like a cat. She pulled out a credit card and put it on the counter.

"Gift wrap the brooch, it's a present. I'll carry the box."

Anos stared at the credit card. His hand shook when he picked it up. The box sighed.

I never bought on impulse. Never. Until yesterday. The stupidest day of my life. I bought an ancient puzzle box for too much money. Me, the queen of pinchery.

No instructions for opening it. Not that instructions would have helped. The thing was so old; time had corroded it shut. The crazy old dude who sold it to me was definitely not Iapetos' son Epi. He was so antiquated he'd look out of place in a steampunk movie. Epi, according to my seemingly chronic delusions, was young and handsome. Too vain to have let himself get that old. But I had the strong feeling that Epi was out there somewhere. Somewhere close. I didn't know why we were connected, but clearly we had bad history.

On the way home I surrendered to what seemed to be a virulent kind of madness. I was definitely headed for a rubber room. I'd lost the strength to fight it. When the Aphrodite voice issued out of my turned off car radio, I wasn't surprised.

Her silky voice crooned, "Of course that was Epi. I knew you didn't love him. If you did, his age wouldn't matter. But, more to the point, I hope you can at least see that it's obvious he doesn't love you."

I knew I didn't feel anything close to love for that moldy, old man and I certainly didn't care how he felt about me. I told her so. The Aphrodite voice lectured me all the way home. She insisted I still had to have it out with Epi. She said I had to make him tell me he didn't love me.

"Sure. Okay." I told her. "I'll make sure I do that." She seemed satisfied with my response.

That night I didn't sleep again. I imagined the box was calling to me. I'd shoved it in the hall cupboard and covered it with towels. I didn't want the aunts to know I had it. Suspicion. Intrigue. My dream life leaked steadily into my real life and I couldn't stop the transmission.

I moved the box from the hall cupboard to the bookshelf in my bedroom and then finally to my bedside table. I slept after that, sinking into crazy dreams. Somebody was trapped in the box, pleading to me to open it.

I yelled at the box. "I don't know how!"

The box shook and rattled and the pathetic wail that burst from it woke me up. I turned my light on and listened to the stupid thing. I knew there was nothing in it, but I shook it anyway. When I put it down and turned out the light, the face in the window of the old guy's shop appeared on my wall, blurry and out of focus. An old man's face morphed into a young man's face. Epimetheus. My husband. I woke up drenched in sweat. There was no questioning it. I had become a raving lunatic. I changed my damp bed shirt, fell back asleep and dreamed again.

In the midst of fireworks gone berserk, I swung a sledge hammer as big as my head at that idiotic box. It bounced off and threw me half-way across the back yard. The box unfolded like an origami gift, revealing a tiny Greek statue. A woman carved out of pink stone, standing straight and stiff, in a plain dress full of pleats, her hair wound up in knots and whorls. I could see her clearly. Nice looking, even by today's standards.

It wasn't until morning, when I woke up, that I realized the statue was me. A much more beautiful me. I was Pandora. Not the Pandora of myth and legend. The real Pandora. Dread sunk through me like a stone. I had to go back. To my old life. I should have known they wouldn't let me stay. I wished I'd known my present life's time limit sooner. Would it have made a difference with Peter? Damned if I knew.

The dream faded like dreams do, but my Pandora-self hung on, so I locked it deep in the dream closet of my mind and made my Autumn-self concentrate on the birthday party.

The birthday started like it always did. The table crowded with a dozen pots of Aunt June's amaryllises, all blooming obediently for the occasion. The aunts plucked every hibiscus blossom from their sunroom forest and pinned them into their hair. I'd never known them to visit the tropics, but every year on their birthday, our house turned into a Gauguin landscape.

I sat on the stairs like I always did, watching them bustle and argue. I took comfort from the fact that the birthday party remained the same. I thought of Peter as I sat there. He hadn't tried to contact me. He'd changed phones so I couldn't text him. He didn't answer my emails. Facebook messages he ignored, but he hadn't defriended me. There was faint solace in that. I knew from his profile page he was still in California with his friend Josh. He'd posted a few photos. Peter and Josh hanging on beach bunnies in a bar. Peter wasn't much of a drinker, but they all looked drunk.

I was wrong about the birthday celebration staying the same. At the birthday dinner, Aunt May always sat like a queen in the one high backed dining room chair at the head of the table and each dish was first passed by her. This time when they called me to the meal and I stepped up to the table, Aunt May, standing behind her chair, beckoned to me.

Aunt May pulled her chair away from the table. "Autumn, why don't you sit here for a change?" There was an unfamiliar sweet tone to her voice.

I reared back like the chair might bite me. "I don't want more change."

"Of course, you do, dear." Aunt April guided me to the chair.

"You just haven't realized it yet." Aunt June patted my shoulder and settled a hibiscus wreath on my head.

I sat. Stiff and tall in Aunt May's chair. Speechless. Birthday buzz filled the house. Color, smells, the aunts seemingly light-hearted and laughing. I ate what they served, my brain bursting with questions, each one a fresh popped kernel of why, going unanswered. I heard Lady Captain Taran's soft voice. *Beware the aunts.* Food and drink tasted strange. Did I think they were going to poison me? Unbelievable.

When it came time for Aunt June to present Aunt May with the gift, she carried the beautifully wrapped brooch in on a silver tray. Aunt May received it with her usual decorum. She unwrapped it carefully. I waited for the customary frown to fold up her forehead. Instead, she burst into tears. She caressed the glass oval that covered delicately woven strands of hair.

"William." She whispered, eyes shut. She passed the brooch to Aunt June, whose cheeks shone with tears.

Aunt June kissed the brooch. "Thomas." Her normally strong voice was rice paper thin. She passed it to Aunt April, whose shoulders were shaking with sobs. "Papa."

The longing in their voices embarrassed me.

Aunt May, tears streaming down her face, looked at me. "Autumn. How could you?"

"How could I what?"

"You don't have to be coy with us, dear. And I'm not saying we don't deserve it."

She sighed deeply and reached over to stroke the brooch. After that they wouldn't talk to me. They murmured and whispered to each other. They sighed and wept. They ignored me.

I served dessert. They ate and wept. After dessert, Aunt June produced an elegant shadow box frame for displaying the brooch. She couldn't have known about the brooch and yet she was prepared for it. She knew about the ether bottles; she's the one who always approved the birthday gift choice. She didn't seem to care that the bottles hadn't appeared.

"Aunt June." I leaned across the table, so she would have to look at me. "How did you know about the brooch?"

She raised her chin and looked past me. "Well, it had to happen eventually, didn't it?" A tear dripped off her chin.

I glanced at the other two. Frowns on both faces.

Aunt May dabbed her eyes. "I hope you're happy." She looked away.

Aunt April drummed with her fingers on the table top. "It would have been much easier if you'd done this earlier."

"What do you mean earlier? You're blaming me? For what?"

"Well." Aunt May sounded huffy. "Play the innocent if you must."

"Huh?"

Aunt June held up her hand. "Please, dear. You're ruining the mood."

I sat down and watched them tinker with the brooch, moving it this way and that. Arguing. Bickering. Finally they positioned it to suit them all and they hung the box on the wall. It looked like it had always been there.

While they cleared away the party, I studied the framed brooch. Three names ringed it. Scripted in extravagant, Victorian, cursive letters. Lieutenant General Sir William Francis Butler; Thomas Pitt, 2nd Baron Camelford; and Eugène Henri Paul Gauguin.

Gauguin was the only name I recognized, because the walls of Aunt April's room were cluttered with Gauguin prints. He was her favorite painter.

Aunt May patted my shoulder. "You want to know what this means? Of course you do. Since it hasn't dawned on you, I suppose we have to tell you."

The other two grinned, but not with humor. Their eyes glittered with a fierce anticipation. They looked like three blackbirds sizing up a meal.

Aunt May pointed to the framed brooch. "William, my husband."

Aunt June stroked the glass behind which the brooch hung. "Tommy. My first and only love."

Aunt April looked adoringly at the shadow box. She smiled. "My papa."

I stared at her. "Your father was Gaugin?" How is that possible? Aunt April smiled dreamily.

Trellos Anoydos paced in the backroom of his shop. Up front he could hear laughter. There were at least a half dozen people wandering around, lifting and touching; poking and prodding. He wished they'd go away. It was not a good day for customers. He wanted to close up. And do what? Go where? The shop was his life. His self-imposed exile. When he falsely confessed to opening the box, he told himself it was to protect Pandora. Truth was, he hadn't done it for her. Her transgression had been convenient. It gave him a way to escape his miserable life honorably. Most of the time he believed the story he told himself about his suffering. About how he longed for her. It was honorable for a Titan to suffer. Truth was, sometimes he went a half century without remembering what she looked like.

Then he'd make her appear. A jolt in a dream, in a desert mirage, in the steam from the tea kettle. And it would be as if he had just stepped away from her moments before. He brought back the smell of her. The taste of her. The sound of her husky voice and the feel of her silky limbs as they tangled and tumbled together. The sight of her stretching and yawning in the morning. He was a man, after all. He'd torture himself with elaborate longing for a few decades. And so it went, from agony to ennui and back to agony again. He loved the rhythm of it.

Then the Bailey girl came into his shop several decades ago increasing the intensity of his suffering when it should have been on the wane. She spoiled his game. He knew the child didn't have anything to do with the beauty he left behind. How could she? But the visions of the other returned the instant the little girl slammed the door. The little wretch put everything out of sequence. Only recently had the visions diminished enough for him to be gently tortured by their loss.

Now, the Bailey girl again. The visions again. He didn't like it. There could not be a connection. The two women weren't similar in any way. The Bailey girl was plain, some might even say, homely. Yet, he had an irrational urge to see her again. Absurd. He felt out of breath. Sometimes old age was not his friend. He made a mental note to reduce his age back down to forty when he opened his next shop. Forty was respectable, containable, but not debilitating.

He rushed to the front counter and tossed the lock-up keys to Joanie. "Shut down early if things get slow."

She raised her eyebrows and gestured into the store. "As if."

He frowned at the half dozen people scattered throughout his shop.

"What's the matter? You allergic to making money?" Joanie chewed on a piece of her untidy, long hair. She grinned at him. She was a good looking girl and cheeky.

"Mind your own business," he snapped at her.

There was no reason to respond like that, but he didn't apologize. He frowned when she winced, ducked her head and whispered, "Sorry."

Last year, when he'd hired her for a ridiculously large salary, she'd teased him with that same question, "What's the matter, you allergic to making money?"

Then, he'd laughed and she'd laughed with him.

"I always over-pay my staff." He'd said. "They stay longer, saving me the tedium of constantly training somebody new."

He liked Joanie. She made him smile. He didn't know why he was suddenly, unreasonably irked by her teasing. Money was nothing to him.

He let the door snap shut behind him. He should have called a taxi, but he didn't want to wait. He strode down the street. He'd catch a bus. The sensible man he had become wanted to know: catch a bus to where? The impulsive young man he'd once been boasted loudly to an elderly woman at the bus stop, "It doesn't matter where she is, I'll find her." To emphasize his resolve he jabbed his finger at the old woman.

She dug into her purse and sprayed him in the face with something vile. By the time he'd stopped choking, coughing and spitting, the bus had come and gone.

"*Kataperdomai!*"

He pulled out his cell phone and jabbed at the taxi icon. It wasn't until he slid into the backseat of the cab that he realized he'd used a Greek obscenity. He hadn't done that... he couldn't remember when he'd last done that. He lied. He *did* know when he'd last used that obscenity. When he ran, like the coward he was, away from a life he didn't know how to live. He knew when Pandora's crime was discovered, they'd use it as an excuse to humiliate him. So he'd confessed to her crime. It made him a hero. It gave him an honorable exile. There was nothing the ridiculous Bailey girl could do to change that. So why was he desperate to see her? He didn't know.

"Where you going, Grandpa?"

"To Hades and beyond, I expect." He muttered.

"You may have to wait a day or two for that trip." The cab driver was good natured. "How about today?"

"Roll down the windows."

The cab driver lowered the seat shield, turned around and squinted at him.

"Not that window. My window. I want to smell the air."

The shield went up and his window came down. He could see the cabbie watching him cautiously in the rear view mirror. Trellos dug around in his deep trouser pockets, pulled out a handful of bills and waved the money where the cabby could see it. Down came the shield again. The cabbie took the money without further comment.

Trellos stuck his head out the window. He shut his eyes. Her smiling face was nose to nose with his. "Catch me if you can." Her sweet laughter tasted like honey. She turned and bounded like a lioness down the street.

"Follow that lion!" he bellowed.

The cabbie turned the engine off, got out and opened the passenger door. He handed the wad of bills back to Trellos.

"Get out." He coughed. "Sir." He added as an afterthought. "If you're high, you can't ride in my cab."

Trellos pushed the money away. He sat back against the seat. "Sorry." He squeezed his forehead. "I'm not high. I'm... I'm in theatre. Practicing my part. I have an audition."

The cabbie stared at him a few moments more, then, "Where's your audition?"

Without hesitating Trellos gave him the address he'd taken from the Bailey girl's receipt.

The cabbie waved the paper at him. "That's residential."

Trellos felt his bluster return. "Of course it's residential. I'm riding to the audition with someone."

The cabbie shut the door.

During the half-hour ride, Trellos turned the day's events over and over in his mind. Prometheus and his goons were baiting him again. Why did he let them do it? He got out of the cab and stood on the sidewalk staring at a rambling heritage house. The cab drove away and the street was quiet. There was nothing familiar about the house, and yet. And yet he knew she was in there. He couldn't fathom why a perfect creature like Pandora would share a roof with the gawky, brash Bailey girl, but he knew she was in there. So what? He didn't care.

His heart pounded in his ears. He felt faint. He turned away and moved down the sidewalk, away from the house. Why had he come? He was a fool. They were doing it again. Prometheus and the others. Dangling a lovely bauble in front of his eyes, trying to mesmerize him into reaching for it. Well, they wouldn't succeed this time.

He sucked in a deep breath and glanced up the street. A person walking a dog approached from about two blocks away. He strolled towards the dog walker, fixing his face bland. He nodded as he tried to pass them. The dog, a Rottweiler, stopped in front of him and wagged her stump of a tail, clearly expecting a pat on the head. He didn't like dogs, but this dog radiated an unexpected beauty.

The owner tugged on the leash. "Pandora. Let the nice man pass." There was worry in her voice.

Trellos stroked the dog's head, looking deep into her liquid eyes. The owner pulled the dog away, mumbling, "I'm so sorry. I don't know what's the matter with her. She's not usually this social."

Trellos stared straight ahead, hot tears streaming down his face. "Neither am I," he croaked.

The dog walker hurried the dog away. Damn them all to Hades and beyond. Let them play on his loneliness; it wouldn't work anymore. It wasn't Pandora he loved. He knew that. It was the idea of her at a distance. An unattainable idea. He didn't want the complication of an actual relationship. Up close that sort of thing was inconvenient, unpredictable and messy. He boarded a bus and went home.

My Aunts confessed to being spooks. Plain and simple spooks. Volunteers from the hereafter. Volunteers to keep me safe for as long as I was mortal. They didn't wish me harm; they just didn't want to go back to the afterlife yet. I told them I didn't intend on leaving them. They didn't believe me. Why else, they reasoned, did I bring the brooch to remind them of the men who pined for them in the afterlife? I told them it was Aphrodite playing with their minds.

Aunt June: "Shame, Autumn. Aphrodite is a golden goddess. She has no time for petty tricks."

The voice that had harangued Autumn all the way home was woven through with petty tricks. She raised her eyebrows at her aunt. "You could be wrong about that. I get the feeling Aphrodite has nothing but time, and an immense urge to meddle in affairs of the heart."

Discovering I wasn't crazy brought me no comfort. I had a frame of reference for crazy; I had no frame of reference for myth becoming reality. The aunts insisted that when Olympus summoned me I would have to go back. They were vague on the details. They said they were only authorized to tell me I had no choice in the matter. I didn't believe them. They were still up to something and I was determined not to be caught by surprise by whatever they had planned.

I watched the aunts and they watched me. Several days passed with no break in tension. Finally, I slipped out of the house and biked over to Wagner Bog. I didn't know if the Fayal would fill in any more blanks for me, but I had to do something. I took the damn box with me. Crammed it into my shoulder pack.

When the Fayal didn't swarm out of the shadows of the evening forest to meet me, I hiked in. I made it all the way to the picnic log before any of them showed up and then it was only Benthi. She perched on my shoulder bag and chattered in my ear.

"We waiting long time for you."

"What do you mean, a long time. I was here three or four days ago."

"Long time we waiting." She insisted. "Now Fayal sick. Maybe die."

"What?"

I'd never known Fayal to be ill. In fact, they insisted they were immortal.

"I thought you guys lived forever."

"Not here, not forever without silver."

"Somebody took your silver?"

"No. Not yet. But if we sleep, they come. No sleep. We die."

"Benthi, that's unreasonable. Can't you take turns guarding this silver?"

"No."

"Benthi, you're exaggerating."

"All Fayal guarding silver. Getting weak."

"That's ridiculous. Where are they? Take me there."

Silly creatures. Moaning and groaning for effect when I got there. No silver in sight. Just a long stretch of wetland with hardly enough water left in it to qualify as one. They couldn't show me the silver. They said only I could point to it.

Naturally I wanted to know: "If only I can point to it, how is anybody else going to find it and steal it?"

"They know how. Flea hear them. They say somebody going to bring a pointer to them. Soon."

"Okay. Fine. How about I stand guard for a while?"

Groans turned into cheers and they circled my head, each one patting my face before winking away. It was a pleasant evening. Quiet. I figured I could use the thinking time. I settled back against a moss-covered fallen log, pulled out a reflector blanket package, shook one out to stretch out on and draped myself with the other. I fell asleep. So much for thinking.

I awoke to a group scold. It was early dawn and the Fayal were reinvigorated and annoyed to find me sleeping. Benthi came to my rescue.

"Big She don't need awake to guard silver. Her ears big."

She lifted a strand of my hair and called them over to examine my ears. As if they hadn't noticed my ears before. Good thing I'm not ticklish. They admired my ears for a few moments, agreed they were sufficient for the task and then flitted off to what I supposed were their assigned guard posts.

I felt remarkably refreshed. Ready for a hearty breakfast and a dozen mugs of strong coffee. When I tucked the blankets into my pack I felt the box. Silly thing. I pulled it out.

Benthi who had been hovering, let out a shriek that pierced my eardrums like a needle. I dropped the box and pressed my palms against my head. It reverberated like a struck bell and I fell to my knees. Before I had the wits to exclaim, Fayal covered my box about six deep. Jumping and whirling and squealing. I was sure they'd gone mad and were taking me with them. I tried to put my shaking fingers into my mouth. I pitched forward as an abrupt silence snapped me like an elastic band. Face down in the soft moss I tried to collect my wits. I turned my head.

"Benthi."

In a flash, she lit on the moss beside me, her tiny face a scowl of disapproval.

"Big She. You got the pointer. Why you not say?"

I groaned and rolled over. I flung my arm over my face. "You bugs are making me crazy." I sat up and wind-milled my arms. "And don't you dare bite me again."

Anos knew it was time to move again. Re-locate. It was the only way to escape the agony of her presence. She was too close. She shouldn't be this close. They brought her to tempt him and they could just take her away again.

He'd been on the North American continent for two hundred years. Perhaps Australia should be next. He rushed to the back of his shop, to his office, powered up his geocoding device and switched on his global positioning system. Sydney. Big town. Over five-million pathetic souls. He could disappear for a few centuries there. Bit of a vacation. Been awhile since he'd visited a southern clime.

He was at the shop the next morning when Joanie came in to open. When she flipped on the light in the office, he was slumped in his chair. Staring at nothing. Not asleep, but not really awake. He heard her come in, but he didn't have the strength or the motivation to turn his head.

"Hey. You scared the beejeezus out of me! Mr. Anoydos. What are you doing here so early?"

Joanie refused to call him, Old Anos. "You're not as old as you think you are." She always said that with a silly grin on her face. She was a silly girl and he didn't know why he kept her. He made himself turn and look at her. He blinked to make his eyes focus.

"You want my opinion, Mr. Anoydos?"

He didn't want her opinion. He didn't want anybody's opinion, but that didn't stop anyone, from the mailman to the grocery clerk, from offering *advice*.

"I'd say you're depressed. You never go anywhere. You never take a holiday. You haven't been to a garage sale this season and the season's half over."

He nodded. Not really agreeing with her, just trying to stave off more unwanted opinion.

"Hey, I know. We got a flyer yesterday. Estate Sale. Big one. Guy lived in Egypt for twenty years. They say he's got some really old stuff."

Old Anos sighed. Maybe he would do that. He couldn't leave the country today.

He nodded his head. "Make the arrangements."

Anos didn't go home to change. He splashed water on his face in the bathroom and went down the street to Alfredo's for breakfast. His head pounded with a pain so severe he could hardly see. He was not accustomed to physical pain and it worried him greatly that he had suddenly become susceptible to a sensation this crude. He didn't enjoy his Eggs Benedict the way he usually did, though the Hollandaise was freshly made with authentic ingredients, rich and light with a touch of lemon; just the way he liked it.

When he got back to the shop, Joanie assured him his taxi would arrive in about an hour. He sighed, relieved. Anos shuffled to the back of his shop and settled himself into the original French Bergère Louis XV boudoir chair he kept hidden behind his floor-to-ceiling magazine shelving. He shut his eyes and waited for the calming influence of his tiny retreat to wash over him. It didn't happen. The small bell over the door at the front announced the first customer of the day. Joanie would look after them. Conversation, louder than usual. He frowned, but didn't open his eyes.

Joanie's voice, clear and stern. "I said, Mr. Anoydos cannot be disturbed."

"Of course he can be disturbed. He's the owner, is he not? Where is he? In the back?"

Anos shrunk down against the chair. He squeezed his eyes tight. Whatever it was. Joanie would look after it.

Joanie, a touch of hysteria in her voice. "Wait. Come back!"

"Epimetheus. Epi. We know you're back there. Yoo-Hoo!"

Anos was out of his chair before he took his next breath. Who knew him by that name? Nobody. He pressed his palms against the back wall of his shop and willed the wall to open and swallow him. Nothing happened.

"Open!" he roared. "I'm a Titan. I command you to open!"

He pounded on the wall with both fists.

"Oh, Epi."

He didn't recognize the voice; he didn't turn around.

"See, girls. Just like Prometheus warned us. He'd try to run."

Prometheus? Anos swung around to face three handsome middle-aged women who seemed to have just stepped out of a Dickens' novel.

A tall, elegant woman with a flawless Dresden-doll complexion waved a gloved hand at him. "Sit down you fool, and don't look so stunned."

A shorter, darker woman turned around and made shooing motions at a flustered looking Joanie. "Go along, girl. Find us some chairs."

Joanie, ever adaptable, soon had the three women seated on serviceable, quarter sawn oak chairs from a dining room set in the store room.

The tall woman removed her gloves and placed them across her lap. "I'm sure you will appreciate there's no time for niceties. I will get straight to the point." She pierced him with a look.

He nodded, his mind racing to place the women. They knew him; therefore, it was only logical that he should know them. He did not.

"First of all, where is the box? We need it."

Anos couldn't make his voice work. He tugged at the collar of his shirt, which was all of a sudden much too tight.

"Oh, for heaven's sake, man. Are you deaf as well as stupid?"

Anos winced. As if it was yesterday, he remembered the last time he had been called stupid. "What do you know of Prometheus?" he croaked.

The tall woman leaned forward, but before she could speak, the woman with skin like warm toffee, smiled at him. "Prometheus told us to tell you he's sorry."

"Sorry?"

The tall woman frowned at the other. Toffee skin returned the grimace with an impish grin.

"Yes. He feels bad that he called you stupid. He didn't mean it. He was just exhausted, he says. His guts were being torn out day after day — I'm sure you remember that — and it was wearing him down."

Anos felt suddenly petulant. "They all called me stupid. Every one of them. They were just jealous, because I got her and they didn't."

"Well, it doesn't much matter now, does it?"

The tall woman fixed a piercing stare upon him and she moved her chair closer to his. He backed his chair up until it touched the wall.

"The box. We want the box."

He crossed his arms over his chest. "If I had the box — and I'm not saying I do — why should I give it to you?"

"Because Prometheus said you must."

"Prometheus is not the boss of me."

That statement burst out of his mouth before he could stop it. He sounded like a four-year old. He lowered his head for a moment. When he lifted it, he smiled. "The box is gone." He said, with unveiled satisfaction.

The tall woman rose half out of her chair. The dark woman put out her arm and shook her head. The tall woman sat back down. She managed to compose her face, but she picked up her gloves and switched her lap with them. Anos knew she would have rather switched him.

The toffee colored woman's smile had not wavered. She leaned forward and patted his knee. Anos jerked his leg away. She touched him. People didn't touch him. If there was touching to be done, he did it. His knee burned where her fingers had been.

"What did you do with it, dear?" Her smile seemed genuine. But so had Prometheus's the day that he had encouraged his brother to confess to the deed when the others accused *her* of opening the box.

"Tell them *you* did it." He'd said. "Zeus knows she did it. He'll get rid of her. She's nothing to him. You can save her. Have you got the orchids to do it?" His smile said Epi didn't have any orchids.

Naturally Prometheus smiled. He planned to be there to comfort the woman Epi would leave behind. Epimetheus didn't care. Prometheus had given him an honorable way to escape.

He folded his hands in his lap. "I did nothing with it. A customer bought it. It was just a box. Nothing more. I don't know what game Prometheus plays with you, what promises he's made. I'm sorry for your disappointment."

He knew he should stand and try to make a dignified retreat. Three sets of eyes pinned him like a bug and he didn't move.

"Who bought it?"

"Call them and tell them you want it back."

"And there's the other thing."

Anos stared at them.

"The silver. We need to know the location of the silver."

"There's enough to share. Prometheus told us how we could use it and it wouldn't interrupt her use of it. He says a dozen of you have used less than that to keep you going for millennia."

"We know the general area where it's been hidden, but some force guards it and we can't get through the barrier. We know you can do it in the blink of an eye. Please."

Most of Epimetheus wanted to say 'yes' to the beguiling eyes and the sweet smiles. But the small part of him that resisted was fierce; he'd been played by many women, many times. He didn't like it. Even so, he knew his regret showed on his face.

"I'm sorry if you've been misled to believe my silver can be of any use to you." He pressed his palm against his chest. "My amulet is attuned to me and not even my opportunistic brother could take advantage of it if it came into his possession."

The women exchanged looks. The tall one stood and waved a hand in his direction.

"Excuse us for a moment, if you would be so kind, Epimetheus. We need to confer."

She swept out of his hide-away followed by the others, not waiting for him to reply.

I got home by eight-thirty prepared to squeeze some answers from the aunts. I burst in the door. The house was empty. They were gone. All of them.

Weird. The kitchen was spotless, like they hadn't stopped for tea and toast. I'd never known them to leave the house before nine in the morning and at that hour it had to be for an important appointment. They hadn't mentioned an appointment to me. I scanned the kitchen, the fridge door and the breakfast nook for a note. I nearly missed it. It was stuck to the toaster with poster putty. In Aunt June's precise hand.

Autumn. You'll have to fend for yourself today. We're on a botany panel at Augustana University this morning. We'll be home late. Don't wait up. A. M. J.

Fend for myself? What did they think I'd been doing since I was nine? I looked at the calendar. *The Circumpolar Symposium on the Use of Indigenous Plants* was scheduled for next month at the University. I knew that because I was helping them prepare their presentation. Their laptop was still in the living room.

They couldn't stay away forever. After I showered and ate I made a pot of yerba maté and carried it to the deck. The fight with Peter, the veil, Fayal hysteria, my visit to Old Anus's shop, the puzzle box. What did I know for sure?

My dream life story was fantastical. As Pandora I'd been following Epi, my lying husband, from the other side of the veil for centuries. Zeus bound me to Epi until he voluntarily released me. From the other side of the veil it made sense. From this side, not so much.

Zeus, the degenerate old fool, called the shots in the immortal world. He blamed me for opening the forbidden box and releasing pain and suffering into the world. As if I would ever do such a thing. Zeus probably did it himself. He loved stirring things up.

There were no answers there in an empty house, so I went back to talk to the Fayal. Nothing coy about them this time. I barely got off my bike before they were on me like a second skin. I jogged them deep into the conifers, shook them off and demanded explanations. I expected one of their convoluted, over-embellished stories; I was disappointed. They led me over to the moss flap and pointed.

Benthi put on her solemn voice: "It's in the box, Big She. You have to open it."

I reached for the flap. A sharp intake of breath from a hundred Fayal. I stepped back. Something had spooked them. I sensed them hovering behind me in a nervous cluster. The moss flap lifted on its own, ripped away and flew over my head. Out of the gapping, dark hole crawled a man. A large, mud-besmeared man. I suppose I should have been afraid. Or at least wary.

But, what came out of my mouth was: "Oh, Great. Now what?"

I backed up to give Mud Man some space. Good thing, too, because he shook like a dog. Fayal got out of the way easily, but I got splattered.

"Hey!"

He wiped back his hair with both hands and squinted in my direction. "Is this her?"

Lady Captain Taran winked into view and hovered in front of my face. "It is." I felt her settle on my shoulder.

He straightened. I looked up. I'm tall. About 5'11". He was taller. Much taller. Maybe 6'5". It was hard to guess his age. Older than I am, but younger than the aunts. Black hair, dark eyes, curly dark beard. And ripped. A gym jockey, wrapped in a sheet like a Biblical prophet. Complete with knee-high sandals that Hercules would envy.

He frowned at me. "Turn around, girl." He made a dismissive motion with his hand. "Let me look at you."

"Excuse me?" I set my fists firmly against my hips. "Who died and made you Elvis?"

I heard the Lady Captain titter in my ear. "Told you she's changed."

I swiped the Lady Captain off my shoulder. Fayal behind gasped in unison. I strode over to Mud Man and jabbed him in the chest.

"Listen you big donkey." I pointed to a fallen spruce. "Sit."

The Lady Captain tumbled in the air, squeaking and chittering. Major Fayal laughter.

Mud Man glowered at me. "What does she mean?"

Captain Taran zapped over and tugged on his ear. "She's inviting you to sit down. Plant your big behind."

He shook his head and the Captain dove out of sight to avoid a mud shower. "She can't do that. I give the orders."

The captain winked back into view. "This isn't Olympus."

"Yeah, but she... but she..."

"You can but-she all you want. You've got no authority here."

Mud Man swatted at the Captain, missing, of course.

I kicked at the tree trunk. "Sit. Damn it!"

He sat, flipping his sheet over his knees. He had scars on his wrists. Looked like he'd been branded with heavy chain. Similar around his neck. He had no piercings that I could see, but the chain scars were impressive.

"Okay. You made your point. You're a tough guy. Good for you. Now, be a good boy..." I made my voice all sweet and syrupy. "and kindly tell me..." Then I yelled. "What the Hell is going on!"

I hollered that last part as close to his face as I dared to go and he winced. I was just getting full of myself when he stood up and raised his ginormous fist. I backed away. The dumb-ass was going to hit me. Crap. I always had to push the envelope.

I was no slouch when it came to defending myself, but I knew better to take on a giant. I leaped out of his reach and prepared to run. I knew all the bush trails in my sleep. I suspected he didn't.

Turned out the Lady Captain had a megaphone voice when she needed it.

"Prometheus!"

Whoah! I looked back. Mud Man had his fist frozen in mid-air and a vicious scowl on his face. He turned his head and spit, lowered his arm and sat on the log.

"Get out of here!" I stared at Mud Man. "You can't be Prometheus." I laughed.

He met my eyes. His hard and resentful. "You dare impertinence?"

I shrugged. "Apparently."

"Does she know why she's here?" His glare didn't waver.

"Not until she opens the box."

The big guy shook his head and pounded it with the heel of his hand. "Yeah. Yeah. I forgot how Hera likes to complicate things." He glared at me. "So. Open the box. I don't like this place. It lacks comfort."

"Open it yourself. I don't know who you think you are, but I didn't sign up for the tournament."

"She talks like a foreigner. Why does she talk like a foreigner?"

"You haven't strolled down here in the mortal muck for a millennium or two have you?"

"Why would I? Humans. They're ungrateful for everything I've done for them. And their world stinks. Don't they know how to pick up litter?"

"Litter?" Colossal slob. "Who are you to talk? The whole time Epi and I lived with you, I never saw you pick up a sock."

"What's a sock?"

I glared at Mud Man.

Mud Man yelled: "She's muddled. She isn't ready. I thought you took care of this?"

Lady Captain: smug. "I did. I got her here. I got you here. That's all my contract requires."

Mud man stood and paced back and forth, muttering mostly to himself. "We're not allowed slaves any more. Our servants are surly. We hire consultants." He swung around and stepped towards me. "I'm a Titan! For the sake of Zeus! Is there nobody who respects me anymore?"

The Lady Captain flew in front of his face. "You're not a Titan; you're the son of a Titan. Spoiled son of a Titan, if I may be so bold as to add."

"You may not!"

I sat back on my heels and I listened to the bickering with fascination. All my senses focused on the big guy and the tiny woman. I was an anthropologist studying an ancient culture. I was a nut bar needing a straitjacket and an intravenous drip of anti-crazy meds. I was Pandora wanting out of a contract I had never agreed to.

The little fairy settled back on my shoulder. "So. Let her open the box. This isn't about you, you know."

"Are you demented? It's always about me. It has to be about me. I made mankind what they are today. I gave them everything. I sacrificed...."

"You never sacrificed a thing in your sorry existence."

"They don't worship me properly; I'm not remembered in great literature. No statues."

I laughed. "Hey, Mud Man. You are remembered." I pulled my notebook out of my shoulder pack. I fired it up. That got his attention, immediately.

"Whose magic is this?"

"Scrappy little human magic, my man. Done without your help, I might add." I Googled Prometheus. "Look. Over eight million hits."

Prometheus stared at the screen with no comprehension.

"I'll show you how you're remembered, Mud Man."

I typed in, *'Welcome to the miserable world of Prometheus'*. My favorite cartoon popped up. The genius of Mark Weinstein. I made a note to email a big thank-you to him.

Prometheus squinted at the screen. "What's that?"

"That's you, brother-in-law. Want to know what it says?"

"I want to know." The Lady Captain vibrated with anticipation.

"See. The first frame. There's you. Chained to a rock. An eagle's come to eat your liver. Again. He's reading something. The eagle says to you, 'I picked up an interesting pamphlet for myself; *Your Rights as a Consumer*.'"

Prometheus grabbed for my notebook. The Lady Captain, squealing with laughter, got in his way.

"You mock me." He thundered.

"Actually the cartoonist mocks you. And thousands of us love it."

"What does it say next? Tell me. Tell me." The Lady Captain tumbled through the air.

"In the second frame, the eagle says, 'I got a pamphlet especially for you.' In the last frame the eagle reads, *Your Rights as the Consumed.*'"

The Lady Captain howled with laughter.

Prometheus roared. "It's an abomination. You lie! It's a trick. I'll smite you. I'll smite you twice."

The Lady Captain kicked him in the nose. "You can't Ox Head. Aphrodite and Hera protect her."

"Aphrodite will pay for this!" Prometheus tried to grab the tiny woman out of the air. She laughed, easily avoiding his big paw.

"Produce the box." His roar had the Fayal cowering in the grass.

"You produce the box." The Lady Captain was not intimidated.

While they bickered, Benthi whispered in my ear. "Box down there."

I pushed past Prometheus and slid down the hole. I landed at the foot of a sandstone pedestal, upon which the box rested. Impressive. The Fayal squealed and chattered, forming a thick, bug cloud around the box.

"Open it, Big She. Then we go home." Benthi's excitement was infectious.

I walked around the chest-high pedestal. The old box did look regal. It also looked impenetrable.

"Open it, Big She!" Benthi perched on my shoulder. I could feel her vibrating.

"Open!" Dredge rammed my cheek with his tiny head, but he didn't bite.

"I would if I could."

"You can."

"How?"

"Don't know. Only you can. Nobody else."

"Wonderful."

I picked up the box. That silenced the Fayal. I studied it. In the indirect light, the surface of the box seemed to pucker.

Patterns formed around a script etched into the metal. Was it Russian? No. It was Greek. Ancient Greek.

ΠΑΝΔΟΡΑ

I recognized the pi and the delta first and then alpha. I whispered the word. *Pandora.* I held the box tight. The name felt like honey on my lips. My name. I caught my breath as a sob escaped. Hot tears dropping on the box. Dropping and sizzling like rain on fresh lava. The metal on the lid sectioned into flower petals. Without hesitation I peeled them back from the center and looked inside. Nothing in it.

Benthi squealed in my ear. "Put box back."

I set it on the pedestal. Dredge dove into the box. Benthi, laughing, followed. Faster than I could count the rest followed. Hundreds of Fayal streamed into the box and disappeared. I waited a few beats after the last one vanished. I lifted the box, carefully. I tried to see inside. It appeared to be empty. I set the box back, my heart racing. Where did they go? It was a trap. To catch Fayal. I didn't move. Hours, days, weeks passed. Okay. It was only a few minutes, but it felt like a month.

Benthi popped back out, disheveled, grubby and grinning. "Path home, Big She. Come."

The air crackled like shook foil. I stepped fully into myself. I was Pandora; I was also Autumn. I backed away from the portal.

"Come, Big She." Benthi hovered above the box.

I shook my head. She waved at me and dove back into the box. I didn't follow. The box snapped shut. I blinked and I was standing in the grass, on the surface. I looked behind me. I tried to lift the moss flap. It didn't move. It was just moss covering a tree root.

Prometheus hadn't seen me yet and I was content to wait until he did. He had one hand pressed against a bleeding cheek. I grinned. Apparently the Lady Captain had bit him. His other hand, he waved erratically in the air, trying, without success, to swat a taunting, jeering Lady Captain out of the air.

He looked like crap. Dried blood on his face and mud in his hair completed his battlefield look. I hoped Aphrodite was watching. She always said there was nothing wrong with Prometheus that a little combat couldn't cure.

Prometheus's silver may have made it possible for me to become mortal. But there was no charity in his gift. I owed him nothing. He did it because he thought I would eventually sleep with him. Not ten minutes after Epi exiled himself to wandering the earth, Prometheus came sniffing around like the horny dog he was. Lucky for me, I didn't have to fend him off for long. Hera took me under her wing and Zeus turned on him, chaining him up as eagle bait for an eon or two.

I cleared my throat. Prometheus swung around. I tilted my head toward him. "Greetings, brother-in-law."

"Good. You've come to yourself. Time to go home." He swiped at his grubby chiton with an even grubbier hand. "It's going to take a thousand years to wash off the stink of this place."

A stick snapped behind me. I whirled around to see Aunt June point her cane at Prometheus.

"Take it to a Laundromat, you spoiled Titan!"

"Aunt June?"

My three aunts stood on the path with a blindfolded Epi on a leash. They ignored me. All three had laser beam eyes on Prometheus.

"We want to exchange this old reprobate for your silver."

Prometheus frowned at me. "Who are these witches?"

"These witches are my aunts." I advanced on them, angry at them for the first time in my life. "Explain, ladies."

They pushed past me. Aunt May hollering at Prometheus: "We demand immortality. It's the least you can do."

Aunt April: "Where's Aphrodite?"

"Aphrodite?" Prometheus growled. He towered over the aunts. They were unimpressed by his height. "You're Aphrodite's minions? Why's she messing with my business?"

The roar of a rocket and a mighty wind knocked me down. Prometheus' robes flew behind him like flags.

Epi yanked the scarf from his face. "Your business?" He snapped the chain that bound him to the aunts. Rage transformed his hound dog face. He became a snarling Rottweiler. He walked towards Prometheus, growing several inches taller with each step.

"This was never your business, brother."

"Epi!" Prometheus ran forward and lifted his brother in a massive bear hug and swung him around.

No longer an old man, Epimetheus pulled free and shoved away. "I'm not your scapegoat anymore, Prom. What are you doing here?"

"I've come to get your wench. You don't want her. Did you think we'd let her rot down here?"

"You can't have her. Zeus gave her to me and I can ignore her for as long as I like."

"Ignore me?"

Epi turned towards me and frowned. "It *is* you, then. I couldn't identify you in that plain wrapper."

"Is that a fact? And you're Mr. Universe, hiding out in a sad, old man's body."

"I can hide out in any shell I like."

He sounded like a whiny kid.

"And I can't?"

His fists hit his hips and he spread his legs like the Jolly Green Giant. "Of course you can't. You need my permission to do everything."

I glanced at Prometheus. He glowered at me.

"You don't have to obey him anymore. He relinquished owner-ship eons ago. It must be obvious; I'm your new master."

Prometheus smirked and jabbed at Epi. "You don't deserve her. Sure, I opened the box. I freed the demons. It didn't matter who did it, you fool. Zeus wanted humanity to suffer. And he wanted us to suffer. So, you've suffered. I've suffered. Game over."

Epi regained his height and breadth. "*You* opened the box! For that I was exiled?"

"You exiled yourself and it hasn't been all fun and games for me. Don't forget the liver-eating eagle."

"You're not funny. You've never been funny."

Epi grabbed the trunk of a spruce tree, yanked it out of the ground and swung it at Prometheus like a baseball bat. Knocked him across the clearing. Prometheus sat there for a moment, blinking furiously, then he lunged for a concrete picnic table, wrenched it off its slab and hurled it at Epi. It struck Epi on the side of the head and he went down.

Prometheus grabbed my wrist. "Come on, time to get you back into your right body."

I bit him. Hard. He dropped my wrist and stared at his arm. "You bit me."

"No shit. I am not going anywhere with you."

Prometheus stared at me. "You can't stay here."

"Why not?"

"You can't do as you please. You're not a Titan. You're a construct. An invention. You have no say. You do as I say."

I folded my arms. "Not on this side of the veil. You don't rule here. I choose to stay."

Prometheus glowered. "You come when I say come."

Epi struggled to his feet. "Pandora. You can't best a Titan."

Prometheus leered at me. "You can choose anything you want, pigeon pie, but see how long you last without my silver." He yanked away the moss and dove down the chute.

"The silver!" Three aunts shrieked as one.

They pushed past me and followed Prometheus down the hole. Suddenly it was quiet. I strode down the trail. I wasn't sure what to do next, but I needed to clear my head.

"Where are you going?" Epi's pathetic wail was hard on the ears.

"Away."

"Without Prometheus's silver you'll just be human. No immortality."

I turned around. "You know what? I don't care."

"But you'll get old. You'll die."

That's when I laughed. "Epi, you moron. I've never been alive. And neither have you. Wandering the earth in a half-life. No friends. No anticipation. No fear. No real emotions. Sure I'll die. But I'll also have a chance to live."

"We live forever. Immortality trumps everything."

"Really?" I walked around him. "Well, it doesn't for me. I haven't taken full advantage of mortality, yet, but I've tasted delight and I've sampled fear and worry."

"When you were in your perfection, I delighted in you."

"You confuse delight with lust. Drooling over pomegranate breasts and cantaloupe bum cheeks. Isn't that what you called them? I was your toy. You were my duty. Not delightful from where I stand. And what about fear?"

"Fear? You're mad. Nobody wants to be afraid."

"Of course not. But it's a spicy emotion. Immortals can know discomfort, but never real fear. Humans fear death. It gives meaning to life. It adds zest to their living."

"Death is grotesque."

"Yes it is."

"You could die tomorrow."

"Yes, I could. And so could you, if you'd take the next step. Become fully human."

"You've lost your mind."

"Perhaps."

"Prometheus won't leave his silver for you."

"I know."

Epi pulled out his amulet and waved it at me. "If you stay with me... my silver."

"You're arguing by rote, Epi. Be honest. You don't really want me."

Epi frowned. "Well, I might if you returned to your beautiful self."

"I am my beautiful self. Do you have the guts to admit you don't want me?"

His eyes widened. "I don't want you." He seemed surprised. "I don't want her." He shook his fist at the sky. "You hear that, Zeus? I don't want her and I never did."

I turned and walked away. He didn't call me back.

Prometheus, of course, had lied to the aunts about the box. He told them they needed it in order to find the silver. The box belonged to Hera and he knew he couldn't touch it or even see it, but if the aunts had the box and he controlled the aunts he thought he would be able to control me. He'd never been able to best Hera, but he was too pig-headed to stop trying.

Hera was so entertained by the whole affair she granted the aunts the option to return to the afterlife right then, or hang out with me for the rest of my mortal life, however long that would be.

Aunt June: "We decided to stay, Autumn."

Aunt May: "Just don't go tempting fate. No dangerous assignments. We'd like a few more years here, if it's all right with you?"

Aunt April: "I didn't really want to live forever. I just got caught up in the moment."

I wasn't sure how I felt about being directly responsible for their second lifespan, but I figured after thirty good years together we could work out the bumps of forty or fifty more.

Epi closed his shop that week. Moving trucks came the week after. I didn't ask his destination and he didn't offer it. I didn't care what he did, but I *was* happy to hear he took his girl Friday with him. She was a cheeky young woman, practical and good natured. She wanted to see the world and I got the feeling she'd developed a genuine affection for the silly fool. You never know what could happen, even to a Titan, when subjected to the effects of real love, no matter how awkward and imperfect it was.

I was determined to discover if Peter and I still had a chance. He finally responded to one of my Facebook messages. I bought a ticket for California on the strength of his agreement to meet me for dinner. Just dinner, and then whatever would be would be. I was scared stupid and stupidly grateful for it. Messy business, mortality, but it beat the alternative.

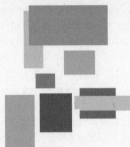

THE THIRD PIECE OF THE PUZZLE

❖   ❖   ❖

Albert opened his eyes to darkness and gasped. "Where are we?"

The Chronicler stood beside him, one more dark shadow, and said nothing.

Albert looked around. The stars were brighter than he had ever seen them. Or perhaps the night was so much darker that they sparkled in contrast. He smelled lilacs and felt the soft touch of grass on his bare feet. The breeze rippled his hair and he breathed deep. He knew where he was.

"Am I still dreaming?"

The Chronicler said nothing.

Albert saw that the old water well had fallen into disrepair, its roof rotted and collapsed. He ran his hand along the lip of the crumbling mortar and stared down into the endless darkness. No water in the well, or he would've seen the night sky's reflection. Or maybe it simply went on forever. 'All the way to China,' his father had told him as a boy.

"How long has it been?" Albert asked.

"Since you were here last?" the Chronicler asked.

Albert paused, unsure if that was what he meant or if he referred to their time at the breakfast table. Both seemed a long time ago. Albert felt as if he was stretched so thin he might snap. He sat on the edge of the crumbled stonework.

"Years," the Chronicler said with a tired, heavy voice.

"I kissed her here, you know. Our first time." He looked down at his hands, and then wiped them on his pants, leaving white streaks. "Our last time, too."

The Chronicler remained silent.

Albert wanted to ask how they had ended up in this park at the developed end of Wagner Bog, miles from his home. The memories blurred together and he wondered which were his real thoughts and which the imposters. He closed his eyes, trying to calm the chaos in his head by focusing on the sounds of the crickets and the soft chatter of the leaves.

He felt something change, but when he looked around, his surroundings appeared the same, though he witnessed them with heightened clarity. Individual leaves glowed in the starlight. The stones surrounding the well refracted the dim light like prisms. Even the mortar holding the stones in place gave off a deep, mild glow. He glanced at the Chronicler.

"Can you see this?" he asked, and then fell silent. The Chronicler swayed with the breeze as if he could blow away at any moment. Although Albert was certain he was the same man, he could see changes. The line of his jaw looked sharper, he held his head cocked slightly to one side, and he stood stooped as if from extreme age. Or had he looked that way before and Albert just hadn't noticed? He shook his head. That wasn't it.

Albert was the one who had changed.

"I don't think I miss her anymore," he said. Like balm to a burn, the realization was calming and sweet. He frowned. The two stories that had emerged from the box wove together into a single tale, which swallowed his memories like a fish devouring minnows.

"What happened to her?" the Chronicler asked.

"She was the one who got away. I thought I wasn't good enough for her. Always one more thing to do. One more accomplishment so I'd measure up. Like she was a prize I had to win. A month became a year. A year, five then ten. Before I knew it, she had moved on."

Albert saw sadness in the Chronicler's face.

"Perhaps she wasn't your destiny."

As a child, Albert had read voraciously. History, geography, biographies. He wanted to unlock the secrets of the world. So many interconnected stories like a spider web connected to every person— living or dead. He had gone into archaeology, received his MA from the University of Calgary and his PhD from Boston College. But it had never seemed enough so he kept throwing up roadblocks in his relationship with Moira.

Albert realized he was thirsty. Not for booze. Hell, he didn't even want to lose himself in the heart-pounding rush of a card game he couldn't afford. What he wanted was the box.

"Do you have it?" Albert asked.

"Yes."

"Give it to me."

The Chronicler stared at him, head cocked to the side. "When I showed up at your door, you wanted to throw me out. Now you treat me — and this — like another one of your addictions."

"You don't know me."

"Sadly, I don't. I know many stories but I don't know yours."

The Chronicler handed him the box.

As Albert touched it, the seams began to glow. Light pulsed, a beacon in the dark. He turned it over in his hand, mesmerized by the light and the letters skating across the bronze surface. Albert touched a letter, moved it to another face. He manipulated the symbols with a practiced touch as if he had solved this puzzle years earlier.

The box removed his pain. He wondered if the stories were antibodies against toxic memories. Filling the void that regret and loss had made.

As he moved the symbols around the face of the cube, Albert wondered if he could move around the pieces of his life until he was no longer a wreck of a man who left disappointment in his wake.

The light intensified and he drank it in.

"You're wrong, Albert. It was never about her," the Chronicler said. "You'll see."

The next Piece of the Puzzle will be revealed after "Angela and Her Three Wishes."

Angela and Her Three Wishes

❖ By Eileen Bell ❖

The Fight

Angela Simonson's day started exactly the same as all the others. She had a fight with her mother.

Angela was in the bathroom finishing her makeup. She spiked a tendril of dyed black hair and ran a ragged, black tinted fingernail under one eye to remove a bit of extra liner, then looked at her reflection. She looked pretty good, but not over the top enough. She needed more.

She reached for her new contact lenses and put them in, smiling as cat eyes stared back from the mirror. *Now*, she thought, *That's perfect*.

She knew her mother would hate the contact lenses, but whatever. Her mother didn't like anything Angela did anymore, as far as Angela could tell. *If only she'd lighten up*, things would be better around here.

Her mother yelled from the kitchen. "I told you to put the milk back in the fridge!"

"I told you I'd do it in a minute!" she yelled back. "I'm getting ready for work."

"We both have to get ready for work, Angela."

Angela turned on the blow dryer to drown out her mother's voice and yelled "What?" over the high-pitched scream. She knew she was acting like an infant, but she couldn't seem to stop herself. The tone of her mother's voice drove her seriously crazy sometimes.

When her mother didn't bother answering, Angela's irritation cranked up another notch. The only thing she hated more than her mother screeching at her was her mother ignoring her.

She slapped off the blow dryer and walked into the kitchen. Her mother stood at the counter, listening to the news on her ancient counter television as she stared out the window.

"It's snowing again. Remember your hat and scarf," she said, without turning around.

"Whatever," Angela replied.

"There's toast. Want some?"

Angela knew her mother was trying to make up with her, but really, when was the last time she'd eaten toast?

"I need caffeine," she said, crossing the floor. As she walked past the small kitchen counter television, the screen flickered and the sound turned to white noise.

"Angela, get away from the TV," her mother said.

Angela knew she couldn't go near a television or computer without causing it to wig out — or blow up — but the reminder fanned the flames of her anger even higher. Another thing in her life that wasn't fair.

"If you'd buy a TV from this century, that wouldn't happen, I bet."

"I can't afford a new one," her mother sighed. "You have another court date coming up and somebody has to pay the lawyer."

"I told you it wasn't my fault," she said, reaching for a coffee mug.

"It never is."

Her mother turned away from the window, looking at Angela for the first time since she'd walked into the room. She gasped and grabbed Angela by the arm, staring at her eyes, her face whitening.

Here it comes, Angela thought. *She's going to go bat shit. Again.*

Knowing she was doing exactly the wrong thing, Angela smiled and batted her eyes at her mother. "You like them?"

"Take those out." Her mother's voice sounded strangled. "Please."

"They're just contacts," Angela said. "What's the deal?"

She pulled her arm from her mother's slack grip and filled her cup with coffee. The carafe chattered against the edge of the mug.

"You know what the deal is," her mother replied. She still sounded like she was choking on her words. "You don't even look human that way."

"I'm just as human as you are," Angela said.

"Then why don't you act like it?"

Angela stared at her mother as she poured her coffee into the sink and dropped her cup in after it. The sound of ceramic breaking made her smile. So did the stricken look on her mother's face.

"I choose not to."

Her mother ran to the sink and picked up two pieces of the cup. When she tried to fit them together, a crack formed in the larger piece and then broke, falling and smashing into what sounded like a million pieces in the bottom of the sink. It could never be repaired.

"Do you have to break everything you touch?" her mother sobbed.

Angela blinked. She'd actually made her mother cry. She hadn't meant to do that. Not really. She opened her mouth to say sorry, but her mother turned on her, and the fury on her face froze the words in Angela's throat.

"Sometimes I wish you'd never been born," she said.

Angela stared at her, the words cutting her to the very bone. "I can't believe you said that. Take it back."

Her mother shook her head. "God help me, I can't."

"You know what I wish?" Angela decided to cut back. Deep. "I wish my father hadn't been the one to die. He would've loved me just the way I am."

"Well, neither of us are going to get what we want, now are we?" her mother replied, then burst into fresh tears and ran from the room.

As her mother's bedroom door slammed shut, Angela grabbed the small television off the counter and hugged it to her chest. It fizzled and wowed and a crack finally zagged across the screen. As acrid smoke puffed from the back, she dropped it to the floor. It landed face down with a satisfying crash, but she didn't feel any better. In fact, she felt worse. Her mother loved that stupid counter-top television.

The Television

Ellen Simonson peeked through the blinds of her bedroom window as Angela kicked through the snow to the bus. The tension in her shoulders eased as the bus sped down the street and disappeared around a corner. Finally, she was alone.

She walked out to the kitchen and saw the shattered television face down on the floor.

"Oh no," she said, and knelt to touch its still-warm plastic case. *Please, please, please let it be all right.*

It wasn't. More tears threatened, and behind the tears, more anger. Anger at Angela. Anger at Angela's father, Arturo. She kicked the broken TV, feeling mean satisfaction when bits of plastic snapped off and bounded across the room.

"I wish you *were* dead, you son of a bitch!"

But she was certain Arturo wasn't dead. She didn't have that kind of luck. Her daughter's father was out there somewhere, in this Realm or his own, doing unspeakable things.

"What a waste," she whispered. "Twenty years of my life lost, trying to keep her from you." Protecting her little girl from that monster, and then watching her turn into him. More and more like him every year. More and more monstrous. In every way.

"I even bought this stupid house," she muttered, half-heartedly taking another kick at the dead television. "Hoping the stability would make her more human." She laughed bitterly. If anything, staying in one place had allowed the differences in her daughter to blossom and grow, like diseased fruit on a poisoned tree.

As Ellen surveyed the mess in the kitchen, her anger collapsed and degraded to something much more familiar. Despair. Utter and absolute despair.

I did everything I could to make a good life for her, and it wasn't enough, she thought. *I shouldn't have run away from you, you crazy-eyed freak. I should have let you take her. At least I'd have my life.*

The Box

Angela got off the bus two stops early, telling herself, as she always did, it was so she could get more exercise.

It wasn't. She didn't want the people on the bus to know she worked at an adult-only video store. She didn't know why she cared, but she did.

As she kicked through the snow, replaying the fight with her mother in her head, she passed an abandoned blue Firebird and saw a glint of something metallic in the back seat. She looked around to see if anyone was watching. No one was. In fact, no one was anywhere near her. She had been handed a rare moment.

She pushed aside a piece of cardboard covering the broken side window and stuck her head inside the car. A small box gleamed in the rays of a shaft of light. She grunted as she pushed herself through the opening, waist deep.

I wonder why no one has stolen this yet, she thought. *Someone monumentally stupid left it here.*

She picked it up, surprised at its heaviness, and wriggled back out of the window. Still no pedestrians, and even more surprising, no traffic.

Mom will love this, she thought as she tucked the box inside her coat, feeling warmth from the box where there should have been cold. She'd give the box to her mother that evening. She hoped her mother would like it enough to forgive her. Ellen was the only family Angela had.

The traffic returned and a bus screeched to a halt not ten feet ahead of her. A dozen vacant-faced people stepped through the doors, and plodded down the sidewalk past her.

Roger Miller, a wire-thin emo with long sideswept bangs, wearing more eyeliner than Angela, stepped out of the bus with the rest. He worked with Angela, and she suspected he was not only an emo, but a cutter as well.

He scuttled over to her.

"Nice eyes," he muttered, looking at Angela's newly acquired cat's eye contacts.

"Thanks," she replied. "I bought them yesterday."

"They look absolutely evil."

His compliment didn't make her feel any better.

"We better get to work," she said.

"I gotta have coffee first."

He pointed at the Starbucks wannabe tucked in a teeny space between the *Slippery When Wet* video store and the karaoke bar across from it, called *Wild 'n Crazy*. The coffee bar was appropriately named *In Between*. "You want?" he asked.

"Sure. Just hurry or Joey's going to get pissed."

Angela walked into the video store and Joey, the eternally angry night guy, looked up. "Late again, bitch."

"Only a couple of minutes," she said as she hung up her coat, tucking the pilfered box inside the sleeve.

"Whatever," he said. He booked out, leaving Angela to clean up the front counter. She snapped on rubber gloves and thought pleasant thoughts as she spritzed with factory strength disinfectant and wiped everything in sight.

Roger arrived with two huge coffees balanced one atop the other. She snatched the top cup and slurped a quarter of it before realizing she had taken his. Triple sweet was downright nasty if you weren't expecting it.

She watched him take a huge gulp of her four shot Americano, black. "How is it?" she asked.

"Great." He set the huge paper cup aside. "Give me mine."

She sipped more of his ultra sweet something girly. "I don't think so," she said. "I could get used to this."

"Yeah. Sure you could. Come on, don't be a bitch. I need my caffeine."

"How can you even taste caffeine in this?" She held the cup just out of Roger's reach. "It's positively fagorific, I swear."

He pulled his arm down and glared. "You really are being a bitch, you know that? Did you have a fight with your mother again?"

"No," she lied, handing him his cup and picking up her own. She took a sip, trying not to think about his germs. It actually didn't taste too awful, and she chugged half of what was left.

"You're lying," he replied. "I can always tell when you fight with your mother. Was it 'bout you rigging the exams again, or something else?"

One year before, Angela had convinced stupid, infatuated Alan Ripley to rig every diploma multiple-choice exam so that only the letter B was correct. She thought it was funny, but her mother didn't, especially when Angela was expelled from school, and then had to go to court over the whole business. Her mother started treating her like she was some sort of demon spawn after their first day in court. That's when she'd told Roger about their fights.

She wished now that she hadn't said a word to him.

"We didn't fight about anything," she said. "Everything's fantastic. Amazing. Now go work the cash like a good boy and leave me alone."

She ignored him, pointedly, and went back to work, determined not to speak to him again for the rest of the day.

They worked in silence for an hour, before three customers came in for their deviance fix. Angela served them with a surliness that neared brutality. Two of them giggled through it all, but the third merely stared at her until she snapped.

"What the hell are you staring at?" she yelled.

"Your eyes," he replied.

"Well, stop it."

"They're beautiful."

"Listen freak—" she began, as Roger trundled out from behind the desk and stepped between them.

"Can I help you with anything?" he asked.

"Fuckin' freak," Angela muttered.

"Ignore her," Roger said, when the deviant frowned. "She's always like that. Means nothing."

The guy shook his head and left. Angela turned on Roger.

"What the hell did you mean by that?" she snarled. "I'm not *always like* anything. Do want me to get Gerald to fire your ass?"

"No," Roger said. "But you shouldn't treat customers like that, you know."

"I can treat them any way I want."

"Whatever," Roger said, then looked down at his watch and turned to the door. "I'm outta here."

"And where do you think you're going?" She felt a small thrill of fear wind through her bitchiness like a drop of ice water. Roger might not be much, but he was the only friend she had. And she did not want to have to explain to Gerald, their boss, why an employee quit on her shift. She definitely did not want that.

"Who are you, my mother?" Roger asked. "Lighten up. It's time for a break."

"So go. Who cares anyhow?" The door slammed shut and Angela looked for something to do. *That guy drives me crazy,* she thought.

With relief, she remembered the box and pulled it from the sleeve of her coat. It didn't look as beautiful as it had in the back of the Firebird, but Angela wasn't surprised.

"Maybe the grass is greener and all that shit," she muttered.

She rubbed her finger along the top, but didn't feel any grooves. It was as though the box had been manufactured from a solid piece of metal. Even though she thought she could hear something moving inside when she shook it — which she did with increasing frequency and severity — she couldn't find any way into the thing.

She was ready to put it aside — actually, she was ready to throw it away — when Roger scared her to the roots of her hair by sneaking up behind her.

"What's that?" he asked.

"Nothing." She tried to hide it, without success. "I thought you were gone."

"I decided to get take out." He held up a paper bag, dripping with grease, and then pointed at the metal box. "What *is* that?"

"Nothing."

"Ooh, a puzzle box." Roger reached around her and pulled the box from her fingers. "I've seen these on the net. But never a metal one. Very cool. Have you opened it yet?"

"No," she said, and made a grab for it. "Not yet. Give it back."

Roger grinned and held it out of her reach. "Let me try. I was pretty good with puzzles when I was a kid."

"No." She grabbed his sleeve and pulled his arm down sharply. "It's mine."

"Yeah, I know," Roger said. "I just wanted to..." His voice faded. "Sorry. It looked like fun."

She grappled the box back. It still looked like a solid piece of metal to her.

"Do you really think you can open it?"

"Maybe," he said.

She returned the box, not allowing their fingers to touch.

"Go for it," she said. "But don't break it. It's a gift for my mom." She winced when she realized she had as much as admitted that she had fought with her mother.

"Hmm," he mumbled. Since he was already well into the wonderful world of puzzle solving, she suspected he hadn't even heard what she had confessed. She found she didn't like it.

But before she could think of a good way to make him pay for not listening to her, a seedy looking customer walked into the store.

"Can I help you with anything?" she asked.

He looked over the top of his glasses, and she was shocked to see that he had the same type of contact lenses she was wearing. She frowned. *Not a great look for an old guy.*

"No," he finally said. "Nice eyes."

"Thanks," she replied. "Back at ya."

"Oh." He laughed and pulled off his sunglasses. "Yes. Thank you. Most people don't like them."

"Really?" The sarcasm rolled thick through her voice, so she tried to dial it back. "I do. I think they look— fine."

"Thanks."

He looked as though he was about to say something more to her — probably was going to ask her out or something, like she needed that bit of horror — when an ungodly scream and a huge puff of smoke billowed out from the back of the store.

"Looks like somebody needs help back there," the man said.

Angela desperately wanted to find out what was going on, but couldn't leave with a customer in the store. "It's all right," she lied. "Anything you're looking for?"

"No," the guy said, and smiled. His teeth were yellow and crooked. *He should have used the money he spent on contact lenses to fix his teeth*, she thought.

"Are you sure?"

"Absolutely," he replied, putting on his sunglasses and opening the door. "That's an awful lot of smoke."

She locked the door after the customer and gasped when she turned around. Green tinged smoke billowed into the store from the back room. What had Roger done?

The Djinn

"Roger?" Angela flailed through the thick smoke and rapped the knuckles of her right hand, hard, on the door jamb. "Where the hell are you?"

"Angela, don't come in," Roger whisper-screamed. "Save yourself!"

"What are you talking about?" she asked. "And how did you start a fire back here…"

Through the smoke she saw Roger huddled beneath the small staff table. The box was on the floor, with the top open, and an eight-foot, oddly dressed man was backed up against the staff room fridge, looking completely out of place.

Angela turned to the tall guy — he couldn't be eight-feet tall, nobody was eight-feet tall — and made her voice manager-firm. "Employees only, pal. You gotta leave."

The guy frowned at her as though he didn't understand.

"Do you speak English?" she asked.

"Yes, I speak English." His voice was so deep it sounded like it came from the basement, and his mouth moved out of sync with the words.

She decided to focus on the positive, which was that he understood English, and not on the negative, which was that it didn't look as though his mouth was actually doing the speaking. "Then you understand me. You can't be in here."

"Is your name Angela?" Mouth and words synced that time.

"What?"

The guy pulled a small piece of paper from a fold in his odd looking trousers. He opened it and squinted, his mouth moving silently as he read. He nodded as though satisfied, and spoke aloud. "Angela Simonson. That is correct, is it not?"

"Who the hell are you?"

"Skip," the behemoth intoned in his basement voice. She snorted.

"Your name is actually Skip?" The big guy nodded. "Bad name, Skippy boy. Now get out."

"I cannot. You summoned me with the opening of the box. I am here to do your bidding." The big guy bowed with a flourish. "Command me, Mistress."

With one eye on the guy, she swung in Roger's direction. "Get out from under there," she said. "And tell me what is going on. Now."

She felt a rush of mean-spirited joy when she heard Roger's head smack against the bottom of the table.

"Jesus," she said. "What kind of a pansy are you? He's not doing anything."

"You didn't see him come out of that box," Roger whispered.

"He came out of the box?"

"Yeah. First the smoke and lightning. Then him." He pointed a shaking finger at Skip, who stood, hat in hand, still as a huge statue. "He oozed out, Angela."

"Oozed?" Angela asked.

"Yes. Like a slug or something." He shuddered. "It was disgusting."

She decided not to go down the 'so frightened you wet yourself' road with Roger.

"How do you know my name?" she asked Skip. "You better explain, and I better believe you, or I'm calling the cops and they will haul your ass outta here, buddy."

She didn't want to have to call the cops. First, most of the cops knew her on a first name basis and always assumed the worst about her. Second, and more importantly, Gerald Becker, the *Slippery When Wet*'s owner, hated the police with a virulence that bordered on insanity. She didn't want to have to deal with his particular form of insanity, because it could mean she'd be looking for a new job by the end of the day. She hoped she'd call Skip's bluff, he'd hit the ground running, and all would be well.

It didn't quite go the way she'd hoped.

Skip hit the ground— but it was knees, elbows and forehead that smashed hard onto the ancient discolored lino. "Milady!" he bellowed. "Please! Don't send me away!"

He rolled back and forth on the floor, howling until Angela reached over with one foot and prodded the top of his head.

"Stop that," she said. "I won't call the cops. Not right now, anyhow. Just stop that noise."

He sniffled once and sat upright. "Gladly, Honorable One. And I understand this will not be one of your official wishes, but a request. Correct?" He swiped at the dirt on his forehead, smudging it. "I am correct, am I not?"

"What the hell are you talking about?" she said, then shook her head. "Forget it. I don't care. Get out. Now."

"But Fantastical One, I must grant you your wishes," he said. "I can't leave without doing that. And you must hurry, or I will be recalled."

He shuddered and wrung his hat in his hands. "I do not want to be recalled."

Angela shrugged. "I couldn't give a rat's ass if you get recalled, Skippy boy." She held up one hand, and pretended to examine her fingernails. "You want a request from me? Here it is. Go back where you came from. Now. I have a business to run, and…"

Her voice faded to nothing as Skip screeched incoherently, and melted.

The pile of ooze that had recently been an eight-foot tall guy named Skip leaked across the floor, then slimed up the table leg to the tabletop, and then across to the small metal box, and into the open top.

"See? That's what I was talking about," Roger said, sounding much more in control than he had moments before.

"Holy crap," she whispered.

Roger stared at the box. "Do you have any idea what this is?" he asked.

"Nope," she said. She stood beside him, happy for his warmth. "Do you think it might be a promotion or something?"

"A what?" He stared at her. "A promotion? You mean like some company trying to sell us something? What the hell could any company possibly be promoting like this?"

"I don't know— a new line of sex aids? You get your wish or something..." Her voice winnowed down to silence. "What do you think he meant by that? The wish thing?"

"No clue." Roger shook his head. "I think you should get rid of it."

"Yeah." She made no move to touch it. "Do you have any gloves on you?"

Roger pulled a glove out of his pocket and handed it to her. "Only got one," he said.

She snapped it over her right hand and edged her way to the table.

"Be careful," Roger whispered, which startled Angela. She jumped about a foot and glared at him.

"Don't *do* that," she cried. "And I *am* being careful."

She touched the open top of the box with one shaking finger, shuddering when a strand of goo stuck to her gloved finger and trailed away like a wet spider web.

"Maybe *you* should get rid of it," she said, backing away.

"No way," Roger replied. "You brought it here, you make it go away."

"Chicken," she said, but still couldn't bring herself to touch the box. "I bet if that Skip guy was here, he'd get rid of it for me."

The box moved.

"Quit touching the table," Angela said.

"I didn't," Roger breathed, behind her.

The box moved again, a half inch.

"What's going on?" Angela asked.

"I don't know."

The box jumped and danced across the scarred tabletop. As Angela screamed and leaped behind Roger, who was doing some screaming of his own, the box skittered toward the edge of the table and toppled on its side, goo frothing from it. More goo sprayed, and something began to push its way out of the box.

"Gross," Angela said, as the box bulged grotesquely and a moaning half-scream emanated from it. She pushed Roger out of the way and headed for the door. "I'm outta here."

"You're not leaving me alone," Roger cried. "Open the door!"

As she scrabbled at the doorknob, Angela could hear something squeezing its way out, slurping through the opening and glopping to the floor.

She turned.

Skip stood in front of them, looking much the worse for wear. "Thank you for calling me forth, Most Gracious One," he said. "Do you have a towel? It's burning my eyes."

The Wish

"So what you're saying is, you are a genie and I made you go back into that box just because I told you to—"

"Please don't request that I go again," Skip said. "I hate it in there."

"Right," Angela said. "No more g-word. Promise."

"And I am a Djinn," Skip said. "Not a Genie. That term is distasteful to us."

"Right. Djinn. Sorry." Angela pointed her tea cup at the box she'd stolen. "So you came here, in this, to give me three wishes. Right?"

"Yes." Skip picked up the cup sitting on the table before him and sipped the hot liquid. "Nice tea," he said. "What is it?"

"Spring Rhapsody," Roger said. "My favorite. The mint gives it something special, doesn't it?"

"Can the two of you shut the hell up for a minute?" Angela asked. "I need to understand what's going on. It has nothing to do with tea."

"Right, Boss," Roger said. "Sorry."

"Yes." Skip hung his head, an eight-foot ball of shame. "I deserve to be beaten, oh Glorious—"

"That's enough," Angela snapped. "Explain why I was chosen to receive three wishes."

"I'm sorry, Most Ebullient One, but I cannot give you that information. I am merely the messenger." He sipped another large gulp of the tea and tipped his head in Roger's direction. "This is *really* good."

"Thanks." Roger glanced at Angela and his eyebrows almost touched his hairline when he saw the look on her face. He turned back to Skip. "Man, no more tea talk, 'kay? She's getting pissed."

"My apologies, Most Fair One," Skip said to Angela. "But I can't tell you anything more about the originator of the wishes. Just that you have them."

She sighed. "So tell me about the wishes, then."

"There are three," Skip said. And then he said nothing for a few infuriating seconds.

Angela stamped her foot. "You are not being helpful. What exactly can I do with them?"

"Anything, Excellent One."

"Cool," Roger said, slurping his tea around the word. "Anything. We should go for a bunch of money."

"Money?" she frowned. *"We?"* Her frown deepened.

"Yeah. After all, I opened the box. Initially." He looked at her, and his face whitened. "Well, I did."

"You were doing it on my orders—"

"I don't think that was an actual order," Roger said. "It sounded more like a request. And you couldn't open the thing." He grinned. "I should get some say. After all..."

"Am I supposed to share?" Angela turned to Skip. "Is there anything in the rules that say I have to share with him?"

"No Mistress. It is for you alone. That is why it came into your possession. That is why your—" His face creased in a frown. "Your servant? Is that what he is?"

"You got it," Angela said.

"I am no one's servant," Roger replied indignantly.

"I'm the boss when Gerald's not here," Angela said. "So, in a way, you are."

You know the only reason you're a manager is because you've been here longer than anyone else. That doesn't make you better than me," Roger said. "Especially not when it comes to things like wishes. I think, in that case, sharing is in order."

"Would sharing get you off my back about this?" Angela asked.

"Yes. It definitely would."

"Then fine. Whatever. We'll share. But I decide how this gets done. Agreed?"

"Agreed."

"Oh Mistress, please." Skip's eyes were pinwheels of panic. "These wishes— they are just for you."

Angela ignored him. "Tell me about the money idea."

"Simple concept, really," Roger said. "Wish for a boatload of cash. Then we'd be set for life. And if we ever run out, we've got two more wishes."

Angela shook her head. "No. I don't think so." It wasn't good enough. She needed to do something that made a difference. Something that her mother would appreciate.

She hated the fact she was thinking of her mother again, but the way the fight had ended had shaken her. Her simply being rich wouldn't take back the words her mother had yelled at her. And she would want to know where the money had come from. Angela knew she'd never be able to convince her that a Genie named Skip gave her a wish. Never.

"Most Glorious Vision, please don't take too long," Skip said. "I was able to get back this time, but I don't know how long I will be able to stay— and I don't know if I'll have another chance."

"All right, sure, whatever," Angela said. She did not want to watch him gloop back into the box. Once was definitely enough.

"So, if it's not money, what's it going to be?" Roger asked.

"I'm going to get rid of homelessness. That's a real problem everywhere. Isn't it?"

"Yeah, I guess. If you want to be all altruistic and shit." Roger pushed his cup away, sounding disappointed.

"The moments are ticking, Most Glorious," Skip said.

"Yeah, right," Angela said, licking her lips.

"Please. The box is beginning to shake," Skip said, fear tingeing his deep voice.

"Wow. It is." Roger skittered back three huge steps, stopping when he ran into the ancient refrigerator skulking in the far corner of the room. "So make the wish already, Angela."

"All right, all right," she muttered. She pushed her chair back and stood. She did it to get away from the quivering puzzle box, but also felt she needed to stand to make the wish work.

More than anything, she wanted to have this wish work. This would be the best gift she'd ever given her mother and she wouldn't have even stolen it or anything.

After all, she thought, *what's more pure than a wish, with good will behind it?*

But as she closed her eyes, she knew there was nothing pure about the wish. She was using it to get on her mother's good side. So she crossed her fingers, hoping that would be enough.

"I wish that all the homelessness in the world would disappear, right now," she said. Then she opened one eye.

"Did it work?"

"It appears that it did," Skip replied.

"How can you tell?" she asked, and looked around the room. Roger was gone. She frowned. "When did he leave?"

"When you wished," Skip replied.

"Why?"

"He was probably homeless," Skip said.

"He wasn't." Angela shook her head. "He rents some dive near Whyte. Took him three weeks to get the smell of cat pee out of the carpet, and they're charging him way too much."

Then the import of Skip's words hit her. "What happened to Roger?"

"You wished for the homeless to disappear, did you not? It appears he went with them."

"But he wasn't homeless. And I did not wish for the homeless to disappear," she sputtered. "I wished for homelessness to disappear. *Homelessness*." She grabbed the big man by the arm and tried to shake him. He barely moved. "What did you do?"

"I did nothing, Most Glorious Star in the Sky. As I said, I am just the messenger. Are you sure you didn't say 'the homeless?'"

"I'm positive," she replied, but didn't feel positive at all. If her wish had made Roger disappear — and he wasn't homeless, he just didn't live in a place he actually owned — then she suspected there would not be many people left in the world, and that was definitely not what she had in mind.

"So, everybody who didn't own a home is gone?" she asked.

"It appears so," Skip answered.

"Do you think everybody left will notice?"

"Probably. You didn't ask that they disappear from the memory of every human left on the earth— just that they disappear."

"Except I'm pretty sure I said 'homelessness'."

Skip shrugged. "Perhaps for the next wish, you should enunciate better."

Angela ignored him, walking into the front of the shop and then outside. She watched the row of apartment buildings across the street from the mini mall crumple and fall, one after another. She whirled when she heard a crash, and watched the hotel across the street from the abandoned car fall in on itself.

"I said homelessness," she cried. "Not this. Not apartment buildings and hotels. Not Roger. This is wrong!"

When she heard the first siren, she wobbled back into the store, and picked up the phone. She dialed the number to the Mustard

Seed Homeless shelter where her mother worked, whispering, "Please pick up, please pick up, please pick up." It rang busy, then disconnected. She stared at the receiver for a long moment before slowly putting it down.

Her mother always answered the phone. Something had happened to her— and to the building. Angela had done something to her mother with the wish. She was sure of it.

She walked through the front of the video store, stopping when she heard small pops behind her and just above her head. She turned and watched the second last of Gerald's televisions begin to spew acrid smoke.

"No! Not now!" she cried, and danced back from the last remaining television so it wouldn't die too. Would this horrible day never end?

When she was certain that the wrecked televisions weren't going to burn down the *Slippery When Wet*, she stumbled back into the employee's lounge. Skip was pouring himself another cup of tea. "Amazing stuff," he said. "I can't get enough of it."

Angela ran her fingers through her hair and looked at Roger's teacup, half full and steaming. She'd erased him. She didn't want him gone, no matter how she treated him. And her mother. What had happened to her mother?

"My mother will hate me," she said, laying her head on the table. "This will prove to her, beyond a shadow of a doubt, that I am absolutely the worst daughter ever. I gotta fix this, Skip. What can I do?"

Skip glanced at her, then turned away and spooned sugar into his tea. "I don't know. Sorry."

"No. You can't just be sorry. Help me."

Skip didn't respond until she reached over and grabbed him, hard, by the nose.

"Please don't do that, Mistress," he cried, jumping away from her grasping fingers.

"Or what?" She grabbed him by an ear, tweaking it. "I thought you were supposed to make sure I got what I wanted. This is not what I wanted."

"Please stop that. It hurts."

Angela tweaked, harder. "I'm sure it does. You better come up with a way for me to fix this, or I'll do it again."

"Use another wish," he cried, dancing away from her. "Ouch!"

"Nope." She pinched him again. "I'm not wasting another wish, fixing something I don't believe I even messed up. Give me a do over."

"What is a do over?" he asked, pushing her grasping fingers away from the hair on his arms, which she was pulling out, one painful hair at a time.

"A do over is— well, a do over," Angela said, enunciating the second 'do over' as though it would somehow help with the explanation. "You set it up so I can redo that wish."

"Oh," Skip said. "You mean a mulligan."

"A what?"

"A mulligan. Please stop hurting me, Fantastical One. I believe I can let you revise your original wish. It will be gone— but you should be able to fix the error."

"There was no error on my part," Angela snarled.

"Yes, yes, I understand. The error was all at my end. Absolutely."

"All right." Angela dropped her hands. "And we can do this right now?"

"Yes."

She stared at him, but he did not move, so she reached out to grab him again— maybe even go further than pinching skin or pulling hair. She felt desperate to make the world the way it was before the wish. She didn't know if it was Roger — and probably half of the population of the earth — disappearing, or not being able to get her mother on the phone, or a combination of the two. All she knew for sure was the way the world was at that second was not what she'd had in mind. "Do something."

"You have to do it over," Skip said, flinching away from her. "You."

"But what if I screw up again?" she whispered. "What if I make it worse?"

"Do your best, Milady. That is all you can do."

She took a deep breath and closed her eyes. "I wish to take back my last wish," she said. "Please."

"Please? When do you ever say please?"

Her eyes flew open at Roger's voice, and she threw herself into his arms. "Are you all right?" she breathed into his hair.

"Yeah," he said, looking confused.

She pushed out of his arms.

"So, how come you're hugging me?" he asked.

"I wasn't hugging you," she replied.

"Yes, you were," Skip said. "I could see the joy on your face as you laid hands on Roger. That was definitely a hug."

"I don't need your help, Skip," Angela said, glaring. All he did was smile, so she turned her back on him, and looked at Roger. "Answer my question. Are you all right?"

"Well, yeah, of course I am," he replied, frowning faintly. "Why?"

"Because when I made the wish— you disappeared." She whispered, half afraid to speak any louder, for fear that her words would make him disappear again. "Poof."

"Poof?" Roger's frown coalesced to a much more familiar look, for him. Fear. "I poofed?"

"Kind of," Angela said, shaking her head. "There wasn't an actual poof— but you were gone. Completely and absolutely gone."

"Where did I go?"

"The Demon Realm, probably," Skip said.

"The Demon what?" Roger asked. "I went to the Demon Realm? There's a *Demon Realm*?"

"We don't know that," Angela said. "Skip, shut up, okay?"

"As you wish," Skip replied.

"And that was not my second wish!" she yelled. "It was a request, or an order, or something. *Not* a wish. Got it?"

"I understand oh Magnificent One."

She ran to the front window of the store and watched the apartment buildings knit themselves back, brick by brick, to their former shoddy glory.

"Did you do that?" Roger had followed her out of the lunch room and stood beside her, staring out the window.

"Yes," she whispered. "Apparently I did."

"Cool."

"There is nothing even remotely cool about any of this."

She turned away from the window and tried phoning her mother again. When she still heard only the busy signal, she slammed down the receiver and went back to the lunch room, Roger trailing behind her.

"This can't come back to me," she said. "There isn't a jail bad enough for someone who disappeared half the people in the world."

She glared at Skip. "So why didn't it work the way it was supposed to?"

Skip shrugged. "I don't know, Most Glorious One."

"Can you stop that?"

"What?"

"Most Glorious One, and all that crap. Please? Call me Angela."

Skip shrugged again. "As you wish—"

"It *wasn't* a wish."

"Right. Yes." He bowed and scraped. "As you request, Angela."

She glanced at the clock hanging above the refrigerator, and her eyes popped.

"It's almost six," she gasped. "Gerald's going to be here any minute. We gotta clean this place up. We gotta hide Skip!" She fought the urge to run in small, hysterical circles around the table. "What are we going to do?"

Roger burst into action. He began cleaning the small room, wiping down Skip's goo trails and straightening the table and chairs.

"You go to the front and get ready for Gerald," he said. "Skip and I will fix everything back here."

Angela felt a distant surprise coating her hysteria. She was going to acquiesce to Roger. She had never done anything like that before. *I'll just go along this time*, she thought. *Because I don't have another good idea anywhere in my head.*

"After we clean up, we'll wait for you at the *In Between*. Then, when Gerald cuts you loose for the night, we can come up with the next step. Sound good?"

"Better than nothing." Then she smiled at him. "Actually, it does sound pretty good. Thanks."

"You're welcome," he replied, batting his heavily eye-lined baby browns at her. "Don't worry, Angela. This will all work out."

"Yeah, sure, whatever," she replied. This day had skittered too far into the *Twilight Zone* for her to believe that the statement 'this will all work out' had any credence whatsoever.

She closed the door and stood behind the counter, waiting for Gerald, the all-time champion of deep running paranoia, to stampede through the door and ruin what was left of her day.

The Bus

"I'm freezing," Skip whined as he, Angela, and Roger walked to the bus stop, forty-five uneventful minutes later. "Can't we go back to the coffee shop?"

"You should have a coat," Angela replied, unwilling to give him an iota of sympathy.

Gerald had filled her ear with what had happened with her wish. As well as being paranoid, he was also a news junkie— and he had his fill on this eventful day.

Angela had listened to him talk about all the apartment buildings, hotels, motels, and, it seemed, most of the old folk's homes collapsing, with all the appropriate death and destruction, and then, fifteen minutes later, everything going back to normal. No one dead or even injured— though it did sound like the numbers of heart attacks worldwide spiked beyond belief in the hour after the "attack".

Hospitals were filling with people convinced they'd been given some sort of drug, after CNN ran a story about the possibility that it had been a worldwide hallucinogenic gas attack. Or something even more horrifying and earth shattering.

Gerald mentioned closing the store for the rest of the night — something almost unheard of — until the deviants, all looking fairly freaked out, trooped in and began cleaning him out of the most disgusting and abhorrent porn they could find. Gerald guessed they'd decided if the world was going to end, they'd watch midgets giving blowjobs to donkeys until it was over, and kept the doors open. He'd even tried to talk her into working a few extra hours, glowering at her when she said she couldn't.

She finally escaped, and decided that everything was Skip's fault. Even the blown up televisions were his fault, though Gerald hadn't complained much after he'd realized there was still one working, and he could still get his news fix. She hoped the cold nipped whatever Skip had for genitals. He deserved that, at least.

"I didn't need a coat, before." Skip tucked his hands inside his jacket and shuddered so hard Angela was certain she heard his teeth rattling against each other. "This is horrible, Mi— Angela. Why do you stay here?"

"Because it's my home," she said.

"It *is* getting cold," Roger said. Like Skip, he was not dressed for the weather. Angela felt even less sympathy for him. "Maybe we should go to my place."

"No," Angela said shortly. "We're going to my place. Mom doesn't get home until nine. You're sure the busses are still running?"

"I've seen a couple go by," Roger said. He pointed at an army tank squatting next to the hotel across the street. The one Angela had seen fall apart, and then reassemble. "You really did all this, didn't you?"

"Yeah," Angela whispered.

Roger smiled delightedly. "Cool. You dicked with the world."

"Shut up."

The Number Eight pulled up to the bus stop, and the three of them piled in with the rest of the great unwashed. They huddled around the back door as the bus lurched into traffic.

"How long to get to your place?" Roger asked.

"About fifteen minutes," Angela replied. She glanced out at the street, cringing when she saw actual soldiers, with actual guns, standing on the street corner.

"At least it's warm," Skip said, grabbing the bar above everyone else's heads. "I do not understand how you can live here. One of your wishes should be—"

"Enough about the wishes already," Angela whispered. "I don't want to talk about it now. Understand?"

"No," Skip replied, but shut his mouth. Angela was glad. The big guy attracted enough attention all on his own, without bleating about granting wishes and such. Angela imagined what might happen if any of the idiots on this bus used their cell phones to upload images of the three of them to You Tube— they would be arrested for shaking the world to its core by first disappearing and then reappearing more than half the people in it.

Yes, she was being paranoid— but at the beginning of this morning, she would have thought that having someone ooze out of a puzzle box and offer her three wishes was impossible, too.

The Mother

Ellen Simonson got off the Number Eight and walked through the crunchy snow strewn over the sidewalk, hoping Angela was home and safe. After the event she hadn't been able to contact the video store where her daughter worked and was afraid something had happened to her.

Event, she thought, for the hundredth time. *Why can't I think of a bigger word for having a building fall on and then rebuild itself around me?*

Ellen's heart lifted when she saw lights on in the living room and she ran up the front steps and threw open the door.

"Angela?" she called.

Angela did not answer.

"Angela?" she called again. She had to be home. Why else would all the lights be on?

"Be right out, Mom!"

Ellen felt a rush of relief, quickly followed by fear, when Angela called from the back of the house. *She's in her room,* Ellen thought. *And it sounds like she's not alone.*

She fought the sudden impulse to run back out the door and hitch a ride to somewhere else in the world — anywhere away from here — and kicked off her boots.

"How are you?" she called, listening to clattering and banging coming from her daughter's room. *Who does she have back there with her?*

"Fine," Angela yelled from her room. "Work was quiet. Not too many deviants out today."

"Understandable," Ellen muttered. She walked into the kitchen, listening to the banging in the back room and trying to keep her tears at bay. She didn't know if they were tears of relief that Angela was all right, or more despair, because Angela was... well, being Angela.

"Why?" Angela asked. Ellen jumped. The girl had appeared beside her, even though she could still hear banging in the back bedroom.

"Do you have friends over?"

"Yeah. A guy from work— and somebody else." For a brief moment, Ellen thought she saw concern on her daughter's face. "Are you all right?"

"Yes."

"You don't look all right. What happened?"

Ellen stared at her daughter in real surprise. "Didn't you see the news?"

Angela blinked twice, slowly. "You know I don't watch that."

Ellen closed her eyes. How to explain a building collapsing and then rebuilding itself around her, to someone who really didn't care one whit about the rest of the world. She decided she was too tired for that. "I had an accident at work."

"Are you sure you're all right?"

Ellen was almost certain she heard real concern in Angela's voice and decided she was projecting. Angela never showed concern.

"I'm fine. Really. Are your friends staying for supper?"

"We already ate."

Ellen looked over at the sink. It was empty. Even the broken coffee cup was gone. Ellen looked around the rest of the kitchen and frowned. It was spotless.

"Where are the dishes?" she whispered.

"Skip — the guy — he cleaned up," Angela replied. "He thought it would be nice for you."

"Skip?"

"Yeah. Weird name, weird guy, but he cleans up after himself." Angela laughed, and after a moment, Ellen joined her.

"So where did you find this weird guy?" she asked. As soon as the words were out of her mouth, she mentally kicked herself. She did not want her daughter to tell her about her latest conquest. Not today.

But Angela was circumspect. "Just a guy I met," she said. "Would you like a sandwich? There are some in the fridge."

"You made me supper?" Ellen gasped.

"No. Roger did. He can make sandwiches like a bastard — sorry, shouldn't have said that — so Skip wrapped the rest up and put them in the fridge. If you'd like."

"Will I be meeting Skip and— Robert?"

"Roger. Maybe. We're doing some research, but maybe later, if you're up."

Angela stared at Ellen until Ellen turned away, reaching for the fridge door.

"Do you think you'll be up?" Angela asked.

"I don't know," Ellen whispered. "Do you want me to be?"

"Like I said, Skip's pretty weird. Might be better for you if you're not."

"Then I probably won't be." Ellen pulled the plate of sandwiches out of the fridge. "You aren't doing anything— illegal, are you?"

"I wouldn't do that. Not again."

"Thanks." Ellen pulled the plastic wrap from the sandwiches. "These look good."

"They are, actually. Roger worked at Subway for a few weeks, and apparently the training stuck."

Ellen felt the familiar ache at the back of her throat. She was going to cry again, but for a different reason this time. This time she felt like crying because this felt so normal.

"I'm going to my room," she muttered. Her daughter did not respond well to tears and Ellen did not want to lose this small oasis of sanity, so she walked away without another word.

Ellen nearly dropped the sandwiches when Angela's bedroom door opened and a young man with dyed black hair and far too much eye makeup stuck his head out.

"Hi," he said, and smiled.

"Hi," Ellen replied. "Are you the guy who made the sandwiches?"

"Yep. You like them?"

"They look good," she replied. "Your name's Roger?"

"Yep. You Angela's mom?"

"Ellen."

"Nice to meetcha." He opened the door a little more. "Wanna meet Skip?" he asked.

Before she could answer, a deep voice boomed "Shut the door, now!"

Roger jumped. "Sorry," he said, as he pushed the door closed. "Guess Skip doesn't want to meet you."

"That's fine," Ellen whispered, through lips that felt frozen. She had recognized the voice. She would never forget that voice. How could she?

In her daughter's room was the person who had helped her escape from Arturo, Angela's father, nearly nineteen years before.

She took a faltering step away from the door. One of the sandwiches slipped from the plate, but she ignored it and skittered to her own room, shutting her door and, as was her custom, pulling her dresser across the closed door so no one — meaning her daughter — could slip in and possibly slash her throat while she slept.

She tossed the plate onto her bed and brayed out a lung busting sob. He was back. He'd promised she'd never see him or anyone from any of the Realms if she just kept her nose clean and lived a good life. He'd promised.

But now he was hiding in her daughter's bedroom like some sort of criminal. What was going on?

If she felt any stronger, she would have marched back across the hall and pounded on her daughter's door, demanding an explanation. But she didn't. A building had fallen on her earlier that day. She just didn't feel up to it. She only had enough strength to crash on the bed and bellow her fear into her pillow.

Another Fight

Angela pushed open her door and frowned at the sight of Skip lying across her unmade bed, crying his head off.

"What did you do to him?" she asked Roger.

"Nothing. Your mom walked by. Then he started that." He pointed over his shoulder at the giant, who was using one of Angela's pillows as a handkerchief.

"Stop it!" she cried, jumping over the junk on the floor and ripping the dripping pillow out of the big guy's hand. "You are disgusting, you know?"

"I am so sorry, Oh Magnificent— Angela." Skip sat up and looked at her with tear blurred eyes, and sniffled, mightily, before using his arm to wipe the rivulet of snot from his upper lip. "I did not realize who your mother was." He sobbed again.

"And how exactly do you know my mother?" Angela asked.

"I— met her years ago." Skip sighed. "Years and years ago." He sighed again. "Years and years and years—"

"Yeah, we get it," Angela said. "How do you know her?"

"I helped her, once." Skip sniffed and hiccupped. "This is all so amazingly complicated. I don't know if I can go on."

"What did you help her with?" Angela asked. "And what makes it so complicated?"

"Please tell me this is one more of your wishes," Skip pleaded. "Please."

"Nope. Simple question. Clarification, if you will. You're not getting off that easy."

"I didn't think I would," Skip mumbled, wiping his nose on his sleeve again. "I met your mother two decades ago. She was having trouble with a man— I guess we can call him a man — and she needed help getting away from him. I provided that help."

Angela's eyes narrowed. "And who was the man?"

"I believe you have already guessed it, Milady— Angela. He is your father."

Angela blinked. "Was," she whispered. "He was my father."

"Is," Skip said.

"Whoa. Didn't you say your dad was dead?" Roger asked.

"Yeah," Angela breathed.

"Well, I wasn't expecting that," Roger said. "Are all the sandwiches gone?"

Angela pushed a pile of dirty clothes off the only chair in the room so she could fall into it. Skip's words had punched the air from her lungs and she needed to recover. Skip answered Roger.

"Shut the hell up, Halfling," he snarled.

"Halfling?" Roger pulled himself to his full height, which on a good day was five foot nine, exactly average for a Canadian male. "Screw you, Tallboy."

Skip rose from the bed, anger blazing from his eyes. "No one calls me Tallboy and lives!" he cried, and leaped at Roger.

Roger squealed as he threw himself into the pile of dirty clothes. Skip banged his head on the light fixture in the middle of Angela's room and crashed onto Roger and the pile of dirty clothes as shards of glass showered down on them in the suddenly dark room.

"Help me!" Angela ignored Roger's muffled cry, focusing on getting air back into her lungs.

"Oh my head," Skip cried. She ignored him too. The news he'd delivered shortly before wrecking her room and falling on her work-mate had frozen her, and all she could think was *breathe, damn you. Breathe.*

"What is going on?" her mother called through two closed doors, and, if Angela knew her mother, one dresser.

Angela pulled in a thin stream of hot, dark air, and let it out in a quick puff. Then she breathed in again, pulling the chaos of her room — and her life — in with it, and felt like she was going crazy.

"All of you need to shut up right now," she said.

She got out of the chair, and out of the room, and then out of the house. She stood ankle deep in the snow blanketing the front yard and cried.

Angela heard the front door creak open and then slam shut behind her, but didn't turn around. She couldn't think of one person inside that house she wanted to see. Quite possibly ever again.

She stared up at the black sky, dotted with stars. She knew she was only seeing those big enough to push their light through the white noise of the city, and thought how nice it would be to live out in the country somewhere, so she could see them all. Way out in the middle of nowhere, away from all the bullshit her life was becoming.

Behind her, snow crunched under boots, and she stiffened. She wasn't going to be able to get away from these people. Then she thought of her wishes. All she had to do was wish, and she'd be so far away none of them would ever be able to find her again.

She wiped her nose on her sleeve and thought about the wish. If she wished herself way, way out in the country— well, that meant more of the cold, right? And animals. There were animals roaming free out there, like wolves and moose and things, and she didn't know if she wanted to meet any of them in the dark. Not without backup.

"Are you okay?" Roger asked.

"No," she replied. "Are you?"

"I think I scraped my elbow, and Tallboy—"

"He didn't like being called that."

"Who cares?" He glanced over at her, as though checking to see if she cared. "All right. Skip. That better?"

"Yes."

"What kind of a name is Skip, anyhow?"

"I don't know," she sighed. "You didn't answer my question."

"I'm all right. He's heavy and I was afraid he was going to crush me but after you left he got off me, so it looks like I'll live."

"Good." Angela turned her gaze back to the sky. Snow crunched as Roger anxiously shuffled his feet.

"What do you think of the country?" she asked.

"What country?"

"The *country*— out there, past the city someplace. Did you ever think about just going out there and living like a farmer, or an animal tracker, or something? Giving all this crap up?"

"No. I would probably never want to do that. It's a lot of hard work, isn't it?"

"I don't know," Angela sighed. "Anything would be better than this."

"Maybe if it was a warm country," Roger said. "But then you have snakes and bugs to think about. Might be all right if you got rid of all the snakes and bugs."

She shrugged, and he frowned. "Are you thinking about using another wish?"

"Maybe." Then she shook her head. "No, not really. I'd have to plan it out better than 'take me to a warm country minus all the bugs and snakes.' I'd probably destroy the ecology of the whole world with a trick like that."

"Probably." He shuffled closer to her, and shivered. "Aren't you cold?"

"Yeah." She hadn't grabbed her coat and the cold was biting her arms and face like a nasty weasel.

"So am I. Maybe we should go inside. You know, and talk. Or something."

"I don't think I can face those two." The words rushed out of her in a steam-filled plume. "Skip knew my mother— and my father. What the hell am I supposed to do with that?"

"I don't know."

Roger's teeth were chattering so hard, Angela barely understood his words. She glanced at him. He was a shivering ball of misery, and the end of his nose had gone a nasty shade of red. She imagined she looked the same.

"Let's go in before you freeze to death."

"Thank you." Roger turned to run, then stopped and touched her arm. "What *are* you going to do about them?"

"I don't know," she replied. "Come on, let's go in."

The kettle was beginning to whistle when they walked through the door and into the warmth of the house.

"I'm making tea," Skip said. "Do you care what kind?"

Angela kicked off her snow-caked shoes without answering him.

"Is there any green tea?" Roger asked. "I could go for some green tea about now."

Skip opened the cupboard that held all Angela's mother's teas. In moments, he held up two boxes and Roger pointed at the one in his right hand.

"And you, Milady?" Skip asked.

Angela ignored him.

"Milady?"

She ignored him again.

"Mi—"

"Knock it off," Roger said. "She's not talking to you, Big Guy. You fucked up."

"It's because I broke her light, isn't it?" Skip asked, looking as crestfallen as only he could. Hugely. "If she'd just tell me where the bulbs are, I could replace it for her. I could replace all the light bulbs in the house, if it would help. Maybe some of those high efficiency ones—"

"You're blathering," Roger said. "Stop it."

"All right," Skip replied, looking relieved. "I knew I was. I couldn't seem to stop myself and—"

"Just shut up," Angela said. "I don't want to hear your stupid voice."

"Ah, Milady, thank you for speaking to me," Skip gushed, scrambling across the kitchen and falling at her feet. "I am so sorry—"

"I am not speaking to you," she said. "Shut up."

"I think she means it, man," Roger said.

"But she must speak to me," Skip said. "It is vital that I complete my mission. Absolutely vital."

"And what would your mission be?"

The three of them whirled and stared at Angela's mother, who had appeared at the end of the hall. Although her nose was red from her recent crying jag, she looked good. Together. More together than Angela had ever seen her.

"You better answer me, Skippy Boy," her mother said. "Now."

The Explanation

"Ellen. I'm sorry. I can't tell you."

Skip scrambled to his feet, narrowly avoiding taking out the old-fashioned sunshine ceiling in the kitchen with the top of his head. "I wish I could, but I can't. You know the rules."

"I don't care about the rules anymore. You broke the big one when you showed up in my house— my life. In my daughter's life, for God's sake. What were you thinking?"

"I didn't know," Skip said, and hung his head.

In spite of herself, Angela was impressed. Her mother looked like she could take on Skip with one hand tied behind her back. Then she remembered what Skip had said about her father, and was angry all over again.

"He's not here for you," Angela snapped. "Leave him alone."

She waited for her mother's face to return to normal— pasty-faced fear. But it didn't.

"That's enough, Angela." Ellen pointed at a chair tucked under the small dining table. "Sit down."

"He isn't yours!" Angela cried.

"Sit down. Now."

Angela started. She hadn't heard that tone in her mother's voice before. Quite possibly ever. She sat.

"Make the tea," Ellen said to Roger. Then she turned to Skip. "Yes, Ellen?"

"Actually, I don't know what to do with you," she said. "You're too big to sit at my table, too powerful to smack the crap out of, and too involved in my family's life to be allowed to crawl away. So just stay right there until we have our tea. And watch your head. I can't afford to replace every light fixture in my house." Then she frowned. "Why *are* you so tall? You were much shorter before."

Skip opened his mouth as though he was going to answer, but snapped it shut when she held up a hand.

"Forget it," she said. "It doesn't matter."

"Yes it does," Roger cried.

"Shut up." Both Angela and Ellen barked the order at the same time, glanced at each other, and then looked away.

"Just make the tea, Roger," Ellen said. He stepped to, and soon there were cups of steaming tea at the table.

"Thank you," Ellen said.

"You're welcome," he smiled.

"Stop it," Angela snapped.

"Stop what?"

"You're flirting with my mother, for heaven's sake. Stop it right now."

"I'm not," he protested.

"Yes, actually you are," said Ellen.

"See? Even *she* can tell, and she's old," snapped Angela.

"Thanks," Ellen said, sarcastically.

Roger looked embarrassed, grabbed his tea, and walked across the room, sitting in a chair against the far wall. He half-turned from them and sipped moodily.

"That tea smells good," Skip muttered, from the floor.

Ellen sighed and handed a cup to him. He took it, burying his nose in the fragrant steam rising from the top before taking a sip. "It is good," he said. "Thanks."

"You're welcome."

"Did you know he's a Genie?" Angela asked, not looking at her mother.

Everyone froze at her words. Everyone. "I asked a simple question. Did you know, Mom?"

"Yes," Ellen sighed. "I knew him, before you were born. He—saved me."

"From my father, right?" She glared at Ellen. "You told me he died before I was born. You lied to me."

"Yes," Ellen whispered.

"Ouch!" Roger cried, melting back into his seat and burying his face in his cup when both women turned and glared at him.

"So my father is alive?" Angela asked.

"I imagine so." Ellen jerked her thumb in Skip's direction. "*He's* back. I can't imagine him voluntarily showing up, otherwise."

"There is truth to that," Skip said, setting his cup down on the table and pulling himself to standing. "I do have my own life."

"So why are you back here then?" Angela snapped. And where is my father?" She turned and glared at Ellen. "Why didn't you tell me the truth about him?"

"The truth?"

"That he's alive!" Angela cried, slamming her tea cup down on the table and slopping the delicately tinted green tea all over the table cloth. "I could have — you shouldn't have — why didn't you tell me that?"

"I was protecting you," Ellen said.

"From what?"

Ellen stared at Angela. "From Arturo." she whispered. "I was trying to protect you from your father."

"Why?"

Skip reached over and placed a hand on Angela's shoulder. She tried to shrug it off, but Skip's hand did not move. "You must trust your mother," he said. "He's nothing you want to know."

"Right. Trust my mother." Angela sneered. "I don't think so."

"I understand you're upset with me," Ellen replied. "You must believe though, I did everything for your own good."

"Uh huh. Sure." Angela stood, and her eyes blazed. "I feel so stupid. I thought you were the best, most honest person I knew." Her voice broke. "And now I find out you're a bigger liar and a cheat than I am. No wonder I can't be the person you said you wanted me to be. *You* weren't. What chance did I have?"

She turned to Roger, who was sitting with his tea cup half way to his lips and forgotten, transfixed by the family drama playing out in front of him. "I'm starting to like the idea of using one of my wishes to teleport myself to a country with no snakes and no bugs," she said. "Screw the ecology of the world. Are you in?"

Ellen grabbed her arm before Roger had a chance to answer. "A wish?" she gasped, then whirled and stared at Skip. "You gave her a wish? From him?"

"Three, actually," Skip answered. "I had to."

"But why?" Ellen cried. "You know how dangerous—"

Skip's face contorted. "I can't tell you."

"You had better," Ellen and Angela said together. Angela turned away.

"Tell us, now," Ellen said.

"He has my family, Ellen," Skip whispered. "He will cause them to be tortured for all eternity if she doesn't make the wishes."

"Tortured for all time?" Angela stared at Skip. "What are you talking about?"

"Your father is not a good man, Angela," Ellen said.

"Truer words were never spoken," Skip murmured.

"There is obviously a ton I don't know, somebody better tell me what is going on, right now," Angela said. "Tell me."

Ellen glanced at Skip, and then at her daughter. "I guess it's time you knew the truth."

"You're going to kill my family." Skip's voice sounded strangled. "Ellen, please don't do this."

"I'm sorry. I have to. She's my daughter, and I've lied to her long enough. We both have."

"This is so cool," Roger whispered, putting his teacup down. "I now get why people get hooked on daytime soaps."

"My life is not a soap opera," Angela snarled.

Although Roger said "Sorry," he meant, "Yes. It definitely is."

Three Pieces of Foolscap

Angela looked at the three pieces of foolscap on which she'd been taking notes. "Are you sure this is everything?" she asked. "I'll have to get more paper if it isn't."

Ellen stopped pacing long enough to glance over her shoulder. "Looks about right," she said. "Can you think of anything else, Skip?"

"I don't believe so," Skip replied, then looked at Angela. "Is there anything you don't understand?"

Angela looked down at the pages, reading them over once more. "It all seems pretty straight forward," she said. "Seeing it in black and white like this."

"This is the most whacked out shit I've ever heard in my life," Roger breathed. "I can't believe you're being so calm about everything, Ang."

"Don't ever call me *Ang* again," Angela said. "Ever."

She straightened the pages and looked up at her mother. "I wish you'd told me about this before."

"And when exactly do you think would have been the right time for this particular talk?" Ellen snapped, sounding more like Angela than Angela wanted to admit was possible. She'd always thought she had the patent out on that particular tone of aggrieved nastiness, but there it was, coming out of her mother's mouth. "It isn't like you were adopted or something."

"True," Angela said.

She stared down at the top page, and reread Point One for the thirtieth time.

'My father is a demon.'

She'd done a lot of horrified screaming shortly before writing Point One. "This kind of beats being adopted all to hell, doesn't it?"

Her mother had resumed pacing for all she was worth. "Can't you sit down, Mom?" Angela asked. "You're making me nervous."

"*I'm* making *you* nervous?" Ellen's voice cracked as she laughed, sounding more than a little crazy. "Girl, we all deserve to feel more nervous than we ever have in all our lives. Live with it." She resumed her pacing. Angela turned her back on her and faced Skip.

"Okay, so whatever. Mom's nervous, Dad's a demon, and you're a Genie."

"Djinn."

"Whatever." Angela closed her eyes and took a quick cleansing breath. "All right. You're Djinn. okay? Did I say it right?"

"Close enough," Skip replied, the ghost of a smile on his face. "Your accent isn't bad, for a human."

"Half human," Roger breathed. "She's half human. And half demon."

"Roger, for the thousandth time, leave it alone," Angela said. "I'm not used to this yet— and I can't take you mentioning it every minute with that look on your face."

"What look?" Roger asked. "I don't have a look."

"You look as though you are even more enamored of her than before," Skip said.

"Shut up, Skip!" Angela cried.

Skip shrugged. "He does."

"I know he does," Angela said. "I didn't want to hear it said out loud. I just wanted him to stop it."

"You don't have to talk about me like I'm not even here," Roger muttered, looking more hurt than enamored.

"Just stop looking at me with those frigging puppy dog eyes. All right?"

"All right," he said, smiling his heart melting half-smile again until Angela wanted to club him. "I won't. But it *is* pretty cool."

"It's not cool," Angela said, her voice cracking. She snapped her mouth shut when she felt her throat close painfully. She was not crying in front of Roger— or anyone else in the room. No way.

She stood and walked over to the stove, staring down at the burners until she felt the pain of the unshed tears recede. She walked back to the table and sat down. She felt if she wasn't careful she would shatter into a thousand shards of glass all over the floor, like the light bulbs Skip kept breaking.

"So, I'm half demon," she breathed.

"Yes you are," Skip said.

"And my father wants me with him," Angela said.

"Yes," Skip replied. "If you can pass his test."

"And these wishes are his way of testing me."

"Yes."

"To see if I'm evil enough to join him."

"Again, yes."

"And I can't just not make the wishes, because your family will be..." She shuffled through the pages. "Tortured for all time."

"Regrettably, yes."

"I'm assuming this would be in the seventh ring of Hell or something?" Angela asked.

Skip snorted. "There is no Hell."

"How can there be no Hell?" Angela asked. "If there are demons, and genies, and wishes— how can there not be a Hell?"

"Knowing there is one thing for certain does not make other things real. I haven't ever been convinced there is either a Heaven or a Hell. Just the four realms."

"Four realms?"

"Yes. Human, Djinn, Demon, and Angel."

"Angels?" Angela stared. "You believe in angels, but you don't believe there is a Heaven?"

"Haven't seen Heaven, so I cannot for certain say there is one. Same goes for Hell."

"But, you've seen angels. Real, actual angels."

"Yes."

"Skip, let it go," Ellen said, sounding as tired as Angela had ever heard her. "This is not the time for a philosophical debate on the reality of Heaven and Hell. If we actually get out of this, we can debate for days. I promise. But leave it alone right now. I can't take it."

"It's because *she* believes there *is* a Hell," Skip whispered to Angela. "And she thinks the rest rolls out from that one supposition. Foolish human."

"Skip!" Ellen barked.

Skip jumped and bowed his head. "As you wish," he said. Angela could not tell if he was being sarcastic or not. "But, perhaps it is not you who should be wishing, but Angela. After all, she was given three wishes. If she uses the next one—"

"Next? She's already wished once?"

"Yes she has."

"What happened?" Ellen asked.

Skip shrugged. "It went about the way you'd expect."

Ellen gasped. "Was that you?"

"Was that me what?" Angela asked, attempting to look innocent and failing, miserably.

"All those people disappearing. Buildings falling down. The White House collapsed, Angela. The President of the United States disappeared. The entire world went on High Alert."

Angela turned to Roger with a guilty smile on her face. "Did you hear that? I made the President disappear."

"And the White House," Ellen said. "I'm assuming this is not what you wanted to happen with the wish. Right?"

"I was trying to make homelessness disappear. *Homelessness.*"

"She disappeared me and my apartment building," Roger said.

"I said I was sorry," Angela said.

"I don't think you did," Skip said. "You just badgered me into giving you a 'do over,' I believe you called it. But I do not think you ever apologized to young Roger here."

"Thanks, Skip," Angela said. "That's the kind of help I need right now, I'm sure."

"Sorry, Mistress," Skip mumbled. "Oh. Sorry, Angela."

"That's enough." Ellen barked. "Skip, did Arturo put any limitations on what she can do with those wishes?"

"None."

"That's good," Ellen said. "Because I think the wishes Angela has left should be used against him. As soon as possible."

"Maybe Angela can send him to some place like Hell," Roger said.

Skip frowned at him. "I told you. There is no Hell."

"Yes there is," Ellen shot back. "And it's a demon's playground, according to my research. It would be like sending a kid to a bizarre theme park."

"Oh." Roger leaned back in his chair. "I got nothing, then."

"Good," Ellen said. "Let the adults deal with this."

"Mom, both Roger and I are adults," Angela said. "And these are *my* wishes."

"I mean Skip and I both know your— Arturo well. We are the logical ones to come up with a plan that will keep all of us safe. That's all I meant."

"Fine." Angela did not feel fine. She still felt as though her mother was talking down to her and Roger, and she did not like it at all. "Whatever."

"We have to make certain that whatever the wish is— it eliminates Arturo from our lives forever," Ellen said. "We cannot have him coming back."

"And make sure it isn't ironic," Roger said. Skip and Ellen both turned and stared at him.

"Ironic?"

"Like the joke about the guy who wished his dick would touch the floor and then his legs disappeared. You don't want that happening. Ironic wishes are pretty funny, but won't help in this situation."

"Thank you, Roger," Ellen said sarcastically. "We will keep it in mind."

Roger backed away, head down. "I was just trying to help," he muttered. "No need to get all mean on me."

"I thought you liked mean," Angela said.

"I do. From you." He smiled, and before she could stop herself, Angela smiled back.

"We do not have time for this," Ellen said.

"There's always time for romance," Skip said.

"There is no romance," Angela said, tearing the smile off her face. "Just back off, both of you."

"That's right," Roger said. "We are compatriots. Comrades-in-arms. Soldiers, fighting the forces of evil—"

"Shut up, Roger," Angela snapped.

"Right, Boss," Roger said. "Shutting up."

"We have to come up with a plan," Ellen said, looking at Skip. "And we have to come up with it now."

"I cannot help you," Skip said. "If I do, Arturo will destroy my family."

Ellen stood tall. "You help me save mine, and I'll help you save yours," she said. "And that's a promise."

Skip lowered his eyes, his throat working. "Angela could wish Arturo had never been born. That might save us all."

"No," Ellen replied. "There is a good chance Angela will disappear as well. That's not what we're going for here."

"Are you sure, Mom? I thought that's what you said this morning," Angela said.

"I was angry." Ellen touched Angela's shoulder. "Can we talk about this later? Please?"

"Whatever," Angela replied, and walked away from her mother's hand.

"So making him disappear is out," Skip said. "What about killing him, then?"

"I would imagine he has safeguards in place for that eventuality," Ellen said. "All he would have to have in place is a quick reanimation spell, three days down, and he'd be right back in the thick of things. But angry, this time,"

"Oh," Skip replied. "You're right."

"And he would assume you told her about him— which breaks your pact with him, and puts your family at further risk."

"Oh." Skip's eyes widened and he put his hands to his face. "I hadn't thought of that."

"Well, what if I use the rest of the wishes just for me?" Angela asked. "Just play them all out as though I don't know about him. Then Skip's family would be off the hook and you'd be safe."

"And Angela would be rich," Roger said. They all turned and stared at him. "Well, she could be, if she makes the right wish."

"That has nothing to do with anything," Ellen snapped. Then she turned to Angela. "Your idea seems good on the surface, but I see two problems."

"And those would be?" Angela asked, trying hard to keep the anger, which was growing by leaps and bounds, from coming out in her voice.

"One, Arturo would still be free."

"And two?"

"We don't know how the wishes would work. Look what happened with the homelessness one. You were being completely altruistic and you threw the world into chaos."

"I wasn't, though." Angela's anger collapsed, leaving only guilt.

"You weren't what?"

"Being altruistic. Not completely." Angela looked down at the floor. "Actually, I wasn't being altruistic at all. I was trying to make up with you, Mom. That's the real reason I picked that as my first wish."

Ellen blinked twice, slowly. "You thought of me when you made your first wish? Even after what I said to you?"

"Yeah," Angela said. "But trust me, it will never happen again."

She watched the quick smile fade from her mother's face, and wished, just for a moment, that it could stay. That smile was for her, after all. For something she'd done.

But she lied to me, Angela thought. *She lied.*

The anger came back, tearing whatever warm and fuzzy feelings she'd had into tiny little pieces as the silence stretched.

"Can someone please come up with a plan before Arturo swoops in here and kills us all? Please?" Skip finally begged. "Anyone?"

"I think I might have something," Ellen said. "And it has to do with what Roger suggested." She looked over at Roger. "I shouldn't have been so quick to say your idea had no merit."

"It's the money one— right?" Roger asked. "She's going to be rich, isn't she?"

"No, it isn't the money. It was the idea of sending Arturo to Hell."

"What happened to Hell being a playground for demons?" Angela asked.

"If you choose the right words, I believe you could make Hell a suitable prison for him."

"And if there is no Hell?" Skip asked. "As I know there isn't?"

"He'd still go somewhere. I think it might depend on whether Angela believes in Hell or not. After all, it would be her wish. Her beliefs would probably impact where he goes. Who knows?

If she read Dante's *Inferno*, maybe he'd end up in the story some-where. Trapped in the pages of a book, for all time. Or maybe he'd go to Angela's version of Hell."

"Are you saying Angela's beliefs could impact reality?"

"Skip, we are talking about wishes delivered by a Djinn, on behalf of a demon, to a half-human. We have crossed so many boundaries I don't see why Angela's imagination wouldn't have an impact on it."

"You have a point," Skip said.

"Let's hope it does work. I just want this done," Ellen said. "I want him out of my life — all of our lives — forever." She turned to Angela and Roger. "Can you see any flaws in my reasoning? Does it make sense? And most importantly, will it work?"

"Sounds pretty solid to me," Roger said.

"Thank you," Ellen said. She turned to Skip. "Besides the whole 'there is no hell' thing, can you see any problems?"

"No," Skip said. "It should work, if the wording is exactly right."

Ellen turned to Angela. "Do you think this will work?"

Angela sighed. "Probably."

"So, we are agreed then," Ellen said. "The next wish Angela makes will be for her father to be sent to Hell for all time, with no chance of escape. Right?"

"Not quite."

Everyone stared at Angela, shock and trickles of fear on the faces of two, and a half-smile on the face of the third.

"I knew it," Roger whispered. "No way she'd acquiesce. No possible way in the world."

Ellen ignored him, concentrating on Angela, who had risen from her chair and pushed her unruly hair back from her face. "What do you mean, 'not quite?'"

"I mean— not quite. I believe that wish would send my father some place far away from all of us. And I think it will save your ass— and Skip's family."

Angela looked apologetically at Skip, but he merely stared at her, his face frozen as he waited for her next words, which were obviously going to contain a 'but' that was going to kick the crap out of him.

"And I am sorry," she continued. "But you are talking about my father. My father, who I thought was dead. Who I thought I would never ever in a million years have a chance to meet."

Ellen opened her mouth to speak, but Angela held up her hand for silence.

"I know he's a demon— but he's my dad." She felt sudden tears touch her eyes, and closed them, taking a quick breath in to get back her control. "He's my dad, and I have the right to meet him and make up my own mind about him."

She pushed her chair back, and stood. Before anyone had a chance to do anything more than think *oh no*, she closed her eyes, raised her hands and shouted, "I wish my father was in this room, right now!"

The Second Wish

The room filled with a hot, heavy mist smelling faintly of patchouli laced with sulfur. Ellen and Skip dropped to the ground, screaming incoherently and Angela, her heart pounding hard, watched Arturo's naked figure materialize.

He was leaning back in a chair with his legs splayed out in front of him and his hands locked behind his head. As the hot mist began to dissipate, he frowned and sat upright, unlocking his fingers and putting his arms down by his sides.

"What is wrong with this sauna, now?" he growled. "I will never buy anything from Cost Kutters again, I swear."

Then, his eyes opened. He did a classic double take, which threw Roger into a quick and hysterical laughing jag that worsened when Arturo squawked like a surprised chicken and ripped the tablecloth from the table, scattering cups and tea everywhere.

"What is going on here?" he bellowed, wrapping the tablecloth around his middle and glaring around the room. "Where am I?"

Ellen and Skip made some of their own 'squawk like a chicken' noises, and Roger brayed out snot and more laughter. Angela rolled her eyes and walked in front of the furious, table-cloth covered figure.

"Hi," she said. "I'm Angela, your daughter. I wished you here. It's nice to finally meet you."

Arturo stared at Angela. She stared back, and frowned.

"Hey, I met you before, didn't I?" She looked into his eyes — strange, otherworldly eyes, like a gecko's — and her frown deepened.

"You're the deviant from the *Slippery When Wet*," she said. "The guy with the wrap-around sunglasses."

Arturo glowered at Angela without answering, then turned on Skip, who was groveling behind a chair.

"You son of a bitch!" he yelled. "What did you do?"

"Nothing, Master," Skip cried. "I did nothing."

"Then how did she know to bring me here?" Arturo pulled the Djinn into the middle of the room. "You better explain fast, Mister, or you are finished living. Got me?"

"Yes, yes, I understand, but this is not my fault, she weaseled the information out of me." Skip tried, without success, to pull his arm from the furious demon's grasp.

"Weaseled?" Angela yelled. Even though her mother had actually been the one to get any information at all out of the Djinn, hearing Skip call her a name stung.

Skip pleaded with his eyes for her to let the 'weasel' reference go, so he could live.

"All right, so maybe I weaseled," she said. "But he was easy to break."

Arturo glanced at her. "Really?"

Angela snapped her fingers. "Took no time at all."

"Hmm." Arturo dropped Skip's arm and walked around Angela, looking her over. "You're very small."

"Sorry," she mumbled.

"Not your fault," he replied. "Your mother was short. Is short." He frowned. "Is she here?"

"Yes."

"Where?"

"Under the table."

"Oh." He looked surprised, and then shrugged. "Can you convince her to come out?"

"Why don't you do it?"

"I am not speaking to her."

Angela put her head down so her eyes were at the same level as her mother's. "He wants to see you," she said.

"I heard him," Ellen replied. "Tell him no smiting."

Angela looked up. "Say it, or she won't come out. She's pretty stubborn about things like that."

Arturo shook his head. "She always was. All right. No smiting, until I get to the bottom of this."

Angela bent back down. "No smiting—"

"I heard him," Ellen shot back as she pulled herself out from under the table.

"We shouldn't fight in front of the child," Arturo said, breaking his own vow about not speaking to Ellen.

"I am not a child," Angela said.

"You are, to me," said both of her parents in unison. They glanced at each other, and then looked away.

"You are," mumbled Ellen.

"You always do like to have the last word, don't you?" Arturo asked. "I think that might be the reason why we are in this situation right now."

"You can't blame this on me," Ellen shot back. "If you'd been honest when we first hooked up, I would have been more careful. This is your fault."

"I was in town having a few laughs when I met you. I wasn't looking to settle down," Arturo said. "And I wouldn't talk about being honest, if I were you. *Roberta.*"

Ellen colored. "All right. So I gave you a fake name. We met in Vegas, for heaven's sake."

"I know. But, Roberta Aroma?" He turned to Angela. "That's why it took me so long to find you. No idea what this woman's real name was." He turned back to Ellen. "I don't think I knew you at all."

"Let's talk about honesty for a minute, shall we? Maybe cluing me to the fact you were a *demon*—"

"*Roberta.*"

"Demon!"

"That's enough," Angela cried. "I didn't wish you here so you could fight with Mom. Work it out later, in therapy or something. I brought you here so I could meet you. Maybe get to know you."

"Fair enough." Arturo shivered and pulled the tablecloth tighter around his middle. "Does anyone have something warmer than this? I am freezing."

"I'll get you something," Ellen said, turning to the hallway.

"No weapons, Ellen. The no smiting deal will disappear if you come out of your room with any type of weapon whatsoever," Arturo said.

Ellen stopped and hung her head. "Fine," she said, and disappeared.

Arturo glanced around the room, stopping when he saw Roger curled up in an easy chair in the far corner of the living room. "Who's that?"

"Roger," Angela replied.

"Minion?"

"Kind of."

"Good for you," Arturo said. "Minions can be hard to gather in this blasted democracy-riddled country. Hang on to him. Looks like he can tote a bale or two."

"Thanks," Angela said, glancing at Roger, who gave her two thumbs up. Bale toting, whatever that was, had never been high on her list of things to do, but she liked the idea of a minion.

She turned back to her father, and they stared at each other for a few long moments.

"So, your name is Angela," Arturo said. Angela nodded. He shook his head. "It should have been Lilith."

"Why?"

"Lilith's a good name. Been in my family for years. Eons, actually." He shook his head again. "Angela. Your mother was covering all her bases, wasn't she?"

"What do you mean?" Angela asked.

"Angela— angel. Looked like she was going for the angel vote, if it came to that."

"Angels? Oh yeah, the fourth realm. Right?"

"Right. Like that would work. You've never met a more judgmental bunch. And *they* can smite like there's no tomorrow, if you anger them." He shrugged. "I try to stay out of their way."

Angela had always assumed that she was named after some long lost aunt or something. She glanced at her mother. Had she used the name to protect her?

"You have to tell me what you did with the wishes," Arturo said. "Was bringing me here your first one?"

"No."

"Well, tell me. I'm dying to know what happened." He grinned. "You went for money, right?"

"No," Angela said.

"I told her to wish for that," Roger said from his chair. "She didn't."

"Quiet, Minion!" Angela yelled.

"What did you wish for?" Arturo's grin slipped.

"I tried to make homelessness go away," Angela whispered. "But I did something wrong, even though I crossed my fingers and everything. It didn't work out the way I wanted at all."

"You crossed your fingers?" Skip asked. Arturo turned on him, glaring.

"You've done enough, Djinn. Shut your mouth, now," he barked.

When Skip hid his face in his hands, Arturo turned back to Angela and grinned hugely, looking even less human than he had moments before. He had many more teeth than any self-respecting human. Many more.

"The crossing of fingers impacts a demon's wish." He laughed and patted her on the shoulder, then pulled her into his arms and swung her around in a giddy-making circle. "But you did well. You brought the world to its knees first time out, girl. Fantastic!"

"Thank you," Angela said.

He swung her around again. "Just remember not to cross your fingers for the next one. It will work exactly the way you want."

"Oh." Angela nodded. "Good to know. Now, please put me down. Your tablecloth fell off."

"Oh." Arturo dropped her and covered himself once more. "Where is your mother? It shouldn't take her this long to find me something to wear."

"She's probably still working out a way to smuggle in a weapon," Roger called from the other side of the room.

"Your minion is quite entertaining," Arturo said.

"He tries," Angela replied. "Too hard sometimes, but he does try."

"All you can ask," Arturo said. "Now girl, come here and let me give you a kiss."

Angela took a step back. She wasn't one for displays of affection, even if it was from her brand new father. "What for?"

"For being the daughter I always dreamed you would be," Arturo replied. "For turning this world upside down with one wish."

"Oh." Angela felt her face heat. She was not used to getting compliments— especially from a parent. She decided it was nice.

The Contract

Angela felt Arturo's lips — inhumanly hot — touch her cheek as Ellen came back into the room, a fuzzy purple housecoat draped over her arm.

"What are you doing, Angela?" she gasped, dropping the housecoat and clutching her hands before her in a gesture of supplication. "Please get away from him."

"The girl can make up her own mind about me," Arturo said, and looped his arm over Angela's shoulders. "After all, she *is* my flesh and blood."

Ellen looked like she was going to cry when Angela did not push him away. "As you wish," she whispered. "I can't stop you."

Angela sighed. Even though her mother had lied about Arturo being dead and everything, Angela didn't want her to feel badly. Not because of her. Not again. She looked up at Arturo.

"Since I did so well with the wish, can you do me a favor?" she asked.

Arturo grabbed the housecoat from Ellen's lax fingers, and cinched the sash. "What favor do you want?"

She pretended to think hard, though she knew exactly what she was going to say. Arturo sighed, impatiently. "Well? Out with it, girl."

"Sign a contract giving my mom and Skip a free pass."

"A free pass?" His eyes narrowed. "A *contract*? I said I wouldn't smite them. Isn't my word enough?"

"I think Mom and Skip would feel better if we wrote everything down, nice and legal. And that would make me feel better."

Arturo started at her, his weird gecko eyes moving independently as he scanned her face. He shrugged.

"If it makes you feel better, then I will. Call it a gesture of good will to my newfound daughter."

He turned and glared at Skip. "You're lucky. Your firstborn was on my list."

Angela scooped up one of the pieces of foolscap and turned it over, so she had a clear page on which to write.

"I'll jot it down here," she said, picking up the pen. "Then you sign it. All right?"

"Certainly." Arturo sat across the table from her. "Is your handwriting legible?"

"It's not bad."

"It's terrible," Roger called from his chair.

"Perhaps he should write it, "Arturo said.

"Good idea," Angela replied.

Roger dropped into the chair next to her and wrote down everything she dictated. He handed the completed document to all interested parties once he was finished, so they could see it was clear, concise, and above all else, kept two of them from being killed at Arturo's whim, forever.

"But they have to stay out of my life from now on," Arturo said. "If they don't, all bets are off."

"Do you agree?" Angela asked Skip and her mother. Both nodded, vigorously.

"Add it in, and then Dad can sign." She looked up as Roger scribbled Arturo's addition to the contract, handed the pen and paper to him, and bowed.

"Don't be a goof," Angela said.

"I can't help it," Roger replied. "This is just so whacked. I love it."

"Glad my family is entertaining you." She turned to Arturo. "Are you ready to sign?"

"I am." He picked up the pen and looked at it distastefully. "Don't suppose you have a quill, do you?"

"I don't think we have one of those, Dad. Just use the pen, okay?"

"All right. But it's not the same."

As Arturo scribbled his signature on the line Roger had drawn for him, Angela sidled up to the kitchen counter and picked up a meat fork lying by the coffee maker. Her mother had filed one of the prongs down to a needle sharp point to clear coffee grounds that sometimes clogged the machine. Angela had a different use for it.

She hid the fork in her hand as she walked back to her father. When he finished writing the date beside his name, she poked his thumb with the sharpened prong.

He yelled and leaped up, rage clotting his face. A single drop of dark red blood hit the piece of foolscap just below his signature.

"What in the name of all that is unholy are you doing, girl?" he cried.

"I am making absolutely sure this is airtight," she replied, looking at the drop of blood. "Looks to me like it is."

His look of rage eased. "Yes," he said. "The blood will definitely do it. Smart girl."

She glanced at her mother, who looked as though she had been frozen. "See?" she said. "Dad thinks I'm smart."

"So do I," her mother croaked. She stumbled back a few steps, then slid to the floor beside Skip, and gave him a huge hug. "I really, really do."

"And I," Skip whispered, hugging her back.

"I think she's fucking awesome!" Roger cried.

"Language," Ellen said.

"Sorry," he replied. But he didn't look sorry. He was looking at Angela as though he had fallen deeply in lust.

The Final Wish

Angela folded the contract and tucked it into the front pocket of her shirt. Then she looked at Arturo. "I didn't hurt you too badly, did I?"

"No." Arturo shook his head. "That was impressive. I don't understand why you are wasting your time working at a video store. You should be a lawyer."

"I can't get into school." Angela shook her head. "I screwed up, my last year of high school. I rigged some of the diploma exams. Well, all of them. People weren't impressed."

"What people?"

"Anyone involved in any way with the school system, actually."

"So, you can't get into any good college—"

"*Any* college," Angela said. "Anywhere. Man, I was surprised. I didn't think they talked."

"Too bad." Arturo glanced at Ellen. "See? If you'd sent her to live with me, this never would have happened."

"Why don't you fix it for me?" Angela asked. Her heart started to pound, hard. Her mother hadn't been able to clean up her mess. Maybe her father could. "You're a demon. Just make everybody forget, or something."

"No can do, sorry Kiddo," Arturo said, shaking his head. "Wish I could help you, but those permanent records are air tight."

"What if I came to your realm?" Angela ignored her mother's sudden gasp and grabbed her father's hands. "I could come with you, go to school there… You do have schools there, don't you?"

"Of course we have schools. Don't be impudent." He tousled her hair. "Sorry, but those permanent records are unchangeable. If the schools here won't take you, no way in the world you'd get into ours."

"That's funny, you thinking demon schools have higher moral standards than human," Ellen said. "I thought you said your father paid your way in. Paid big, if I remember the story correctly. What about that?"

"I hadn't applied myself, Ellen. That was all. I didn't do anything that couldn't be undone with the help of a smart minion and a rich father. I bent the rules. She broke them. No coming back from that."

"Well this sucks," Angela said. She felt tears prick her eyes, and scrubbed at them, causing her makeup to smudge disastrously. "A lot."

"But, *you* could fix it," Arturo said.

"How?"

"With your final wish. You do have one more, don't you?" Arturo asked.

"Yes." Angela said. "Yes, I still have one wish."

"Not the wish," Ellen whispered.

"What about the money?" Roger cried.

"Shut up, Roger," Angela said absently, thinking of the possibilities. "I'd have to make sure it worked the way I wanted it to. Everyone needs to forget what I did, so I can go to a good college, get a degree and have a life."

"A life in my realm, if you like," Arturo said. "We'd take you, once you clear up that mess."

"I could have a real life, with you," she said. She tried not to listen to her mother sob.

"Yes," Arturo said, pulling her into his arms. "You could have everything you want. With me."

She leaned toward him, preparing for another kiss, when the look on his face changed from joy to puzzlement. He pulled her closer to a light and roughly tipped her head back so the light shone full into her eyes, making them tear. "Do you have contacts in?" he asked.

"Yes." She struggled. "You're hurting me!"

"Take them out," he said. "I need to see your eyes. Now."

She wrenched herself free and popped out the contacts. "There," she said. "Satisfied?"

Arturo gasped in horror and Ellen put a protective hand on Angela's arm. "Leave her alone," she said. "This is not her fault."

"But look at her." Arturo grimaced as though the sight of Angela caused him physical pain. "How can you stand it?"

"What do you mean?" Angela asked, pulling her arm from her mother's and walking in front of Arturo, trying to catch his eye with hers. He refused to look at her, so she turned to her mother. "What's wrong with my eyes?"

"They're blue," her mother said.

"So?"

"They are considered— unclean by his people."

"Unclean?" Angela whirled, looking at Arturo. "My *eyes* are unclean?"

"Yes." Arturo glanced at her and shuddered. "Don't look at me any longer. I feel sullied."

"Sullied?" Angela snorted. "What are you, a girl?" She turned to her mother. "Is he for real?"

"I'm afraid so." Ellen turned to Arturo. "Tell her what you called our relationship when you realized *my* eyes were blue?"

"Slumming," Arturo replied. "So what? By the time *that*," and he pointed at Skip, "told you all about me, you didn't want to be with me any longer anyhow. Remember?"

"Yes," Ellen whispered. "I remember."

"I was banned for life from that casino for your little tantrum, you know."

"Arturo, I wasn't the one who caused that. You did."

"Maybe, but you were the one who pushed me into it. You know that."

"What happened?" Angela asked.

"Please, just leave this alone," Ellen said.

"No," Angela replied. "Tell me what happened."

"He beat me," Ellen whispered, closing her eyes as if reliving a nightmare. "Right on the floor of the casino. Skip finally stopped him."

"Yes. Helpful, helpful Skip." Arturo turned and glared at the Djinn, who stared, shaking, at the floor. "I made you pay for that one, didn't I Djinn?"

"Why would you do that?" Angela asked Arturo.

He shrugged. "Ask her what she did," he said. "Then you'll understand."

"What did you do, Mom?"

"I called him a name," Ellen said. "All I did was call him a name."

"Yes," Arturo sneered. "And tell her what name you called me. In that casino, in front of all those people."

"I called him— dung man," Ellen whispered.

"What?" Angela asked.

"Dung man," Ellen said. "Skip had told me about his— background. About the Book of Books. According to the myths, humans are made from dust. Djinn, from air. Angels from fire, and Demons…"

"From dung," Angela said. "Well fuck me."

"Language."

"Sorry." Angela shook her head. "But really, Dad. Sticks and stones and all that crap."

Then she thought of the times she had overreacted to a real or imagined slur. Even the Exam Incident that got her kicked out of school had started with Jeremy Rutherford calling her stupid. She'd decided to prove him wrong. Sticks and stones. Just like dear old Dad.

"I'm sorry, Mom," she said. "This is my fault."

Ellen grabbed Angela and hugged her, hard. "No it's not," she said. "I wish I'd told you the truth about him, even though it was easier to pretend he was dead."

Angela momentarily stiffened in her mother's arms, and then relaxed. Her hug was nice, she realized. Almost as nice as her apology.

"I wish I'd told you everything…" Ellen's voice faded, and Angela felt her arms stiffen. She turned and saw Arturo speaking to Skip in low tones. Skip looked terrified.

"What are you doing?" she asked.

"Nothing," Arturo replied, glaring at Skip. "Tell her nothing."

"He wants me to take away your last wish," Skip whispered, shaking with fear. "He says the test is over. He doesn't want you anymore."

"He doesn't want me?" Angela squeaked, outrage driving her voice up to soprano range. "*He* doesn't want *me*?"

"It's nothing personal. I just can't have you showing up in my realm looking like that," Arturo said, keeping his back to Angela. "I would lose such face…"

"Gee, that would be too bad," Angela said. "Losing face can be a real bitch."

"You don't know the half of it," Arturo replied. "Those people are vicious. You'd be treated terribly. I'm doing this for you too— not just for me. You know?"

"Oh yes. I understand completely," Angela said. "Skip, do I still have a wish?"

Skip nodded.

"And it won't screw with the contract he just signed, will it?"

"It shouldn't, Mistress."

"I have good lawyers!" Arturo cried, pulling the purple house-coat around him and standing tall. "I swear, Skip, I will spend the rest of my life looking for a loophole and taking you down if you give her that last wish."

"Then I guess we won't let you contact your lawyers," Angela said. "But first, here's a tidbit your fancy demon schools obviously did not teach you. Genetically, blue eyes are recessive."

"What?"

"In order for me to have blue eyes, there has to be blue eyes somewhere in your bloodline. You weren't the only one in your family to go slumming, Daddy dearest."

She smiled as he screamed in outrage and horror. She really did love the sound of breaking.

"And now," she said, "It's time for you to go."

She held up her hands and closed her eyes. She heard Arturo run toward her, and she heard her mother gasp "Angela," but she didn't move. She concentrated hard on the next words she would speak. And she made certain her fingers were not crossed.

Arturo's hands grabbed at the front of her shirt as she screamed, "I wish Arturo was a full time janitor in Hell, forever and ever, with no way out!"

She felt Arturo's hands disappear and opened her eyes. He was gone. There was nothing left but condensation on the windows and a whiff of sulfur to show he had ever been in the house.

Then the rest of the people — and the Djinn — jumped and screamed and cried and held each other in wild celebration.

Angela let everyone hug her, and even laughed when Ellen and Skip danced around the room clinging to each other as they whirled in happy little circles.

"That was pretty cool, wasn't it?" she said to Roger.

"Yeah. Coolest thing I think I've ever seen."

"So why do I feel so let down?"

Roger patted her arm. "You finally met your father— and he rejected you. On top of that, you found out your mother was right. Either one would be hard to take. You got slammed twice."

"Yeah, I guess." She glanced over at Skip and her mother, who were now doing their own pathetic versions of either the *Electric Slide* or the *Chicken Dance*. "At least they're safe. That's a good thing. Right?"

"It is." Roger shrugged. "A lot of money would have been nice too, though."

"Yeah." Angela laughed. "Looks like we both have to go to work tomorrow."

"That's all right with me. Just as long as you're there." Roger smiled his dreamy half-smile and Angela poked him in the ribs.

"You have that look on your face, again."

"I can't help it. You sent your dickhead dad to Hell. As a janitor. You are evil, but in the best possible way. I think I might actually be in love."

"Shut up."

"I'm not kidding. We should get matching tattoos."

"Shut—" Angela stopped in mid-word, and thought.

"Maybe," she said. "But I get to pick the design."

"You got it, Boss," Roger said, and when he pulled her into his arms, she did not resist. "You got it."

The Box, Again

In the back room of the *Slippery When Wet*, the puzzle box popped out of existence. Gerald would have been in paranoid heaven if he'd seen it happen, but was watching the news on his last remaining television and missed it all.

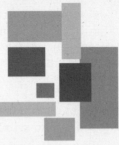

THE FOURTH PIECE OF THE PUZZLE

❖ ❖ ❖

The stairs groaned under his weight, and Albert could tell the house hadn't been disturbed for years. A thick layer of dust blanketed the hardwood floors. Like the rusted water well, this place was lonely and forgotten.

Albert stepped down onto the landing, clutching the banister. He knew it was unnecessary, but did not want to let it go. He felt so empty he was afraid he would blow away, as light as the dust on the steps.

Looking into the living room, he observed the Chronicler gazing into the cold hearth like he was admiring a crackling fire. Another step and the floor squeaked, lifting the older man from his reverie.

"Ah, there you are, my boy. I was imagining a fire in the fireplace. A Christmas tree over in the corner. Candles. Laughter. Wouldn't it be wonderful?"

"I used to live here," Albert said.

"I know."

"I thought you didn't know my story."

"I know the broad strokes but not the fine touches."

Albert walked the last three steps into the living room. The box rested on the mantle. He pushed past the Chronicler and took it into his hands.

"I have to understand," he muttered. Letters formed then coalesced in the bronze. He let the characters spill across edges, watching the motion as if it were a snow globe. It was as if he saw his life laid out in those details. First bike ride. First kiss. First fight. Then he frowned. There, in his early years, he saw a malignant hole, with cancerous strands at the edges, veins of poison spreading across his life.

Albert inspected the rotten strands as though reading the morning news. "These aren't it," he said. "It's this hole." He tried to concentrate, bring the hole into sharp focus, but couldn't. The more he gazed into the emptiness, the more it slid away from him.

"What's in this hole?" Albert asked. He was surprised at how calm he was. In the past, introspection had led to drinking, gambling, ruin.

"Or what's not in the hole," whispered the Chronicler. "Only you can answer that question."

"But I can't see it. Not really." Albert wondered if he could fill the hole with the puzzle box. If he plugged that gaping maw, would he be whole again?

"Who made this box?" Albert asked, and glanced at the Chronicler. He was shocked to discover that much as he could not see into the hole in his life story, the Chronicler now also defied him. He shook his head in frustration. "What is going on here?"

"You are getting to the quick of your tale. That is all."

"And why can't I see you? Really see you?"

"You need to know where to look. But why would you want to chronicle the Chronicler?"

"Because it's important," Albert said. The Chronicler took a small step toward him, and Albert's vision began to clear.

"It may be too late, my boy."

Albert stared at the Chronicler and for the first time thought he recognized him, but Albert wasn't sure if could trust his own memories.

"How long have you been doing this?" Albert asked.

"I do not know." The older man frowned and this time Albert *did* recognize him, or more to the point, recognized his look. He leaned back in surprise, tendrils of fear surrounding him. That look had frightened him every day of his life, growing up in this house.

"Who gave the box to you?" Albert asked the question with suddenly dry and parched lips. He wasn't sure if he wanted to hear the answer, but he listened, intently. Because sometimes it is not what you want, but what you need. Had the Chronicler said that to him only the night before?

"It found me."

"It found you?"

"Just as it found you."

"But... It was sitting forgotten on a back shelf in that warehouse. There wasn't even any documentation for it. Nobody remembered it. I found it." But even as he said the words, he knew he wasn't speaking the truth. He'd felt it, even then. The box *had* found him.

Because he could no longer look at the face of the Chronicler, not without feeling overwhelmed, he stared at the letters coalescing on the glowing box. And finally, the box showed him his story:

Albert stared at the oaken door, a glow emanating from beneath the door. That light called to him, and he considered going into his father's study, though he had been forbidden from ever going into that room.

Albert disregarded that rule and pushed open the door.

His father sat at his desk, a glowing box sitting before him. When his father noticed Albert, he tried to hide the box by pushing it into his lap. "I told you never to come into this room!" his father roared. "Get out! Get out now!"

Albert retreated, slammed the door shut, then leaned against it, sobbing into his hands.

It was the last time he ever saw his father.

The final Piece of the Puzzle will be revealed after "Ghost in the Machine."

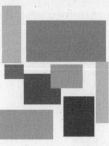

Ghost in the Machine

❖ By Ryan McFadden ❖

She didn't belong in my world.

Maybe it was the shopping bags that gave her away— an art show was generally a destination, not a stop on a day-long expedition. Or maybe it was the way she looked at the illustrations on the wall, her forehead creased with puzzlement as she tried to understand why comic-book art necessitated evening gowns, the occasional tuxedo, and paper plates mounded with appetizers. I had blown my budget on those appetizers so I couldn't afford a tuxedo.

I tried not to be obvious watching her, the guy beside me talking about the last art show in Montreal.

"Excuse me," I finally said, trying to break away from him.

"You know her?" he asked.

"No, not yet."

I ignored the voice in my head yelling *flee, flee, flee*. I didn't approach women, at least not like this. I preferred the 'sit back and hope they somehow notice me' approach. That had never really worked.

I wanted to say something eloquent. The perfect opening line, but when she smiled I had absolutely nothing but knew I couldn't retreat. Failure to act would relegate me to another of the nameless crowd and that wouldn't do.

"That one won the gold medal from the Society of Illustrators," I said, realizing my error immediately.

"Sounds like a big deal. Are you the artist?"

"Ah, no. You see those three, tucked away in the corner from the high traffic areas? Those are mine."

"They look so lonely."

"They probably are. My name's Sam."

"Lucy." We shook hands and I hoped she didn't notice my nervousness. "I'd like to take a look, Sam," she said.

We wandered to the back. I should've been introducing the background of my works but instead I let her scrutinize them in silence. She took her time, not being pressured by my presence to render a quick verdict.

"They're nice."

Nice. The polite way of saying that they looked like pretty much every comic book out there but without the accompanying sticker shock. Other than the illustrators and the fans, who could detect the subtle differences, these works did look pretty much the same.

"Thanks." I should've been trying to push the sale but I knew she wasn't a buyer. Curiosity had drawn her here. Besides, I didn't want a sympathy buy. In the past I hadn't been too proud for that, but I didn't want that from Lucy. Instead, I asked, "What are you doing right now?"

"Are you asking me out?"

"That sounds really official. How about we grab a coffee?"

"I don't drink coffee."

"Neither do I."

She smiled. "Can you leave in the middle of the show?"

"I think my three prints will manage without me. What do you say?"

I expected her to say no. Hell, I'd say no if some geek asked me out in the middle of an art show. Luckily, I was wearing my finest (and only) suit so I looked like a presentable human being.

"Sure," she said.

Two hot chocolates led to a peck on the cheek and her phone number. I called her a day later which led to another date. And another. I fell hard and fast. Then, three months in she confessed that she was in a long-term relationship with someone else. I should've picked up on it earlier, but I wondered if I hadn't wanted to know.

I should've ended it then.

I didn't.

We sat on the floor around her coffee table and ate fondue and drank too much red wine. I leaned over and kissed her, tasting the Shiraz on her tongue. The kiss lingered until she pushed me away with her palms. "I have to pee," she said.

"You're such a romantic."

"That's what you get for trying to get me drunk."

"I don't have to get you drunk to get into your pants."

"I'll meet you down there." She pointed to her bedroom, then climbed out from beneath me and bounded down the hallway into the bathroom.

I waited in her bedroom. The room smelled like her— the scent of lotions, soaps, hair sprays. She kept her room neat but not obsessively so: some dirty clothes on the floor and the bed sheets rumpled. I walked around, intrigued.

Despite our three-month relationship, we rarely ended here. In fact, when I thought about it, I'd only been in her house a handful of times. I inspected the pictures on the walls. I knew her family only through these pictures; we hadn't met. I didn't see any pictures of the other man and I wondered if she hid them for my benefit or if he and Lucy were simply so detached that the only thing that held them together was the concept of being in a relationship.

I read the titles of the books on the shelf. I didn't know everything about Lucy. Not yet, but half the amazement of being with her was discovering who she was.

A metal box sat on her night table.

The box looked old, the metal tarnished from the acidic touch of fingerprints and overhandling. I judged it empty from the weight.

I tried to twist it, turn it, but couldn't open it. I couldn't even get the first step.

"Having fun?" she asked, closing the bedroom door behind her.

"What is it?" I tried prying it apart.

"It's a box."

"I can see that. What's it for?"

"It's a puzzle box. It takes thirty-seven steps to open."

"Show me." I tried handing it to her but she wouldn't take it.

"And reveal all my secrets?"

"What's inside?"

"Stuff." She fell into the bed.

"What kind of stuff?"

"The usual— my heart, my soul, my dreams."

I shook it next to my ear. "Is your heart empty?"

"That's what I've been told."

"No, really, what's inside ?"

"I have no idea. I can't open it."

"Then why do you have it?"

"Because it's nice to look at and I like pretty things," Lucy said. "That's why I keep you around."

"Trying to seduce me?"

"For heaven's sake— would you get in here and make love to me? You have obligations you know."

"How could I forget?"

She was ready for me, her body molding to mine and I felt the arousing sensation of her breasts against my chest as her legs wrapped around mine.

"Gotcha," she said.

"I'm not going anywhere."

"Shut up and kiss me."

"Sorry, that doesn't usually happen," I joked.

"Wow. I hope that happens all the time," Lucy said, her naked body entwined with mine. The covers lay crumpled on the floor, our bodies covered in a light sheen from our exertion.

My hand traced delicate patterns on her back and we settled into a comfortable silence. Her breathing became steady as she drifted toward sleep. I wasn't ready to relent so easily, however, and my gaze settled on the box on the nightstand.

"So you've never been able to open it?"

"Open what?" she murmured.

"That box."

"Aren't you supposed to be sleepy after sex?" Her eyes closed and her voice softened.

"Not always. I can finally think clearly with all the static gone."

"You're a strange creature. Do you act this way with all your girlfriends?"

"Ah, my other girlfriends. I have so many. Why don't you ask your boyfriend about it?"

I sensed the tension, perhaps from her silence or maybe I sub-consciously picked up on a barely noticeable shift of her body— a roll of her shoulders or maybe her breath hitching slightly.

"You haven't talked to him?" I asked.

"I promised I will."

"You've been promising for three months. Is there something going on here?"

"Of course not, Sam. I love you. But it's complicated."

"No, it's not."

She sighed and pulled away, retrenching on the other side of the bed.

"It *is* complicated. You don't know Alan. He's got a temper."

"You're scared of him?"

"Not in that way. It's going to be messy. I've got to make sure everything's in order. You don't walk away from someone you've been with for five years."

"Sure you do. Alan — you're out. Sam — you're in."

"You're already in, Sam. You know that."

"Do I?"

"I love you, Sam. No one else but you." She held my gaze, guiding my head with her hand on my cheek. "Only you. Do you believe me?"

"Of course." The tension in my gut signaled that I might've been lying.

She kissed me, hard. "Good, now leave me alone." She fell back into the bed. "Don't guys go and play video games or something? This is your perfect opportunity. All my girlfriends complain about their husbands spending too much time in front of the TV playing games."

"I want to spend time with you."

"I know, that's the problem." She tossed the pillow and I ducked.

"Besides, I don't play video games."

"You're so sensitive. Now get the hell out."

"Fine, I'll amuse myself."

Pulling on my boxers and T-shirt, I watched her falling asleep and wondered if maybe I should climb back into bed.

"I can feel you staring," she said, eyes closed.

"I'm just admiring, that's all."

"Hmm." She smiled and my emotions grew so large I thought they'd overwhelm me.

I had been married once. A foolish thing when I was far too young and far too stupid. I had fallen more for the concept of being in love rather than for her, mesmerized by the intimacy and the closeness but when the inevitable friction began, we didn't have a foundation to get us through the rough patches. Sometimes, I had wondered if I was incapable of anything more than infatuation. Lucy proved I did.

I picked up the puzzle box and admired the design. Though old, the craftsmanship was excellent. As I pried, a section of the box disengaged and twisted around itself like a Rubik's cube.

"Ah," I muttered. Except that quick victory was only a decoy and I didn't get much further, my frustration growing and I wondered if perhaps video games wouldn't have been a better choice than playing with a stupid box.

"Who gave you this?" I asked.

"You're going to talk all night, are you?"

"Until I open this damn thing."

"Maybe you should get a hammer. It might be—" Her voice caught. I looked over, Lucy having retreated further up the bed, the sheet pulled protectively over her breasts and her gaze fixed on the now open door.

An intruder stood in the doorway, his dark hair disheveled and wet, clothes soiled and tattered, and face unshaven. Dried blood caked his cheek and neck from where it looked like his ear had exploded. His nose was alarmingly crooked.

He held a shotgun, finger on the trigger, the barrel dull and pitted.

Alan. The other man. I had seen him in pictures but never looking so wild. In the pictures, he had been clean cut, together. The kind of guy who was probably a jock back in high school and hadn't let himself go. Nothing like the man standing in her bedroom doorway.

We stood that way for several long breaths. I needed to say something. God, I needed to say something so badly, as if the right words would shatter this dream and the man and his shotgun would pop like a bubble and disappear.

I opened my mouth but said nothing.

"Alan?" she finally whispered.

The shotgun blasted and Lucy jerked, her chest erupting red, the sheet shredded. She fell back, her head bouncing off the wall with a hollow thud.

Why wasn't I doing anything? She tried to inhale but her damaged lungs wouldn't allow it. Her eyes fluttered.

The room fell into a suspended animation. I couldn't breathe. I wanted to scream her name, run to her, save her. I wanted to do *something*.

Smoke curled from the barrel of the shotgun. Alan frowned, mouthed something to himself. He stared at the gun as if not quite understanding that he had pulled the trigger.

"Lucy," I gasped.

Alan blinked, wakening from his stupor. He turned the shotgun on me and my insides felt like water. I needed to do something. Some semblance of a final defense. But I couldn't move. I met Alan's gaze— my last pitiful resistance. I saw bewilderment, not a madman.

"It wasn't supposed to be like this," Alan said. I wondered if I'd hear the shotgun before it tore me apart, or whether everything would just go black. But he didn't shoot me. Alan turned the shotgun on himself, his lips sizzling over the heat of the barrel, then he pulled the trigger, the shot liquefying the back of his skull and splattering it onto the ceiling. He crumpled and the shotgun clattered to the floor, a fine red mist fogging the air where he had been standing.

I tasted the blood in the air. Looked from Alan's body, over to Lucy.

Lucy.

A mental circuit breaker blew, disconnecting my emotions from my consciousness. I knew I was screaming but it registered as if watching a TV with the sound turned down.

I climbed onto the bed, and I rocked her back and forth, her blood glue-like against my hands and face.

In the five days it took the medical examiner to perform the autopsy and stitch Lucy back together, I was a passenger in my own body as if my brain had dosed me with anesthetic. I relied on instinct to get me through. On the day of her funeral, that instinct got me showered, shaved, and dressed in the same suit I had been wearing that day in the art gallery.

I hadn't been asked to be a pall bearer because Lucy's family didn't know me. When I approached Lucy's mother, she stared at me with puffy eyes, not understanding.

"I'm Sam," I said. "Lucy and I..." My throat constricted, preventing me from saying the final words. *Loved each other.* Couldn't say them because they were past tense. Lucy's mom's face wrinkled as she battled back an onset of her own grief, then composed herself.

"She never mentioned you," she said. Something else swirled in her expression— accusation.

I wanted to tell her about us. I wanted to tell her that if she could've seen us that night on the Beaches, she would've understood. How we had watched the kids flying kites, tails snapping on the wind whipping in from Lake Ontario. I finally convinced a kid to sell me his kite— so I could impress Lucy. Instead, the thing tangled in the air and broke itself on the rocks. The kids mocked me and so did Lucy. We held hands and walked. We hadn't wanted that night to end. So many nights were like that.

But I couldn't tell her anything, because it felt like a hot coal was stuck in my chest.

The minister spoke about how much Lucy loved her family: her mother, her sisters, her friends. He never mentioned me.

They put Lucy in the ground. Someone handed me a flower and I tossed it onto the coffin. It slid off the polished mahogany. *It contains my heart and my soul.*

Afterward, we ate sandwiches in the parlor. I held a plate while my sister Cami stood beside me, encouraging me to eat. Eat? I hadn't eaten since Lucy had died.

Cami put her hand on my neck.

"You know I'm here when you want to talk," she said.

I wanted to let her help me with the awful burden. But I wasn't ready. Didn't have the faintest idea how to process the horror. Occasionally, my mind reconnected my emotional centers like a mechanic running a set of diagnostics. The resulting flood of raw emotions would hit my nervous system like battery acid until my brain, thankfully, cut the connection.

Lucy's family cast accusing glances at me and I heard the threads of conversation.

"The other man."

They whispered it with accusations sharp as knives, like I had been the one with the shotgun. They blamed me for not stopping it. Because I should have, shouldn't I? I should have saved the day or at least died trying.

Cami stayed with me for three more days before she flew back home. My friends took over, trying to ensure that I wasn't alone. Except I wanted to be alone. I hated how their looks of sympathy gradually turned to pity. Eventually, I knew that pity would become scorn. They didn't believe that after only three months I had loved her. I started locking the door to prevent them from getting in, then disconnecting the phone to stop the telephone calls. They called the police because they assumed I was suicidal.

Am I suicidal? I looked at the bottle in my hands. I had been drinking for days. When the merciful numbness had worn off, grief, anger, and loneliness mixed into a toxic stew.

I was trapped in a box with the sides and top nailed tight. I couldn't get away from that damned scene. Over and over, Lucy's chest erupted with blood while I stood and did nothing. Sometimes, my mind played tricks on me and allowed me to save her. The more I drank, the more heroic I became. But when the booze ended, reality drowned me.

I reached for the whiskey bottle and knocked it to the floor. I cursed and tried to retrieve it before too much spilled.

A brick-red snake uncoiled from the bottle and struck me three times. *Snick, snick, snick.* It coiled around the bottle, those glittering eyes fixed on mine, a black diamond-pattern overlaying its deep-red scales.

I was paralyzed, not from venom but from a potent blend of booze and impossibility— a viper from the whiskey bottle had bitten me three times.

Drip, drip, drip.

The blood from my hand brought me back.

I cursed and scrambled up until I was sitting on the back of the couch, my vision locked on the viper. It grew bored of me and slowly slithered back into the bottle.

I heard blood rushing in my ears, my vision swirling like someone had shaken a snow globe.

A fucking snake bit me.

Impossible. I stared at that whiskey bottle, the spilled booze leaking through nail holes in the floor while I bled on myself. My fist wouldn't loosen. I breathed deeply, tried to calm myself and then willed my hand to open.

As my pulse raced so did the bleeding. This wasn't a snake bite. *Dear God.* I couldn't tell how deep the cut was because of the blood.

I hoped I didn't need stitches. Christ, I was in no condition to be stuck in an emergency room for four hours. The blood bubbled through my fingers.

Then I saw the knife. For the first time in weeks, there was something other than my grief. Fear. Fear because I couldn't trust myself. Fear because I wasn't in control. It was a steak knife from my counter block, white handle smudged with bloody fingerprints undoubtedly belonging to me. I had done this, cut myself and imagined that a snake had struck to cover my own tracks. I fell back into the couch.

"Look what you've done to yourself," Lucy said.

"Lucy?"

You can't trust yourself, I answered. But that *was* her voice, and it had come from the bedroom. When I stood, my head swam from the shock and booze.

"I'm coming," I whispered. I wrapped a cloth around my hand and then followed the voice into the bedroom.

It wasn't my room.

It was Lucy's. The bedding had been stripped, the mattress stained with blood that had darkened to the color of chocolate. The headboard was spotted with buckshot around a silhouette of Lucy. Sections of the carpet had been removed and the ceiling was spotted with the remains of Alan's liquefied brain and bits of skull.

Lucy had died right there on the bed.

The booze gurgled in my gut and I knew I was going to puke.

I barely made it to the toilet before vomiting a burning mix of alcohol and bile. I heaved until there was nothing left, my eyes stinging with tears. I flushed the toilet and rested my forehead on the cool porcelain. I cried and couldn't stop.

"I miss you so much," I said. I wanted to stay huddled against that bowl like it was my lifeline, but I knew I couldn't because I was crying in Lucy's bathroom. I had to pull it together and fight my way through this maze.

I drew several deep breaths, then rose to my feet and returned to the bedroom. How had I ended up here? The police had left their markings— tripods, equipment cases, and plastic sheeting. I was intruding in their investigation, but what was there left to investigate?

'*Why does no one know you?*' they had asked me. I tried telling them that we loved each other but like her family, they didn't believe me. *Did you touch the shotgun? Did you kill Lucy? How did you know Alan?* They had confiscated my computer and my cell phone. They would see our love letters and our sex emails but I didn't feel exposed or embarrassed because finally someone would believe me. Finally. I didn't even get a lawyer as I sat through the questions from their psychologists and investigators. *We'll be in touch.* Except they never were. They never explained why Alan had ended up in that room with a shotgun, turned it on her, then took his own life.

No one would give me answers.

This room was all that was left of Lucy. The pictures, the stained floor, her toiletries, the silver-plated hair brush. As I sat on the bed far from the chocolate-colored stains, I contemplated the impossibility of my situation. How had I gotten into Lucy's house? Hell, how had I even left my apartment? I was wearing my jacket but didn't have my wallet. I must've walked over and used her hidden key to get inside.

You've fucking lost it, Sam.

Was this how it was going to end, with my sanity in tatters while I slowly killed myself?

The puzzle box sat on the night table where I had left it, except I could clearly see a panel had been displaced. *Step one.* Had I done that the night Lucy died? No, it was a different panel. Someone else must've been playing with it. Who would do that at a crime scene?

"What's inside?"

"Only my heart, my soul, my dreams."

I picked it up and my touch displaced another panel. *Step two.* Despite myself, I began playing with the box and for the first time in weeks, I felt no pain, only a resolve to solve the riddle. A stupid kid's toy gave me a needed diversion and the lack of hurt was sweet.

I pried, twisted, and poked at the box. *Click.* A piece of metal slid to the right allowing the box to twist upon itself.

Movement out of the corner of my eye.

I looked, but saw nothing. *More mind tricks?* The skin on my arms tightened with goose bumps. *Keep yourself together, Sam.* I was alone and wasn't about to let my mind trick me again.

"Sam," Lucy whispered in my ear. *No, don't believe it,* I answered myself.

Sweat dripped into my eyes and my head pulsed as my drunkenness relented to a raging hang-over.

Click.

The box opened, two panels opening like metallic gates. I gazed inside.

It was as if God flicked a switch on my reality.

I sat on a stone floor, my back against a fungus-covered wall, water dripping into foul pools while a naked incandescent bulb dangled from the ceiling. No bed, no chairs, just a bucket by the open door. I realized I was in a windowless prison cell. But the door was open so was I not a prisoner?

Vertigo crashed upon me and I slid sideways, hyperventilating. I squeezed my eyes shut. *Don't trust yourself.* And yet, what could I trust if I couldn't trust my senses? I gasped for breath, waiting for the dizziness to pass.

When I opened my eyes, the lights in the hallway flickered and popped. I didn't call out because I wasn't sure if I really wanted anyone to know I was there.

Wherever there was.

The slick fieldstone walls dripped with moisture, jagged white marks engraved in the surface. They weren't in a recognizable language but the symbols looked familiar like something I might've seen in a book once.

I realized I was missing the puzzle box and a spike of panic jolted me.

I discovered the box in a corner but couldn't remember seeing it moments earlier. Had the box been there all along, or just when I had thought about it? It had brought me here, hadn't it? I used the wall to help me stand, dizziness threatening to spill me to the filthy floor. I inhaled deeply and tried to still the spinning world. Gradually, the vertigo subsided. I felt deep grooves in the wall through my palm.

My fingers traced patterns over the symbols. Alien in nature, yet somehow familiar. The work was extensive, thousands of symbols etched into the rock, the entire cell an encrypted tale. Why did they seem so familiar?

I heard the sound of hard boots on stone marching down the hall toward me. I pressed myself up against the wall by the door hoping that whoever was coming would pass by though I had a terrible feeling that those boots were coming for me. I tried to shrink further, wishing I could've melted into the stone. As I shifted, I stepped on something the size of a small rock.

A ring. I recognized that ring and my vision flared hot and white.

I retrieved it, momentarily forgetting about the approaching boots because that ring belonged to Lucy. A delicate gold band with an emerald setting.

Had Lucy been here?

Impossible— she's gone.

I heard talking outside my door, the words mostly muffled though I caught stilted fragments, so emotionless that it sounded robotic. *Not human.* I tucked the ring into my pocket so I could figure out its mysteries later.

The box. My only way out. I tried opening it but the pieces had reconfigured themselves back to the original form. Frantically, I tried to recall how I had solved it earlier. Slide, twist, depress. I pulled at it, too hard, and I heard a crack. *There's no time.*

A jailor stooped through the door, head brushing the ceiling as it straightened. Its white skin gleamed like fish scales, its body lanky, arms too long. When it turned to face me, I thought my legs would fail.

Its eyes had been scooped away, replaced with jutting copper wires that looked like sea urchins, electricity arcing and sparking from the tines. A tight iron grill was bolted over its mouth and its nose was a mess of ruined flesh.

"Where is Alan?" the metallic voice asked. Three more of the abominations entered, each carrying a blunderbuss— a long rifle-like weapon with a flared nozzle. They circled the cell as if someone could be hiding in the hairline cracks of the fieldstone joints.

"Alan was here?" I asked in a whisper.

"How did you gain entry?"

"He has escaped," one of the nightmares said to another. Then they communicated with a series of clicks and whirs that must've been created by mechanical means.

I had no chance to solve the box. Even if I had had time, fear froze my hands like ice. I dropped the box with a metallic clatter and their electronic chatter stopped.

I only had one chance.

I stomped on the box. It held. The first jailor cocked the hammer and leveled his blunderbuss at me. I struck the box again and it cracked.

"Stop," the electronic voice commanded.

A stomped a third time and the box shattered, metal pieces scattering like building blocks. Springs, cams, and gears. *Too late.* As I looked up, the blunderbuss fired, the blast an echo to the broken box. I flung my arms up, muscles clenched defensively.

I stood in Lucy's room and the prison and the inhuman jailors faded like a sunspot.

A second wave of vertigo broke upon me, and I thought I'd fall forever. The ground hit me too soon, my teeth knocking together and I lay stunned, watching the ceiling light spin as if it were fastened to a rotary blade. Eventually, that blade slowed and stopped.

I didn't move. I worried that if I did my sanity would unravel. Because that was the only explanation, wasn't it? I was teetering on the edge of an abyss and if I took one more step, I'd fall into a permanent dementia.

I didn't want to close my eyes, fearful of what I'd find in the dark. Had the drinking and sleep deprivation finally caught up to me?

Lucy's ring, the one I had found on the floor, was pressed into my palm.

Impossible.

No, not impossible. I was in Lucy's room. I must've retrieved it from her jewelry box, my brain concocting a nightmarish tale. Except why couldn't I bring myself to believe that? Maybe because I didn't want to accept the conclusion: that I was insane. But was that any better than the alternative: that I had been trapped in a jail guarded by nightmares?

I sat up, the broken pieces of the box scattered around me.

I had to get out of here. Get back to my apartment so I could try to think. *Think!* Put away the booze, try to reason through this problem.

I put the broken pieces of the box into my coat pocket and stumbled through the house. Outside, the crisp, frigid air burned my lungs, an invigorating sensation as I focused on the tingle in my cheeks and the numbness in my nose. I walked quickly, my first exercise in weeks. Hell, I couldn't even remember venturing from my apartment since Lucy's funeral. The elation lasted three blocks until the cold returned me to reality. I shivered, teeth chattering, calculating that I had easily another hour on foot. Luckily, I had enough coins in my pockets for bus fare and I took the twenty-four-hour bus home.

I took a seat near the front, sharing the ride with two other passengers near the back who were more concerned with making out then paying attention to me. I became hypnotized while I watched the street lights flare by the window.

Am I losing my mind? Is it already gone?

I pulled the ring from my pocket. Lucy's ring. Why did I have it? Perhaps my emotions played tricks on me, creating complex stories about how Alan and Lucy were somehow trapped in that alien world and that the box could take me there.

Except even if that were true, I had broken the box.

I staggered from the bus stop to my apartment. The door was open, Cami sitting on the couch in her coat, her luggage dropped by my bedroom. Seeing her sitting on the edge of a cushion was as surreal as anything I had encountered all night.

"Cami?"

"Your friends called me. They were worried. I was worried." She hugged me and it felt good. I didn't want her to let go. All I had to do was ask and Cami would've held me for hours. But I didn't ask.

"Oh, my god, Sam, your hand." The blood dripped down my fingers. "What happened?"

"I don't... remember." I was the child hauled before the principal.

"You don't remember?"

"I was drunk," I lied.

"Does it need stitches?" she asked. She tenderly took my hand and unwrapped the cloth.

"I don't think so." I hoped it didn't. I needed space to process and a room full of sick people wasn't the place to do it.

Cami sighed and I actually felt sorry for her. Sorry that she had come all this way to look after me because I had become a burden no one else could handle. I hadn't asked her to come but knew that she would. I wondered briefly if that was what had happened— that I had needed myself to hit rock bottom so Cami would save me. I discarded these thoughts. This wasn't a plea for help.

"I wish I could make it better," Cami said. "But I'm here as long as you need me."

Tears ran down my cheeks. I hadn't even realized I had been crying. "You can't stay here forever."

"You'll live through this," she said.

"Sometimes I feel like I don't want to."

"I remember." She was talking about the pain of losing our parents. Our mother had died of breast cancer when I was ten. The cancer was so aggressive it killed her in two weeks. Five months later our father got pancreatic cancer and died within the year. Just like that, we were orphans. The grief got so big it felt like it would swallow me whole. "You need to get some sleep, Sam. You're coming apart at the seams."

I tried convincing her to take my bed but she insisted that I take it. I think she wanted the couch because then she could make sure I didn't leave the apartment.

I fell into my bed.

I load the shotgun. Two shells. Click, click. The snap of the barrel shutting. I walk up the front steps of Lucy's bungalow. The front door is open so I slip inside past the screen. I hear murmured voices from the bedroom and my stomach twists. Am I too late? I can't be too late. I can't be. Not after all I've done.

I pad down the hall, open the door.

Lucy is in the bed. My brain shuts off at seeing her. I feel only one thing. Rage. Pure, hot, white.

I level the shotgun and she says my name.

I pull the trigger.

The sound of the shotgun wakened me, the echo dying in the ether. I was alone. It was dark and I saw the alarm clock numbers flashing as if from a power outage.

There would be no real sleep tonight, just like all the nights since Lucy had died.

I took the puzzle pieces out of my jacket pocket and laid them on my bed. It looked more like a jigsaw puzzle now.

The intricacies of the mechanics astounded me. Springs, cams, and hinges. So many parts that worked as one unit. I tried reassembling them but the task seemed impossible and I surrendered after an hour.

I pushed the parts away and sat spinning through the possibilities of yesterday. Even with time, nothing seemed plausible. Alan couldn't be alive. And yet...

I picked an outfit from my closet but it didn't fit. I had lost so much weight over the past weeks that all my clothes hung from me. Before I left my room, I piled the pieces of the box into my top drawer.

When was the last time I ate?

I tripped on Cami's shoes, bumped a lamp off a table but managed to catch it before it hit the floor. Cami popped up amazingly fast. I told her to go back to sleep. She resisted initially but must've been satisfied when I told her I was only making myself some breakfast. I defrosted a bagel, swiped it with some suspect cream cheese, and washed it down with orange juice. One of my typical breakfasts really.

I couldn't get the images of that prison out of my head. They kept swirling. I'd close my eyes and they were there. I needed a release before my head exploded.

When I slipped into my winter jacket, Cami was instantly alert.

"Where are you going?"

"To my studio."

"Sam?"

"Honestly. This is a good thing, Cami. I've been in a bad place..." I shook my head. "For far too long. I'm okay. Really. I'm glad you're here, Cami. But right now, I need some time. Let me do my thinking and clear my head."

She smiled. "I'm not trying to be Mom."

I took her hand in mine. "I know how you must feel. But this is my journey and I have to take it alone. You being here has already helped more than you could know. I need to go to my studio and try to get some of this junk out of my head."

"I'll come with you."

"You can't live my life for me. I know you're worried but do you trust me?" Her hesitation was answer enough. "Cami, have you ever not trusted me? Please, believe that this is what I need to do. This is what I *have* to do."

She exhaled and nodded. "Take your cell phone. At least give me some say in all of this."

"Fair enough. Now go back to bed. You look like hell."

"Thanks," she said.

"Just being honest."

I took a cab the ten city blocks to my studio. The metal door slid open on a rickety wheel-and-track system. The place was cold and still, in suspension since Lucy had died. I flicked on the lights, turned up the thermostat, and removed my coat even though it would take at least an hour for the cast-iron radiators to move the temperature upward.

Prints in black frames hung on the walls: Toronto Life, Maclean's Magazine, and Captain Cheetah — a character I created for a UK supermarket chain. On the opposite wall hung my movie prints — mostly straight-to-video titles. And then some of my prints that I sold at conventions across the country. Comic book mash-ups featuring the Green Goblin battling Batman in a black-and-white fight to the death. In another, the Hulk warred with the Terminator.

I retrieved a sheet of nineteen by twenty-four Bristol paper and placed it on the blue glass of my drafting table. I unscrewed the Black Magic Ink bottle and chose a Hunt Crow Quill nib pen from the under-mount sliding tray. I let the ink guide me. Normally, I began with pencils but this wasn't a typical illustration. This one was for me alone— as if transcribing it would somehow give that place some form of reality.

Seemingly disconnected lines and shapes merged into discernible patterns. My pen worked, my fingers and palm soon stained with ink. I became careless, smudging lines and blurring segments as a picture formed amongst the disconnected lines. I let the image flow through me so I was as much a passenger in the creation as any observer would be. An image formed. Lines coalesced into definable shapes. Curves turned those shapes into faces and figures.

I recognized segments and as the picture became clearer, an icy drip of water trickled down my back.

I drew eyes, a nose, a face. My ink strokes became more frenzied. The clarity dropped but my pen attacked the paper with spastic strokes.

I was drawing a picture of me. I wasn't alone. The other person came into focus.

Alan. The two of us entangled together. A rocky background, my hand on his face, trying to push him into the stone while his hands encircled my throat in a death grip.

Alan is dead.

I saw him die. I saw the back of his skull liquefy. And yet, why did I have doubts? Wasn't my experience last night the culmination of grief, booze, and self deprivation? I didn't believe it. I wondered if I wanted to believe that Alan was alive because then Lucy could be alive too.

I crumpled the paper and tossed it. I wasn't crazy. Lucy was alive, and the puzzle box was the key.

I retrieved a clean sheet. Began drawing again, this time a technical drawing with straight lines. Springs. Cams. I was drawing the box, the pieces laid out like schematics, both disassembled and assembled. Multiple angles and cutaways. I inked it in far more detail than my knowledge should've allowed. When I finished, I knew. I knew how to reassemble the box.

I took a cab back to my apartment. Cami yelped when I threw open the door.

"Jesus Christ, you scared me," she complained.

"Sorry." Then I looked around. "Oh, wow."

Cami had cleaned the place. Something I hadn't done in weeks. Vacuumed, tidied. Hell, she had even done the dishes. I smelt frying food and my mouth watered. But I didn't have time.

"I have to lay down, Cami."

She didn't ask me if I was all right, probably because she knew I wasn't. Instead, she asked if she could bring me anything and I mumbled something about an upset stomach and disappeared into my room.

I retrieved the pieces of the puzzle box from my drawer, then scattered them around me. I understood the configuration, how the pieces interrelated, how each part became a foundation for three others. My hands worked independently of my mind, twisting and turning the myriad pieces.

The final part clicked into place. I frowned as what I held in my hands looked slightly different than what I recalled. Was something backwards or upside down? The longer I tried to remember what it had looked like before I had smashed it, the more it flitted away.

Only one way to find out.

Nine moves later and the box opened.

God flicked a switch.

I stood in a deep forest, a thick canopy of branches concealing the sky, the trees old and twisted, crowding each other for a rare slice of sunlight.

The gnarled roots wound together like serpents as if each tree somehow plugged into a larger network. Creamy-white mushrooms, the biggest I had ever seen, were fastened parasitically to the tree trunks. Colonies of lichens and molds undulated in the breeze like sea anemones.

The forest was dense and oppressive, the air thick with an amalgam of spores and humidity. I couldn't see a path, only limitless trees that were all broken and twisted upon themselves. *The box.* What if I had messed up? What if I had put the box together incorrectly? I didn't even have it now and without it, how would I get back? I searched frantically, hoping that maybe I had dropped it upon arriving and it had bounced away on a tree root. I found no sign of it.

Trapped.

Trapped where? A dream world? Alternate world? Did it even matter? I closed my eyes and tried swallowing the surging panic. I came here to find Lucy and that was what I would do, with or without the box. My quest had not changed.

I took a step and sank ankle deep in moss and brackish water. I retreated up onto a tree root, careful not to touch the undulating fungi fastened to the tree base.

I hadn't even begun and already I was lost. No path. No guides.

I used my apartment keys to mark the trees and leave myself a trail, though retracing my steps to this spot didn't seem helpful but at least it would give me a starting point.

I picked a direction. I slipped from the network of roots and sank to my knee in the sucking quagmire. When I withdrew my leg, I was shoeless.

"Son of a bitch." The oppressive forest swallowed the echo. I reached into the muck and recovered my moss-and-sludge filled shoe. I emptied it as best I could before slipping it back on.

My shoe gurgled with every step. I stepped carefully, fearful that if I fell off the roots I would disappear forever into the morass. The minutes passed into hours. My feet ached and my calves burned. I gasped for breath, the air so thick it was like breathing through a hot, soaked cloth.

I slogged through the dead wood, wet shoes slipping against the gnarled roots. Endless trees. I etched so many hardened trunks that I ground away my keys.

My thirst began as a tickle but expanded into a maddening desire so great that I knelt beside a dark-green pool of brackish water. I used my good hand to cup water and lifted it to drink but the water teemed with life. Tadpoles, squirming nymphs, larvae. I wasn't that thirsty. *When will I be that thirsty?*

Beneath my thirst something else bubbled: despair. I was trapped, certain I could not return home. Lost in my own permanent hell. Destined to walk these woods forever. Since Lucy's murder, everywhere felt like Hell to me. Was this endless forest any different?

When she had walked into the art show that day, I had been divorced three years. I had married my high school sweetheart. Married her far too young and the dissolution was a slow and tedious process. By the end, we said our goodbyes and simply parted.

Then, when Lucy came into my life, I was able to experience falling hard for someone. The wonder of her becoming a part of me, seemingly more important than breathing. And right in the middle of that glory, she was murdered.

I rested in the crotch of a tree, my forehead pressed against the trunk.

When I opened my eyes, a triangular head floated a foot from my face. I startled, nearly falling from my spot as two unblinking serpent eyes stared into mine. The snake stretched down from the upper boughs. A red reticulated pattern covered its golden body— a strangely beautiful sight after hours of muted earth and ashen trunks.

"These woods are not safe and the night approaches," the python said with a sibilant lisp. I stared dumbstruck at the reptile for some time, deciding that it was both real and speaking to me. *Now I'm talking to snakes— and they're answering back.*

"I'm lost," I whispered.

"What other reason would there be for you to be here? What brought you to these woods?" The serpent's tongue tasted the air with several quick flicks.

"I'm looking for someone."

"Yes, we are always looking. But why come here? This is the last place most people look."

I ran my hand through my sweat-soaked hair. "Where exactly am I?"

"You do not know?" The head drifted closer.

"I told you, I'm lost," I said, wishing I wasn't pinned against the tree.

"Of course, of course."

"And I'm thirsty."

"It is fortunate you did not drink the brackish water. The parasites grow at an alarming rate— they would've devoured you quickly. I know of a pool. Crisp and clean and free of the parasites. It is where I drink. I can take you there."

"Why are you helping me?"

"You are that untrusting of help in a strange land?"

"Of talking snakes? Yes."

"A wise decision, probably. However, if I would've wished you harm, I could've dropped upon you from above, constricted you, squeezing until your heart exploded. Then I would've devoured you whole."

"That doesn't put me at ease."

"I am offering you help. These woods are without end. I guide the lost and the misplaced to the fresh water so they may slake their thirst."

"Others have passed through here?"

"You are not the first."

"I'm looking for someone," I blurted. "Her name is Lucy."

"I do not think she has been here."

"How do you know?"

"The path is long to the pool and night will be coming soon. You do not want to remain lost when it is dark. Evil daemons walk these woods at night." The snake poured from the tree and slithered to my right, its body elongating until it stretched forty feet.

"Serpent, you didn't answer my question," I said, scrambling to catch up. "How do you know that she hasn't been here?"

"Unfortunately, most lose hope and throw themselves into the swamp. Or they foolishly drink the water. Or fail to find shelter when the daemons come at night. Many simply lie down and give up."

"Well that doesn't answer my question," I said, but the snake was ahead of me, wending its way through the gnarled network of petrified roots and stumps. Its body was the perfect form for navigating the difficult terrain.

"What shall I call you?" I hollered as if I was at the back of a train and trying to call to the engineer.

The snake slowed and the bulbous head swung around. "You may call me Shiloh."

"That's a strange name."

"It is the only name I have. Now come, I can hear the daemons beginning to stir."

"I don't hear anything."

"You won't. We must reach the pool before nightfall. Your safety depends on it." The snake slithered so quickly that I nearly lost sight as it twisted around obstacles.

I struggled to keep pace, my fatigue overwhelming me. I banged my shins on roots with every slip ending with my foot in the sucking mud — which sapped even more energy to struggle free. I had stopped sweating — a bad sign.

"How much longer, Shiloh? I can't go much further."

"We are almost there. Do not despair. Not yet."

I tripped into a tangle of roots. I wanted to close my eyes and sleep. Perhaps I may have even done that. The heavy body of the snake slithered over me and wakened me from my stupor.

"I can't go any further," I said. The snake's head hung close to mine. If it decided that it would rather make me a meal, I had no strength to resist.

"The pool is beyond that tree. We are there. It will refresh you."

I used the last of my reserves to climb to my feet— if I fell again, I didn't know if I'd get up. I focused only on the next step, and then the next.

I followed Shiloh around the tree.

The pool was so clear that I could see the bottom. The surface looked like ice— motionless. Had I ever seen anything so beautiful? I tumbled to my knees and drank. The water was the sweetest thing to have ever touched my tongue. With my thirst quenched, I sat on the shore and stared into the waters.

"Was it not exactly as I had promised?" Shiloh said.

"Yes. What place is this?" I gazed around the oasis. The petrified trees had drawn back in a ring so that I could see the orange sky of sunset.

"This is the sanctuary. I bring the lost and the misplaced here so that they may rest. The daemons may not enter this place of tranquility. You may close your eyes and sleep if you wish. Nothing can harm you here."

"Where do others go when they leave?"

"I do not know," the serpent whispered.

"You don't follow them?"

"Why would I follow them?"

I didn't trust the serpent— as I doubted anyone could truly trust a talking snake. Shiloh had guided me to this oasis, however, which gained him some credibility. I laid back and inhaled the sweet smell of the soft grass. My thoughts turned to finding my way out of this forest— knowing that Shiloh wasn't going to guide me.

I'll close my eyes for one moment.

I awakened to moonlight in my eyes. I scrambled to my feet, and saw that the murky trees had encroached upon the pool.

"Shiloh?" I hissed knowing full well the snake had abandoned me.

Movement caught my eye, pale skin flashing in the glow of the moonlight. It ran on two legs, humanoid, but not human. The creature froze next to an over-sized trunk, the camouflage so perfect that if it hadn't already given itself away, I never would've spotted it. It stared at me with eyes as big as saucers set in a toad-like head, large round mouth opening and closing like a fish out of water. Was this one of the daemons that Shiloh had warned me about?

How many others watched me? I scanned the trees but couldn't penetrate either the darkness or their camouflage.

A blaze of light.

The pond glowed. I gazed into the rippling waters and the observer became unimportant as I watched orbs of light dancing in its depths. They burned white with pink coronas and I marveled at the dripping fires, at the way they flitted effortlessly in the waters.

"*Sam,*" said a sing-song voice from the water. *Lucy.* We played cribbage, that stupid game, for hours. She cheated better than me so she usually won. Then she'd taunt me and I'd end up kissing her. We made love on the couch beside the board.

The fires faded and my stomach tightened. God, I didn't want to be in the dark again. I didn't want to be alone.

"Don't go," I said. I waded into the pool, the cold water sending a shiver through me. The fires intensified, circling as if performing a choreographed dance. I waded further out, the water rising above my waist but the cold faded. They'd make everything better— their lights burning away my loneliness and my despair.

"They are called Demon Fire," said someone from the shore, the gravelly voice breaking my trance. The water was up to my shoulders, ice cold. I was shivering and my feet and hands were numb. The fires dwindled with the interruption but remained like suspended sparks.

On the bank, an old man stood stooped, as if forced over by both the weight of time and his full-length suit of mail. The Templar cross was embroidered onto his chest— the insignia worn by the Knights of the Crusade. A braided rope fastened a sword to his waist. He held a burning lantern in his hand, the flame banal compared to the Demon Fire.

"Though they are not demons," the man continued. "They are the damned. They cannot gain access to Heaven because of their sins on earth. Nor will the devil take them into Hell. Time ground their bodies into ash leaving their souls as balls of energy to lure the lost and the despairing."

"Who are you?"

"My name is Elijah." The man did not drop his gaze or the lantern. "You must decide. You may follow the Demon Fire into the pond where you will drown, or you may come onto the bank with me."

"I don't know who you are." I gazed longingly to the suspended fires.

"You know me no less than you know the Demon Fire."

The chill— I sensed it overwhelming me.

"But they are so beautiful," I whispered.

"And I am just an old man."

My euphoria faded and the hardness of reality crept back. My muscles, fatigued from the grueling hike earlier, were numbed by the cold and I knew if I didn't turn back now, I would be lost.

I struggled back to shore and the Demon Fire faded until only the old-man's lantern kept the night at bay. My teeth chattered uncontrollably as I crawled onto the bank. The man put his lantern on a stump and he retrieved a blanket from his pack, then draped it over my shoulders.

"I shall start a fire."

"There are creatures out there," I said.

"My steel will keep them away," Elijah said, slapping the hilt on his waist though he looked as if his best fighting days were well behind him.

"What are they?"

"They are called the Thrage. They are a malicious folk who have a tendency to gnaw on human flesh. You are foolish to be here so late at night."

"A snake brought me here."

"And you were foolish enough to trust a snake?"

"It spoke to me."

"You trusted a talking snake?"

I fell quiet, watching as Elijah built a pyramid of wood then started the fire with steel and flint. The kindling smoldered and he nursed it to life.

"Take your clothes off and place them over on that root. They'll be dry by morning."

I stripped then huddled under the blanket by the fire. "Where are we?"

"You do not know? I suppose you would not, otherwise you would not be here. You have wandered into the Sourlands of Quedmore Wither."

"Who's Quedmore Wither?"

"I think it's a menacing name to warn people like you away."

"It was an accident. I didn't want to be here."

"Perhaps you do not wish to be here, but it was no accident."

"I must've made a mistake with the box. Put it together wrong."

"A box? A box does not bring anyone anywhere. A box does not do anything. It does not grant wishes or signal the way home. You can put things in it. Or open it and close it, maybe lock it to keep out thieves. But a box did not bring you here. You brought yourself to this lowly place."

"How do I get out?"

"You leave, of course."

"I've been walking for hours. Maybe for days. It all looks the same."

"Some wander for months. Others fall victims to the Daemons, the Thrage, or the inner demons that plague them. Some sink into the bog. Sometimes a man finds himself alone in his despair. He sinks deeper until he imagines doing that which is most heinous. In those times, sometimes he just needs a hand extended to pull himself free."

"For what it's worth— thank you."

"Hmm, yes." The man dug through his pack and retrieved a pail wrapped with cloth. He unwrapped it and produced a loaf of buttered bread and several strips of jerky.

"I must apologize for the basic food. I was not expecting to have a guest at my fire tonight." Elijah handed it to me.

"What about you?" I asked.

"What about me?"

"You didn't leave any food for yourself. I can't take all of it."

"I do not need to eat," Elijah stated. "You can tell me, however, that if you didn't desire to be in these woods, what you are doing here?"

"I'm looking for someone."

"God, you mean?"

"No, hardly. I'm looking for a woman."

"Ah, yes, a woman. The elusive unicorn?" He must've read my confused expression. "The unicorn— the mythical creature that we always pursue but can never attain."

"Not quite. She's gone."

"Kidnapped for a hefty ransom, no doubt."

"Murdered."

Elijah considered for some time. "Unfortunately, being dead is usually rather final."

"I think she's here."

"I have not seen her."

"How do you know? I mean, the snake told me the same thing."

"Well, you cannot trust a snake."

"But I can trust you?"

"Weren't you praising me for saving your life? How quickly a savior becomes a traitor in your eyes."

I poked at the fire, mesmerized as sparks crackled and spun into the night air. "I didn't mean it that way."

"How did you mean it?"

"I don't want to believe that you haven't seen her. That she isn't here."

"I never said she wasn't here," Elijah said. He drew his sword and I tensed but the man groaned, his knees popping as he plopped himself onto a log on the other side of the fire. He began sharpening the blade with a whetstone.

"So she's here?"

"I'm truly having a hard time keeping up with your train of thought, lad. I do not know that she's here. I do not know if she's not here. In fact, I don't know anything about this unicorn at all."

"Her name's Lucy."

"No matter her name, this is not the place to be looking for a unicorn. No, no, no. This place is hopelessness and that pool is the ultimate pit of despair."

"The box broke," I explained.

"The box, right. The box made the mistake. Let me tell you something even though you don't want to hear it. You're here— because you're here."

"Very metaphysical."

"Where is this box now?"

"I don't know."

"How did it get you here, then?"

"I solved it."

"You solved a box and it brought you to these woods?"

"Not here." I told him of the prison. Showed him the ring that I thought Lucy had left behind. "This belonged to Lucy. I think she dropped it... or maybe left it as a clue for me to find. But I don't know why she would've been there."

"You were in Gardizael prison. You are fortunate that you escaped. It is as vile and evil a place as you'll find in any world. The Jailors' depravity knows no bounds."

"Who are the prisoners?"

"The unfortunate."

"What crimes did they commit?"

"That's the problem. No one really knows. There are murder- ers, rapists, and adulterers. There are priests and saints. Who knows what the Jailors deem to be crimes?"

"The cell I was in— it wasn't my cell. It belonged to someone else." I told him about Alan and how he murdered Lucy then escaped Gardizael prison.

"You are hunting Alan, not your unicorn?"

"What? No."

Elijah lit his pipe and took several quick puffs. "Is this a story of revenge or redemption?"

I sighed, resting my head in my hands. "I don't know what it is." Uncomfortable with the conversation, "Tell me about yourself, Old Man. If this is a place of hopelessness, why are you here?"

"I'm a questing knight. I cannot lay down my sword until I complete my quest and sometimes my journey takes me to places of ill repute."

"What's your quest?"

"I'm searching for something." Elijah gazed into the fire. "I'm looking for a unicorn."

"Oh. I'm sorry," I whispered.

"For what?"

"You said… you're looking for your unicorn. We're talking about a woman, aren't we?"

"Of course not. I'm looking for a unicorn. A horse with a horn. I think your brain is addled from the cold waters."

Before I could complain, he asked me about my world. As I told him tales of technology and politics, he remained quiet. Thoughtful, his bushy eyebrows scrunched at my descriptions. Finally, he had heard enough.

"Try to sleep. I will watch over you for tonight."

I didn't argue. Exhausted, I laid my head on my arm and before I realized it, I fell into a dreamless sleep.

Water. It flowed down my mouth. I was gagging on it, it choked me, filled my nostrils, clouded my eyes. I thrashed but someone held me down.

Elijah. Trying to kill me.

"Calm down, lad! I'm trying to save you. Now don't waste anymore and drink it down."

I don't know how much I swallowed and how much filled my lungs. It tasted salty. Elijah abruptly climbed from me and gave me some space to hack and wheeze my way to a kneeling position.

"Trying… to kill… me," I coughed.

"You were poisoned, lad. The parasites were already growing in you."

He screwed the lid on his canteen. He shook it, heard that it was almost empty and frowned. He muttered something to himself before stowing the canteen in his equipment.

"Parasites?" I wheezed.

The sun beat down on the pool. Except the pool had become an algae-infested bog. Frogs bigger than my fist swam lazily through the slime. Not normal frogs. These had scorpion tails or lobster claws.

"What happened to the pond?"

Elijah frowned. "Nothing happened."

"But the water was clear last night."

"Let's not focus on last night too much, shall we, lad?"

The liquid Elijah had doused me in turned sticky as it dried. I tried wiping my mouth and neck but managed only to smear dirt onto my face. "You could've told me to drink it," I said. "You didn't have to force it down my throat."

"Perhaps. But you seem the untrusting type. It is time for breakfast."

Elijah had set a small cast-iron frying pan over the coals of the fire. Two eggs sizzled and popped beside a hunk of meat that looked quite similar to a frog. I glanced at the pond, and shuddered. I had drunk that water.

Elijah scooped the food onto a plate and handed it to me. My stomach rumbled and my mouth watered, overpowering any queasiness about eating mutated frog. "Don't worry, boy. The fires burn off all the parasites. It's as good as meat as any."

"Thank you," I mumbled between bites. Elijah handed me a canteen of water. It passed the sniff test and I drank my fill. "I want to leave this place," I said when finished.

"Of course. Sober second thought," Elijah replied. Before I could ask what he meant by that last remark he said, "The path is over by those trees. We should be out within the hour."

"I was close," I said. "To getting out, that is. Perhaps Shiloh did help me."

Elijah's face darkened. "You were close to ultimate despair, Sam. This wood is only as big as you make it." Before I could question him, he held up a hand. "Clean the dishes. It is a good traveling day and I do not wish to dally too long."

I scoured the dishes with a bar of sand stone and repacked the supplies. When finished, I joined Elijah at the edge of camp. He sat on a root but didn't look up while I waited. I cleared my throat and broke his trance.

"Ah, there you are," he said. "I was thinking of your tales from last night."

"You think me mad?"

"Perhaps. Perhaps. But that would make me a figment of your imagination. I am not particularly fond of that explanation. I have another theory."

I sat across from him.

"Imagine two streams in a forest flowing side by side. Each one teeming with life. If the streams do not touch, do the inhabitants even know of the other stream? After all, in their experience, there is nothing to suggest that there is another river right beside them. They spawn, eat, live, die all within the confines of their banks. Without evidence, they'd grow to believe that they are the only stream in existence. Over time, even if they began as identical ecosystems, they would evolve down different paths.

Soon, the streams would be alien to each other. Different life. Different topography.

"But what if those streams suddenly touched? Would the fish migrate from one stream to another? What would seem commonplace for the first stream, would seem unbelievable, maddening for the others because it is beyond their experience.

"What if your world and my world are two realities flowing side by side in the same universe but never touching? Your world is as foreign to me as this place is to you."

"A Next World?"

He grunted and we sat contemplating his theory. Like solving the puzzle box earlier, I tried fitting the pieces together.

"The puzzle box is a conduit," I said.

"A conduit?"

"It would be a tributary from one stream to the other stream. A way of crossing back and forth."

"Very intriguing. Then how did Lucy come to be here?"

"Death." I saw his questioning look. "What if death isn't the end? What if there are thousands of streams? And what if death is simply a way of crossing from one stream to another? A one-way trip. From here to there."

"I doubt this is Heaven or Hell, my friend."

"It's neither. It's just a river. Flowing beside my river."

"And yet you say that it is a one-way trip. Your quest has already failed."

"The box changes everything. I never died, Elijah. That box gives us the ability to go back and forth. I can take her back with me."

"You do not have the box."

The excitement of the discovered theory faded. "That is a problem."

"Or you really are mad," Elijah said.

"Then you are simply a figment of my imagination."

"Yes, I see. If you are truly mad then no task is fully impossible to you. After all, you are trapped within your own mind— limited only by your imagination."

I considered for a moment. "That sounds reasonable."

"Then I must show you something."

He slung his pack over his shoulder. Less than fifty paces later, we emerged from the infernal woods into a land with a fiery sky, reds and oranges extending over the low heavens as if the world was awash in flame.

"What's wrong with the sky?" I asked.

"Beautiful day, isn't it?"

"Does it always look like this?"

"Not always quite so breathtaking."

A mountain rose before us, so out of place in the otherwise flat plain that it looked like it had been thrust from the earth in defiance to the heavens.

"What is that place?" I asked.

"That is the Hammer of the Gods." He turned his gaze upon me. "At the peak is the prize that can get you your unicorn. The Blue Rose of Quintes. It blooms once a century for but a single afternoon. It grants the ultimate gift— immortality."

"I don't want immortality, Old Man."

His brows twitched. "Not for you. For anyone. Think of the gift."

For Lucy.

"Can... that bring her back?" I asked.

"How would I know? I've never plucked the rose. No one has. But I wonder— maybe it can bring back your Lucy."

"I just have to climb a mountain," I said dubiously.

"Thistles and nettles cover the approach, their poison so toxic that one scratch will liquefy you from the inside out. High in the crags nest the harpies, the wicked bird women, who will swoop down and steal you for their nefarious appetites. You do not have climbing equipment, or any equipment for that matter."

I stared at the Hammer of the Gods. Me, climbing a mountain? Not possible. But a lot of things hadn't been possible.

"Are you coming with me?" I asked.

"My unicorn lies in another direction. This is where we part ways."

"Thank you, Elijah."

"I merely showed you a choice."

"Thanks anyhow."

Elijah bowed low and his back cracked. I had to help him straighten.

"Right then," Elijah said. "I have but one more thought before we part. It is our theory of the two streams again. It occurred to me, Sam. When two streams touch— often, the very nature of *both* streams is changed. Be wary of the forces you are playing with."

"I won't stop until I find her, Elijah."

"Good luck in your quest for the unicorn."

"And you yours."

Elijah saluted smartly then headed off along the edge of the swamp. I turned back to the mountain. Was that the key to getting home? With no other path available, I decided to head toward the Hammer of the Gods.

I found an overgrown path and I walked in one of the old ruts, the ground so compacted that the grasses and weeds hadn't overgrown it. I walked for hours and yet appeared no closer to the mountain than when I started. How far away was it?

The plains gave way to a sparse forest.

"Don't move," a voice to my right demanded.

I didn't see them immediately— the shadows from the trees gave them plenty of opportunity to hide. My eyes adjusted: several men huddled in the culvert running beneath the road. Another man crouched at the edge of the ditch.

"Are you talking to me?"

"You, bloody bobber. Who else would I be talking to?" A jagged scar ran from the corner of his mouth to one ear. His left arm ended prematurely at an elbow covered in bloody bandaging. He pointed a revolver at me with his other hand, the kind of weapon that a gunfighter from the Wild West would've used except this one was antiquated and rusted, though I didn't want to find out firsthand if it worked.

My gaze drifted to the other men. All missing limbs. A foot there, an entire leg from the man on the right. Both hands. All amputees.

"What the hell happened to you?" The hairs on my neck were standing up and I knew the situation was about to go sideways. Nowhere to run and no way to defend myself.

"Are you alone?" he asked.

"I am now."

"I was told to shoot you on sight." I stole a glance at the revolver. "What's your name?" the scarred man asked.

"Sam."

"My name's Hector."

"Are you going to kill me?" I asked. "You're making me nervous."

"I haven't decided. Do you know why anyone would tell me to kill you?"

"I have an idea."

"Perhaps you should share it."

"The man's name was Alan, wasn't it? He's trying to get you to shoot me because he's afraid of me."

"You don't look like much. Why would he be afraid of you?"

"Because I know what he's done. He's a murderer."

"Funny, he said *you* were the murderer, and a liar. Said that you'd probably say the same thing about him. Two days ago, I would've believed him and killed you on the spot. Today, I'm not so sure."

"Why's that?"

"Because he abandoned us. Where the hell are we supposed to go?"

"You're from the prison?"

"That's right. Look at us— we're broken men. If we venture onto the plains, the Jailors will nab us. If we go back, the swamp waits. We have nowhere to go except we're not going back to prison."

"I'd say you can come with me, but I don't think you'd make the journey."

"To the Blue Rose of Quintes," Hector said.

"How'd you know that?"

"Because we were spinning tales the first night with your friend. I told him about the rose. Next morning, he was gone. He's after that rose, like you. Except he has a two-day start."

I cursed. It hadn't occurred to me that Alan could be striving for the same thing. What if he got it before me? More importantly, why did he want the rose? To get back to our world?

"Shite," Hector said, staring over my shoulder. "You've brought them down upon us, bobber." I whirled and saw seven riders tear around a thick stand of trees. *Jailors.* Only moments away.

Those who could, ran. Those who couldn't, tried to hide.

Hector swung the revolver's cylinder out, inspected it, then flicked it back in. "I only have three bullets, Sam." Hector turned and shot the man closest to him. A bullet to the head. He went down without ceremony. The man lay there like he hadn't even known it was coming. Hector cocked the gun and aimed at another of his men. The bullet hit him in the forehead and he fell still.

"What are hell you doing?"

"Sorry, friend. You're on your own." Hector shot a third man.

Horses galloped past me, one so close it grazed my shoulder. A horse skidded next to me, grit bouncing against my legs. I faced the Jailor, and realized Hector hadn't murdered his companions— he was giving them an escape.

"This is a mistake," I whispered. My legs turned rubbery.

The second rider leveled a blunderbuss at me and I held up my hands in feeble defense.

"You escaped Gardizael," the metallic voice stated.

"I'm not your prisoner. You're looking for someone else." Alan was the man they were looking for. Alan was the murderer.

The blunderbuss fired a net with a puff of smoke, the weight sending me stumbling to the ground. The metallic mesh electrified, my teeth snapped together and my muscles locked. I smelt burning, burning, burning.

"Hit him again," the metallic voice commanded.

Another jolt powered through the netting and like a tripped fuse, my nervous system disconnected. My vision flared white then collapsed into black but I heard my own agonized cry through clenched teeth.

God had flipped a switch again.

Someone was knocking on the door. I tried to orient myself. I sat on the floor of my bedroom, the puzzle box in my lap. My bedroom. No Jailors. Just me and that box.

"Open the door!" Cami yelled from the other side.

"It's not locked," I stuttered.

The knob turned but failed to catch. Cami twisted it, banged on the door again. I wanted to let her in but the vertigo overpowered me. The knob caught in its housing and Cami stumbled into the room.

"What were you doing, Sam?" I saw something in her expression I hadn't seen from her before: distrust.

"It's a puzzle box," I said, pushing it aside like she had caught me with a murder weapon. I rubbed my eyes in a an attempt to rid myself of the disorientation. "What time is it?"

"It's noon."

"Noon…" *Two hours.* I had only been gone for two hours.

"Why'd you lock the door?" she asked.

"I didn't lock it. It can't lock."

"You didn't answer."

"I must've drifted off, Cami." A terrible lie and she couldn't hide her disbelief.

"The police are here for you, Sam."

"The police?"

A man wearing a well-worn brown suit pushed past Cami. A rut of a scar disfigured his face.

"I'm Detective Hector."

"I know you," I said. The man from the other world who had shot his own men.

"I questioned you the night of Lucy's murder," he said. "We have a warrant to search your apartment and seize all computers and electronic devices." He flapped an official-looking form in my face and I took it but didn't look at it. They had already taken my stuff. What was going on? I felt intoxicated and I couldn't focus.

Outside the room, uniformed police began to pull apart my apartment.

"Please hand over your cell phone and any other portable devices," Hector said.

"I don't understand."

"You should contact a lawyer."

"Why are you here?"

"It's part of an ongoing investigation."

"What investigation?"

Hector stared at me warily. "The murderer of Lucy Busby and the disappearance of Alan Harrison."

"Alan?" I croaked.

"You going to tell me where I can find him?"

"I need to sit down." I sat on the edge of the bed. *Alan is dead*. Was Elijah's theory true? Had the two independent streams touched— perhaps altering both? If so, was Alan hiding here, aware of what he had done to Lucy?

"Where's Lucy?" I asked.

"I need to speak with my brother," Cami said. She grabbed me by the arm.

My head swam with the possibilities. The box had changed reality. Made it different.

Cami pulled me past the clusters of police out into the hallway. Finally away from earshot, she pushed me against the wall.

"What the hell is going on here, Sam?"

"I don't know. Where's Lucy?"

"This isn't time for games. Your place is crawling with cops. What have you done?"

"Is she alive?"

"Enough of the crap!" she snapped, then caught herself and lowered her voice. "How are you involved in this?"

"I'm not, Cami. I promise."

"How did you injure your hand, Sam?"

"My hand?" I held it up. "I told you…" I trailed off because I knew what she thought— that my wound was from a struggle with Alan.

"Call your lawyer."

"I don't have a lawyer."

She opened her cell phone and dialed. "I'll get you one. Don't talk to the police without a lawyer."

"What do you think I've done, Cami?"

"Nothing, Sam. I'm being careful, that's all." Except I saw the lie on her face and it cut me deeply. I needed her to be on my side.

"Lucy's dead," I stated. She didn't dispute me so I assumed this was still true. "And so is Alan."

The phone wavered at her ear. "Don't say another word, Sam. Do you hear me?"

"You think I killed him?"

"I never said that."

"Alan killed her."

"God damn it, Sam. Has the trauma rattled your brain? You've got to listen to me— don't say another word. Not to me, not to anyone until you have a lawyer. This is serious business."

"I haven't slept," I confessed. "I'm so confused."

"You're exhausted, Sam." She called her local friends scouring for a lawyer. Fifteen minutes later, she finished her calls.

"I have someone coming."

"They're taking my computers," I said, watching as police removed sealed boxes.

"They won't find anything, right?"

"Of course not." Except I didn't know what else was different. The only thing I could be sure of was that Lucy wasn't in this world. Not yet. But what else could I change? *The Rose of Quintes.* What if I could pluck that rose? Would it bring her back?

Except waiting for me on the other side were Jailors.

"Sam? Are you all right?" Cami snapped her phone shut.

I tried to focus. Even though I couldn't be sure I wasn't either crazy or a murderer, I didn't want Cami believing I was because I needed her to be on my side. She was all I had right now.

"This is all happening so fast," I said. Hell, I was still trying to get my bearings from the other world. I didn't understand how I had gotten back without the box.

"You won't talk to anyone, right? Right, Sam?"

"Right. Won't talk to anyone."

"What have you gotten yourself into?"

I wanted to tell her. Wanted to tell her so damned bad. But what would I say? Instead, I said, "Lucy and I loved each other, you know."

She sighed. "I know, Sam."

I slid down the wall into a sitting position. "She was going to break it off with Alan." The thought made my stomach churn and I buried my face in my fists.

She crouched and kissed the top of my head.

"I'm sorry."

"You would've liked her."

She straightened. "I'm going back inside until the lawyer gets here. Make sure the cops aren't overstepping that warrant."

"Thanks. I can't face them right now."

She left me alone and I listened to the hum of the elevator and the squeak of police shoes in the stairwell. I got lost in the sounds, let them carry me away. I closed my eyes.

I've never fired a gun but this feels natural. The barrel is pitted from years of skin acids eating at the metal. The shotgun is a two-barrel side-by-side configuration. I break it open and load two shells. My pockets overflow with more ammunition.

The front door is partially open and I push it the rest of the way with the muzzle. I wait in the front hall, listening. I hear the click of a door closing further in the house. My pupils dilate and my heart thumps. My hands are sweaty and I wipe them on my thighs.

I know there is no turning back now. I lick my cracked lips.

I take three steps, stop, and listen. I hear nothing but I know I could be walking into a trap. Movement. I turn, too late, and he is upon me. I see the mask of rage as he plows into me. The drywall cracks behind us, leaving an impression of our bodies. I am trying to bring the shotgun up but he's too close. His fist comes from below and cracks me on the jaw. My teeth snap together.

I club him in the face with the shotgun and he staggers backwards. It's enough of a break for me to pull myself from the wall. He's drawing a pistol. I turn the shotgun on him. The guns go off simultaneously.

I jolted awake but didn't open my eyes. The world swayed. The sounds didn't match my location. No more elevator or the hum of police as they tore my place apart.

The crack of whips, the snap of electricity, the creak of wagons, and the moaning of the anguished. I thought I might've been one of the ones moaning.

I smelt the pungent odor of decay.

"I know you're awake," a girl said.

I sighed because I couldn't delay any longer. My eyes fluttered open. I sat scrunched in a caged wagon strung together with vines and bamboo. Though primitive, the bars looked solid. I shared my cage with the wounded— casts, missing limbs, stained bandages. This was one wagon in a long train, each filled with the crippled and the maimed.

Mounted Jailors escorted the wagon train, quick to use their whips though I saw no signs of resistance. The prisoners kept their eyes downcast, each caught in their own private torment.

Amputees crowded the wagons. Some were missing a hand or an ear. Others entire arms or legs. I.V. bags were tacked to the outside of the bamboo bars, clear plastic lines looping to those too weak to move. Why would the Jailors bother to keep anyone alive?

My hand. It was wrapped tightly in gauze. A stab of panic— what had they done to me? When I unwrapped it, I saw that the Jailors had not only cleaned and bandaged it, they had stitched it up, thick black thread looping through my flesh like a sea serpent on the old style globes. The skin was white and wrinkled but I saw no signs of infection.

"They don't want it to infect," the girl said.

"Mercy?"

"No," she said. She couldn't have been older than ten. She wore a blue flowered dress with golden hair tied into a ponytail. She belonged skipping through a field of wild flowers rather than stuffed into this cage. "My name's Tegan. What's your name?"

"Sam."

"You're not from here. Where are you from?"

"Another place," I said.

"What a silly answer. Of course you're from another place. We're all from different places."

"Where are we now then?"

"The Jailors are taking us to Gardizael. You've been sleeping for nearly a day."

"Why is everyone..."

"The Jailors use us piece by piece. They take only what they need. They think they're being merciful."

"My god... what are they doing with the limbs?"

Tegan didn't answer.

Were the Jailors going to do that to me? Cut me apart piece by piece and leave me as half a man? Hysteria clawed at the edges of my already frayed sanity.

Laughter. Before I looked around, I realized it was coming from me.

"Is something funny?" Tegan asked.

"I think I've gone crazy," I said, wiping a tear from the corner of my eye.

She put her hand in mine. "I'm afraid you're not, Sam." My laughter stopped. I considered asking where her parents were but I was afraid of the answer and remained quiet.

I had to get back. *The box.* I needed the puzzle box to go home. Except I had already gone back and forth without needing it.

"What are you looking for?" Tegan asked.

"A box." I made a shape with my hands, as if that would help her remember.

"I'm sure it's gone."

I slumped against the bamboo bars. *Trapped.*

"Was it important?"

"It brought me here."

She giggled. "Don't be silly. A box is just a box."

Except you're wrong.

We rode in silence for hours. The sun never moved in the sky. Were days longer in this place? I craned my head, searching for the men from the culvert.

"Are you looking for someone?" Tegan asked.

"No. Yes. I don't know."

She giggled, the sound odd in this place of suffering. Her's wasn't the sound of cynicism or madness but actual mirth. I worried that she'd draw attention and my gaze darted to the mounted Jailors. They didn't appear to notice her.

"I met some escapees—"

"Was it Hector? He has a large scar on his face." She made a motion from the edge of her lip to her ear. At seeing my expression darken, her excitement died quickly. "What of the others?"

I shook my head, nearly imperceptible but she noticed.

"They are dead then? They are fortunate."

"Tegan, I need to get to the Hammer of the Gods."

She frowned. "That is not a good place. You want to escape the prison so you can head to another bad place? That doesn't make any sense."

"I know, but it's my only way of saving Lucy."

"The Jailors captured her too?"

"I don't think so."

"You don't know much."

"It's complicated."

My mind registered the sound of a snapping whip before I felt the streak of fire down my back, the pain so intense my vision distorted, the bars of the cage flaring out then sucking in. The bamboo cage thrummed with the time of my heart. When my vision cleared, a Jailor sneered at me, keeping pace with our wagon, a whip dangling at his side.

"You are the one who helped Alan escape," the metallic voice said.

"I didn't help him escape," I said through clenched teeth. My eyes watered from the trail of liquid flame down my back.

The sea-urchin eyes sparked and the Jailor went rigid as if focused elsewhere.

"You are Sam Madison," it said. "You escaped from our prison."

"I wasn't supposed to be there."

"You were there because of Lucy."

"Yes," I said, practically exploding at the bars. I pressed myself up to them. "Is she here, have you seen her?"

"Lucy would not be here. Only you. And Alan."

I opened my mouth to argue my innocence, and an arrow materialized in the Jailor's neck, the shaft protruding through his throat like a magic trick. He slid off the back of his mount but the horse never missed a step. I scanned the forest looking for the archer.

"For the glory of the Empire!" Old-man Elijah burst from the wood on a horse so beat-up that surely its knobby knees would crumple under the weight. Elijah's plate armor gleamed, sword raised above his head, shield grasped in the other.

Hector ran onto the roadway. A cloud of smoke puffed from his revolver accompanied by a sharp retort. Another Jailor crumpled from his horse. More men tumbled from the forest like a carnival act. They were a sorry lot of amputees and broken-down flesh. Arrows whistled. A horse reared, a shaft protruding from its flank, sending its rider flailing, then rampaged off the path. The terror spread through the other horses. The roadway became a tangle of wagons and horses.

"Hector!" Tegan jumped to her feet, head brushing the top of the bamboo cage. "I knew he'd come for us," she confided. "I just knew it."

Elijah charged to our cart, he and his mount carrying themselves like they were half as old, as if the lure of battle awakened long dormant energies.

"Stand back from the door," Elijah commanded. He swiped at the lock with his sword and sliced it in two. Hector and a one-armed man helped crack the door open.

"We don't have long," Hector said. "Reinforcements from the front and back of the train will be coming and we don't have the numbers to fight them off for long."

Other wagons were liberated and the wounded and the hurt staggered into the woods. Jailors arrived from the front of the train. A firing line of men met them using captured blunderbusses. A concussive boom and they repelled the first counterattack.

Tegan jumped into Hector's arms and his knees buckled from the onslaught.

"Easy, girl! There will be time for reunions later."

An organized troop of Jailors used scimitars and blunderbusses to break through the beleaguered firing line.

"Fall back!" Hector shouted.

"There are so many others that need help," I said.

"We will not forget them. But this war is just beginning." The rescue squads broke from the wagons, leaving the trapped reaching through the bars, pleading for salvation that would not come today.

"I will hold the line," Elijah said. "I will meet you at the rendezvous point."

Hector was about to disagree but Elijah's hardened stare must've dissuaded him.

Elijah patted his decrepit mount and whispered something in her ear. Her tail swished and she pranced backwards. "That's right. Songs that will fill the night sky." He turned his mount to face the hard-charging Jailors.

"He'll die," I said.

"No, he won't," Tegan replied.

"Follow me," Hector said then retreated into the petrified wood.

"I'm not going back in there," I said. I remembered the miles upon miles of trees and the never-ending hopelessness.

Tegan placed her hand in mine. "It's okay. You won't get lost. It's easy to find the way out once you know where it is."

I planned to stand my ground but I found myself walking then running beside her. I chanced a glance back and saw Elijah charging into a pack of Jailors. He didn't stand a chance. Each was his physical superior. Taller, wider, strong. The old man's battle cry warbled from aged vocal cords. The sun glinted off his sword as he and his mount dove into the fray. Belying his age, he moved with fluidity and grace, blade arcing, slicing, chopping.

Then we ran past the tree line and the oppressiveness fell like a sheet of rain, the brilliance of the sun a memory. Biting gnats buzzed me, the humidity so thick that the air clogged my lungs. The wounded splashed through the bog. An earless man slipped on a tree root and disappeared into the swamp without even leaving a cloud of bubbles in his wake.

They were the sorriest bunch I'd ever seen but somehow they had survived. Staged an attack against the Jailors and broken free.

We reached a spot where the trees weren't quite so dense, the air not quite so heavy, and the bugs not quite as thick. Tents made of burlap and canvas had been crudely erected and campfires burned. The inhabitants that greeted us were the ones that were too incomplete to assist in the rescue— the legless, the blind, those that were no more than living torsos.

And yet, there were smiles, claps on the back, and hugs all around as the survivors straggled in.

"Why is everyone so happy?" I asked.

Tegan stared quizzically. "Why wouldn't they be happy?"

"All those people in the wagons…"

Tegan didn't answer.

Despite all the suffering, the camp's mood remained upbeat, almost jovial. I wanted to ask Hector how he and his men had escaped the Jailors earlier but there was no time for that. I helped where I could, assisting in moving patients, setting up more tents.

"Incoming," someone yelled and those who were capable readied weapons.

"Friendly," A voice answered back.

"One of ours," someone else confirmed.

Elijah stumbled into camp. He dragged his sword behind him in the mud and he tripped and tumbled into a tent. People rushed to greet him, including Tegan and Hector. The crowd nearly crushed him in their excitement.

"Everyone back!" Hector finally hollered. "The man needs some air."

Elijah plopped down on a root, his face ashen, eyes downcast. Hector squatted, whispered something to him and Elijah lifted his gaze.

"I'm not as young as I used to be," he confessed. "My future looked bleak, and alas, poor Dulcinea succumbed to the demons in our battle. She fought valiantly— saved my life, no doubt. I promised her that her name would be remembered in songs of this mighty day."

"Are you hurt?" Hector asked.

"Hurt?" He scrunched his bushy eyebrows. "Do I look hurt? I fought them tooth and nail. Broke three knives and they sundered my shield. I felled nine of the demons if I slew three. I'm not as young as I once was. These heroic tasks are far more tiring than back in WW2."

"You fought in World War Two?" I asked.

"World war what? What are you talking about now, boy? Honestly, I'd think it was you who came out the wrong side of a battle with thirteen Jailors."

"Glad to have you back, old man," Hector shouted.

"You... you thought I wasn't going to make it back?"

"The thought had crossed my mind."

Elijah tried to spit in disgust, but couldn't muster any saliva. "Damn it. My mouth is dry," he muttered. "Never doubt a man on a quest. Never."

"We move out in an hour," Hector shouted to the camp.

"Where are we going?" I asked.

"We're going to create a base camp away from the Jailors. Tend to the sick and wounded. The Thrage and daemons wander this forest at night and we need to be better prepared for them. And the war with the Jailors is just beginning."

"I can't go with you," I said.

"Well you can't stay in the swamp," Hector said.

"He's chasing a unicorn," Elijah interjected.

Hector nodded. "I wish you luck then."

The old man stood, his knees popping. He extended his hand. "This is where our paths part. Again." I took his hand, Elijah's skin calloused and weathered like tree bark. "I cannot offer you much," he said, breaking contact and digging through his pack. He produced flint and steel and handed them over. "To light your way, of course." The old man returned to his root with another creak of his joints. "Remember, the harpies prowl the skies above the Hammer. If they catch you, they'll take you back to their nest where they'll feed you piece by piece to their young."

"You forgot to mention the poisonous thorns," I said.

"I did not. I merely hadn't gotten around to it," he replied.

Hector pulled the antique revolver from his waistband. He handed it to me, pearl grip first. I was hesitant to take it but he motioned it closer.

"There are five shots left. The bullets are old and prone to misfire, so make them count." I took the gun-metal blue revolver from him. The weapon felt foreign in my hand. My experience with guns had been a single trip to a firing range years ago.

"Thank you, Hector."

"Do you know the way out?" Tegan asked.

"I think I do," I said. "It's over there. I can't thank you enough. I owe you my life."

"From one questing knight to another. Good luck, Sam," Elijah said, attempting a bow from where he sat. The others hugged me, wished me well and I left the camp, pausing at the tree line to glance back. Hector nodded and Tegan waved goodbye.

I hurt. Everywhere. But another emotion bubbled to the surface, an emotion that had been a stranger for a long time. Hope. Hope that maybe I was beginning to take control of my life— as crazy as it had become. I wondered about the box. I hadn't needed it to travel between the worlds. Building upon our theory of two streams— had I become a citizen of both streams, able to flow between the two at will? Would I be able to eventually think myself between the worlds?

As Tegan had said, once you knew the way out of the woods, it was easy. I stepped over a root and onto a plain at the base of the Hammer of the Gods, the mountain so mighty that clouds shrouded the summit. Lazy specks circled the sky beneath the cloud line— the harpies.

Thickets surrounded the mountain base, their thorns as big as shark's teeth, the edges serrated and dripping a milky-white liquid. As I neared, one of the bushes trembled as if sensing my presence. When I retreated, it relaxed. I began circling the mountain base hoping to find a path but all I found was the impenetrable field of thorns that bristled with my approach.

The mountain could take days to circumvent. I sat cross legged in the tall grass and rested my head on a fist, contemplating while the winged creatures circled like vultures riding a thermal draft.

"Hello, friend," a sibilant voice said. I hadn't noticed the snake slithering around me. Now Shiloh's head bobbed at eye level. "You abandoned me at the pool," he said. "No doubt the Old Man talked you into leaving. He cannot be trusted."

"Funny, he said the same thing about you."

"Did he now? I knew I should've eaten him when I had the chance. It is unwise to be out in the open," Shiloh said. "The harpies will find you and take you to their nests."

"Yes, where I'll be fed to their young."

"Is that what Elijah told you? More lies from the Old Man. No, they will not just feed you to their young. They will bind you, and torture you, and milk you of your seed."

"They'll milk me?"

"Until you are a broken, bloody mess. But I have found a path for you. A way that is clear so that you cannot be harmed by the thorns."

"Will you take me there?"

"Of course, friend. Remember who brought you to the clear pool when you were dying of thirst. Shiloh is your friend."

"Then let's go."

"The way is not far." Shiloh slithered through the tall grass. After a half-hour, Shiloh led me to another section of impenetrable thorns.

"Am I not your friend? Here it is. The path to the top."

I saw thorns. "I don't understand."

Shiloh's head bobbed from me to the thorns. "Right there. The path. Can you not see that the way is clear?"

"Of course," I lied. I gazed into the sky at the circling harpies. "The path is clear. I cannot thank you enough."

"That is what friends do."

"I must prepare for my journey. Can you give me a few moments?" I asked.

"Yes, yes. Prepare."

I waded through the tall grass and collected twigs and kindling. My walk around the base had proven one thing— there was no path through the thorns. I assembled the wood as I had seen Elijah do that night in the forest. I crouched low over it and dug his flint and steel from my pack.

"What are you doing, friend?"

"I am lighting a fire."

"You will bring the harpies down upon us!"

A spark and the kindling smoldered and caught fire. My campfire snapped and popped.

"You were going to lead me to my death, Shiloh. There is no path just as there was no clear pool. You were deceiving me again."

The circling shadows grew smaller but more focused— the harpies would be upon us soon.

Shiloh's head flared like a cobra's. "You are an idiot, blinded by your own emotion. Do you think plucking a rose will bring her back? Do you think she'll fly into your arms at seeing you?"

"This is my journey, not yours."

"They are here," Shiloh said, and curled himself into a protective loop. My stomach constricted and I dared not look or my courage would fail.

Their wings stirred a sour wind, loose black feathers swirling around me.

"He is so pretty," one said.

"Oh, what a prize. So sweet!"

Claws snatched me around the shoulders and we took flight. Two of the bird women descended upon Shiloh. He tried to strike but they were faster. Their claws pulled at him, rending his flesh. He flopped and twisted but they cut him apart, fighting over him like two birds on a worm. I looked away.

What have I done?

I reached for the revolver though I knew it was too late. The bird woman holding me had flown so high that if we fell now I'd surely perish.

"I am taking you to meet my daughters," she said.

The face craned down to look upon me— the face of a goddess. Gorgeous blue eyes, long blonde hair, and a perfect white smile. "We shall make love for days upon end. We will fulfill your every fantasy." The tip of her tongue licked her moist lips.

But as we soared upward, I saw their bodies, a map of open, sucking wounds. Scaly, over-sized breasts flopped loosely on their stomachs.

The harpies took me past the thorns, into the clouds and toward the top of the mountain. One step closer to the rose and to restoring my life to the way it was. Back when it was good. The beautiful faces gazed upon me, licking their lips with desire.

I had no escape plan. This was an act of faith to let them carry me skyward. Faith that an escape would present itself at all.

God flicked a switch.

Vertigo.

I stood in my hallway, hands on knees, trying to catch my breath. The faded floral carpet pulsed and I steadied myself with the wall. Behind me, the stairwell door opened and I heard hard-soled shoes on the tile. More cops?

I tried to remember what I had been doing moments earlier. I recalled something about flying— a strange hallucination of beautiful women with fiendish bodies. *I am crazy.*

I wanted to call to Cami but I couldn't breathe. Damn, I needed the world to stop spinning. A set of shoes entered my vision and I raised my head.

I crashed to the ground before I registered the sickening crunch of my nose breaking. Alan stood over me, the shotgun held white knuckled. He had smashed me in the face with it. My eyes watered and I tasted the rush of blood, bits of broken teeth floating in my mouth. Then the agony hit. I wanted to rise but vertigo and my busted face kept me grounded. Alan held all the cards and from the way he had that shotgun jammed into my neck, he knew it.

But what did Alan know of his place in this saga? That he had liquefied his skull in Lucy's room? That rather than death he found himself in the Next World, trapped in a prison of nightmares that I had released him from?

I spit out a wad of bloody phlegm laced with my teeth.

"Do you know where I was, Sam?" he said.

"You don't know me," I replied.

"I was in that cell for a lifetime. They did things to me— made me forget, burned the memories out of me."

"You killed Lucy."

He frowned, his eyes unfocused. "Killed her? No, I'm here to save her. From you."

The butt of the shotgun hit my right shoulder and my arm went numb. I fell flat and a cold sensation spread from the impact point and I wondered if he had shattered my collarbone. I gasped for breath through the sheets of pain.

As I lay in a ball at Alan's feet I realized a revolver was tucked into my waistband. How did I get it? I remembered something— a man with a scarred face had given it to me. The more I tried to draw the memory to my consciousness, the more it broke apart like vapor.

Sensation crept into my right arm but I knew I wouldn't be able to draw, cock the hammer, and fire before Alan would blow me apart. If I had any chance at all, it meant I had to use my left hand. My uncoordinated hand.

"I love her. Do you understand?" Alan said. "I'd never do anything to hurt her. I remember terrible things but that wasn't me."

"You killed her."

He knelt beside me, shotgun at his side, looking confused. "I remember things." He shook his head as if trying to clear away nightmares. "But she's alive. I'm going to get her now."

"Don't go, Alan." I pulled myself to a sitting position, my right arm limp at my side, trying to adjust so I could reach the gun with my left and keep it concealed until I drew it. "You don't need to do this."

"I'm saving her, Sam. She's meeting me tonight. We're leaving. Getting away from you. Because you're the one—"

I yanked the revolver from my waistband and caught Alan flat footed. I fired before he brought the shotgun around.

My aim was off, a bullet hole in the wall opposite me. Alan flinched and the shotgun punched twin holes beside me. He fell back, a bloody streak along his jaw— I hadn't missed entirely.

I frantically tried to pull back the hammer for a second shot.

Alan recovered but mustn't have liked his chances. He surged down the hall and disappeared into the stairwell. I fired blindly at the door.

I cursed. People peered out from their apartments but seeing my revolver, the doors slammed shut again. No cops came running and I knew they had abandoned my apartment earlier.

Lucy was alive. *My god, she's alive.* I had to get to her before Alan did.

I crawled to my feet and wiped my face with my shirt. Blood, lots of it. I couldn't breathe through my nose so I was pretty sure he'd broken it. My right arm was sore but I could move it.

I pushed through the stairwell door and gave pursuit.

God flicked a switch.

I landed awkwardly, taking the brunt of the impact on my right shoulder and my face. My nose broke and my shoulder went numb.

Somehow, I hadn't dropped the revolver. *Alan.* I rolled, aiming for an enemy who was no longer there. Harpies landed around me.

"I want him first."

"Let me have a lick."

"He'll be delicious."

The first harpy shambled at me, her wounds opening and closing like tiny mouths. I pulled myself to the edge of the nest— a two-foot tall embankment of straw and mud interlaced with bits of bone and clothing. A glance behind revealed a sheer drop down the mountain face. They ignored my revolver and I wondered if they even knew what it was.

I had five shots left. Not enough to fight my way out.

Before the harpy reached me, two others intervened.

"He's mine. I saw him first."

"You can have him second."

"Harpy!"

The argument exploded into violence. Other harpies joined the fray until the nest boiled with feathers, splashes of blood, and black wings. Kicking, spitting, talons rending. They screeched and danced.

My chance.

Except there was no chance. A straight drop behind me and a sheer wall in front of me.

The battle had been decided and the mass fell back, leaving one harpy opposing me. *Dear God.* Her face, splashed with blood, was unmistakable. Lucy. The harpy had the face of Lucy. The sight of her beautiful smile attached to such a hideous creation nearly destroyed me, and the world filled with static like an old-style TV signal. If I could've surrendered, if I could've closed my eyes and let the world wash away, I would have.

With one flap, Lucy launched herself high above me, extended her wings so she blotted out the sun, then dove upon me like an eagle upon a hare. Her wings folded around us like a cocoon.

"I am your princess," she purred, talons raking, shredding my bloody shirt and tearing ribbons from my chest.

I gripped the revolver tightly. My options dwindled. Soon, I'd have to try to fight my way out. I could kill one, maybe two before the harpies tore me apart in their sexual frenzy.

Lucy dove at my face, her beautiful teeth snap-snapping. "Just one kiss. Just one kiss."

"Yes, a kiss," I said through my tears.

Confusion distorted her expression of lust. Before she could act, I leaned in and kissed her. Her breath tasted like Lucy, her lips felt like Lucy's, and her tongue played with mine like Lucy's used to do.

Except this wasn't Lucy. This was a mind game to destroy me. I wasn't sure I had the strength to resist.

"I've missed you," I whispered. Because I did. God damn it, I did.

"We are together now," Lucy purred and her talons rested on my thighs. *Not Lucy.* "We can be together always."

"Yes," I choked. "But not here. Not with them watching."

"It is safe in our cocoon."

"You know that's not true. You saw the way they looked at us. They want to take what we have. They want to destroy our love." She cocked her head to the side. Her eyes weren't quite right. They darted too quickly. Like a bird's, I realized. "But we can be together," I said. "Take us toward the summit where we can be alone."

"But the nest…"

"It can only be this way," I said. "Take me. Take me now."

Her talons fastened to my shoulders and with a whirl of feathers, she lifted me from the nest. The other harpies squawked and screeched but didn't follow.

"Do you love me?" the fake Lucy asked.

"More than anything."

"What would you do for me?"

"Anything."

We flew toward the summit.

There.

A lone man climbing. Alan. He was, at most, two hours from the summit. I thought he may've glanced in our direction but I couldn't be certain. My gaze switched to the peak of the Hammer of the Gods.

"Take us to the summit," I said.

"We cannot go there. It is forbidden."

"Can't you do it for me?"

Her eyes regarded me but she shook her head sadly. "We will start a new family. Over there. It is close to the summit."

The new nest looked like a jagged tooth cast sideways from a jaw, a tenuous length of rock that had no realistic approach by foot. Flight was the only option and perhaps the reason the harpy chose it. While she wanted to please me, she also wanted to keep me separated and alone— servant to her desires only. Once there, I'd be trapped. I had to act. Now.

"Kiss me again," I said. Wings flapping, she leaned in, eyes closed, mouth parted, delicate tongue so inviting. We kissed. It *was* her. Except I knew it wasn't.

I shot her. My guts clenched. *Not Lucy.* We plummeted. We were falling, twisting, and we landed and her body broke beneath me with a sickening crunch.

We lay in a heap. I couldn't breathe, couldn't get my equilibrium, but I couldn't stay with that monster. I rolled away, the pain in my shoulder flaring.

When the air returned to my lungs, I cried. What torture was this? How much more anguish could I endure? I wiped my eyes with the back of my hand.

I climbed to my feet like a newborn foal. My legs wobbled and I steadied myself on a rock wall. I hurt everywhere. My joints throbbed, my head pounded, and I was covered in a thousand cuts. But I had survived the fall.

"My love," Lucy whispered.

Dear god, it's still alive. The beast reached for me, tears streaking her face. *What have I done?* I aimed my gun at her, knowing that I should pull the trigger— end the mockery. But as I looked into its eyes, I couldn't.

I ran from her because I was a coward.

I wondered if that was why Alan had turned the gun on himself that day. In a rage he had killed her, then when he had realized that he had destroyed the one good thing in his life, an avalanche of regret overwhelmed him.

I had crash landed two-hundred difficult feet from the summit. I saw no direct path so I'd have to climb, jump, and pray my way to the peak. I tucked the revolver into my waistband and set out.

I had three false starts before finding a negotiable route over an outcropping. I pulled myself up, twisted across an open chasm, then folded down.

I heard a curse and the scrabble of falling rocks beyond the next ledge. I shimmied closer to the edge and peered over. My breath caught.

Alan. Twenty-feet below, trying to climb the steep hill, his back to me. He wore shreds of mismatched clothing, shotgun strapped across his back in a makeshift holster. He looked like I felt— beat up, worn, tired. A thorn niggled at my brain but I pushed it aside.

I drew the revolver, the smoothness of the well-worn grip comforting in my hand. There was no urge for honor or grandstanding. My pulse raced and my palms sweated. I needed to do this. Alan had already murdered Lucy and had destroyed my life. And now it was my chance to make it better.

Alan worked his way up the steep embankment. I watched him searching for the perfect toeholds and then cursing as he realized he had to descend and try another approach.

I pressed myself against the rock, steadied my wrist with my other hand. Closed my other eye and took aim. All I had to do was squeeze the trigger. A simple pull. *Quit thinking about it and do it!*

Click. No bang, just the sound of the hammer falling on a dead bullet. *Misfire.*

Alan must've heard the empty sound and he dropped from the wall as I cocked the hammer and fired again. A live round and a puff of smoke. The bullet hit a foot to his right, gouging the rock and spraying Alan with splinters.

He brought the shotgun up. I rolled back and the lip of the ledge exploded. I only had two bullets left. The situation had gotten complicated.

God flicked a switch.

I stood in the hallway of Lucy's bungalow, the door open behind me. Lucy's jacket was thrown over the back of the entrance bench, her keys dropped by the front door. Music filtered through the walls from her bedroom. My heart hammered and the coffee-colored walls shimmered. I tried blinking away the strange vision.

Lucy was alive. Here and now. I had arrived in time.

"Lucy?" I called but she didn't answer. Alive. Alan hadn't gotten to her yet. I tucked my gun into the back of my waistband.

I resisted the urge to sprint down the hall. I wanted to see her, touch her, taste her. God, I wanted that more than anything. Yet, I couldn't quell the rising anxiety, as if building to a crest I wouldn't be able to control.

I padded down the hall and stopped outside the door. I wanted to burst in, to catch her and spin her as she jumped into my arms. My shoulder ached and I wondered at the pain spreading into my hand. How had I injured my shoulder? *Alan*. Except I remembered something else— crash landing with a monster that looked like Lucy. I pushed away those strange memories for they were only wisps left from old nightmares.

What would Lucy say when she saw me with my broken nose and welts across my shoulders? How could I explain without her thinking me crazy? It didn't matter. The only thing that mattered was protecting her.

I pushed the door open.

Lucy was in the bed, smiling, the sheet pulled protectively over her breasts. But she wasn't smiling at me. I followed her gaze and my stomach lurched. Alan stood by the nightstand, wearing boxers and holding a puzzle box. Lucy gasped when she saw me and when I looked back to her, there was no greeting in her expression — she blanched. That look — I understood what it meant. She didn't want me here.

"Yeah, but I think I can open it," Alan said unaware of my presence. When Lucy didn't answer him, he looked over and saw me.

"Lucy?" I said, feeling like I was underwater, unable to breathe and my vision liquid.

"Alan, I can explain," she said.

Alan, I can explain. Not, 'Sam, I can explain.' Because if she would've said that, I would've known that I was the one she was afraid to lose. But she didn't. She was begging forgiveness from Alan.

Alan, the one who murdered her.

"You said you loved me," I said.

The pressure in me built— like the initial rush of air as a subway approaches. My head thudded in time with my heart and my world collapsed to a single tunnel. And in that tunnel I saw the truth— I was the other man. Not Alan. I was the indiscretion, the one that Lucy hid away from the world, secreted from her friends, her family. Kept me hidden so that no one would discover the relationship because she had never intended for it to last.

The pressure pulled at my hair, ripped at my face and nearly blinded me. I struggled to stay upright against it.

I hated her.

All her lies. Her deception. Did she tell all her friends about me the next morning, giggling, dissecting our lovemaking and critiquing it with her friends?

That *look*. Her expression of shock.

I clenched the smooth pearl grip of the revolver. The pressure ballooned until my head was ready to explode. I needed to do this before I ruptured in a geyser of flesh and emotion.

Her look didn't change when I aimed the gun at her.

"We've done this before," Alan said. His voice startled me because I had forgotten he was here. "I was there and you were here." He offered the puzzle box to me. "You think this is yours, don't you?"

I didn't answer.

"Your name is Sam." He frowned at me. "How do I know that? How is that possible?"

Images piled atop each other: snakes, daemons, harpies. Every time I tried to focus on one of the images, it slipped away as if the memory was built on ice.

"You don't have to do this, Sam," Alan said.

"Shut up." My head throbbed.

"A box is just a box."

"You're not okay, Sam."

"I am your friend."

"Chasing your unicorn."

"Put the gun down," Alan said.

"Quiet!" Why couldn't I think clearly?

"How many times do we have to do this?" he asked.

I had lost my mind.

God flicked a switch.

"Do you think this will change anything?" I yelled.

He yelled something back but his words were lost in the winds.

I stood tight against the wall, hoping that Alan couldn't get to higher ground. I also knew that I couldn't stay here or he'd loop around and beat me to the rose. I had lost sight of him earlier and now we hunted each other through the passes and corridors etched in the mountain.

"You murdered her." I thought I said it, but I heard the words come from him.

The stone beside my face vaporized and grit stung my neck. I dove to the ground, wondering if I'd feel the follow-up shot or if everything would just go black. I thought I had good position— tight confines with a clear view to the path to the top. Except almost getting my head taken off indicated that he had a better position.

"Do you think you know me?" he said. I lay supine, scanning the upper passes but saw no signs of him.

Harpies circled high overhead, probably hoping to pick the bones of the defeated. I tried reading their patterns, hoping to discover Alan's position like I had seen in all those old Westerns, when the cowboy would know where the Apache had ambushed the stage coach from watching the clouds of vultures, but I couldn't decipher their circles.

I checked the revolver. Two shots, assuming they were good rounds. Alan's shotgun was a two barrel. He had more stopping power and didn't have to worry about accuracy. The odds were in his favor. Pushed that from my mind. I wasn't going to fail.

I lay that way far too long. Maybe he had circumvented my position and decided to go straight for the rose rather than taking me out first. I stood, waiting for the kill shot that would splatter my skull over the rock.

When it didn't come, I edged forward, paused and wiped my sweaty palms on my thighs. The air tasted thin. Altitude or fear?

A stone bounced past me, a careless mistake on Alan's part. He waited behind the next corner. Before my courage fled, I spun around the rock.

Alan turned at the same time. Face to face, weapons drawn. I fired first but my bullet jammed and the gun exploded. Searing pain as shrapnel tore my hand apart. My fingers were ruined, white bone protruding from exposed joints. The flesh had been flayed and burned.

No time to worry about my hand, the nerves thankfully numb from the shock. I turned, trying to make myself a smaller target. The shotgun roared. The close range saved me. Another two feet and the shotgun blast would've shredded me.

I staggered backwards and hit the rock wall. If I fell, I wasn't getting back up again. Alan cracked open the shotgun, feeding in two more shells. In no condition to counterattack, I stumbled up the path and around an outcropping. Rock sprayed my face from an errant shotgun blast.

God, don't look at it. I cradled my hand tight to my body. If I stopped I was a dead man. But a man has limitations and I was at mine. I veered from the path, knowing that I had to rest or I'd collapse. My hand hurt but it came from far away. *Thump, thump, thump.* The whole world kept time with my pulse that raced far too fast.

But my hand is ruined. I am ruined.

I found a spot. I closed my eyes and took a deep breath.

God flicked a switch.

Lucy — oh god — she was in a bed splashed with blood, sitting against the headboard, eyes vacant.

I was too late — Alan had beaten me to her. Given my chance to redo that night, I still had failed.

"Lucy," someone said. The sound snatched me from my detachment. I wasn't alone. I sensed Alan standing to my right and when I was finally able to pull my gaze from Lucy, I saw him in his boxers and T-shirt. He held a puzzle box that matched mine. I was holding something too but when I looked at it, it didn't make sense.

I was holding an antique revolver that stank of cordite.

I stared at the pistol, trying to work my way through the maze. Why had I been pointing the muzzle at Lucy? My hand trembled as I remembered a strange dream. A dream of a rose atop a mountain. *Alan.* Just a dream.

"What have you done?" Alan asked. His eyes wide, face colorless. Shock.

"I didn't do this," I stammered. Why would I hurt Lucy?

I already knew the truth. I flicked out the chamber. Four shells. Back to Lucy and saw the four dark rings on her chest. One bullet left.

What have I done?

My world crashed. Her blood crept along the sheet.

I couldn't breathe.

One bullet left.

I turned the gun on myself.

Click.

I stepped from the path onto the summit.

Alan waited for me, calm and collected, the shotgun held loosely at his side. I shivered, my vision wavering. Shock from my ruined hand. The pain didn't quite belong to me. I sensed it but the delirium kept it locked away from my last mental reserves.

Not that it mattered now. My hand was ruined and my revolver scrap metal. Alan stood twenty-five paces away. Too far for me to cover before he'd shoot me down.

Behind him, the single rose stood against the blasting winds, the flower growing from a small patch of moss on the desolate rock. Three leaves with a tight flower bud. The petals opened slowly, revealing a forest of blood-red stamens thick with pollen.

"I wonder if it could end any other way," he said, scanning the horizon. "The two of us on top of this mountain." Sadness dripped from his voice even though he held all the cards.

"We're locked in this loop-to-loop that'll never end. You solved the box, didn't you? Because I solved it, too. It took me until I reached the top of this mountain, but I remember that box. Probably the same one that got you here. Don't look so shocked. I know because I've walked in your shoes."

"I love her," I said.

"Isn't that the perfect reason for killing someone? When all that love is turned bad and it floods your system like battery acid. I loved her too."

"I would never hurt her." *Except I would.*

"Are you sure? I killed her, then woke up in that cell. I know you've been there too."

I shivered but I was unsure whether it was from the shock or from the sense of inevitability.

"I lost track of time in that cell, the years bleeding together into a limitless nightmare. Do you remember the strange writing on the walls, Sam? Do you remember that?"

The writing on the prison walls— I had been unable to decrypt the strange set of symbols and scratchings. I said nothing.

"In my loneliness, I deciphered those messages."

I knew too. *How do I know? How could I know?*

"They were from you, Sam. You had been there before me. Locked in that very room for your own lifetime. You had developed your own system of writing— perhaps to fool the Jailors or perhaps because you had gone mad. Or maybe I devised it and you were the follower before me."

"That's not possible."

"Not possible or you don't wish to consider it? Look at us, battling for this." He gestured to the rose. "Is any of this possible? You were in that cell before me. And probably I before you. Looping. Can't you see it?"

"I'm going to get the rose," I said. The world twisted on itself. A numbness pervaded me. I stared down at my ruined hand, at the bone protruding where fingers used to be.

"I won't stop you from getting the rose. What will you do with it? When you bring her back— what will you do?"

I wanted to tell him that I would fix it. That I would make it right. But I never got the chance.

A shadow passed over me followed by a waft of sour wind. A flight of black feathers accompanied by the screech of a harpy. It flew overhead in a broken path, shattered wing tucked behind its back. I saw Lucy's face on that broken harpy and I realized that she had come to save me. I had tried to kill her and yet, here she was— coming to my aid.

Alan didn't raise the shotgun. His expression matched that of when he had killed Lucy those weeks ago. Bewilderment. His gaze fell to me. No panic, no fear. He pursed his lips and gave me a quick nod.

Then Lucy slammed into him and they were ripped from the summit— a whirl of feathers, arms, legs.

And I was alone.

How long did I stand like that, willing myself to move? So long that I saw the petals begin to close. I stumbled forward— determination taking me those last few steps before I collapsed beside the rose, smelt the delicate scent in the harsh winds.

I reached with my ruined hand but couldn't grasp the stem. Used my good hand and I plucked the Blue Rose of Quintes.

Click.

There was no gun in my hand. I steadied myself on a nearby desk while the disorientation passed. A man in a suit talked about the latest art show in Montreal. Gradually, my world righted itself and the guy never missed a beat.

Patrons browsed the work on the walls while carrying tiny plates of appetizers. The appetizers probably cost more than I'd make with my exhibit. But I was trying to make an impression. Wasn't my art the most important thing in the world?

The door opened and my breath caught as Lucy stepped from a dream into the gallery. My vision imploded around her. *The Rose. Dear God… it worked.*

Alan, swept from the summit. I clenched my hands. Whole again.

A gift from the gods.

She glanced around the gallery and her expression clouded with momentary confusion. *Because she's realized that she's in the wrong place.*

"Sorry," I interrupted the guy mid-sentence, and left him without waiting to be excused. I greeted Lucy while she inspected one of the prints.

"The Incredible Hulk battling Superman," I said.

"Pardon?"

"It's unique because they don't actually exist in the same world." I tried to compose myself. My hands were shaking. "One is DC and the other Marvel. Sometimes, we try to jam the two worlds together— but the worlds are never meant to come together."

"Of course," she lied. We stood gazing at the picture, trying to act interested but for different reasons. I breathed in her scent, closed my eyes and tried to fight back the emotions. I wished we could've stayed that way forever. But we couldn't.

"You're not supposed to be here," I said.

"Oh, I'm sorry," she said blushing. "I thought this was an open gallery."

"I mean you're not a comic book fan. You're here on the wrong day, aren't you?"

"It's that obvious?"

"Insider knowledge," I said. I wanted to reach out and tuck the loose strand of blonde hair behind her ears.

The door opened again. Cami. She beamed when she saw me. I smiled to cover my sudden doubt. *So it's changed. A do over.*

"Great turnout," my sister said. "I'm so happy for you." She hugged me and I held her tightly. She looked at me quizzically, as if asking me what was wrong. I gave a quick shake of my head.

"Cami, this is…" I gestured to Lucy, waiting for her to fill in the blank.

"Lucy."

"Lucy," I repeated. My throat constricted. *We don't know each other.* She stood right here in front of me.

Ask her out.

"My name's Sam." We shook hands and her grip felt perfect in mine. I didn't want to let go.

"It's nice meeting you, Sam." And she waited. Did a small part of her remember me from another lifetime? Did a small part of her know that we were destined to be torn from each other? *What will you do, Sam?*

I smiled and nodded, probably looking goofy but trying to buy some time so that the lump in my throat would subside. Finally, "Nice meeting you, Lucy. Maybe your... boyfriend might like something?"

Just like that, the romantic tension between us popped. Her gaze momentarily darted away but there was something different there. A disconnect.

"He's not really into comics," she said.

I nodded because I knew I wouldn't be able to speak without breaking down. She wandered away, spending a few moments trying to act interested. Lucy left without looking back.

"She was cute, Sam. You should've asked her out," Cami whispered.

God damn it. I didn't try to hide my tears.

"Sam?" Cami's hand was on my shoulder. "Is everything okay?"

I nodded, wiping my eyes. I couldn't hold it together any longer. I hid in the bathroom and cried.

Cami knocked on the door after fifteen minutes.

"Are you okay, Sam?"

I splashed cold water over my face while she called my name. There was no hiding the red-rimmed eyes or swollen cheeks so I opened the door.

"Dear God, Sam. What's wrong?"

"Not now. I can't tell you now."

I hugged her and I felt her confusion in her stiffness. Then she softened and hugged me back.

"I'm glad you're here, Cami. I wouldn't have been able to do this without you."

She hesitated and I knew it was because she didn't understand. She said, "I'll always be here for you, Sam. You know that. I wish you'd tell me what's happening."

"I will. But not now."

I took ten minutes to compose myself before returning to the party. I sleepwalked through the last of the gala before the night thankfully drew to a close. People spoke with me but I couldn't remember the conversations. And there was Cami, hovering but not pressing.

When the last of the patrons left, Cami waited for me at the front door. "I forgot my folio," I said. "I'll be right back."

My body felt waterlogged, my steps heavy and ponderous. My eyes burned with fatigue. I flicked on the switch in the back room and saw the puzzle box. I paused, knowing that it shouldn't be here and that it had disappeared a lifetime ago, but it couldn't surprise me anymore.

The top panels were open.

I didn't know how I knew, but the box, the conduit, was closed to me. Now, it was a simple box. Here I was, alone. What had this box given me? Could I say that those three months weren't worth the carnage? Could I weigh them and say doing the right thing felt good?

I gazed inside the puzzle box.

The Rose of Quintes lay at the bottom of the tarnished metal. I plucked the rose and the box folded back on itself like a Venus flytrap.

Cami waited for me at the front. She wanted to ask me what had taken so long. I could see the questions on her face.

She cupped my cheek with her palm. "Sam, everything's going to be all right."

"Right now, it hurts like hell."

She frowned briefly before it disappeared in the softness of a smile. "This too shall pass."

I handed her the rose. "I want you to have this."

"It's beautiful." she said.

"It's all I have left," I said.

"Left of what?"

"A life left behind."

The Final Piece of the Puzzle

❖ ❖ ❖

Finally, Albert understood.

There was no going back. His loss of Moira and everything else in his life had been on him. His decisions. His actions. There was no one else to blame. Not even his father for abandoning his family, leaving his young son scarred with a chronic sense of inadequacy. It was Albert himself who had made a mess of that abandonment. He could have moved on. He could have used it as a sword rather than a crutch. In his dream, the story, the memories in the box, the man had gone back and changed his life. He had sacrificed the love of the girl, Lucy, and in doing so had saved them all. But that was not Albert's story. For Albert there was no going back. Only forward.

Albert also understood about the box.

The puzzle box wasn't a construct. It didn't belong to any time or place, but belonged to every tick of the clock. It couldn't be measured by any of the primitive mathematical equations that defined the universe.

Perhaps it is the universe, Albert thought.

And maybe that was why it exhibited itself as a puzzle. Because there was no answer. No way to apply a formula to solve its mysteries. No linear experiments or ways to measure and define it.

Albert didn't know where the box ended and he began. Earlier, if he had been told of his journey, he would've considered it a parasitic coupling, with the box stealing his identity, claiming his own story for its never-ending legacy. Now, he realized it was a symbiotic joining, one that made him whole. That malignant breach in his life had been plugged, his life now braided with the reality of the box.

All he had to do was let go. Release the feelings of inadequacy and abandonment. The memories within the box showed him how.

Albert looked at the empty bottle of Jim Beam on the table and felt no desire for a taste. In a detached sort of way, he marveled at the power it used to have over him.

The Chronicler sat across the table from him, a different man than when he had intruded upon Albert's life. He suspected that the older man hadn't changed at all— but rather, last night, Albert simply had been unready to see, or accept, who this mysterious visitor truly was.

As if from afar, Albert remembered his past life, all the travails that seemed so important then. Now, they seemed like grainy photographs at the bottom of a shoebox.

The man sitting across from him was different from the one he remembered as a child. In Albert's memories he was taller, with perfectly cut features and an air of infallibility. Now, he just looked old. The stubble on his chin was grey, his skin leathery, his facial muscles sagging beneath the weight of time.

"Will I ever open it?" Albert asked.

"Someday."

"How will I know when?"

"You'll know, just as I did."

"What was inside?"

The Chronicler smiled a genuine look of contentment. "Among other things it brought me here, to you." He pushed the small box across the table, much like the bartenders who used to slide drinks to him. "It is yours now, son."

"Thank you— Father."

Someone pounded on the door. It should've startled Albert, but he wasn't sure if anything could surprise him anymore.

"It was never about you, Albert," his father said, the only apology he would ever receive. "Not really. It was my burden, my problem, but I didn't know. Didn't realize. You understand that, don't you?"

"I do. Now."

A tear welled in the older man's eye. "It took me twenty-five years to discover that. It took you one night. You are a better man than I ever could have been."

From the other side of the door, Morley Van Rosen shouted, "Open the door, Albert, or we'll break it down."

"I should go," Albert's father said.

Albert didn't ask whether he'd see him again because he knew that he would; his father had become a part of the puzzle.

The Chronicler smiled. "It's good to finally meet you, Albert. The real you."

The door broke with a staccato crack. Van Rosen's two goons kicked aside the splinters. Van Rosen followed them in, wearing his pressed white suit with matching fedora. The two goons flanked him.

"Mr. Van Rosen," Albert said calmly. "So good to see you."

"Who were you talking to?"

Albert breathed deeply. He felt a twinge of something but it was whisked away like a leaf on the wind. That life of regret and loss was over. He wondered briefly if he was a new person. Some vestiges of him remained because Van Rosen recognized him.

"I'm alone," Albert replied.

"We heard you talking to someone."

The two goons walked around the table and stood on either side of him. Van Rosen sat down at the table in the chair where moments before Albert's father had sat. He shook his head.

"Albert, you know I'm a businessman. I didn't want it to come to this. I gave you extensions and leniency."

Albert ignored his words. They meant nothing to him any longer. "I have something for you, Mr. Van Rosen."

The man's eyes narrowed, perhaps wondering about Albert's boldness. Albert was never bold. "But not money. That will not do."

Albert knew that the men on each side of him were here to break him. They would shatter his legs, perhaps snip off fingers. And they would enjoy doing it. But he felt no fear or apprehension. They could do nothing to him that mattered. Not any longer.

He placed the box delicately on the table between them. The two goons exchanged glances.

"What the hell is that?" Mr. Van Rosen demanded.

"It is everything," Albert said.

"This some kind of joke? I want my..." His sentence drifted into oblivion as his eyes settled on the box, his gaze unfocused.

"I have a great gift for you, Mr. Van Rosen. Now I ask you: what do you want? What do you really want? You don't have to say. It already knows."

"I... I..." Van Rosen reached for the box, his goons stuck in a strange suspended animation.

"Tell me, Mr. Van Rosen," Albert whispered. "What would you say is the greatest gift I could give you?"

Our titles are available at major book stores
and local independent resellers who support
Science Fiction and Fantasy readers like you.

EDGE Science Fiction
and Fantasy Publishing

**Our titles are available at major book stores
and local independent resellers who support
Science Fiction and Fantasy readers like you.**

Alphanauts by J. Brian Clarke (tp) - ISBN: 978-1-894063-14-2
Apparition Trail, The by Lisa Smedman (tp) - ISBN: 978-1-894063-22-7
As Fate Decrees by Denysé Bridger (tp) - ISBN: 978-1-894063-41-8
Avim's Oath (Part Six of the Okal Rel Saga) by Lynda Williams (tp)
   - ISBN: 978-1-894063-35-7

Black Chalice, The by Marie Jakober (hb) - ISBN: 978-1-894063-00-7
Blue Apes by Phyllis Gotlieb (pb) - ISBN: 978-1-895836-13-4
Blue Apes by Phyllis Gotlieb (hb) - ISBN: 978-1-895836-14-1

Captives by Barbara Galler-Smith and Josh Langston (tp)
   - ISBN: 978-1-894063-53-1
Children of Atwar, The by Heather Spears (pb) - ISBN: 978-0-88878-335-6
Chilling Tales: Evil Did I Dwell; Lewd I Did Live edited by Michael Kelly (tp)
   - ISBN: 978-1-894063-52-4
Chilling Tales: In Words, Alas, Drown I edited by Michael Kelly (tp)
   - ISBN: 978-1-77053-024-9
Cinco de Mayo by Michael J. Martineck (pb) - ISBN: 978-1-894063-39-5
Cinkarion - The Heart of Fire (Part Two of The Chronicles of the Karionin)
   by J. A. Cullum - (tp) - ISBN: 978-1-894063-21-0
Circle Tide by Rebecca K. Rowe (tp) - ISBN: 978-1-894063-59-3
Clan of the Dung-Sniffers by Lee Danielle Hubbard (tp) - ISBN: 978-1-894063-05-0
Claus Effect, The by David Nickle & Karl Schroeder (pb) - ISBN: 978-1-895836-34-9
Claus Effect, The by David Nickle & Karl Schroeder (hb) - ISBN: 978-1-895836-35-6
Clockwork Heart by Dru Pagliassotti (tp) - ISBN: 978-1-77053-026-3
Courtesan Prince, The (Part One of the Okal Rel Saga) by Lynda Williams (tp)
   - ISBN: 978-1-894063-28-9

Danse Macabre: Close Encounters With the Reaper edited by Nancy Kilpatrick (tp)
   - ISBN: 978-1-894063-96-8
Dark Earth Dreams by Candas Dorsey & Roger Deegan (comes with a CD)
   - ISBN: 978-1-895836-05-9
Darkness of the God (Children of the Panther Part Two)
   by Amber Hayward (tp) - ISBN: 978-1-894063-44-9
Demon Left Behind, The by Marie Jakober (tp) - ISBN: 978-1-894063-49-4
Distant Signals by Andrew Weiner (tp) - ISBN: 978-0-88878-284-7
Dreams of an Unseen Planet by Teresa Plowright (tp) - ISBN: 978-0-88878-282-3
Dreams of the Sea (Part 1 of Tyranaël) by Élisabeth Vonarburg (tp)
   - ISBN: 978-1-895836-96-7
Dreams of the Sea (Part 1 of Tyranaël) by Élisabeth Vonarburg (hb)
   - ISBN: 978-1-895836-98-1
Druids by Barbara Galler-Smith and Josh Langston (tp)
   - ISBN: 978-1-894063-29-6

Eclipse by K. A. Bedford (tp) - ISBN: 978-1-894063-30-2
Even The Stones by Marie Jakober (tp) - ISBN: 978-1-894063-18-0
Evolve: Vampire Stories of the New Undead edited by Nancy Kilpatrick (tp)
   - ISBN: 978-1-894063-33-3

Evolve Two: Vampire Stories of the Future Undead edited by Nancy Kilpatrick (tp)
-ISBN: 978-1-894063-62-3

Far Arena (Part Five of the Okal Rel Saga) by Lynda Williams (tp)
- ISBN: 978-1-894063-45-6
Fires of the Kindred by Robin Skelton (tp) - ISBN: 978-0-88878-271-7
Forbidden Cargo by Rebecca Rowe (tp) - ISBN: 978-1-894063-16-6

Game of Perfection, A (Part 2 of Tyranaël) by Élisabeth Vonarburg (tp)
- ISBN: 978-1-894063-32-6
Gaslight Arcanum: Uncanny Tales of Sherlock Holmes
  edited by Jeff Campbell & Charles Prepolec (pb)
  - ISBN: 978-1-8964063-60-9
Gaslight Grimoire: Fantastic Tales of Sherlock Holmes
  edited by Jeff Campbell & Charles Prepolec (pb)
  - ISBN: 978-1-8964063-17-3
Gaslight Grotesque: Nightmare Tales of Sherlock Holmes
  edited by Jeff Campbell & Charles Prepolec (pb)
  - ISBN: 978-1-8964063-31-9
Gathering Storm (Part Eight of the Okal Rel Saga) by Lynda Williams (tp)
  - ISBN: 978-1-77053-020-1
Green Music by Ursula Pflug (tp) - ISBN: 978-1-895836-75-2
Green Music by Ursula Pflug (hb) - ISBN: 978-1-895836-77-6

Healer, The (Children of the Panther Part One) by Amber Hayward (tp)
  - ISBN: 978-1-895836-89-9
Healer, The (Children of the Panther Part One) by Amber Hayward (hb)
  - ISBN: 978-1-895836-91-2
Healer's Sword (Part Seven of the Okal Rel Saga) by Lynda Williams (tp)
  - ISBN: 978-1-894063-51-7
Hell Can Wait by Theodore Judson (tp) - ISBN: 978-1-978-1-894063-23-4
Holy War (Part Nine of the Okal Rel Saga) by Lynda Williams (tp)
  - ISBN: 978-1-77053-032-4
Hounds of Ash and other tales of Fool Wolf, The by Greg Keyes (pb)
  - ISBN: 978-1-894063-09-8
Hydrogen Steel by K. A. Bedford (tp) - ISBN: 978-1-894063-20-3

i-ROBOT Poetry by Jason Christie (tp) - ISBN: 978-1-894063-24-1
Immortal Quest by Alexandra MacKenzie (pb) - ISBN: 978-1-894063-46-3

Jackal Bird by Michael Barley (pb) - ISBN: 978-1-895836-07-3
Jackal Bird by Michael Barley (hb) - ISBN: 978-1-895836-11-0
JEMMA7729 by Phoebe Wray (tp) - ISBN: 978-1-894063-40-1

Keaen by Till Noever (tp) - ISBN: 978-1-894063-08-1
Keeper's Child by Leslie Davis (tp) - ISBN: 978-1-894063-01-2

Land/Space edited by Candas Jane Dorsey and Judy McCrosky (tp)
  - ISBN: 978-1-895836-90-5
Land/Space edited by Candas Jane Dorsey and Judy McCrosky (hb)
  - ISBN: 978-1-895836-92-9
Lyskarion: The Song of the Wind (Part One of The Chronicles of the Karionin)
  by J.A. Cullum (tp) - ISBN: 978-1-894063-02-9

Machine Sex and other stories by Candas Jane Dorsey (tp)
  - ISBN: 978-0-88878-278-6
Maërlande Chronicles, The by Élisabeth Vonarburg (pb)
  - ISBN: 978-0-88878-294-6
Moonfall by Heather Spears (pb) - ISBN: 978-0-88878-306-6

Of Wind and Sand by Sylvie Bérard (translated by Sheryl Curtis) (tp)
  - ISBN: 978-1-894063-19-7
On Spec: The First Five Years edited by On Spec (pb)
  - ISBN: 978-1-895836-08-0
On Spec: The First Five Years edited by On Spec (hb)
  - ISBN: 978-1-895836-12-7
Orbital Burn by K. A. Bedford (tp) - ISBN: 978-1-894063-10-4
Orbital Burn by K. A. Bedford (hb) - ISBN: 978-1-894063-12-8

Pallahaxi Tide by Michael Coney (pb) - ISBN: 978-0-88878-293-9
Paradox Resolution by K. A. Bedford (tp) - ISBN:978-1-894063-88-3
Passion Play by Sean Stewart (pb) - ISBN: 978-0-88878-314-1
Petrified World (Determine Your Destiny #1) by Piotr Brynczka (pb)
  - ISBN: 978-1-894063-11-1
Plague Saint by Rita Donovan, The (tp) - ISBN: 978-1-895836-28-8
Plague Saint by Rita Donovan, The (hb) - ISBN: 978-1-895836-29-5
Pock's World by Dave Duncan (tp) - ISBN: 978-1-894063-47-0
Pretenders (Part Three of the Okal Rel Saga) by Lynda Williams (tp)
  - ISBN: 978-1-894063-13-5
Puzzle Box, The by Randy McCharles, Billie Millholland, Eileen Bell and Ryan
  McFadden (tp) - ISBN: 978-1-77053-040-9

Reluctant Voyagers by Élisabeth Vonarburg (pb) - ISBN: 978-1-895836-09-7
Reluctant Voyagers by Élisabeth Vonarburg (hb) - ISBN: 978-1-895836-15-8
Resisting Adonis by Timothy J. Anderson (tp) - ISBN: 978-1-895836-84-4
Resisting Adonis by Timothy J. Anderson (hb) - ISBN: 978-1-895836-83-7
Rigor Amortis edited by Jaym Gates and Erika Holt (tp)
  - ISBN: 978-1-894063-63-0
Righteous Anger (Part Two of the Okal Rel Saga) by Lynda Williams (tp)
  - ISBN: 897-1-894063-38-8

Silent City, The by Élisabeth Vonarburg (tp) - ISBN: 978-1-894063-07-4
Slow Engines of Time, The by Élisabeth Vonarburg (tp)
  - ISBN: 978-1-895836-30-1
Slow Engines of Time, The by Élisabeth Vonarburg (hb)
  - ISBN: 978-1-895836-31-8
Stealing Magic by Tanya Huff (tp) - ISBN: 978-1-894063-34-0
Stolen Children (Children of the Panther Part Three)
  by Amber Hayward (tp) - ISBN: 978-1-894063-66-1
Strange Attractors by Tom Henighan (pb) - ISBN: 978-0-88878-312-7

Taming, The by Heather Spears (pb) - ISBN: 978-1-895836-23-3
Taming, The by Heather Spears (hb) - ISBN: 978-1-895836-24-0
Technicolor Ultra Mall by Ryan Oakley (tp) - ISBN: 978-1-894063-54-8
Ten Monkeys, Ten Minutes by Peter Watts (tp) - ISBN: 978-1-895836-74-5
Ten Monkeys, Ten Minutes by Peter Watts (hb) - ISBN: 978-1-895836-76-9
Tesseracts 1 edited by Judith Merril (pb) - ISBN: 978-0-88878-279-3
Tesseracts 2 edited by Phyllis Gotlieb & Douglas Barbour (pb)
  - ISBN: 978-0-88878-270-0

Tesseracts 3 edited by Candas Jane Dorsey & Gerry Truscott (pb)
- ISBN: 978-0-88878-290-8
Tesseracts 4 edited by Lorna Toolis & Michael Skeet (pb)
- ISBN: 978-0-88878-322-6
Tesseracts 5 edited by Robert Runté & Yves Maynard (pb)
- ISBN: 978-1-895836-25-7
Tesseracts 5 edited by Robert Runté & Yves Maynard (hb)
- ISBN: 978-1-895836-26-4
Tesseracts 6 edited by Robert J. Sawyer & Carolyn Clink (pb)
- ISBN: 978-1-895836-32-5
Tesseracts 6 edited by Robert J. Sawyer & Carolyn Clink (hb)
- ISBN: 978-1-895836-33-2
Tesseracts 7 edited by Paula Johanson & Jean-Louis Trudel (tp)
- ISBN: 978-1-895836-58-5
Tesseracts 7 edited by Paula Johanson & Jean-Louis Trudel (hb)
- ISBN: 978-1-895836-59-2
Tesseracts 8 edited by John Clute & Candas Jane Dorsey (tp)
- ISBN: 978-1-895836-61-5
Tesseracts 8 edited by John Clute & Candas Jane Dorsey (hb)
- ISBN: 978-1-895836-62-2
Tesseracts Nine edited by Nalo Hopkinson and Geoff Ryman (tp)
- ISBN: 978-1-894063-26-5
Tesseracts Ten: A Celebration of New Canadian Specuative Fiction
edited by Robert Charles Wilson and Edo van Belkom (tp)
- ISBN: 978-1-894063-36-4
Tesseracts Eleven: Amazing Canadian Speulative Fiction
edited by Cory Doctorow and Holly Phillips (tp)
- ISBN: 978-1-894063-03-6
Tesseracts Twelve: New Novellas of Canadian Fantastic Fiction
edited by Claude Lalumière (tp)
- ISBN: 978-1-894063-15-9
Tesseracts Thirteen: Chilling Tales from the Great White North
edited by Nancy Kilpatrick and David Morrell (tp)
- ISBN: 978-1-894063-25-8
Tesseracts 14: Strange Canadian Stories
edited by John Robert Colombo and Brett Alexander Savory (tp)
- ISBN: 978-1-894063-37-1
Tesseracts Fifteen: A Case of Quite Curious Tales
edited by Julie Czerneda and Susan MacGregor (tp)
- ISBN: 978-1-894063-58-6
Tesseracts Sixteen: Parnassus Unbound edited by Mark Leslie (tp)
- ISBN: 978-1-894063-92-0
Tesseracts Seventeen: Speculating Canada from Coast to Coast to Coast
edited by Colleen Anderson and Steve Vernon (tp) -ISBN: 978-1-77053-044-7
Tesseracts Q edited by Élisabeth Vonarburg and Jane Brierley (pb)
- ISBN: 978-1-895836-21-9
Tesseracts Q edited by Élisabeth Vonarburg and Jane Brierley (hb)
- ISBN: 978-1-895836-22-6
Those Who Fight Monsters: Tales of Occult Detectives
edited by Justin Gustainis (pb) - ISBN: 978-1-894063-48-7
Throne Price by Lynda Williams and Alison Sinclair (tp)
- ISBN: 978-1-894063-06-7
Time Machines Repaired Whie-U-Wait by K. A. Bedford (tp)
- ISBN: 978-1-894063-42-5

Trillionist, The by Sagan Jeffries (tp) -ISBN: 978-1-894063-98-2

Vampyric Variations by Nancy Kilpatrick (tp)- ISBN: 978-1-894063-94-4
Vyrkarion: The Talisman of Anor by J. A. Cullum (tp) ISBN: 978-1-77053-028-7

Unholy Science (Part Ten of the Okal Rel Saga) by Lynda Williams (tp)
    - ISBN: 978-1-77053-046-1
Urban Green Man edited by Adria Laycraft and Janice Blaine (tp)
    -ISBN: 978-1-77053-038-6

Warriors by Barbara Galler-Smith and Josh Langston (tp)
    -ISBN: 978-1-77053-030-0
Wildcatter by Dave Duncan (tp) - ISBN: 978-1-894063-90-6